Land I Have Chosen

Land I Have Chosen

BY ELLIN BERLIN

THE BLAKISTON COMPANY

Philadelphia

76 45

PRINTED IN THE UNITED STATES

Acknowledgments

The author extends thanks to the publishers for the privilege of reprinting the following quotations:

Irving Berlin, Inc.—for lines from the songs "I'll Get By," by Roy Turk and Fred A. Ahlert, and "There's a Rainbow Round My Shoulder," by Al Jolson, Billy Rose, and Dave Dreyer.

Harcourt, Brace & Company, Inc.—for lines from *Heinrich Heine: Paradox and Poet,* by Louis Untermeyer.

T. B. Harms Company—for lines from the song, "Who," by Otto Harbach, Oscar Hammerstein II, and Jerome Kern.

Mills Music, Inc.—for lines from the song "I Can't Give You Anything But Love, Baby," by Dorothy Fields and Jimmy McHugh.

This is the story of a world I knew. To make that world and its time seem real again I have described actual places: cities and summer resorts here and abroad. I have not described any people I have ever known. If the reader thinks he recognizes in these pages any living people he is using his memory, not mine. I have told a story that might have happened, not one that did happen.

Contents

BOOK I

The Beginning

I

LISA BLESSING walked up Fifth Avenue in the bright June sunshine. New York was beautiful in the sunlight. Lisa lifted her eyes to the tall towers. In Europe you could not imagine the towers. Skyscrapers, you said, and smiled at American exaggeration. But these buildings did seem to touch the sky. The towers, because of their narrowness, seemed taller than mountains. In Europe you could not imagine the towers. You could not imagine America. A serene, sunlit land. Here the people were free of fear. There was no shadow over the peaceful year of 1928. The war years were part of the past, forgotten. Nineteen eighteen belonged to another time. Lisa's mind turned from the memory of that year, that dark December. In Europe, even after ten years, the dark days were still easily remembered.

There were small clouds in the blue sky—just such soft, white clouds had floated in the blue German sky over the children's festival in 1914. Do I really remember? Lisa wondered. Do I really remember that one summer day when I was six? Or—did I make one picture of all the sunny days, a picture of the perfect day, which I held in my heart through all the dark years? And now suddenly in this strange, foreign city the little white clouds remind me of that day—of all the days of my German childhood.

Her grandmother had kept Lisa's childhood carefully German. "For your mother's sake," Frau Blessing had said. "Rosa wanted a little German girl. I shall not let my American ways alter the childhood that Rosa planned for you."

Lisa remembered the pictures—the pictures in the storybooks and in the songbooks; the star princess and the dew fairies; the root children in their flower dresses. The root children marched right across the wide pages. And the poor little Moor and St. Nicholas. And, in the songbook, the three princesses in the garden; and the fir tree of winter—how green are thy leaves! There were beautiful pictures in the books which Rosa had kept so carefully for the daughter she would one day have, the daughter she was never to see. Little Lisa had loved the pictures. She had learned them by heart while she listened to the stories and sang the songs.

And now, Lisa thought, I am older than Rosa. How strange to be older than your mother. She remembered Rosa's picture in the nursery. It had been the picture of a grownup—a pretty grownup who had mysteriously turned into an angel. Now, in Lisa's bedroom, it was the picture of a young girl—younger than Lisa, for Rosa had died at nineteen and Lisa was twenty.

Rosa's photograph, in her bridal gown, had looked down on Lisa and her grandmother as they told the stories and sang the songs. Did you know, Lisa wondered, and were you pleased with your American mother-in-law for teaching your daughter the German ways?

Because of my American grandmother this could be my city, Lisa thought. This land was Granny's and her father's.

Lisa could not remember her great-grandfather, Dan Hanauer. He was a photograph in her grandmother's sitting room—a formal photograph of a gentleman, lovingly and inappropriately framed in pale embroidered silk. He was a photograph. And he was a brave, sad story, a story too remote to be frightening. The story of a great ship sinking in the icy sea and Dan Hanauer standing stiffly like the photograph—standing not alone—standing with the others and singing "Nearer, My God, to Thee!" It had been a story and a picture—the big ship and the wide, black sea and the voices raised to the dark, distant sky. In those long-ago days death and sorrow had not been frightening. They had existed only in song and story. The story of the *Titanic* had been as unreal to Lisa as the fairy tales and the songs. In those days it had been as difficult to believe in sorrow as to imagine darkness in the sunshine.

Now, as Lisa walked north on Fifth Avenue, the sunshine was everywhere. It danced on the golden general upon his fine horse. It shone on the trees in the park, still bright with the clear green of early summer. This could be my country, Lisa thought. It would be pleasant to live here in this bright, young land. And I can. I have the right. This, too, is my heritage.

The golden general looked proudly at the golden palm leaf that was borne before him. His pride reminded Lisa of her grandfather, Wilhelm Blessing. He, too, had liked the palm leaves and the laurel. He had been the great man of German poetry.

Wilhelm Blessing had rejected his wife's American heritage. "The Hanauers are good German stock," he had asserted. "Never forget that, Lisa. They were only briefly in America. One man's lifetime cannot alter the blood—the heritage."

Lisa smiled as she remembered the old man's disregard of his wife's American fortune, the fortune which had luxuriously supported his greatness. Lisa smiled at him. It was hard not to smile at the dead, not to think of them gently. Not so had Wilhelm Blessing thought of his only son. Lisa turned her mind from the dark memory, from Siegfried Blessing, whom in death the old man's song had transformed. She turned her mind from the hero in whose name her grandfather had lifted the bloodstained sword of song—the *"Heldenlied."* Not that false image would she remember in this June sunlight, but her father as he had been—her father, the professor, as she remembered him in the little years before 1914.

"Even so do I teach my pupils, Lisa," he had said.

"Like this, Father, with a pointer and a blackboard?"

Lisa remembered the corner of her nursery where had stood the little blackboard. It had been big then. She had had to look up at it. Her father had listened as she read from her book. It had not been too hard to read the single words, to say "The egg—the eggs," when the pictures beside the words so conveniently illustrated the difficult letters.

Her father had watched the children's festival at Waldenberg in 1914. "You and Sophie Braun were the best—absolutely the best of all the angels."

Rosy with pleasure, Lisa and Sophie had grasped each other's hands and had sung once more for the professor:

> *"Now I lay me down to sleep,*
> *Fourteen angels watch do keep . . ."*

"Were we really good, Father?" Lisa had asked. "Do you think that one year soon I might be Gretel?"

"I hope so, my child—indeed I hope so."

He must have known that this would be the last of the summer festivals. But Lisa and Sophie had not known. Proudly they had sung again:

> *"Now I lay me down to sleep,*
> *Fourteen angels watch do keep . . ."*

"May they watch over you, little Lisa—and the dear God, too!"

Her father had known but Lisa had not. Lisa had not known that there was fear against which one prayed. She had known that God was there somewhere beyond the angels. She had prayed from habit and from politeness, not from need. There was no need of God. There was Granny and there was her father, the professor, and there was her mother who was one of the angels. God was remote. The picture of Him was confusing. Sometimes He was patriarchal like Grandfather Blessing. And sometimes He was young. Sometimes a baby younger than Lisa. But always He was the God of Peace of whom you were not afraid. You brought Him birches in the spring and pine branches in the winter, you brought Him bright flowers in the spring and bright candles in the winter. And always there were small songs from the books and prayers that rhymed.

After that summer of 1914 God had changed. Lisa had remembered the God of Peace and she had wondered how He had changed into the God of War—the God of War who marched beside the All Highest's conquering armies. Lisa had wondered and she had learned to pray, not in gentle verse, but desperately in hidden, silent fear. "Not my father, dear God, not my father."

The sun was bright now. Beyond the low wall Central Park was fair and green. Lisa turned her mind from the darkness. It was over. For him it was over. Even after ten years Lisa had forgotten for a moment that, for her father, it was over. He would not want her to remember the darkness in the sunshine.

Perhaps he would want her to have always this American sunshine. Perhaps he would want her to stay. He was, after all, half American. No, that is not true. Lisa shook her head. He was German as I am. Where you are born, what your heart remembers—that is what you are.

"Well, Lisa, what are you doing, shaking your head so gravely? Rehearsing?"

"No." Lisa smiled at Harry Millard. She had not seen him approach. "I had forgotten that I'm an actress. This lovely day made me forget. It made me remember long ago before I was an actress. Except, of course, in a very small way. Being an angel was the beginning, I suppose. Even then I wanted to be Gretel—to have a big part."

"You look like an angel to me," Harry said. "I never imagined quite such a fashionable angel, but you have the red-gold hair and the transparent look. And angels should be tall like you, Lisa, and move lightly as though they could fly and only walk because they choose to."

"Why, Harry, you're very poetic for this time of day."

"Maybe this fine day has gone to my head, too. But I've got the future on my mind—not the past. How about lunching with me at the Casino in the Park?"

The Casino was crowded. The women in their pale silks and chiffons were like flowers in a great conservatory. Beyond the wide glass windows was the cool green of trees and lawns. Lisa remembered the restaurant in Budapest where she and Franz von Erlencamp had lunched.

"What a curious idea, Franz," Lisa had said. "A restaurant in a zoo."

"It is nice, you will see," Franz had said proudly. He had been pleased that there was something in Budapest that Lisa did not know, something beyond the world of the theater where she was beginning to have success—a success that Franz could not share. They had lunched on the terrace and beyond them was the park and out of their sight the fairground. They had heard the shrill, distant music of the merry-go-rounds.

"It's nice here," Lisa said to Harry Millard. "It reminds me—it's quite different—but it reminds me——"

"Please don't be reminded, Lisa," Harry interrupted. "This is now, and I want you to concentrate on me."

"I do," Lisa said, but her eyes dropped to the ring on her left hand. Franz had given it to her at the end of that day in Budapest. . . .

"Look, Lisa—you must have known I was working round to this."

Harry Millard spoke earnestly. "All these months when I've been practically your shadow."

"Please don't, Harry." Lisa wanted to stop him. "I didn't think you were serious. I thought it was just fun for you to be friends with an actress. You seem so young."

"That's my silly, pink, baby face." Harry blushed a deeper pink. "But I'm not young. I'm twenty-one and my own man—and I love you and I want to marry you. And you know, Lisa—I don't like to talk about it," he stammered, "but I mean we'd be all right. I'm—uh—pretty well fixed."

Poor Harry. Lisa smiled at his embarrassment. He doesn't want to boast and yet he is afraid that, as a foreigner, I may not know he is offering me one of the great fortunes of America.

"I'm sorry, Harry."

"You could be happy here," he continued eagerly. "Everything's great here—not like Germany—well, I mean in Europe you never know. Anything can happen."

"I know, Harry, but——"

"And I wouldn't want you to stop acting. I mean, unless you wanted to. If you marry me you can have everything you want——"

"I'm sorry, Harry." Lisa stretched out her hand to him.

He looked at the round ruby surrounded by diamonds. "But, gee, I thought you just wore that. I thought it must have belonged to your mother or something."

"It belonged to his mother," Lisa said gently. "The man I have promised to marry."

"Is he a German?"

"Yes."

"And do you love him?"

Lisa looked at the park beyond the glass. She remembered that other park in a distant city, that other day almost a year ago.

She and Franz had walked together through the gardens. They had watched the fair, they had ridden in the tall Ferris wheel and had looked at the two cities that bordered the Danube. That night after the performance Lisa had gone with Franz to a restaurant. They had listened to the music and watched the river. In the darkness one could imagine that it was blue.

"I'm going to New York, Franz," Lisa had said. She had waited all day to tell him. "Gerald Michaels, the American manager, has a part for me. It's not a big part but it's a good one—it can mean a great deal."

"Must you go?"

"I have promised Michaels' agent——"

"But you will come back, Lisa—I shall not lose you to the Americans?"

"I'll come back."

"You have waited all day to tell me this. And I have waited, too."

Lisa remembered his hand as it held the ring. His hand had trembled, and his voice.

"I've waited, too, Lisa, I've waited this whole year to tell you that I love you."

"And I have waited, Franz, since that first evening in Baden-Baden. I knew then and I have waited."

"I have so little, Lisa, only my name. I am proud of it, but I know it's not much as things are nowadays in Germany."

"Don't say it, Franz." It had hurt her to have him humble. He needed his pride. It was his armor against the world. Lisa would keep it bright for him. "It's a great name. Any woman would be proud to bear it—and I love you. Without the name I would love you. And with it I am proud." Her pride would strengthen his. "It is no small thing to be the Countess Erlencamp."

He had put his mother's ring on her finger. He had kissed the ring. "All that I am or ever shall be I pledge you with this ring."

Now, in New York, Lisa remembered that night. She looked at the ring and remembered the lighted terrace and the dark waters of the Danube—and Franz beside her. In Europe today his name meant little. In America it would mean nothing at all. In America he would be defenseless.

"You're pretty quiet, Lisa," Harry said. "I mean, are you sure you love this guy? I mean, after all this time and all . . ."

"I love him," Lisa said. "After all this time. After all the time there'll ever be. That's how it is with me."

"Lucky guy." Harry pulled a flask from his pocket. "I could use a drink—and I'll drink it to you." He lifted his glass. "Be happy. You rate the best."

"I'm sorry, Harry. I should have told you sooner. I liked having you as a friend, and so I didn't let myself see."

"I'm all right. Matter of fact, I think I'll stay right in here pitching. You don't mind if I stick around?"

"I'd like it. Just so you understand——"

"Well, you never can tell. You might get to like America enough not to want to go back."

"I do like America. Almost it tempts me to stay."

"Does it, Lisa? That's swell. What do you like?"

"Lots of things. I like the gaiety and the luxury. The luxury that in this prosperous land doesn't make you ashamed. I like your American sunshine and your American gift for staying young. I like all the things that any girl of twenty likes and that here she can have so naturally, so easily."

"I guess it's a pretty good country at that. I'm used to it so I never think about it. What else do you like?"

"The pattern of liberty that is so plain to see. The people who face one another here. They look not up, not down, but straight into each other's eyes. All the people equal in a country that really belongs to the people—that has always belonged to them. Here there have never been kings nor crownless substitutes for kings. Here everyone can be what he wishes to be. You were right to put stars on your flag. Here the stars are within every man's reach."

"You're a little romantic about us, Lisa, but just so you like us, it's all right with me."

A tall, thin man approached.

"Hello, Lisa. Hello, Harry. Sorry to interrupt, but I'd like five minutes with this young lady if you're through lunch."

"You're not interrupting," Harry said sadly. "I wish you were."

Lisa rose. "I must go anyway. You called a three-thirty rehearsal of the last act on account of the new boy. Or did you forget, Gerald?"

"How can I forget that my cast are dropping away? Ted off to Hollywood and you, Lisa, refusing to go on the road. Come on, I'll take you to the theater."

"All right. Good-by, Harry."

Harry held her hand. "Think of what I said. Meantime I'm sticking around."

As they drove away from the restaurant Gerald Michaels asked,

"Is Harry Millard the reason you won't go on the road for me?"

Lisa shook her head. "I'm going home."

"You won't do better than Harry. He's a nice kid and he has tons of money."

"No, it's not Harry. It's that I mean to go home. I told you that when I came."

"But we didn't know then that you'd be a hit. Look here, Lisa, you go on the road with *The Newcomers* and next season you'll play a lead for me."

"No, Gerald, thanks a lot, but I'm going back to Germany when we close in New York."

Lisa recognized the finality of her decision by the ease with which she spoke it. This is what I really want, she thought, to go home. It's what I intend to do. Even though I have the right to stay. Dan Hanauer gave me that right, and my grandmother. No, she gave me the right to be a German when she made my young heart German.

"I think you're making a mistake," Gerald said. "You've got a great future here. Most girls would be pretty darn grateful to have your chance."

The taxi was halted by the traffic that crossed Fifth Avenue at Fifty-eighth Street. Lisa watched the motorcars. She watched a young girl who drove a bright blue car with red wheels. She wore no hat. Her short curls were bright in the sunlight, bright as the metal fittings of her shiny new car.

"That girl, for instance," Lisa said, "with her small, proud head. Look at her, Gerald, how pretty she is—the one in the blue motor. She looks like a magazine cover, but more eager, more determined— like a poster, if one can imagine a poster small and elegant."

"She's on her way all right," Gerald said. "Listen to her press that klaxon!" The blue car shot noisily down Fifty-eighth Street and disappeared in the stream of traffic.

"America belongs to girls like that," Lisa said. "They are really young and free."

"And you, Lisa, aren't you young and free?"

"Young, yes. Though I can remember when I thought twenty a great age."

"And free, in spite of this?" Gerald touched the ring on her ungloved hand.

"That's a pledge, freely given, freely kept." Lisa held her hand so that the sunlight shone on the crimson stone. This was her choice. Her beloved choice. She would return to Franz, her German love. In Germany, too, after the darkness, there was light. There, too, the peaceful years would make the pattern of liberty. And she and Franz and their children would be part of that slowly emerging German pattern.

> *I had long since a lovely Fatherland.*
> *The oaks would gleam*
> *And touch the skies; the violets would nod.*
> *It was a dream.*

Lisa remembered her father's sad voice as he taught her Heine's verses. For him it had been a dream—a dream destroyed by war. The evil, ancient gods had walked again in Germany. But now in the peaceful years the dream could be true. Lisa and Franz would see the dream, the lovely Fatherland.

II

THE QUEENSBOROUGH BRIDGE was crowded. Anne Brooke pressed the horn of her bright blue car. She was caught in the stream of Friday's traffic. It would take forever to get to Southampton.

Anne wondered why she was hurrying. At the end of her journey there was only another party. Another party. Anne remembered when every party had been this party. Then every day had been this day— this new day in which the world might change for her, in which she might get a glimpse into the secret heart of things, find the reason for painfully and eagerly growing up, for growing old and dying. She shivered. Then she smiled at herself in the mirror on the windshield. Twenty-one was a long way from age and death. But it was the last of the goals in time. "When I'm sixteen," she had said. "When I'm twenty-one, when I'm grown up." Now she was grown up. There were no more years to wish for. Nineteen twenty-eight was just another year, another year in Southampton. And tonight there would be another party. Another party and Paul Craven. Soon she must decide about Paul.

Anne had known Paul always. She did not remember a summer without him.

She remembered the long summers of childhood. The early summers when the afternoons had been spent at the beach or playing under the trees beside the lake at Mary Winton's. Paul had been part of all the summers. And when the years had begun to be grown up Paul had still been part of them. Because of Paul, Anne's first New York dances had not been frightening. Among the strange, stony-faced little boys in their first dinner jackets, Paul had been her friend. He had brought his friends to her and he had seen to it that they had danced with her.

Paul had protected her at those first parties as he had protected her in the ocean when she was little. He was three years older than she and he had always been strong. She remembered how in the surf he had taken her hands from the rope to which she clung while the waves pushed her and the sand slid quickly, roughly away beneath her feet. "I'll take you out to the barrels," he had said. "Don't be afraid with me." She had put her hand on his shoulder and she had not been afraid.

But it's not enough, Anne thought. Just not to be afraid isn't enough for a lifetime.

She drove along the shaded Long Island road. Bruce Craven, Paul's uncle, lived near by in Westbury. Bruce Craven was enormously rich and Paul was his heir.

Paul's rich now, Anne thought, with what his family left him. And that, too, is security, but it isn't enough—it isn't enough for a lifetime.

Anne remembered how she had tried to explain to Paul. He had brought her home from a dance and they had stood together in the summer night.

"We're friends, Paul, but that's not enough. There must be something more—a reason for all this." She had gestured vaguely at the starry night that surrounded them.

"A reason for the sea and the stars in our small hearts? Could be, Anne. You're the reason in mine. Always have been."

"No, Paul, don't you see? We've known each other forever. We're only friends."

"I'm more than friends. But I'll wait—only not forever. Just till you're sure. Don't let it be too long."

Anne wasn't sure. She liked Paul, and she liked him to kiss her. But that wasn't love. That wasn't what the poets promised. That was second best. Anne remembered girls who had had to take second best because they couldn't get their first choice. Pale brides of whom the wedding guests said: "Funny, I thought she'd make a lovely bride. She's such a pretty girl!" Then, afterwards, the not quite happy brides seemed to be all right.

Anne turned into the Middle Country Road. She hated this dusty, hot part of the drive. The sweet, sickly scent of the dry scrub pines was suffocating. She had left the traffic behind. She drove quickly. She drove quickly towards another party in another June. Perhaps tonight would be different. Paul's voice on the telephone had been urgent. "You'll surely be there?" he had asked. "I've got to see you."

Anne remembered his voice and wondered if tonight she might have to decide. She tried to analyze her reluctance to decide, to choose this one path of life. It would be a pleasant path, a smooth and safe path. She had said that, too, to Paul. "It would be so easy to say yes—to move from one Southampton dune to another. To take the easy, expected path with you. To choose forever the pleasant places that I've always known."

"You like the pleasant places, Anne. They're all you've ever known."

"Sometimes I think I'd like something I haven't known."

"The unknown might be dangerous, Anne. You'd be safe with me."

"Perhaps I'm tired of safety—perhaps I'd like danger."

"In a book or a play, maybe—with a safe ending; or, if it's not a safe ending, you can close the book or leave the theater."

Anne had stood on the steps of her mother's house and looked out over the resort that engulfed the village, that spread out over the hills of Shinnecock. Here and there lights were still burning in the houses of the summer people. Anne knew every house and every lane in Southampton. It held all her summers.

"I'll wait, Anne," Paul had said again.

But he would not wait forever. Anne's time of choice was running out. In the end she supposed she would choose Paul. She wasn't sure that she wanted Paul but she was sure that she didn't want to lose him.

At eleven o'clock that night Johnny Payne drove Anne up the hill to the golf club. Paul had gone to another dinner party. She would meet him at the dance. The lights of the clubhouse were bright above the Shinnecock Hills.

Another party, Anne thought as she danced with Johnny. Another party. Not this party. Not this night. Not the beginning—the beginning that you imagined when you said: "Someday, next year, tomorrow."

" 'Lo, beautiful," Tom Webb cut in. "You're looking pretty cross."

"Not really, just thinking."

"Party's no place to think."

"Oh, for all the thinking I do . . ." She giggled and followed smoothly an intricate step.

This is fun, she thought. What a fool looking for tomorrow on a Friday night at Shinnecock. Expecting every party to be Cinderella's ball. It's high time I got over that.

Tom twirled her dexterously beyond the reach of an approaching stag.

"Seen the new visiting fireman?"

"There isn't one. At least not one that's new to me."

"You haven't seen this. He's a wop but a nice guy."

"When you say 'wop,' do you mean he's an Italian or that he didn't go to Harvard and looks like Valentino?"

"No, he's Italian. He was at Harvard Law with Bill Winton and Pete Smithers. Good-looking feller but a swell guy. He's some royalty or something."

"You mean nobility, don't you? Southampton would hardly take royalty so calmly."

"Gosh, you know what I mean. Title or something. His father or his uncle or someone was a count. He's staying with Bill Winton. I'll tell old Bill to fix you up."

"Never mind."

"I can't give you anything but love, baby . . ."

The orchestra leader's soft voice was clear above the sound of the instruments.

> *"Dream awhile, scheme awhile,*
> *We're sure to find*
> *Happiness and, I guess . . ."*

I guess, Anne thought. Happiness seemed sure in the stories, but they were fairy tales. In the songs I sing now it's uncertain. The best I can do is guess.

> *"Gee, I'd like to see you looking swell, baby.*
> *Diamond bracelets Woolworth doesn't sell, baby . . ."*

Mrs. Brent danced by. Against her partner's black coat her arm was bright. Narrow line bracelets of diamonds, of rubies, of sapphires formed a jeweled sleeve from her wrist to her elbow.

Paul's right, Anne thought. I'd hate to have to settle for Woolworth's.

Paul cut in. "Right on cue. 'Gee, I'd like to see you looking swell, baby.' And I do, baby." He smiled at Anne's flushed face. "For a girl who's been heard to say she's tired of parties, you're looking very swell indeed."

"It's a pretty swell party."

It was a gay party. Gaiety was all you could ask of a party. Anne looked up at Paul and sang:

> *"Dream awhile, scheme awhile,*
> *We're sure to find*
> *Happiness and, I guess . . ."*

"I guess," Paul interrupted cheerfully. "Happiness, ours, yours and mine, that's what I want to discuss. But not here, not in a ballroom festooned with drunks. Come on, we're getting out of here."

"But I've just come. Let's not go yet."

"This is important. I'll tell you in the car. I have news."

He drove her down the winding road and turned towards Southampton. He drove down a road toward the ocean. When he reached the beach he turned off the engine. She heard the roar of the sea.

It was dark under the moonless sky. She could just distinguish the pale edges of the waves as they broke.

She did not need light to see Paul's face. She could see him in the dark. She knew his face by heart.

"Sorry to drag you away from the party, Anne—and you dressed up for it so pretty."

"That's all right. It was just another party. I used to hope . . ."

She hesitated. Put into words, the hopes sounded silly. They were silly. They were born of nursery fairy tales—and they had been nourished at school on a rich diet of nineteenth-century poetry.

"That you'd be pretty? Was that what you hoped, Anne, because——"

"No, that didn't matter."

"It matters to plain girls. You're completely pretty. I was watching you on the dance floor before I cut in and I thought you looked like a young Greek boy. That short white dress is like a tunic."

"Not a goddess?"

"You'd hate that—great full-blown creatures. Pretty passé nowadays. No, a boy—a beautiful, discontented boy done by a fashionable Athenian sculptor. Listen to you! You're purring like a small white kitten—which you also resemble."

"What else am I like? I like talking about me."

"A wax doll with absurd big blue eyes and yellow hair. Only yours is gold." He touched her short curls. "Not just the color of gold. In the dark it feels like metal—cold and smooth."

She moved her head under his hand.

"I don't think I like the wax doll."

"Sorry. I'm only talking to put off saying the important thing."

He took out a cigarette.

"Oh, Paul, I wish——"

"That you were in love with me? Wishing it is beginning to be it."

"Then it's been begun for ages. I like you. And"—she smiled at him in the brief bright flame of the match—"you have the sort of looks I like. I like those broad shoulders, too. You're square and solid without being dumb."

"Will you please learn, Anne, my girl, that stockbrokers, football players, and large men don't have to be dumb."

"I know they don't have to be, but they are a lot of times. And you're not. That's the wonderful thing. But about your looks——"

"For gosh' sake, Anne! You're just talking, too—to put me off. But tonight you can't put me off."

"It isn't that I want to put you off; it's just that I'm not sure."

"I think you'll never be surer than this—and now I've got to know. You see, I'm off tomorrow."

"Off where?"

"On an inspection trip for Uncle Bruce—to our offices in Chicago, San Francisco, and points between. I'm seeing him tomorrow to get my final instructions."

"But isn't this sudden?"

"Not exactly. I just didn't want to say anything unless it came off."

"It's important then and good?" She couldn't see his expression but his voice sounded pleased.

"I'll say it's good. It means the old boy is going to push me ahead. It isn't just the money. It's the responsibility. Uncle Bruce wouldn't pick me, only nephew or no only nephew, to take his place eventually if he hadn't confidence in me."

"Paul darling, it sounds wonderful. But I'll miss you. How long will you be gone?"

"Till September anyway."

"Oh, Paul."

"Do you mind?"

"You know I mind. I can't imagine a summer without you."

"And I can't imagine a lifetime without you. And now that my life is beginning—I can tell from Uncle Bruce's attitude that this is the beginning—I want you. The waiting's over, Anne; you've got to decide."

"Not yet, Paul. I don't want to decide yet."

"You don't know what you want, sweet, but I do. I know what's best for you, so let's get it settled—about us, I mean."

"No, Paul, you see——" She didn't want to have things settled. Not yet. He stopped her protest with a kiss. It was hard to think when she was close to him. She moved into her corner of the car.

"Don't you see, Anne darling, I can't be worried. About us, I mean. I've got to be able to pay strict attention to business. I've got to make good for both our sakes." Paul described his trip. "In Chicago I'll see Bennett, of course, and the Mathewson bunch."

Anne tried to understand her reluctance to promise. Perhaps she was just afraid of being grown up.

"Well, Anne, how about it? I'm serious now. I've got to settle down and I want you with me. I mean it this time. If you say no I'll accept it. I can't go on like this."

Anne thought he meant it—or might mean it when he got away. She didn't want him to go. She hadn't ever meant to let him go for good.

"You have to decide, Anne. Is it yes?"

This was the first time he had required an answer. He would let this be her final answer. She looked at him. He sat staring stolidly ahead. His shoulder was stiff. It didn't move against hers. He spoke without turning his head.

"Well, Anne, are we set?"

"I think so." Not the final word, not yet. "Let's not have anything official yet."

"All right. We won't announce it until I come back and then we can get married in October, say—or November?"

"November, perhaps." She didn't believe on this June night beside the sea that November in New York would ever come. The thought of that other time and place touched her mind but not her imagination. In the beginning of the summer the cold death of the year had no reality.

"Atta girl. That's a promise."

It isn't. I just said "perhaps." He can't make "perhaps" a promise by calling it one. But she did not speak her denial.

"And no last fling in my absence, young lady."

"A fling in Southampton. Don't be ridiculous. Who with?"

"You never know. Just don't let it happen. I'd break his neck."

"And marry me anyway?"

"And marry you anyway." He pulled her toward him. "I'm not worried—not really. Not now that it's settled. And this should keep you in mind of me." He kissed her.

When Anne awoke the next morning, she moved uneasily in her bed. There was something—something important. Paul and I. Paul and I. She sat up. She was surprised at her cheerfulness. It was fun to be engaged. It was nice to have it settled—well, practically settled. She had always meant to marry Paul. She wondered why she had hesitated. She was fond of Paul, and she liked him to kiss her. That was love, no matter what the poets said. Perhaps unrequited love was different: more romantic, since it wasn't real. And the romantic marriages—they didn't turn out so well always. A good marriage, however it began, settled into a partnership of friendship and affection. Paul and I have that and a little more. Anne touched her lips. A lot more. She smiled as she rang for her breakfast. All my romantic ideas. I suppose I was waiting for Lindbergh or the Prince of Wales. And if you could achieve it, that sort of relative glory mightn't be such fun.

She ate her buttered toast and licked her small fingers greedily. Paul's new job is pretty swell. It'll be fun being rich and young. It's usually people's families who are rich. Old rich people are stuffy. Heavy houses and stiff gilt-chair parties. Young rich people are gay. They have fun. Paul and I will have fun.

"You're looking very pleased with yourself. I thought you were ill. What happened to you last night?" Mary Winton stood in the doorway.

"Mary darling. Oh, Paul had to go home early. He's leaving for the great open spaces. His uncle's sending him on this God-awful trip for the rest of the summer."

"Poor Paul. I mean, you don't look very sad."

"Well . . ." Anne stopped. Not yet. She wouldn't tell anyone yet. Not even Mary Winton. Anne loved Mary. She trusted her. She would never trust a man as she trusted Mary. If only Jim Forrest would fall for Mary. Mary had never said anything but Anne thought she was in love with Jim. Boys liked Mary but they didn't fall in love with her. Fools they are, too, Anne thought impatiently. You can fall in love with boys but you can't really like them. They are such fools. Mary isn't pretty. But her face has good bones and her figure will last. She's tall and straight. She'll be better-looking than I am when we're both forty. Not that it'll matter then. But Mary is brave and clever. Boys are fools.

"Aren't you going to tell me, Anne?"

"There isn't anything." Only in my mind. Nothing is true until you say it and I haven't said it—not even to Paul really. "You know I always tell you everything."

"Today I'm going to tell. That's why I'm here at this unearthly hour. I have news."

Anne stared at Mary. Today she was not plain. She held herself proudly. Her eyes shone and her mouth curved in a new soft smile.

"It's Jim. He's asked me to marry him. And he wants it announced right away, tomorrow night."

"Oh, Mary——"

"You knew I was in love with him. Everyone knew, I guess, except Jim. And he was afraid to ask me. I can't believe it." Mary sat on the edge of Anne's bed. "You don't know what it's like to be plain Jane and to be dragged to the parties. Parties aren't meant for plain girls. You're one of the lucky ones, Anne, one of the lucky, pretty ones."

I'm not lucky, Anne thought. I'm not because I can't be sure, not with the sureness that's shining in Mary's eyes.

"Anne, you're crying. You mustn't cry. Everything's all right for me now."

Anne wiped her eyes. "It's just that I'm afraid for us all, beginning our lives."

Why is growing up sad? Anne wondered. Why do we imagine it will be different? Each one of us, pretty or plain, planning her life—her different life. And all the lives are the same. But for Mary at least the beginning is different. Happiness that is bright like a flame, not quiet, content . . .

"I'm going to be married in September," Mary said, "and I want you to be my maid of honor."

"Thank you, darling, and I'll want you, too, when I—if I——"

"Still not telling?"

"There truly isn't anything."

"Then don't tell me or anyone. Especially not yourself. Don't tell yourself something is true when it isn't. Be sure. I am—and it's a good feeling. It's worth all the waiting."

When Mary had gone, Anne lay still against her pillows. She remembered Mary's face, as though a light were shining. For Mary at least the beginning was different. But in the end the marriages were the same. Anne thought of the middle-aged lives she knew—the

Wintons, the Moreheads. Contentment was the most you could hope
for in the end. And that Paul and I have now, Anne told herself.
That we have now.

III

WHEN ANNE ARRIVED at Mary's engagement dinner, Tom Webb
joined her. "Nice timing on my part, what? How about me as a sub
for Paul?" Tom took her arm. "But wait till you see Marco Ghiberti.
I won't have a prayer."

"Who's he?"

"You know, the guy I was telling you about, staying here, friend
of Bill's and Pete Smithers'."

The room was crowded when they entered.

"Jim, congratulations. It's grand. Hello, Mr. Winton. How do
you do, Mrs. Winton."

"Anne dear, this is Marco Ghiberti, Bill's guest. Bill's late as usual.
Take care of Marco, will you?"

"Would you like a cocktail, Miss—Miss——"

"Brooke. Anne Brooke. No, I don't want one."

They stared at each other. This isn't meeting. This is recognition.

"Have you been here long?"

"No, I came only yesterday."

"Are you staying long?"

What could you say when you couldn't say anything? When you
couldn't hear what you said because your heart pounded as though
you were at the end of a race? Was there really a race, a prize to win?

"I shall be here some time. You see, Bill is my friend. Mrs. Winton
has been most kind."

Not most kind. I shall be most kind. All the words were new—
"kindness" and "delighted" and "meeting."

"You must come to us. Get Bill to bring you to swim tomorrow.
It's nicer than the beach club." Her voice sounded flat.

"Marco, I want you to meet——" Mrs. Winton took him away.

"Well, is he something or is he something?" Tom was triumphant.

"He's something," Anne smiled. She was glad that her voice was flat. It did not betray her. Perhaps, after all, she was one of the fools to whom this happened alone. Don't let that be true. Please don't let that happen to me.

She went in to dinner with Tom. Mary called to them to come to her table.

Anne didn't see Marco. He was behind her. "May I join you, Mary?" He sat down beside Anne.

"You've met Marco, Anne?"

"Yes, I've met—we've met."

So that was true, too. You couldn't say the name without betraying yourself. For that one word, your voice would not obey. But this couldn't be happening. You didn't fall in love like this, suddenly. Not at a dinner party—not with a stranger in this familiar room. She looked at the room, the dark curtains, the pale walls. Everything was the same. Only she was changed. She turned her head slowly. Marco was watching her. He smiled a little. She knew she was not alone. So it happened like this suddenly. It was this party—this night—this time for which she had waited. There was, after all, a reason in your heart. A reason for the stars and the sea. A reason for all the beauty you had ever seen. An answer to all the questions.

After dinner the victrola was played, and the piano. It was a gay, noisy evening. Anne moved quietly through it. Marco was beside her. When the party separated them, he watched her.

She felt as though her heart was stretched too tight. She could not stay any longer.

Marco followed her through the front door. "May I help you find your car?"

His hand touched hers as they walked. It's as though he touched my heart. It's as though I had never been touched, never been kissed—as though it were new.

"How early, tomorrow, may I come?"

"Oh, any time—any time at all, Marco." The last word caught in her throat.

"Anne." She heard his voice change, too, with her name. "Anne, let's not wait until tomorrow. Let me talk to you now."

She stood beside the car. "Not now—not yet."

"I know. We have time or do I only think we have time, Anne?"

"One thinks lots of things at night. The day is better for talking."

She got into her car without giving him her hand. It made it easier to leave him.

"I let you go because you do not want to go." He turned away and then stopped. "For me, too, you know, this is the first time."

He walked back through the darkness into the bright doorway.

Anne drove slowly home by the ocean. Like a silly lovesick girl, she thought; or perhaps they aren't silly. Perhaps they're all like me. The first time. It's not just the first time. It's the only time.

Anne had never before lain awake all night. She felt neither tired nor restless. Her body was light. Her thoughts were like dreams. They moved through her mind without her control. She saw Marco's dark head against the pale green wall of the Wintons' dining room. Then he moved so that the red curtain was behind him. How queer that that long-remembered room should be now forever the frame in which she had first seen Marco. She stood beside him under the trees. In the darkness the trees loomed big as they had been when she and Mary, as children, had played under them. She remembered playing there once after the rain, the leaves slippery with light. Bill had come, and Paul.

Anne moved away from the thought of Paul. Her body felt heavy under the covers. She must tell Paul.

It was beginning to be day. She watched the light spread slowly through the room. On the chair her blue dress was colorless in the pale light. I'm glad I wore that. A new dress in honor of Mary's party. A new dress in honor of Marco. A new dress with soft chiffon drapery that trails below the short skirt. The pretty new fashion. I'm glad there are pretty fashions to wear for Marco. "Anne dear, this is Marco Ghiberti . . . Take care of him . . ." The party moved around her again, like the dream of a ballet, a masked ballet—except for her and Marco. They alone could see one another's faces.

Anne went down to the beach early, long before she could expect Marco. The sand and the dune grass were bright in the sun. Very bright, as though they were newly washed. No, not that. Anne groped for an exact description. Newly seen. As though a thin veil or an imperfect pane of glass between her and the earth were gone.

When Marco came Anne was sitting on the wooden steps that led from the dune down to the beach. "Am I too early? I could not leave before."

"No, not too early."

He sat beside her.

"This is the first thing I remember."

"The sea, Anne?"

"No, the dune. Being hot and tired and having to climb it. The steps were so tall and the boards were rough when I fell. It sounds flat as I tell it. That's because I'm not remembering it now, just remembering the memory. But I want to tell you about me. I thought I might start when those steps were high and the dune grass was tall. I used to be afraid that the dune wasn't big enough, that the waves would come in and in and never go back. I didn't see why they ever turned back. Why they didn't swallow all the land. I didn't understand about tides."

"Do you now?"

"No, I suppose not." She stopped remembering and turned to smile at him. "I take them for granted." Her eyes dropped.

"Look at me, Anne. Don't be frightened at what has happened. It has happened to you, too, hasn't it?"

"Yes, I think so—to me, too."

"You know it, Anne. That is why you try to tell me about yourself, about the little girl you were. You want me not to be a stranger. It's frightening to love a stranger."

She did not answer. She was afraid. This was happening too quickly.

"Don't be afraid. I'm not a stranger. I'm not a stranger here in your country. My own country is strange to me. I have been away at school in Switzerland and then here. I cannot go back."

"But I thought Italy was wonderful now. I mean the trains and everything. Everything so orderly and peaceful."

"That, yes. Also death is orderly and peaceful. I do not judge. I have been away too much. I know only that it is not for me. I shall live here. I shall be American. You are so American, slim and golden, with a small eager face."

"But your family—do they feel as you do?"

"There is only my mother left. My little mother. I wish you could see her. She is small and gentle. When I was a child she was very gay. Pretty, with shining dark hair that matched her eyes. Now she is tired. Her hair is white. Since my father died she has grown old. It was not easy to bring a little boy through the war years. She lives now in a convent near Naples with the sisters. She accepts the world beyond the convent walls. She is too tired not to accept. All but the very young are tired from the war. A tired people accepts much. But my mother knows that for me acceptance is not possible. She knows that America is right for me. Liberty, equality. Not even the dream of those things exists in Italy. But in America—America is the dream."

"Do you talk like this to Bill and the others? They don't talk about liberty and things."

"They take them for granted as you do the tides."

"Is it me you like or America? I don't want to be a symbol."

"You, Anne. Love, not like. I knew I loved you right away. Mrs. Winton said, 'Mary's best friend there in blue!' And I saw you and I thought, 'This happens only to the poets, not to me.' "

He held her face in his hands and looked at her. "You might make a poet of any man."

"You look like a poet." Her voice shook. "Oh, Marco, I feel so funny." Tears stung her eyes. He kissed her eyelids and then her lips.

After a while he said, "Your family—should I?"

"There's only Mother. You'll see her at lunch. Let her get to know you before we say anything."

"Let you get to know me, my poor Anne. But I can tell you a little. I am to work in September for Danforth and Kane."

"Oh, Mother knows Mr. Danforth. He's a sort of cousin."

"That is good. And Mrs. Winton and Bill and Pete Smithers know me well. I have a little money that my father left. It's not much, but soon I shall be earning——"

She put her fingers to his lips. "Someday you can tell my mother all that. But let's talk about us. Not our families and money."

"My father——"

Anne interrupted. "Would he have approved of me?"

"Of course, and my mother."

"And my mother will, too. But it'll take time. And in that time let's not be practical. Let's talk about us. We have so many years to make up, so many lost years."

Anne wanted to think only of Marco himself. But she couldn't help wondering about the grandeur on which he had turned his back for the love of a dream. And she was part of the dream. His mother would like her. It would be fun to visit her someday. My mother-in-law. She has retired now to a convent. Anne imagined the old lady behind the gray walls. My mother-in-law, the Countess. Tom had said something about Marco's being a count. Perhaps with his funny democratic ideas he wouldn't use the title. She would find out from Bill. It would be fun to have crowns embroidered on things. These thoughts were on the edges of her mind. In the center was Marco.

"You look a little like a poet, Marco—more like a soldier. A soldier who would fight only for liberty, of course." She laughed.

"You are lucky to be able to laugh when you speak of liberty, Anne."

"Well, you know it is rather a joke. What with prohibition and taxes. Mr. Bruce Craven says——"

Marco's face was stern. Anne stopped speaking. Then he smiled. Anne thought, His face is beautiful when he smiles. I never thought I should like beauty in a man.

He took her hands. "I forget that you are young. I have noticed that Americans stay young a long time. I should like my sons to be Americans." He tightened his hold on her hands. "I cannot believe that your hands are mine to hold—that you will be mine."

He stood up. "Perhaps if you would present me to your mother, she will think it strange."

"She has given up thinking that anything I or my friends do is strange. You'll meet her at lunch."

Mrs. Brooke liked Marco in spite of herself. Her anxiety was a wall against him. She had never thought Anne too impressionable, but today there was something in her manner that was new. Sometimes Anne had seemed hard but since the war all young people . . . Mrs. Brooke's thoughts trailed away into a vague uneasiness as she watched Anne's soft, bright face. The young man was charming. He liked America—really liked it. None of that kindly condescension—I-don't-mean-you-dear-lady sort of thing. The English were the worst, but Mrs. Brooke wished this boy were an Englishman, not an Italian. She wished he didn't exist at all. She wished Paul Craven might have brought that look to Anne's face.

"What are you young people going to do this afternoon?"

"I don't know," Anne said. "Sit around here for a while. We'll wander over to Mary's later, I guess."

"I must go there myself sometime today." Mrs. Brooke put down her coffee. "I think I'll just drive over there now. I want to congratulate Mamie Winton and Mary. Did you send flowers, Anne?"

"No, but I will. Marco and I can do that now and then we'll go to the Wintons'." Anne did not intend to have her mother question Mrs. Winton.

Mrs. Winton was a small, faded woman. Under her soft exterior was strength—strength that she used for her children against the world. She's like Mother Wolf really, Anne thought, strong and fierce for all that gentle, gray-haired prettiness.

"You stay here, Mother. It'll be better. I'll come back and report all the excitement and everything."

Anne dined alone with her mother that evening. After dinner she asked, "Well, Mother, how do you like the Wintons' Italian?"

"The Wintons' Italian? I was afraid he was ours."

"Yes, and Mrs. Winton would have thought so, too, if I'd let you go over there. She's very sharp, is Mrs. Winton. I like her but I don't trust her. No one can. No one young, at least, except Mary and Bill. I guess she'll relax though, now that Mary's settled."

"Anne, you're talking too much. Are you trying to avoid telling me about this young foreigner you produced at lunch?"

"I didn't produce him. He's staying with Bill, and Mrs. Winton dotes on him. I found out all about him. He's good family——"

"Darling, you know I don't care about those things."

"Yes, you do, angel. Everyone does. Family or money. Preferably both. Well, Marco will have both. He'll earn one and he's born to the other. He belongs to the Neapolitan branch of the family. It seems his father was a younger son so they haven't a title, but in Italy Marco would be Don Marco. Bill explained all the ramifications. I couldn't follow it very well. But if it satisfies Mrs. Winton, that's enough. She's the snob of the world. And he's got a job with Danforth and Kane, starting in the fall, so you can find out all about him for yourself when Mr. Danforth gets back from Scotland."

"Anne, are you serious about this boy? I thought you and Paul——"

"Paul!" Anne's eyes widened. "I must write Paul."

"Paul's such a dear," Mrs. Brooke said. "I've always hoped——"

"Mother, honestly, there's nothing to worry about. Do you mind if I go now? I've really got to write to Paul."

It was a difficult letter. Anne wrote and rewrote it. In the end, it was only a note. She did not mention Marco. "I said 'perhaps' and you thought I meant 'yes.' But I didn't. I'm afraid even 'perhaps' is too much. I'm sorry, Paul, because I do like you. 'Like' is too small a word for my affection for you. But I don't love you. And liking isn't enough. I'm sorry. Don't answer this and please forgive me."

By the time Paul's answer came from Chicago, Anne had almost forgotten her own letter. She had forgotten the time before she knew Marco. The old time of waiting and compromise.

She read Paul's letter as she waited for Marco. "There's nothing to forgive. I don't believe you. You're just scared. All brides are nervous. That's all that's the matter with you. You'll be all right when we're married. And we'll be married when I come home. I've made up my mind and I think you have, too, even though you don't know it. Don't write again. Writing, like talking, is no good between us."

Paul was part of the past. Anne put his letter away. She waited for Marco.

"Anne, must we really go to this great dinner and dance? You look very beautiful for it. But couldn't you look like that just for me?"

"Of course we must go to Mrs. Brent's. It'll be fun. And it would be mean not to."

"Would Mrs. Brent mind?"

"Maybe not, but Tom Webb would."

"I don't understand. Is he perhaps a relation?"

"No. But he wants to build her house. He's a budding architect."

"I know that, but what have we to do with that? What has the party to do——"

Anne wondered if she could explain to Marco. Marco refused to distinguish between American fortunes through complete simplicity or superb snobbishness. Sometimes Anne suspected the latter. Surely he knew there was a difference between New York and the Middle West. "Our voices, Marco," she had tried to say, but he had insisted that the variety of American pronunciations added to the richness of the American scene.

"Look, Marco, Mrs. Brent—well, for one thing, people feel that she has too much money."

"Now you are silly, Anne. How could one have too much money?"

"You can't, of course. But you can show it too much. Perhaps you can have too much cash. And you shouldn't make it in funny ways. You know—Brent's plumbing. It makes people laugh. Money should make you respect it, like banks and things."

Marco looked blank. "You ought not to go to this lady's house if you laugh at her, Anne." His voice was grave.

"Oh, I like her. I feel sorry for her. It must be awful to be that age and have the conquest of Southampton one's ultimate victory. Poor thing, she tries so."

Marco said, "You are kind, all of you. Even if you laugh."

"Kind? Maybe. Live and let live anyway. And then, there's Tom."

"Tom?" Marco asked. "You mean you will speak for him. At a party—that seems hardly the place to speak of business."

"If there's a chance to do it tactfully." Anne did not try to explain. Marco would not understand that the presence of Tom's friends would plead his cause. Mrs. Brent would be pleased with Tom if his friends were nice to her. Otherwise she might go, next summer, to Maine or Rhode Island; she might find another resort with another Tom Webb whose local friends might be kinder.

"Anyway, it'll be a good party. Mrs. Brent has taken a lot of trouble about the bands and everything. It would be mean not to go."

"You are a kind little thing." Marco smiled at her. "You are all kind, only you are ashamed to admit it. And you live in a strange world. It's a holiday for me but for you this rich little corner of America is your whole life. I wonder what Mama would think." His voice was gentle as it always was when he spoke of his mother. "Little Mama, with her tired hands that now can rest. She would be astonished at the carefree luxury, the clothes and the jewels, the cars and the houses, all the lovely, expensive things that seem as though they had been not earned, but created by a wish. Mama has never seen anything like your shiny, brand-new, fashionable world."

I bet she saw plenty of luxury before she retired to that convent, Anne thought, but Marco doesn't remember. He was too young. Little boys don't notice clothes and jewels.

As they drove home after the party, Anne stopped the car and pointed to the small red church on the dunes. "That is where I've always meant to be married. I had planned everything about my wedding except you."

"But, Anne, that is a Protestant church."

"I never thought." She stared at him and at her own stupidity. "Of course, you're a Catholic. All Italians are."

"Yes. Devout or anti-clerical. We are born in the Church, we marry in it, and we die in it."

"You've talked politics so much. I mean democracy and those things. I never thought you were religious."

"It's not that I am devout or not devout—that's what you mean, I think. It's that I belong. I don't often speak of the Church. I don't always consciously believe. But always, I belong. Do you understand?"

"You say, '*the* Church,' not '*my* Church,' as though you admit no other. That's really belonging, isn't it?"

"Would you mind, Anne? Would you mind being married in the Church?"

"I haven't thought about it but I will if you want it." Mother will mind, or perhaps not, since Marco isn't American. Marco doesn't think Americans are snobbish. And this particular snobbishness he would find incredible. I never thought of marrying a Catholic, but for Marco to be a Catholic is romantic. I expect I'd think that for Marco to be a heathen Chinese was romantic.

"Anne, you're not listening to me."

"No. I'm not listening. I'm loving you."

"Darling." He drew her to him. Then he stopped himself. "But you must think. You must listen. You must know me and all my heart and mind before you trust yourself to me."

"No one knows anyone else, really, and I love you, Marco, and I trust you. We have all our lives to learn to know each other in. We have only this short time for the beginning of love."

He kissed her and they talked no more that evening.

IV

JULY SLIPPED AWAY and it was August. Marco and Anne were alone as much as Anne could manage.

"There's no point in being conspicuous." They were sitting in the afternoon on the steps, watching the sea as they had watched it on their first morning.

"We are more important, Anne, than what those others think."

"It isn't that they're important. It's that I want to keep us apart from them. Not have them talking, thinking too much. And even when we're with them, we're always alone. Alone as we are here."

He put his arms around her.

Presently he lifted his face from hers. They stared at the sea. Almost two months had passed since that first June morning. Anne looked back, trying to separate the days. The days had slipped by like beads on a smooth thread. This kind of happiness joined time together.

"We don't know each other, Anne."

"We know bits and pieces. In the end we'll know everything."

She had talked of herself more than Marco had talked of himself. Marco's voice was sad when he spoke of his boyhood.

"Were you unhappy when you were little?" Anne asked.

"No, I was not unhappy. No one could be unhappy with Mama. But I cannot remember any more without knowing what I know now about my poor Italy. So even the memory seems sad. Italy is beautiful. The sea near my home. If you could see that water, your Atlantic would seem gray. This thick northern blue. Near Naples, from the convent garden, my mother can see the bay. You can see the bay, too, from the house where I was born."

"The Castella Costa?" Anne asked. "I know. Bill told me."

"The Di Costas were very kind to us always. It was as though my mother were their daughter. Her own parents were dead and so the Countess di Costa took her back before I was born. She looked after her, had her own doctor——"

"Was it beautiful—the castle?" Anne asked.

"It was more a villa than a castle, but it was very pretty, white with a scarlet roof. I went there sometimes when I was a little boy. From the terrace you could look far out over the bay. Now my mother can see almost that same view from the convent garden."

Anne imagined them—the gay little castle shining in the sunshine, and the gray-walled convent, and beyond the different buildings was the bright blue water. Church and aristocracy side by side, in a distant, romantic land.

Anne watched Marco as he looked out at the Atlantic. She wondered if he was remembering that other sea. Could your heart really choose a new country completely? A country couldn't be just ideas. It must be the feeling of the air and the color of the land, sounds and smells. Nationality was remembering. But someday Marco would remember this, the bare shore and the northern sea. He would remember seeing them with her when they were young.

"What are you thinking about, Anne?"

"About us. When we're old. We'll know each other then."

"But we should now."

"We know enough, Marco. We know our love."

"Yes, that we know—all the time. It makes us alone whether there are crowds or not. Your face I know." He touched her cheek. "And the feeling of holding you in my arms."

She put her fingers against his mouth. She remembered when Paul had told her she was as beautiful as a Greek boy. That had been a compliment. She knew she had a bright, fresh prettiness, but not beauty. Marco had beauty. The curve of his mouth . . .

"Anne darling, we can't live forever in this golden summer. We must plan."

"It's the first summer. The first time in my life I've ever known joy. Fun, yes. But not joy. Happiness that is sharp like pain and underneath steady like faith."

"I know. I, too, would rather not break the enchantment. But we must. We must learn to know one another. Our minds. Not just our hearts and bodies."

"I know quite a lot about your mind, Marco. Your political ideas, anyway. I can't help knowing them. You're almost as much in love with America as you are with me."

"But America makes our love possible. In Italy it could not be."

"It could be anywhere."

"I think not—though you would try. Bill has told you of my family background. You always stop me."

"Yes, Bill has given me the picture." She looked at him thoughtfully. He was afraid that his mother wouldn't accept her.

"You think, Marco, your mother will approve of me?"

"I was thinking of you, Anne, not of my mother. With her it naturally wouldn't be disapproval. She would be only afraid for our happiness. She believes in class distinctions. To her they are part of the natural order."

So it certainly isn't from his family that he gets his democratic ideas, Anne thought. Perhaps it's lucky for me he has them.

She spoke lightly. "Well, I suppose, Marco, in Italy you keep people in compartments. But even so——"

"That's it!" Marco interrupted. "In Italy one thinks in those terms. Here there are no kinds of people. There are just people."

"My poor innocent. I hope that when you know us better you'll still love me and America."

"It's you who know neither yourself nor your country. But about my mother. I wish I could make you see her. And my father, too, though I hardly remember him."

"Bill's told me."

"Yes, with Bill I have spoken much of Mama. You are different from her, but when you know her you will love her."

"Look, Marco darling, it'll all be all right. When Mr. Danforth gets back next month he can tell Mother the whole situation."

"There is no situation, Anne. It is just that——"

Anne stood up. "Please stop worrying." She frowned into the sun. Old lady Ghiberti must be a terrific snob who knew nothing about America. Mr. Danforth could settle her. In the meantime she would continue to keep Marco off the subject. It made her angry.

Anne managed August as she had managed July. Even Mrs. Brooke didn't realize how much time her daughter spent with Marco. It's natural, she thought, that Anne should be attracted by the young foreigner. The child can't sit home because Paul's away, and Marco has the charm of novelty. That will wear off and then Paul will come back.

During the last week in August, Phil Sinclair spoke to Anne about Marco. They were sitting on the terrace at the Wintons'. "What's all this about you and the visiting fireman?" he asked.

"Nothing for your column, Phil."

Phil had grown up in Southampton with Anne and the Wintons

and the rest. He had meant to be a lawyer, but one summer he had stumbled into the position of assistant to Lorraine Van Clef, the society editor of the New York *Star*. Phil had not gone back to law school. He had continued to work for the *Star*. And now he wrote the Peter Pierpont column on the *Express*.

"Not for my column, Anne, for me. I like you and you're one of my old friends who doesn't disapprove of my job."

"Well, I like to be in your column. The others just pretend they don't."

"And their disapproval is supposed to be the convincer. But about you and Marco, Anne? Not for publication."

"It still isn't anything."

"I don't believe you—you've changed this summer. You look the way you did when we were kids. You were an awfully pretty little girl."

"Are you breaking it to me that I've lost my looks?"

"No, but it was as though they had got frozen into a pattern. And this summer you're different. But I'm worried. I have an idea you're walking around in a fog. Look here, Anne, how much do you know about Marco?"

"I know enough." Anne wanted to ask Phil if he knew anything about Marco's mother. Perhaps she had some special reason to dislike Americans, but the question might betray her secret. To tell Phil would be to tell the world. She was not yet ready for that. She would wait for Mr. Danforth's return.

"Anne, hang on even if it's tough. Don't let people stop you if this is what you really want. Money, position, they're not such a much."

"They're handy to have," Anne said.

"They don't last, you know. You ought to have a look at the old Peter Pierpont files before my time. You wouldn't recognize more than a handful of the rich, important names."

"Well, jot Marco's name down for future records," Anne said proudly. "He's going to make history."

"I think he will. It may be tough at first, but you hang on." Phil's thin, sallow face broke into a grin. "I don't know why I'm pleading Marco's case. I guess I'm not. I guess I'm pleading yours. It looks to me as though this is for you and I don't want you to lose your chance. Take your chance, Anne."

"Thanks, Phil. And, not for publication, I know it's my chance. The chance I'd almost stopped believing in."

Marco came through the french windows. Anne rose to meet him. "Good-by, Phil, we're going to New York. Mary's having Lisa Blessing, the actress, to dine. You know, she was in *The Newcomers*."

As they drove towards New York, Marco and Anne were silent. The talk with Phil had made Anne uneasy. The summer had been a dream and now it was ending. This was the beginning of reality. It is the end, she thought, almost the end. This summer seemed so long when I promised Paul.

They were on the Middle Country Road. She breathed the sweet dry smell of the scrub pines.

"Usually, Marco, I hate this part of the drive, but now I'm grateful to it. It still holds our summer in its dusty heart."

"Don't be afraid, Anne."

"I didn't say I was afraid."

He smiled at her. "That is one of the things the summer has given us. We have no need to say everything to one another."

Anne stood beside Marco in front of Tony's in West Fifty-first Street. They waited for someone to open the grill in the upper panel of the locked door.

"I bet you hate this," Anne whispered. "You're more law-abiding than I am. I love speak-easies even though I know they ought to make me feel creepy. I guess they do or I wouldn't whisper."

"Darling, your heart is always right. If you would only listen to it."

"Now don't tell me you believe in prohibition. I couldn't bear it."

"No, but I can see what they were trying to do. Young countries try all sorts of things. Sometimes it's splendid, sometimes absurd."

The door opened. Lisa Blessing stood beside Mary near the doorway.

Lisa Blessing looks the way we'd all like to look, Anne thought. Dead white skin and bright hair and thick dark lashes that shadow her eyes. She shines in this dingy little room as though she had all the lights of the theater.

"This is Lisa," Mary said. "And Harry Millard of course you know. Sit there, Anne, will you, beside Jim."

"Hi, Harry." Anne turned to Jim Forrest. "Goodness, he must be in love again. He looks like a stuffed robin."

"Don't tease him. The poor guy knows he hasn't a chance."

Anne smiled at Jim's innocence. Of course Lisa Blessing will marry Harry. She'll never pass up the Millard millions.

"I wish you could persuade Lisa to stay, Jim," Mary said. "She's going home right after our wedding. She didn't really mean to stay that long."

"I didn't know you were going back, Lisa." Jim sounded astonished. "What for? You can be a terrific star over here."

Lisa smiled slowly. "You are very kind."

Her voice is low, not a blond voice, Anne thought. Everything about her is unexpected. She's tall, but not a Valkyrie. A Lorelei or Undine seen through still water. A tall, gray-eyed Undine with red-gold hair.

"I must go," Lisa said. "Mary understands that I want to go home."

"We all understand you," Harry interrupted. "But we'd still like to change your mind. You like it here and—I mean—well, things in Germany——"

"Dear Harry," Lisa spoke quietly, "I know what you mean. Even so, I must go."

"Lisa's beautiful," Anne murmured to Marco. In the noisy little restaurant it was possible to talk privately. "But not quite what I'd pictured. I think of Germans as bouncing, rosy people. Too many cheerful, brightly colored fairy tales in my youth. Thank goodness people my age didn't learn to hate the poor things."

"Nor to understand them," Marco said. "The Germans aren't a simple people. Your fairy stories weren't very well illustrated if you have forgotten Grimm's dark forests. But you can't understand Europeans. Americans are the only sunny people, really. You, for instance. You have a clear, innocent prettiness that is typical of your countrywomen."

"Typical? Marco, I don't like that adjective about myself. Nobody does."

Jim Forrest interrupted. "I think you better talk to me, Anne. I have news for you."

"That sounds pretty solemn. Good or bad?"

"That's for you to say. Paul's back in town."

Anne steadied her right hand on the table. Now she would have to tell Paul and her mother. This was the end of summer. She had known this time would come but she hadn't imagined it clearly. Now that the moment was here, she was frightened. She clenched her left hand in her lap. She wanted to feel her nails sharp against her palm. She wanted to feel something besides her heart, which pounded heavily in the emptiness inside her. She looked down and was astonished to see that her dress was motionless against her breast.

"You take it pretty calmly. Did he get hold of you?"

Anne shook her head.

"I didn't tell him you were dining with us. He sounded excited and I don't care for scenes. I think he's gone straight down to Southampton."

"I didn't expect him to come back so soon."

"Don't explain to me, Anne. But you'll have to explain to Paul— or are you really through with him?"

"If I were, don't you think I ought to tell Paul before I tell you?"

"So you haven't said anything to Paul about Marco? Someone has." Jim looked at her kindly through his glasses. "I hope you aren't too involved, my dear. I feel responsible."

"Why? Responsible for what?"

"For Bill and Mary. They're too impulsive. These foreigners! Poor old Harry—although he's safe. I don't think the fair Fräulein will have him. And, after all, she is someone, in a way. She's a darn clever actress and her grandfather was the grand old man of German poetry. But you and Marco, if you're serious . . ." He paused. Anne was silent. "What I mean, he's a nice feller and all that, but he's pretty much of an unknown. I just thought—I don't want anyone hurt because Bill got too hospitable with a guy he doesn't know all about."

"How do you mean?"

"Well, Paul said—I don't know. I've always had confidence in Mrs. Winton, but Paul sounded pretty upset. He said a lot of things."

"He would." Anne knew how Paul would behave about a foreigner. She had heard him on the subject. "These handsome fellers with their second-rate titles, looking for American dollars to patch their crumbling castle walls . . ." Her mouth tightened as she imagined Paul's contempt.

"Thanks, Jim, for telling me about Paul." Her small competent hands fumbled awkwardly with a cigarette.

Mary watched Anne anxiously. She hoped Jim wasn't being tactless about Marco. Jim didn't approve of foreigners.

"Suppose we go to the Montparnasse where we can dance," she suggested. "It's stuffy here."

Anne went with Marco.

"Is something wrong, Anne?" he asked when they were alone. "You look suddenly tired."

"Not exactly. Paul Craven's back." She realized that she had told Marco very little about Paul. "You know he's the man that Mother wants me to marry."

"Yes, you have said his name. But you are not afraid of your mother?"

"It's hard to upset her plans, not to do what she expects. I hoped she'd get to like you."

"I think she doesn't dislike me. The important thing is that she loves you. She will want you to be happy."

"I thought it would happen some easy way." She stared at Marco. Her light eyes were almost black as the pupils grew big.

"Poor Anne. It was a summer dream and now it's real. It's natural you should be afraid."

"I mean it to be real."

"Of course, and I will help you. To displease your mother, to displease even this Paul will be hard for you. I understand. To imagine being brave, that isn't difficult for any of us, but to be brave . . ."

"Marco, I'm scared." Her voice shook. "I kept thinking something would happen. That Paul would meet someone else, that Mr. Danforth would persuade Mother."

"Nothing is ever easy. Nothing will happen that you don't make happen. It is time now for courage."

"I'm brave. Well, not very. But with you to help me it won't be too bad."

She knew that her mother loved her. And she knew one thing about her mother that Marco did not know. Mrs. Brooke was romantic. She had been happy in her short, young marriage. Mrs. Brooke wanted to be practical about her daughter's marriage but Anne thought that she, more easily than most mothers, could see love and marriage with the eyes of her own youth.

"I guess I'm just a silly coward, Marco."

"No, my darling. You are young and nothing has ever been hard for you."

"Anyway, the silliness and the cowardice isn't all of me. Loving you is all of me."

He stopped the car near the Montparnasse and took her in his arms. He interrupted her protest. "If they do see, what does it matter? They will know soon anyway."

They danced to the summer's tunes—tunes that at summer's end had taken on the sweetness of familiarity, the beginning of memory.

"This is the end of the enchantment, Marco."

"And the beginning of reality. That will be better. You will see."

They danced in breathless silence. Anne was not afraid.

Lisa Blessing watched Anne and Marco. While she talked with Jim Forrest, she watched them. She saw Anne's lips move as she murmured the words of the song the orchestra was playing.

> *"I'll get by as long as I have you.*
> *Though there be rain and darkness too . . ."*

For her too, Lisa thought, there is a song, a little song for falling in love.

> *"What care I, dear? I'll get by*
> *As long as I have you."*

"It surprises you that I have no accent?" Lisa asked Jim. "But I have always spoken English as well as German. My grandmother is American. She brought me up."

"I didn't realize that you lived with your grandfather; 'der Dichter,' as he is called."

"Germans speak of him so. It would have pleased him that even here . . ."

She smiled as she remembered how the great man had enjoyed his greatness. With his own hands the laurels as Napoleon the crown. Fame, praise, the consciousness of his own genius—had they made up, she wondered, for happiness and grief? Even his sorrow for his only son had added to his glory, or at least had popularized it. *The Death of Kings* and the other tragedies were more admired than read. But everyone could sing the *"Heldenlied."*

"I'm not much on poetry," Jim said. "But I've heard the *'Helden-lied.'* It's a stirring tune."

The Montparnasse orchestra was playing "Who."

"Your American music is more lighthearted," Lisa said. That tune belonged to her and Franz. They had danced to it on their first evening together in Baden-Baden.

> *Who stole my heart away?*
> *Who makes me dream all day?*

"That? That's an oldie," Jim said, "but it's still a darn pretty tune."

Lisa was grateful for the American music. While it played she could not hear the other music—the music to which her grandfather's words marched in two-quarter time.

> *From our bright swords the evil blood shall flow,*
> *From lifted blades the alien——*

Not those dark words. Lisa listened to the American music. She remembered the night on which she and Franz had first danced together to that tune—to those words.

> *Who means my happiness?*
> *Who would I answer yes to?*
> *Well, you ought to guess who.*
> *No one but you.*

That American song had been the beginning for her and Franz.

V

WHEN LISA REACHED her hotel room, she went to the desk and took from the drawer a letter from Franz.

. . . Why do you not stay in America, Lisa? Since Gerald Michaels is so anxious that you remain. Things are no better for me here. Once in a while I write a political article for the *Morgenpresse*. But really it is my name that is useful to them to obtain advertising. The department-store owners' fat wives are pleased if I go to their dinners.

They say that in America anyone can be successful. Perhaps even I. It is worth trying. Let me join you. In that new country we can make our life. Germany is finished. Under the present government we are only a third-rate, defeated nation—after ten years, still on our knees. The old Germany will never rise again. Why should you and I, my darling, stay in this new Germany which has taken my birthright? Perhaps in America I might start again. I might offer you more than an ancient name whose glory is forgotten. There is no place for the Erlencamps in this middle-class republic. It belongs to the shopkeepers.

Lisa put down the letter. To reread it made it no easier to answer. Her hand lingered on the envelope. She imagined his long-fingered hand as it held the pen and wrote her name. Perhaps it is for me that he wants to come here. For my sake he is impatient for success. If it were not for me, Franz von Erlencamp would never desert Germany. If I let him make such a sacrifice, he would not be happy. He and his people are too deeply rooted in Germany.

A photograph of Franz stood on the desk. Photographs are no use, Lisa thought. When you see them suddenly, yes, but when you are used to them they get between you and the person. Dear Franz, I saw you more clearly tonight than I have for a long time. Those two reminded me. One sees it so rarely, that bright, concentrated look— two people alone, however crowded the place. Anne and Marco have it. What you and I have, Franz. What we shall always have.

She remembered the way Anne placed her hand on Marco's shoulder when they first danced together. Lisa curved her hand as she tried to recapture the soft possessive gesture. The most casual gesture, when one loved, had significance.

Lisa remembered when she and Franz had first danced together. It was two years ago at Baden-Baden. He had been staying with his aunt, the Baroness Billingsloeven. The Baroness had a fashionable appreciation of celebrities. She had driven from Baden-Baden to Waldenberg to call on Frau Blessing. The Baroness had taken Lisa back to Baden-Baden to dine. "My nephew, Franz, will be so pleased." Franz had been indifferent.

Lisa remembered.

Franz danced with her to please his aunt. He stood before Lisa, tall, dark, a little sullen. "Gracious Fräulein, may I have the honor?"

Lisa knew. Before he took her in his arms, she knew. She knew that this was the beginning for her. She smiled and rose from the table and gave him her hand. It was strange that it should be this unfriendly boy. She had not imagined him so. But this was he for whom, unknowing, she had waited.

They danced. Her hand was light on his shoulder. He was smiling when they returned to his aunt. She spoke amiably to Lisa.

"We must see each other a great deal, my dear. Not just on your grandmother's account, though she is, of course, almost an historic figure. You, yourself. I saw you in that Reinhardt production. Only a bit, of course, but you were charming. You will go far—and not because of your grandfather's fame and your grandmother's fortune."

The Baroness talked and the music played. Lisa watched Franz.

"And not only as the widow of the poet is one interested in Frau Blessing," the Baroness continued, "but she herself. She represents an epoch. She has that elegance. She reminds one of those happier times. There was no court in Europe to equal that of William II. Not even the English. Theirs is a bourgeois royalty, overshadowed by the counting houses of the City. The Emperor and his sons were soldiers. Ours was a truly royal court. It had a saber's brightness. Strength as well as grace. A court of princes and officers. I remember seeing your grandmother there when I was first presented. She wore white and diamonds. One dressed in those days."

Lisa smiled at Franz. He saw her a little, now. The orchestra played.

> *Who stole my heart away?*
> *Who makes me dream all day?*

Franz and Lisa danced. Lisa knew that now he saw her, that now he held her in his arms. This was the first dance. This was the beginning.

Franz lengthened his visit to his aunt. He came often to Waldenberg to see Lisa.

After his second visit Frau Blessing asked Lisa, "Is it he? Is he the prince on the white charger? You have just met him. And am I already too late with my warning?"

"Your warning, Granny? You mean, you think that your money . . . ?"

"No, not that," Frau Blessing smiled, "although the Baroness looked about her with appraising eyes. But since the war no one is sure about German fortunes. We live simply so no one, I think, is aware that I have managed to preserve the greater part of what my father left me. It's safer, perhaps, that people should not know."

"What can you fear nowadays, Granny? Now we are all safe."

"We thought that once before, Lisa. We thought we were safe."

Outside Frau Blessing's sitting room the branches of the pines gleamed in the sunlight. The warm summer air came through the open windows. Lisa looked at her grandmother. With them in the sunny room was the memory of fear. The memory of that December day when fear had been finally realized.

"There can be nothing more." Lisa took her grandmother's hand. She held it as she had held it long ago. "Now we are all right. The whole world is all right now."

"I hope so, my child. However, I didn't mean to speak of a great fear but only of a little one that troubles me. I'm afraid of Franz von Erlencamp's pride."

"Surely that's a good thing in a man."

"Pride implemented with strength, yes. My father had that." Frau Blessing pointed to Dan Hanauer's photograph. "And Wilhelm was proud. Even as a young man your grandfather was proud. And he had strength. He believed in his own greatness and created it."

Lisa looked at her grandfather's photograph. The young, fair-haired Wilhelm Blessing, whom only Granny remembered. To Lisa, Wilhelm Blessing seemed always to have been the white-haired, white-bearded patriarch. The great man.

"Even his pride, Granny . . ." Lisa hesitated. Not willingly did she turn back to the darkness. "The '*Heldenlied*.' That was pride turned to hate."

"Poor Wilhelm," Frau Blessing sighed. "His pride turned to hatred, to bitter, wounding hatred. Your father was his immortality. His fine son. His only son. One can only pity Wilhelm, but you are too young to know that. And one can pity, too, the Franz von Erlencamps. They were taught their pride—a pride in forgotten glories, a pride that looks back, that turns away from this postwar world."

"Poor Franz. They brought him up wrong. His pride is not his fault. It's not of his making. They gave it to him."

"I don't blame him, my child. I don't blame any of the lost young men who refuse to find their way in a strange, new world. But pride is no weapon against fear. Fear can change pride to greed—to ruthless greed. And I am afraid for you."

Her grandmother had been wrong. Lisa smiled at Frau Blessing's photograph, that stood beside Franz von Erlencamp's. With me to help him, his pride will turn to courage, not to fear. He will see the true German pattern, the pattern of peace, not of war. He will learn to love the Germany of which my father dreamed—the Fatherland of Goethe, of Schiller, of Heine. The lovely Fatherland.

Lisa began to write. Her fingers moved easily in the German script, the script of her childhood. To write it was to be, a little, home again.

I, too, my dearest [she wrote], miss you. It is like you to think of my career. But truly, this sudden leap forward is an accident, even here. It happened that Gerald needed a very young actress for the part. And because I am new, the critics spoke much of me. Also it is fashionable in the theater to be a foreigner. It was luck and a very fine play that made me important. Even for my career, it is better that I go home to study. It will be slow but it will be safer.

I am tempted by this city. It is so new. It was built yesterday. It will be rebuilt tomorrow. It belongs to the young. Here one can begin again with no burden of memories—of ancient evil. Here our life would be new—new as our generation is. It tempts me. It would be a good life. But not good enough for you and me. However bright the foreign land, it would be for us shadowed by exile. We are born to love Germany. We are too German, you and I, to break the bond to the Fatherland. These are your words, Franz, that I quote. I know your German heart as I know my own. This is an exciting city. This is a beautiful country. But it is not ours. For us there are no hills, no valleys, no earth that is not German earth. We could not live transplanted. As exiles we should be but half alive. For us there is no homeland but Germany. And in Germany we will build our home.

Lisa put down her pen. What I say is true. Truer for him, perhaps, than for me. Only now, without me, he is lonely and afraid. He shall never know that I know he is afraid. It is not his fault. They brought him up wrong. Only his pride they gave him. Well, his pride will keep him safe until his courage grows stronger. His pride and I.

She stretched out her hands toward Franz. She looked down on the city from the high hotel window. She imagined the harbor she could not see—the harbor that lay beyond New York's dark towers. From there, the ship would sail to take her home. Now the darkness was over. In Germany the sun shone bright. She and Franz would build their life in the light, in the Fatherland.

VI

BILL WINTON and Pete Smithers had dined alone in Southampton. They sat in the Winton library and talked about Anne and Marco.

"Hell, Pete, I don't remember what I told her about Marco. It was way at the beginning of the summer. But, you know, I gave her the story. Doesn't wish to be called Don Marco over here. That was a fancy touch. Doesn't mention his grandfather's title on account of his democratic ideas. He has those all right."

"It's a little tough on Anne. I've an idea she's fallen for him—and she's a snob."

"Serve her right then."

"Well, not really, Bill. Girls probably think a count's romantic. I mean an Italian would have to have some sort of a title to rate with the girls we know."

"Nuts."

"No use being sore. That's how girls are brought up to think. And when Anne finds out that Marco's mother was the Countess di Costa's maid until she married—and that Marco's father kept a little restaurant in Naples . . . Well, you can imagine. Anne's going to be plenty upset."

"He's probably told her."

"He may easily never have mentioned it. I mean, with her knowing you so well, he probably thinks she knows. And he doesn't think things like that are important in America. He's a smart guy, but in some ways he's awful innocent."

"Well, what did you want me to do? I didn't know Anne was going to fall for him when she asked me. And when we'd taken all this trouble to put Marco over in Southampton, I wasn't going to wreck everything. Anyway, he's a great guy."

"We both know that doesn't prove anything or we wouldn't have thought up this damn-fool idea."

"You know, Pete, this might be pretty tough on Marco."

"Light dawns."

Bill and Pete discussed their handiwork without satisfaction. It had seemed a smooth idea to invent an aristocratic background for Marco. It would force Southampton to give Marco a good time. That had been the beginning. A beautiful by-product of the scheme had been the joke on Southampton's complacent snobs. Now it was becoming evident that the joke would be on Marco. They hadn't meant it to turn out like that. They liked Marco.

"Suppose John Kane or old man Danforth hears about it and thinks it was Marco's doing. They know Marco's family history. Say, Pete, the poor guy might lose his job."

"I'll say."

"Can I help?" Phil Sinclair came quietly into the room. "I'm considered bright if not quite respectable."

"Have you been listening?" Bill asked.

Phil's pale face reddened slightly. "You make it pretty plain that you think I'm a heel."

"Well, it's a heel's job—writing about your friends."

"You'd be surprised how many of my friends don't mind. Besides, it's a well-paid job. Suppose I had sweated my head off at law. What would have happened? There have to be jobs as cushions for the fannies of guys like you who have what are elegantly called connections, but my connections aren't that good. They went overboard with my old man in the panic of 1907. Peter Pierpont is a living. And I don't earn it with my ear at the keyhole. In fact, a good many people call me up to tell me the news about themselves. Anyway, I earn money. And money's the big objective in this year of grace 1928, isn't it? Aren't we going to elect Mr. Hoover so we can all have plenty of money? All right, so I cash in on my friends. Well, that's what I'd be doing if I was selling bonds. That's what a lot of the boys from law school will do."

"Not Marco," Bill said. "It wasn't pull that got him his job with Danforth and Kane. And they're one of the best firms downtown."

"That's why they're one of the best firms. Because they take the Marcos—not just names for window dressing. But I don't kid myself. I'm no Marco. Because my father went there I let Mother start to put me through law school. Not a pretty picture, now that I look back on it—me accepting the silver platter that she couldn't afford. I like Peter Pierpont better than that. And I like to be the one in my family who provides the silver platters." Phil reached for a drink. "But let's get back to Marco. I take it that this war council is about him. Have you got in a little too deep with your practical joke? Don't look so blank for my benefit. I know all about the Ghiberti restaurant, and about the Ghibertis—and the Di Costas."

"How did you find out and what do you mean to do about it?" Bill demanded.

"Do? Nothing. Marco's a right guy. How did I find out? I asked him and he told me his life history. You should have let him in on your little plot."

"We couldn't," Pete explained. "He wouldn't have stood for it."

"I should think not. Most completely idiotic thing I've ever heard of. You like the feller so you figure out a way of making him inevitably appear a heel. He's in love with Anne. She isn't in on this, is she?"

Bill shook his head.

"You boys have certainly fixed everything up dandy for Marco. I don't see why he hasn't caught on, though."

"Well," Pete explained, "I guess no one but you said anything to him. Bill and I fixed it so the old girls down here would think it would show up their own ignorance not to know all about the Ghiberti family."

"I see. And the poor guy's in a fog anyway over Anne. Also the population of this handsome resort spend their time playing games instead of talking and thinking. I mean, they don't even gossip if it requires an intellectual effort like adding two and two." Phil held out his glass to be filled. "And since no one mentions the Hoyt soap or the Morehead carpets, I suppose Marco doesn't expect them to discuss his family's business. But how did you explain the big welcome to a plebian foreigner—from Southampton, one of the snob places of the world?"

"He thinks all Americans are like that. I mean, he thinks there are no classes in America—that we're all born equal. He takes the whole thing seriously from the Declaration of Independence to Abraham Lincoln."

"Don't think he's a Red though," Pete put in. "He isn't."

"I don't think so. But I'm surprised you don't. Why didn't Mary stop you?"

"We couldn't tell her the truth. She'd have made Bill tell his mother."

"She'd have made you make sense. So would Mrs. Winton. You underrate your mother, Bill."

"No, I don't. She'd have been fine with Marco, only—well . . ." Bill hesitated. "She'd have thought it was swell of me to have him for a friend and she'd have told everybody how democratic I am. You know Mother—always adding jewels to my heavenly crown. She'd have been fine but she wouldn't have taken Marco for granted. You can see, Phil."

"I've seen, all right. It's been a masterly exhibition of stupidity to watch."

"How long have you known?" Bill asked anxiously.

"For a couple of weeks. It's my business to find out things. If I'd known in time, I could have stopped you."

"Well, what'll we do?" Pete mopped his damp forehead. "We never thought at the beginning——"

"You guys never think at the beginning or any other time. You better tell Marco and tell him quick. My spies tell me Paul Craven is hurrying home. He's probably heard about Anne and Marco. It looks as though your practical joke was about to blow up in your faces— hurting no one but Marco. And possibly Anne, though I don't suppose that would bother you. You haven't noticed Anne this summer, have you? She's quite a different young lady."

"Can't we keep it quiet? You won't print it, will you, Phil?"

"I can promise you I won't use the story. But it may break in spite of me. Lorraine Van Clef or someone may get hold of it and play it up. News is scarce these days. You better get busy. You can't do much tonight. Anne and Marco have gone up to New York to dine with Mary."

"He's driving back. We'll wait up for him."

When Marco returned from New York, his friends greeted him with solemn faces.

"What's the matter with all of you?" Marco asked. "You should have come to town to Mary's party."

"Look, Marco——"

"The thing is——"

Pete and Bill spoke at once. They turned to Phil. "You better tell him."

Phil explained.

Marco stared at them. "I don't understand. You were ashamed of me?"

"Hell, no. It wasn't that."

"Was it then on account of Mary, or your mother, Bill?"

"No, it was—well, it was a sort of joke."

"The joke is on me, I think. People will not believe that I was such a fool as not to know."

"Oh yes, they will," Bill said.

"Thanks. But I'm afraid not. They would have to accept, too, my ignorance of certain American viewpoints that to them would seem unbelievable. I could not have imagined a situation like this. You see, I don't yet understand why such a joke should be necessary, why it should be even funny. This is America."

"This is the world, Marco," Phil said gently. "We have our classes same like any other country. Of course, sometimes our system of classification seems odd to foreigners. Boy, I remember, a few years ago, Long Island was pretty annoyed with the Prince of Wales. He couldn't seem to grasp our fine distinctions."

"Mrs. Winton will mind." Marco spoke slowly.

"Don't worry about Mrs. Winton," said Phil. "She likes you and that's that. She makes her own rules."

"Even so, she will not like being the butt of a stupid joke. Thank God, Anne—but I haven't told her. I thought she knew." He stopped. "Did you tell Anne all this nonsense?" Marco looked at them. "I see you did."

"Mother'll help you with Anne. And she can talk to Mrs. Brooke."

"I know Anne won't mind. She never wanted to talk about my family. I was afraid it was because they weren't grand enough. I did her an injustice, as you do." Marco smiled at them. "I guess you made the Ghibertis elegant but tiresome. Anne isn't a snob. She was bored with the relations you gave me. Anne won't mind."

"She may not mind when she gets used to the idea. But I'd go a little carefully," Phil suggested.

"Anne is the one person I understand—the one sane creature in this craziness you have made."

"Gosh, Marco, I'm sorry. Is there anything Pete and I can do?"

"It's all right. You meant no harm. It's so late. I must stay here tonight. But tomorrow——"

"You're not going to leave. I don't blame you for being sore."

"I'm not." Marco laughed. "I am, of course. Sore as hell. I'll get over it. But I don't like to stay here. It was not I who deceived your mother. But she has been deceived and I am the deception."

The next morning Mrs. Brooke came into Anne's room. "You'd better get up. Marco Ghiberti's here. He wants to see you. He seems excited."

Anne smiled lazily at her mother. Her new courage was as strong by daylight as it had been by night.

"Sit down, Mother, and prepare for a shock."

"It's not a shock, dear child. But it is a disappointment. I always hoped that you and Paul—we don't know anything about this boy."

"I do. I know from Bill. Marco hasn't said much, but I gather that his mother may be a little snobbish about us."

"Well, really——"

"It's all right, Mother. You can floor her with the lords of the manor and all the rest of it."

"Are you serious, Anne? Do you mean to marry Marco?"

"I can't imagine not marrying him. I've been scared. Scared to tell you. I wanted to keep Marco and me outside of real life." She remembered Paul's words, "Close the book or leave the theater." He had been right about her then, but not now. "Now, Mother, it wouldn't be life at all without him."

"He's a foreigner."

"Not really. People of our class are the same the world over. And it isn't as though I were going to live over there. Marco's determined to be an American. I know it's kind of an unexpected marriage but it'll be all right."

"What will you live on?"

"Well, Marco has a little something. And there's my trust fund. And Uncle Norman Brooke will help. He's always said that when I marry——"

"But Marco must be a Catholic. That's enough to make your Uncle Norman wild. Particularly this year: he's already so upset about Al Smith."

"Uncle Normie will get over it when Hoover is elected. It's not religion with him. At the moment it's politics, and usually it's snobbishness and a pretty démodé snobbishness at that. Marco's titled forebears will soothe him."

"Don't be absurd, Anne. Some of my best friends are Catholics. But aside from any—well, feeling I may have——"

"Prejudice, Mother darling."

"All right, prejudice. I think Marco's religion is a difficulty. I think that, in marriage, Catholicism is like a wall. It can enclose and shelter you both or shut one of you out."

"If it shelters Marco, it will shelter me. You see, nothing matters except Marco and me. We have something . . ." Anne paused. "It's no use, I can't describe it."

"I know." Mrs. Brooke's eyes were bright with remembrance. "The poets have tried but even they——"

"And all they said was true. I hoped that, but I didn't believe it. And all the things I thought no one could promise. In sickness and in health—that's all true."

"My dear little Anne, I hope Marco is everything you believe him to be. You do love him, don't you?"

Anne nodded her shining head. It hadn't, after all, been hard to tell. Courage grew when you opened your heart to it.

Marco was waiting for Anne in the library. She paused before she crossed the room. All I ever hoped, all I ever wanted . . .

"Shall we go outside, Anne?"

They sat on the steps. The sand and the waves were bright in the hot sun. Only the clear air and the heavy white clouds showed the beginning of autumn.

"Anne, there has been a misunderstanding about me. I don't quite know how to begin. My family——"

There it goes again, Anne thought. They must be something.

"Marco darling, I'm sure your ancestors were wonderful. And your mother has every right to be proud of them. But, really, she's not marrying me. You are."

"I know, Anne. I know you won't mind. But still, I feel like a fool. I've never told you about my family. It was Bill."

"Bill mostly. But your reticence spoke volumes. Don't be scared, Marco. Your mother will approve of me when she knows about me. She probably thinks that you've let your enthusiasm for democracy affect even your choice of a wife. It'll be all right." Anne enjoyed comforting Marco. He was always the brave one. But he's afraid of his mother—of his distant connections. He can't escape that European, patriarchal thing.

"I never meant to mislead you, Anne. This whole thing is a stupid joke of Bill's and Pete's. My mother isn't grand. She and my father— and their parents before them—were simple people like me. My grand-parents were peasants and fishermen."

Anne picked a piece of the dry dune grass. She twisted it carefully around her finger. She did not look up.

"Bill just pretended that ours was a noble family. Actually——"

"But why?" Anne asked why as a child does: not to know a reason but to delay an incomprehensible conversation until her understanding could catch up with it.

"He and Pete Smithers did it for a joke. I suppose that it's funny in a way." Marco laughed uncertainly.

Anne was silent.

"Anne, you see, Bill thought—I don't yet understand very clearly what Bill thought. Anyway, these are the facts—the facts I thought you knew. My father kept a restaurant. My mother, before she married him, was the Countess di Costa's maid. Surely I told you that. It seems to me I remember talking to you about it—about the Castella Costa where I was born."

Anne snapped the blade of grass in two. Now she saw the pattern. It had been there clearly all the time. When she was a child Anne had seen a floor of mosaic. At first she had seen nothing but the colored bits of stone. Then, one by one, she had found the pictures hidden in the pattern of stone. Once she had seen the pictures plain, she wondered at her blindness.

It was like that now. She was amazed at her blindness. Marco had told her, but she had not heard. She had been deaf and blind, lost in a bright fog of enchantment. She had accepted the false pattern Bill had shown her and she had looked no further. But Marco had told her.

"My little mama with her tired hands." Hands did not grow weary in aristocratic idleness.

"All the things you said, Marco, I misunderstood. When you spoke of class distinction, I thought——"

She stared at him. He hadn't changed. That aristocratic look was accidental. But it was there. The proud, upward line of his eyebrows, the curve of his mouth.

"My poor Anne. They have played a joke on us. But they meant no harm, Bill and Pete. Have they done harm?"

Anne shook her head. She held her trembling lips together.

"Anne, you don't mind about my parents? This hasn't changed us?"

"No, Marco. I don't mind. Of course, my mother——" Anne's voice was shaky. She stood up.

"Would you like to speak to your mother now?"

"No, I want to think."

He put his arms around her. She held herself stiffly. She moved away from him.

"Let's go to the beach club, Marco." She wanted to escape from being alone with him. There was no bright enchantment now. There was only an ugly joke.

When they reached the beach club, Anne knew it was the last place she wanted to be. As she walked down the narrow path of boards between the umbrellas, she heard her name and Marco's. She turned to one side. She stumbled through the sand between the umbrellas. Marco followed her. She found a place at the edge of the crowd.

They know, Anne thought. Of course they know. Why did I come here? To sit at the edge of the laughter and give it point.

"They know, Marco," Anne said.

"Naturally. That much I required of Bill and Pete. That they put an end to this deception."

Over her head Anne heard Mrs. Hoyt's voice booming, "I haven't laughed so since that Russian prince turned out to be a soda clerk from Yonkers. But Mamie Winton ought to be more careful."

Anne sat beside Marco under the bright umbrella. Betty Morehead walked by. She sang, " 'I can't give you anything but love, baby. That's the only thing I've plenty of, baby.' "

"That's for us, Marco," Anne said. "We even have a theme song like a talking picture."

"I'm sorry, Anne." Marco's voice was gentle. "This is hard for you."

"It's only the beginning."

He put his hand on hers. "Poor darling."

She moved her hand. "Not in public, please." Her voice was sharp.

Mrs. Brent, with Tom Webb at her elbow, stopped beside the umbrella. "Hello, Anne. Don't forget my cocktail party this afternoon." She smiled at Marco. "I want you, too, of course." She moved on.

"That woman patronizing me!"

"Why, Anne." Marco stared at her. "She's trying to be kind. But you—you sound——"

"Sorry." Anne held her voice steady. "I just can't stand Mrs. Brent playing the gracious lady at me."

"Anne." Marco sifted the sand through his fingers. He watched it falling smoothly. "You mind this very much."

"No." She looked at his dark, bent head.

"Too much, I think. Shall we go?"

"No." She wanted to sit still under the small shelter of the umbrella. She didn't want to walk with Marco past all those eyes.

Mary and Bill wound their way through the umbrellas. "There you are. Boy, is that water cold!"

"My tactful brother. Showing that all is well. Sorry about this mess, Marco. But it'll blow over. It will blow away with the summer."

"We're lunching here," Bill said. "The family's coming."

"No, I——" But Anne didn't move. She didn't want to stay but she was afraid to move.

At lunch Anne sat beside Mr. Winton. He and Mrs. Winton rarely came to the beach club for lunch. "Barbarous, really, these half-dressed young people. And sand over everything. Mamie and I do this only once a year. But then I'm old-fashioned. I liked the beach when it was simple."

"Surely this is attractive. The pool and all."

The club was good for a few more sentences. Then what would they talk about? Not Marco. Anything but Marco. The Wintons were being kind. Mary was being kind. Anne looked at Mary's thin hand with Jim Forrest's emerald blazing in the sunshine. Easy for them to be kind. Easy for them to smile benevolently on Anne's courage. They had no need of courage. They were safe.

"Next thing they'll be having a jazz band. To my mind this sort of thing belongs in Florida or Atlantic City. Southampton used to be a quiet place. Hate to see it getting so brassy. Never cared for brass. Nor for plush."

"Now, Willie, stop your nonsense," Mrs. Winton interrupted. "Southampton has to change. There are nothing but old fogies left in the summer places that haven't changed."

"Don't like change. Don't like new things. And I particularly don't like new people." Mr. Winton bowed to Mrs. Brent, who edged her way toward them. "Mamie's wonderful with them, though, and perhaps she's right."

"Indeed I'll be there, dear Mrs. Brent. I can't promise for Willie. He likes his golf, you know, and that makes him so late." As Mrs. Brent left, Mrs. Winton smiled at her husband. "Certainly I like new people. It's a change from watching myself and my contemporaries grow old. That's a depressing masquerade. Besides, Mrs. Brent is a nice woman. And she's being kind to my godson. Tom's going to build her house. Even you must admit that's one advantage of new people. They build and they buy."

"These are times when everyone can build and buy," Mr. Winton said. "And if the American people show their good sense, we'll keep on having good times. Seen these? Here—take one."

Anne looked at the small imitation gold coin. On one side were the words "Vote for Hoover" and on the other "Good for Four Years of Prosperity."

"You keep it, Anne." Mr. Winton smiled at her. "You must be old enough to vote."

"I am."

"Good, we need all the votes we can get. Got to hold the line. I never thought I'd be on the same team as Tom Heflin, but in a crisis like this you can't afford to pick and choose. After all, those Ku Klux fellers may swing the South for us."

Anne held the coin. You could vote for prosperity and for safety. A country could vote itself security. It was easy enough. She looked at the inscription on the coin. But where could you find a talisman for yourself alone?

She turned to Marco. "I've got to get away. This heat. My head."

"Yes, Anne. You have to get away. I'll go with you." He walked with her to her car. "Shall I come with you, Anne?"

"No, not just now."

"I'm sorry, Anne. You know that. You are upset. But we must talk."

"Not now, Marco."

"Tonight, then. The Wintons expect you to dine with them. We can talk then. And soon I must see your mother. There is much to explain."

Anne nodded.

"Is it too much, Anne?"

She stared at him. Her eyes were wide with tears. They mustn't spill over.

"Is it too much, Anne? Just tell me. I shall understand. But you should tell me."

Her tears blurred his face. She didn't want to see him since he hadn't changed. Everything else had changed. He should have changed, too. He should stand revealed as common, as too handsome. He should be different. She listened to his voice. It had not changed.

"I am the same, Anne," he said. "But the picture in which you believed is gone. Is everything gone with the picture, Anne? Was the summer enchantment all? Is reality too hard?"

His hand gently brushed the tears from her eyes. "Is it too hard, Anne?"

She could not speak. He looked at her. "Perhaps I, too, saw a picture of someone who was not there."

He turned away. She watched him walk down the road toward the Wintons' house. She drove home.

Anne met her mother as she entered the house.

"Why, Anne, what's the matter? You're as white as if you'd seen a ghost."

"It seems I've been in love with one. Marco doesn't exist. Bill Winton made him up." She pushed past her mother up the stairs into her room. Mrs. Brooke followed her.

"Anne darling, what is it?"

"All that fairy tale I told you about the noble Ghiberti family. Marco's father kept a restaurant. His mother was a lady's maid. It's enough to make anyone laugh." What a comic thing it would be if it happened to someone else. If it happened to anyone else, she would laugh herself sick. Great tearing laughter that would rip her heart like sobs.

"Stop it, Anne." Mrs. Brooke shook her. Anne continued to laugh.

Her mother looked at her helplessly. "Oh dear. I don't know what Norman will say. And to think of that nice-looking boy being such a liar."

"That's it, Mother." Anne's eyes moved away from her mother's. "He let me believe—I feel so awful that he let me believe all that."

"My poor child. Such a shock."

"If he hadn't been ashamed of it, Mother."

"I know, my dear. You'll just have to forget."

"I will." Easy to say. She moved her head abruptly away from the image of Marco's remembered face.

"Is there anything I can do?" Mrs. Brooke asked.

"Get me out of dining at the Wintons'. Say you're ill."

"I certainly will. And I don't have to say I'm ill. I'll tell Mamie Winton in no uncertain terms——"

"No, Mother. Just say you're ill."

"But, Anne. You're not going to see this boy again."

"No. I don't know. Just leave me alone."

To get rid of her mother, Anne laid herself down on the bed. "I have a blinding headache."

"Poor lamb." Mrs. Brooke tiptoed from the room.

When her mother was gone, Anne carefully relaxed. It was no use. She could not remain still. She wept. She wept unwillingly and angrily. She tried to stop. This grief was humiliating. Marco was a comic figure. Marco had deceived her. Even if he had not meant to deceive her, he had been the deception. The summer's golden enchantment had been a paradise only for a fool. And she, Anne Brooke, was that silly, lovesick fool. She pressed the pillow against her wet, sobbing mouth. She would not cry for this. Crying for ridicule, for shame, was a hateful thing. If Marco were dead . . . For a moment, she wept for Marco's death. She would have loved the dead Marco. But Marco, alive, was a clownish figure. She felt no pity for herself or him. She controlled her sobs. She would not cry. Tears were no defense against her world's loud laughter. She lay still. Her eyes were hot and swollen. She forced herself to stop crying.

She sat up. She stopped the laugh in her throat. It was the echo of other people's laughter. She did not propose to be the butt of that laughter. She had always been contemptuous of boys because they were so easily trapped by obvious beauty and charm. Now she had been caught in the same trap. But since she recognized the trap, she could escape it. She must think. She could still put things right.

The telephone rang. She had forgotten to switch it off. She let it ring. When the bell stopped and she knew that someone else had answered, she cautiously lifted the receiver. She heard Paul Craven's voice.

"Hello, Paul, it's me. I heard you were back and I wondered why you didn't ring up." She forced warmth into her voice. Paul could be her escape. He was security, the security she had so nearly lost.

"I didn't know you'd want me to. I've heard you were rather busy."

"Don't tell me you believe everything you hear." She managed a laugh.

"What about your letter?"

"What about yours? Or didn't you mean it?"

"Gosh, Anne, I mean it all if you want me to."

"Come over this evening and we'll discuss it."

Mrs. Brooke left Anne and Paul together. This would be the solution for the child. This always had been the solution.

"Well, Anne?" Paul's voice dropped as he said her name. Anne recognized that. Long ago, her voice had done that. Long, long ago. Long ago—I used to play that song on the nursery piano. The black notes moved before her eyes. This is maudlin. I'm not . . . I won't be . . . Not ever again.

"What about this phony count?"

"Paul, that wasn't serious. Marc——" She licked her lips. "He was just someone to play around with."

"And that letter you wrote me? Didn't he have a little something to do with that?"

"Why, I don't know that he was even here when I wrote it. I was just—oh, Paul, you know how I hate being pinned down."

"There's been plenty of talk about you and that Italian."

"That's because he's divine-looking." She closed her eyes against the sudden memory. "And all the girls wanted him. He liked me best and that was fun. But he always knew we were engaged."

"And are we?"

She smiled at him. "Almost."

He put his arms around her. He kissed her. She clung to him. He was what she wanted. With him she could escape from the trap into which her heart had betrayed her.

"I said I'd marry you anyway." Paul held her face between his hands. "And I will. But I'd kind of like to break that guy's neck."

"Truly, Paul, it wasn't anything."

"Wasn't it, Anne? Well, just so it's over. And now I'm going to tell your mother that we're engaged."

"Not yet. Let's keep it our secret for just a little while."

"That hasn't worked too well. I'll be down next week end. We'll announce it then. And I'm going to tell your mother now."

"All right, Paul." This is safety. This is my life that I want. "I'll drive up to town with you in the morning and we can discuss it at lunch."

"No more discussion, but we'll tell Uncle Bruce and I'll buy you a ring. I think I'd better put a No Trespassing sign on you." He kissed her again.

When Paul left, Anne stayed in the library. She looked at the red leather bindings of her father's books. They were handsome books. They looked particularly well in firelight. A fire was becoming to any room. It would soon be cold enough for a fire.

This is the way, Anne thought. I'll keep looking carefully at real things and after a while I won't remember Marco's face. She walked noisily around the uncarpeted edge of the room. I won't ever hear his voice.

The next afternoon Anne drove back from New York to Southampton with Paul's ring on her finger.

Bruce Craven had been pleased with the news of his nephew's engagement. "I thought you kids would never make up your minds. I'm glad it's settled. I'm planning big things for Paul."

The big things would be for her, too. They were what she had always wanted. The other hopes had been a dream. A dream that had turned to a nightmare.

Anne drove along the familiar road. Soon she would turn south into the cool air from the ocean. This part of the road was dusty with the summer's heat.

It had been easy to manage Paul. He loved her. That was fair enough. She loved him—with the sensible love that would last a life-time.

It's more than most people have, she thought. And this other. This other isn't love. It's a pain. It's an illness. Just now it's hard. But only now. Things remind me now. The road and the time of day and the summer's tunes that run in my head. Soon they will be old forgotten tunes like the nursery song, "Sing me the songs that to me were so dear, long, long ago, long, long ago."

She looked at her ring and held it out for the sun to shine on it. This is new, she thought. Soon everything will be new. When everything is new there will be nothing left to remind me.

Mary Winton's car was parked outside the Brooke house. Marco will be there. And I've got to tell him. He must have driven over. Anne coasted quietly to a stop. She sat still. She had meant to write him a note. It would have been easier than telling him. She tried to plan her words. "You see, Marco, my mother . . ." She couldn't tell him the truth. He saw things too differently. He could never see the complications that made up the truth for her. He thought there was black and white, good and bad, truth and falsehood. But it isn't like that. Don't you see, Marco?

Anne took off her ring and put it in her pocketbook. Slowly she got out of the car. Slowly she walked into the house. Phil Sinclair was waiting in the living room.

"There's a note for you from Marco. I took Mary's car and brought it. Marco's gone."

Anne stood still. She twisted her narrow belt around her waist as though she would break herself in two. Slowly she reached out her hand for the note.

It was, after all, the summer's enchantment. And it has no reality. I do not make you tell me. That would be too hard for you. No one can do what is too hard. Good-by, Anne.

                                                          MARCO

"Has he gone, Phil?" Anne lowered herself into a chair. Her knees were weak as if she had been ill.

"He's gone but you can bring him back."

Anne shook her head. "I can't bring him back. He didn't exist. Bill and Pete made him up."

"Anne, believe me, that part isn't important. People will laugh. They'll be unforgiving for a while. And you'll be insecure for a while, but it won't be too hard—you can take it."

"We'll never know if I can or not. You see, I'm going to marry Paul."

"You can't do that, Anne. You're in love with Marco. It was plain to see."

Anne took Paul's ring from her bag and put it on her finger. "This is plain to see."

"Look, Anne. I like Marco, but I'm more concerned about you. I'm even concerned about Paul. We three have been friends since we were kids. You can't do this."

"It's what I've always meant to do. This summer was just an interlude."

"Maybe it was." Phil looked at her gravely. "Maybe it was. But you don't believe that. And you know you're not in love with Paul."

"Since when have you been an advocate of romantic love?"

"You can't advocate love any more than you can advocate spring, but you can recognize it. And I recognized it between you and Marco this summer."

"Whatever it was, Phil, it was just this summer. One summer can't change all the years."

"Maybe you're not in love with Marco," Phil said slowly, "but I think you are. And, much more important, you think you are. But you're afraid. So you're selling out. And believe me, Anne, you're buying the world too dear. You're buying money and position. And you're paying too much for them. And for all your life you'll value them at the price you've paid. And in the end they'll be all you'll have."

"At least I'll have them, and they last."

"Let's hope so, for your sake. But what about Paul? He's a good guy. He's not getting much of a deal."

Anne smiled. "It's what he wants. Ask him."

"It's what he wants. But he's paying too much, too. Buying half a loaf at an exorbitant price. Poor guy. But at that I'm sorrier for you. Half a loaf is still better than no bread at all."

"Don't be sorry." Anne turned her eyes away from Marco's note, which was crumpled in her lap. She looked at her ring. She stretched her hand into the sunlight that came through the west window.

"It's very handsome," Phil said. "The first of the beautiful things. You can pile them up, the lovely, shiny, expensive things, but they won't be enough and you'll be buying them too dear."

Phil stood up. "Well, I've said my piece. And I've given you Marco's note. You'll write him? About you and Paul. That's the least you can do."

Anne nodded. The least . . . That was all that was left to do. The least.

"Good-by," Phil said. "Sorry if I've talked too much."

Anne held out her hand. "Aren't you going to wish me luck?"

"Yes, Anne, I do. All the luck in the world. You're going to need it."

Anne walked outside with Phil. She stood on the porch and watched him drive off. Marco's note was crumpled in her hand. Without unfolding the paper, she tore it into pieces. She tore the pieces again and again until they were as small as confetti. The wind was blowing from the ocean. She jerked her hand. The tiny white scraps swirled in the wind and vanished.

Soon there will be nothing left to remind me, Anne thought. They won't play this summer's tunes any more and I'll forget them. This summer will be just one among all the summers. I won't remember it at all.

There is only the letter left to do—the least I can do.

Anne walked into the house. She sat at the desk in the library. She stared at the blank sheet of note paper. How did you write the last letter? What did you say when there was nothing left to say? When only the least was left.

"Dear Marco: I want you to be one of the first to know." She would use the familiar pattern. Nothing she could say would tell him. He knew. He had known yesterday at the beach club. She saw his dark head bent over his hands through which sifted the white sand. "My mother is very happy. She has always wanted this marriage." It was fair not to appear too ugly. She held the pen and thought of her signature. How did you sign the last letter? She had never written the last letter before. Here, too, the pattern. "As ever, Anne." That was how you signed all the letters that didn't count. Ever, always. Forever, never.

She sealed and addressed the letter and left it on the hall table to be mailed. She walked upstairs. She moved her hand along the smooth wood of the banister. As ever, Anne. As ever, Anne. She pushed the phrase from her mind. She counted the shallow stairs as she walked. She counted her steps as she went down the hall to her mother's room. She did not want to be alone.

VII

ANNE DID NOT see Marco again until Mary's wedding day. They met in the Wintons' Southampton house where they had first seen each other.

Anne stood in the receiving line. Her diamond engagement ring flashed as she smoothed her pale blue dress. The dress was the same soft color as the one she had worn on the night of Mary's engagement dinner. She tried not to remember the day she had chosen her maid-of-honor dress. "Let's have blue, Mary. It's a lucky color for me."

Mary had not told Anne that Marco was to be at the wedding. Mary had not been sure that Marco would come. She had asked him to bring Lisa Blessing. "If not for my sake, come for Bill's, Marco. He feels so badly over what he has done."

Southampton was mildly surprised to see Marco.

"Fancy his turning up," Mrs. Morehead murmured.

"It's just like dear Mrs. Winton's kindness to ask him," said Mrs. Brent.

"Kindness! Mamie Winton just thinks she can get away with anything. She can, too," Mrs. Morehead added resentfully. "If anyone but Bill Winton had attempted such a hoax—— Look out, here comes Anita Brooke. I'm sure there was a good deal between Anne and that foreigner, even though Anita was clever enough to get her engagement announced so opportunely. Anita darling, how lovely your Anne looks."

Anne stood in the line and smiled steadily. She accepted congratulations. "So you're to be next, my dear. Isn't Mary a lovely bride!"

Anne looked up and saw Marco. It was like the first time. Doesn't the heart learn? She pressed her flowers against the sudden pain. He had not changed. Her heart recognized that nothing had changed. His hand touched hers in a formal greeting. It was like the first time. Marco moved down the line and out of her sight.

"How do you do, Mrs. Hoyt. Doesn't she look lovely?"

"So you're to be next, my dear. When is it to be?"

"In November, we plan."

"Isn't Mary a lovely bride!"

She spoke lightly. Her heart pounded heavily.

Anne danced with Paul. "The nerve of that feller showing up. I'll cut in if he has the cheek to dance with you."

Anne did not leave the dance floor. Once with Peter Smithers she danced close to the window beside which Marco was standing. She need only smile. She need only move her hand. She did neither. She did not want him to dance with her. She did not want to begin again what was finished. If Marco cut in she would make an excuse. She didn't want him to cut in but her heart waited for him. She would not let her heart betray her again. She would protect herself against her own heart and against Marco. She danced every dance. Marco did not come near her.

Anne stood beside Bill Winton to drink the bride's health. She looked across the bridal table at Marco. He looked past her and lifted his glass to Mary.

I don't have to explain, Anne thought. I don't need any excuse. Marco will never ask for it. Well, this is how I want it. Even though it hurts, this is how I want it.

Mary went to change her dress. Anne danced with Bill. The music was loud in the crowded room. This summer's tunes. In September they were already last summer's tunes.

> I'll get by as long as I have you.
> Though there be rain and darkness too,
> I'll not complain. I'll see it through.

She had danced to that song, with Marco last summer. Long, long ago. "Sing me the songs that to me were so dear, long, long ago. Long, long ago." Her childhood's tune was a countermelody in her head. It beat against the tune the band was playing. Because it's now, I mind. When this is long, long ago, I shan't mind any more.

She watched Marco standing beside Lisa Blessing. He had been with her all afternoon. Southampton is not being very kind to him. I shall be kind. I shall be most kind. I thought that long, long ago.

Anne watched Lisa as she danced with Marco. Anne looked for Harry Millard. He was not there. Lisa better be careful, Anne thought, or she'll lose Harry. She doesn't want to do that. Even if you're beautiful and talented you have to be careful if you want to be safe.

Tom Webb cut in. " 'Lo, Anne. And you're to be next."

"So it seems."

"Prove it. Here comes Mary. Catch her bouquet."

Anne held out her arms. The white flowers fell into her hands.

Paul came up. "That's a good omen." He tucked her arm into his. "We'll see Mary and Jim off and then I'll take you home."

As she walked toward the car, Anne looked back. The crowd had scattered. Marco was standing alone in the doorway. The doorway was bright in the September twilight as it had been in the June night. Anne walked under the dark trees with Paul.

A neat ending, she thought. She would keep her mind crisp and clear. Paul was what she wanted. She pressed her hand against the sleeve of his jacket. Her heart and body could not deprive her of the life and the world of her choice.

Anne was quiet during dinner. Mrs. Brooke watched her anxiously. The child looks dreadful. I always thought Paul was the right person. It's so hard to know what to do.

Anne started to go upstairs after dinner.

"Don't go, my dear. I want to talk to you. Are you sure that you and Paul——"

Anne wearily followed her mother into the living room. "Could we please not discuss it? I know what I'm doing."

"But, Anne, if you don't really love Paul."

"Please, Mother," Anne said irritably.

"I've tried not to be a managing mother, but this is your happiness," Mrs. Brooke bravely continued. She was afraid of her daughter. Anne was so much more competent than Anita Brooke had ever been.

"I know. I don't mean to be cross. You're a perfect mother. You shouldn't be, according to the book. Widowed mother and only child. What a setup for the Freudian boys."

Mrs. Brooke kissed her daughter silently. Widowed mother. That was what she was. Nothing was left in anyone's mind of the young Anita Howard whom Tom Brooke had loved and married. No one remembered Tom any more. His youth and charm were frozen in stiff photographs. They were funny photographs, she supposed. Just as the times of her youth were funny. Prewar, people said as they said Gay Nineties, and laughed.

Tom had died when they were both young. Their youth had remained whole in her heart. She had slipped unnoticingly into the middle-aged present. It was queer to be so much older than Tom. Why, she was as old as her own mother had been when she and Tom had been married. She had come a long way in time without Tom. It was lonely.

"Anne," Mrs. Brooke persisted, "I saw Marco today."

"He didn't even dance with me. Not that I wanted him to."

"But you watched him. Whenever I looked you were watching him. My dear, I like Paul. I've always wanted you to marry him. I thought that Marco was just an interlude."

"So he was."

"But today when I saw you looking at Marco——"

"Oh, Mother, for heaven's sake."

"I thought perhaps you really loved him. And if you do—well, it's not what I'd planned, but I want your happiness."

Anne stared at her. "You'd like that?"

"No, I'd hate it. His family sound dreadful and all this business of concealing them. But people forget. I can't pretend I'd like it. But I'd get used to it. You have a right to marry the man you love. I did. And I want you to."

"But it was easy for you. I mean, everyone approved—I mean, after all, the Brookes——"

"No marriage is easy. I should think that, without love, it would be impossible."

"Marriage is pretty impossible anyway nowadays. At least it isn't a life sentence any longer." Anne's voice was harsh. She stopped herself. "I sound cross. I don't mean to."

"It's all right, Anne." Mrs. Brooke hesitated. "I don't mind your being cross; I only mind your being frightened. You're right, it was easy for me."

"Then surely you see. Even if I loved Mar——" Anne stumbled over the name. "You wouldn't want me to marry the sort of person he is. You'd want me to marry Paul. You've always wanted Paul."

"Perhaps because Paul is like your father. And I loved your father. I don't like to think it's because of his money, or Bruce Craven's power."

"But you've always wanted me to have those things, Mother."

"I think I've taken them for granted. No, I've wanted them for you, but not to have you pay too much for them."

Poor Mother, Anne thought, like all her generation, she is unwilling to face an uncomfortable fact. Truth should be decently, even fashionably, clad.

She smiled at her mother. The smile must be a grimace. A muscle beside her mouth twitched. She was tired of smiling.

"It's all right, Mother. Paul is what I want. The other was just an interlude."

"And you're not frightened, Anne? It isn't for security that you're marrying Paul? Because there is no real security, you know."

Mrs. Brooke remembered the lifetime of happiness in which Anita Howard had believed. Anita Howard and Tom Brooke had planned to live happily ever after. So should all stories end. "Until death do us part" had been only solemn words. They were the words that had come quickly true.

"It's all right, Mother." Anne was speaking. "Paul and I have as much safety as anyone can have. And safety is happiness, don't you remember?"

Mrs. Brooke remembered. She remembered walking up the aisle of the little New York church to safety. She had thought she would be frightened of her wedding. Shyness could be an agonizing fear, and all the people were watching. Their heads turned with her passing as though a wind were blowing. Anita Howard had not been afraid. She had seen Tom Brooke waiting at the altar. The watching people hadn't mattered. Only Tom had mattered. Because of him she had been unafraid.

Mrs. Brooke touched her daughter's hand. "Security can be the sign of happiness. When your heart is not afraid, you know."

Anne withdrew her cold fingers. She kissed her mother. She walked slowly up the stairs to her room.

Anne was glad the day was over. She was tired. She opened the window. The roar of the surf pounded in her ears. That rhythm had been the familiar accompaniment of all her summer days. Now the sound reminded her only of this summer. Of all the summers, only this one was vivid and whole. Soon it would be last summer. It would fade. It would be forgotten.

Anne was determined to move quickly to New York. This place reminded her. In town she would forget quite easily. She would have much to do. She would arrange her wedding. She would plan the life which she had chosen.

VIII

A FEW PEOPLE were left at the Wintons' after the wedding.

"Stick around, Phil," Bill suggested. "We'll be gloomy if we're left to ourselves."

"I'll interview Lisa Blessing. Actresses in Southampton are still news."

Lisa asked Phil about Marco. "He and Anne seemed so happy. Mary explained, but I still don't understand. After all, this is America."

"Americans are just people. We also enjoy our little social distinctions."

"Well, to Europeans it seems queer. Our distinctions, at least originally, were based on birth. And we've never outgrown them."

"Come now, my dear. Lineage is in proportion to a country's age. We have our comparatively ancient families. And our newcomers are contemporary robber barons. Our aristocracy springs from the same source as yours. The lucky ones want to keep things as they are. Make privilege a right. And abroad, as well as here, elegant ancestry has to be implemented with money."

Lisa thought of Franz. His pride was an empty sheath that the sword of his life must fill.

"Still it's different in America," she said.

"Not different enough. At least, not in this neck of the woods. Luckily for me, I guess. My job is to chronicle the doings of the upper classes. I should be the last to want to do away with them. Actually, my column's a bulwark of conservatism. Nothing is real, nowadays, that isn't in the newspapers. Society should be more grateful to me than it is."

"I still don't understand about Marco. He can't really be unacceptable. Take Mrs. Winton, for instance. She is very *grande dame*. And she likes Marco—really likes him, I mean. Not just to please Bill and Mary."

"Oh, Mrs. Winton. She likes Marco and that's that. She really is free. That's one of the qualities that gives her power. She makes her own rules. And she breaks even these if she has a mind to. The ones who make the rules can be free. It's the ones who accept other people's rules who are caged."

"But your young people are free. And there is nothing against Marco. This foolish joke of Bill's was not Marco's fault. Why can't he and Anne Brooke be married?"

"Southampton's daughters just don't marry foreigners with lower-middle-class backgrounds and no money. Now, if the Ghibertis owned the Fiat works, or if Marco were one of Mussolini's up-and-coming young Fascists, that would be different."

"You mean that Anne's mother will not allow this marriage."

"She certainly wouldn't encourage it. But Anne herself——"

Betty Morehead stopped beside them. "Talking about Anne Brooke? She certainly never took her eyes off Marco today. I guess she still has a yen for him."

"You think then, after all, they will be married?" Lisa asked.

"Good heavens, no. Anne isn't a fool."

"You see," Phil said as Betty moved on. "That's what Anne can't buck: the judgment of her peers. There are lots of Betty Moreheads who accept the rules. And Anne thinks they're the world."

"Poor Anne, she doesn't see. She looks so clear-eyed, but she's blind."

"Blindfolded. Like the pretty girls in the Old Gold advertisement." Phil looked around the room. "Most of them are blindfolded. They have deliberately chosen not to see. Maybe they'll never have to. I wouldn't know. Maybe they can live forever in the slick-paper world of the advertisements, of the rotogravure, of the shiny magazines. Could be they'll never need to look beyond it."

"It's like the English fairy tale my grandmother read to me about the prince who couldn't see beyond the confines of his court. *The Happy Prince.*"

"Gay, not happy, but that's almost as good. And if you're not gay you get drunk. And when you're drunk you're gay as hell. Listen to them."

Pete Smithers and Tom Webb leaned against the piano and sang

> *"There's a rainbow round my shoulder*
> *And it fits me like a glove.*

"Come on, Betty, you sing. Everybody sing.

> *"There's a rainbow round my shoulder*
> *And a sky of blue above!"*

"You see, Lisa," Phil said. "They've got a rainbow. At least, some of the time they have the rainbow. And they've always got the pot of gold. The gold's paper, too, most of it. I hope it's good. I've got quite a lot of it myself. Anaconda, U. S. Steel. The new alchemy. Base metal to paper to gold."

"Come on, you two," Pete interrupted. "Come on, Marco. Everybody sing.

> *"I can't give you anything but love, baby.*
> *That's the only thing I've plenty of, baby."*

"Come on, Marco." Lisa touched his arm. "We can leave now."

Lisa carefully kept pity out of her voice as she talked to Marco on the way to New York. She spoke of Mary and her mother, of the charm of the little church.

Marco answered in monosyllables. At last he said, "I'm sorry to be bad company. I—things have been rather difficult."

"I know. Please speak to me or not as you wish. I'm sailing for Germany in three days. It's sometimes easier to talk to a stranger."

"I can talk to you. You aren't a stranger, you aren't American. And I thought I understood them."

"I think these are special Americans, cut off by an act of their own will from their fellow countrymen."

"I should have recognized them. I knew them in Europe, the rootless rich who are loyal only to one another. They pay allegiance to a class, not to a country. It's not good when they take over a country. They've taken over Italy."

"They might have taken over Germany in the inflation. Germany's danger then wasn't theirs. It wasn't the Junkers, it wasn't the industrialists, it wasn't the generals, who stood in line, who stood clutching the paper marks. The paper marks that dwindled as the people waited to buy bread and shoes."

"And they wouldn't stand in line here if the bubble burst."

"No, I suppose they wouldn't." Lisa spoke slowly. "If the bright bubble burst they'd manage somehow after a little while. There's an old man in *The Newcomers;* he has a bit in the last act. He lost his savings in the Florida boom. Gerald told me about it. He told me the carriage trade wasn't hurt. They still go to Palm Beach and the shrunken values are useful for tax purposes."

"Then you, too, Lisa, are disappointed in America."

"No, Marco, I'm not. I'm disappointed in one little group, but they're not America. They haven't the strength of a class. In America there is no ancient framework to give them strength."

"But if this prosperity should after all be only paper, Lisa, if this boom is a bubble that must inevitably burst. In the moment of danger they might become strong as they did in Italy."

"No, Marco, they can't. The bubble isn't America. America isn't a stock boom or a land boom. America isn't paper. It's all the wide, deep land and it's all the people. Don't be frightened of the group we saw today. They're the ones who are frightened—frightened in the midst of security, greedy in the midst of plenty. And not all of them. They aren't all like that. Mary and Bill aren't. Mrs. Winton isn't. They're what I believed all America to be."

Marco stared ahead. "But Anne—I thought she was like Mary and Bill. Even today I hoped. Against my judgment I hoped for a sign from Anne. I was mistaken; there was no sign."

"I'm sorry."

"I don't understand. I was so sure of Anne." He was silent.

"Even though this hurts," Lisa said, "you don't want it to end. But it will."

"I was so sure. All the long summer I was so sure."

Marco was driving too fast. The brakes screeched as the car slid to a stop just in time. "I'm sorry. I might have hit that truck. I wasn't paying attention." He drove more slowly and carefully.

"That is it. You will see. You will have lots of things to pay attention to. You're a lawyer, aren't you?"

"Yes. I'm with Danforth and Kane."

"You like it?"

"I'm going to try to stick it out."

"For a while, I think you are right. I know Mary said it means a great deal to be with that particular firm. Then, perhaps, you will move on. I think you will find what you are looking for in America."

"I think I'm a little too late to find the things I believed existed here. They've packed them all away in the history books."

"Every newcomer, every frightened, lonely immigrant must have thought that sometimes. But the generations of immigrants brought America with them. America is a coral island that they have built."

"I used to hope——"

"You will again. You will find what you came here to seek. You will give what you have brought."

"Why don't you stay here, Lisa?"

"No, I must go home. It's where I belong. There are things I can do there."

"In Germany it may still be possible to work for freedom. In Italy the prison gate is locked. But I think I would have chosen America no matter where I was born."

"That is why all Americans have come."

"You are right, Lisa. These people have made me forget. All Americans have chosen. Even the frightened ones who were driven here by oppression or starvation chose the unknown. They deliberately braved the greater fear. No one is American by accident. He or his forebears came here by an act of the will. America is the land of choice. It could be your choice, Lisa. Are you sure you aren't drawn back to Germany by a hope born of memory? The memory of your childhood? The saddest childhood is sweet to remember. Recollection pulls at the heart."

"The sadness is over, Marco. It's over in Germany. The new Germany is different. The dark years are over. Germany, too, is part of the new world."

"I hope so, but . . ." Marco hesitated. "Once in Germany I saw something. Shabby men and a shabby leader. They weren't part of something new. And the song they sang. The '*Heldenlied.*' That's no anthem for a new world. That's a song for evil on the march."

Lisa remembered the men who had sung the "*Heldenlied.*" The empty-eyed young men, the shabby, middle-aged leaders. The hooked cross. The cross of terror. They had frightened her, those men who sang the song. They, too, on a dark night in an empty street. She heard their quiet steps and the sudden noise at the end. She saw the stranger fall, as her father had fallen.

"I remember the men of the crooked cross," Lisa said. "I saw some of them a few years ago. They frightened me, too. But they have almost disappeared. Some said they had secret backers. My grandmother said they had. She said their money must come from somewhere. But the money wasn't enough. The men of the crooked cross couldn't capture Germany. Their leader was put in jail. We Germans are not like him, any more than the '*Heldenlied*' is like my father."

"Lisa, I'm sorry. I forgot it was about your father."

"It's all right. It wasn't really. It's a song to him, not about him. It is Grandfather's sorrow and anger. And that we have no right to judge. Grandfather tried to make it a glory when Father was killed, but he lived only a very few years after Father's death. He did not understand Father as Granny did. Perhaps he loved him less, but Father was his future, his immortality. When Father was killed, I think Grandfather knew suddenly, clearly, that he, too, would die. No one can live long when that knowledge becomes constant and vivid. We have to feel immortal to live at all."

She shivered as, for a second, time closed in. All the years became this one bright moment of light—the bird flying through the hall from darkness to darkness.

"I hope the glory was a comfort, poor old man."

When Marco left Lisa at her hotel, it was late. She stood in the lighted room and remembered the dark December afternoon of ten years ago.

Her grandmother's sitting room was warm after the cold outdoors. The reflected fire danced on the glass of the photograph frames. So many pictures, framed in velvet and brocade. Faded photographs on pale embroidered silk. Gilt frames twisted into elaborate bowknots.

The screen by the door with the big photographs. The hand-colored, long-ago pictures. Father when he was a little boy, and Grandfather, a fair-haired young man. Lisa's mother in her wedding gown, and Granny's father, stern and tall.

Lisa ran to her grandmother. Frau Blessing sat stiff in the blue velvet chair by the fireplace. Her hands were empty. Usually she embroidered. It showed off her small white hands. The last of her vanities, Granny said. Downstairs, behind the heavy glass, the young Frau Blessing stood, unchanged. On the drawing-room wall hung Granny's portrait. The fashionable young woman with the tiny waist, the beautiful, straight young woman with her hand holding back the carefully painted fold of a red curtain; with her smoke-black hair and her red lips and her smooth white bosom, she was a crisper, more elegant Snow White. That had been Granny. Lisa had looked at the portrait on her way upstairs. Now this was Granny. This was the Granny Lisa loved, but she tried to believe in the beautiful painted lady. She knew it pleased her grandmother that one should believe in the portrait. Frau Blessing sat still in her chair. Her empty hands turned outward in a tired gesture. She drew Lisa to the stool beside her. The arm around Lisa's waist was trembling.

"Your father will not come back from Munich, Lisa. He will not come home. Never again. Your father is dead."

Lisa had not known then how hard it was for Granny. My son, my son, her heart wept, but she said "your father" and sheltered the little Lisa's grief.

"But the war is over, Granny. There is to be no more killing."

"Poor little Lisa. The first of all your dead. Since you don't remember your mother."

"I'm afraid. If it had been in the war . . ."

Lisa had never said how afraid she had been when Father was fighting in the war. Grandfather had been proud. And Granny, too, had seemed brave. Had everyone really been as she, Lisa, had been? Had all the prayers been the same? Not my father, dear God, not my father.

"But now, Granny, when I thought we were safe. I'm afraid, I'm afraid. The world is bad. Never safe. Never safe."

"Hush, Lisa. It is hard to grow up at ten. It is hard when you first learn. For a child to lose her parent—one doesn't believe it. It doesn't happen. Nor does a young son die. Hush, Lisa. Now you know anything can happen. To both of us the unbelievable sorrow. Weep, my child. You are learning what the rest of us know. Anything can happen. Hope is born again and again. Despair waits quietly."

Wilhelm Blessing came into the room. He did not wish his women to weep. "Anger, brave, unforgiving anger—that is what we must feel," he told them. "Never forget to hate them. For that your father died—that Germany may remember. That the new Germany may learn to hate and, in that hatred, be reborn. They killed him in the dark of night. Ten of them. And he alone. An officer and a gentleman; they, the Red scum."

Lisa stared at her grandfather. His dark words made a picture. The Red scum. Blood is red. My father's blood, red against the snow. In the dark of night. There is no color—only darkness. The dark blood flowing on the dark ground.

Lisa screamed. Her grandmother drew her closer and put her finger to her lips. "Hush, Wilhelm."

"No, Elisabeth, she must know. Your father, an officer of the German Army, was ordered to Munich. There, in fulfillment of his orders, he patrolled the dark street. And in the dark they set upon him. The Reds, the alien interlopers. They stabbed him in the back as they and their like stabbed the Fatherland."

Lisa clung to her grandmother. She tried not to hear the old man's words. She tried not to see the picture.

When they were alone, Granny said, "Don't try to imagine the end." Lisa saw the cold, dark street. She heard their quiet footsteps. Then the sudden rush. She pressed her knuckles into her eyes—not to see.

"It was quick, Lisa. He never knew. Don't hate them. You will forget him in hating them."

Grandfather hated them. He spoke often to Lisa of them and of her father. "The young, blond Siegfried has died as a hero. For this, unknowing, I named him. He, the soldier, has shown to Germany her new enemies. In Siegfried's bright spirit Germany lives. The dark enemies of the world would destroy Germany. They must destroy her to conquer the world. Siegfried's memory shall keep bright our German swords. From our bright swords shall drip the evil blood."

Lisa listened unwillingly. That was not Father.

"So I pretend to be a soldier, Lisa. The professor in uniform that ill becomes him." Lisa remembered her father when he came home on leave. "Sh, Lisa, don't tell Grandfather, but it is the professor, pretending to be a soldier." And she had prayed. Not my father, dear God, he does not like killing. Let him not be killed. He is not really a soldier. Only soldiers, dear God, are supposed to be killed.

Grandfather had been pleased when Father received the medal. From the All Highest himself. But Lisa had been afraid. "The Iron Cross, Father. You must be a soldier, Father, to win it. A real soldier, Father." She had looked at him anxiously.

"No, Lisa. Just lucky. Luckier than those others, poor devils. And, of course, I behave outwardly like a soldier. It wouldn't do for the General to know that I am only the professor, pretending."

Grown suddenly wise, grown up at ten, Lisa knew that Father had been playing a game with her. A game that would, he knew, soothe her fear for him, her fear for a soldier—one of the soldiers who were meant to be killed. But he had liked the game. He had liked to laugh and to make small jokes. He was not like the bloodstained heroes of the *Nibelungenlied*. Grandfather was changing him.

Lisa hated Grandfather's song. It frightened her. The dark, bloody end blotted out all that had been before.

"I can hear them, Granny. I hear when they run suddenly. I want to call to him to warn him. When it is dark, I hear it all so plainly. Over and over—the rush and the noise at the end. And I cannot stop them."

"Lisa, don't torment yourself. There is no end to imagining what we cannot ever know. Remember what you know to be true. Remember him as he was."

The song made it hard to remember him. It changed him. He would be remembered all wrong.

"Only you and I will remember, Granny. Why did Grandfather write the '*Heldenlied*'? I hate it."

"Hush, Lisa. Let your grandfather have his song. It's not much to have instead of a living son."

"But it's such a hating song. Father never hated. Not even the enemy. I know now he was brave—but not the way the song is."

"Yes, he was brave. And not like the song. But perhaps it is better to be remembered wrong than not to be remembered at all."

"I shall remember him right." And Lisa kept the song and the memory apart. Until the song did not hurt her. It would not have hurt her father. To him it would have been a continuation of the secret joke between the child Lisa and the professor who pretended. "Don't be afraid of the *'Heldenlied,'* Lisa. It's part of the past. The shabby, frightened men cannot make of it the future. The gilded hero, Siegfried Blessing, shall march with his music to Valhalla in my place, Lisa. I should hate Valhalla. I shall find a kinder heaven more suited to my quiet taste."

Lisa came back to the present. It was good to remember Father so plainly. In the hotel room she smiled at him across the years. The *"Heldenlied"* was no longer frightening, since there were none left to sing it. It was part of her childhood years—a bitter part. But the years must be remembered whole, to be remembered at all.

Lisa was still smiling as she began to pack. It is foolish, she thought, to begin in the middle of the night, but this is the beginning of going home.

Lisa sailed for Germany on a sunny morning. She stood on deck and waved to the friends who had come to say good-by. "I will come back," she called, and waved. The ship moved away from the dock. The faces grew blurred and featureless as the faces of strangers. The ship moved out into the harbor away from the land of strangers. Soon she would be home. As her heart grew light, she knew that it had long been heavy with homesickness. The alien shore receded. Soon she would be home. She remembered Mignon's song that longed for the south, "Know'st Thou the Land?" A different land but the same sadness. The sadness of the stranger who remembers another time and place. She thought of the American song her grandmother used to sing, ". . . Land where my fathers died." For me that land is Germany. Where my father died. Where I have lived. Where I have loved—the different kinds of love. My father and Granny and now Franz. It is good to live where one has been a child. The dark, sweet pines and the great river. And the little, gentle streams. The heavy, ancient houses reflected in the still stream.

Lisa looked away from the horizon against which the ship seemed to stand still. She looked directly down at the water. Beside the ship the blue was a different color; it was clear like glass—glass being made—glass drawn out into swift shining motion. As she watched the bright, rushing water, she could feel the ship cutting through the sea, bearing her swiftly home.

IX

THE AUTUMN came quickly to Southampton. The summer people began to leave. The clear autumn winds blew across the dunes. The sun was still hot, but in the shade there was the chill promise of winter. On the beach the bright cluster of umbrellas grew smaller until, overnight, the last ones were gone. The beach club was closed. The sand from the deserted beach blew against the light-colored walls. The building was no longer gay with the people and the paraphernalia of summer. It was shabbily unreal like scenery seen from the wings. It was forlorn as tropical houses are when the rains come. On the dunes and around the lake, the houses stood empty and blinded by boards and locked shutters. The fashionable shops on Main Street were closed. Otherwise the village was unchanged. Summer people were a seasonal phenomenon. They came and went with the summer. The natives knew that the summer people were not part of Southampton. They were not part of any place. They were seasonal everywhere. They were native nowhere.

Anne was glad to feel New York's pavements hard and smooth beneath her feet. The noise of the traffic was a welcome change from the lonely, pounding surf. September in Southampton was enough to make anyone sad—September anywhere. The end was sad. The end of summer. The end of the year. October was the beginning of the year in New York. This clear blue and white autumn belonged to her and Paul. The evenings were gay with parties in their honor. The days were filled with things that must be done before the wedding.

Anne moved tirelessly through the shiny heart of the city. She plundered the shops on Fifth Avenue and Fifty-seventh Street. There was so much to do, so much to buy. She chose her apartment. She chose the furniture that Bruce Craven's lavish check would buy. She

ordered the linens and the clothes for her trousseau. Silk and lamé
and velvet for the evening. Silk and wool and velvet for the day. Furs
and gloves and shoes and hats. Nightgowns, intricately pleated and
shadowy with lace.

Anne stood on a carpeted pedestal while the fitters crept around
her, cutting and pinning the gleaming satin of her wedding dress. Like
a queen, she thought. The Snow Queen. You weren't supposed to
like her, but I did. White and cold and fair and beyond the earth.
For me, Gerda never won.

Anne was the young queen of her own world. Her mother and her
uncle were pleased with her. They petted and praised her. No one
limited her extravagance. "Your uncle Norman has been very generous. We don't choose to do less than Bruce Craven," Mrs. Brooke
said. "And besides, my dear, you have only one wedding. I want
everything to be perfect."

As the wedding day approached, the Brooke house overflowed
with presents. There was the constant rustle of unfolding tissue paper.
Miss Paterson made order out of the expensive chaos. Miss Paterson
was the secretary who had been engaged to see to all the details of
the wedding. The presents were her triumph, too. Miss Paterson liked
to feel that her brides were important, worthy of tribute.

"Wait, Miss Brooke. No, don't touch it. Let me," Miss Paterson
would say. "You might break it or lose the card. Ah, a Paul de
Lamerie cake basket from Mr. Gordon. He always gives silver. This is
particularly nice."

Mr. H. P. Gordon's present was given a prominent position. The
card was conspicuously placed.

Miss Paterson carefully removed nests of thin, curled paper. "Look
at these exquisite crystal trees. We haven't any like that."

Anne looked with pleasure at the loot of 1928 that was spread
before her—the rich and complicated loot of a rich and complicated
time. It was fun to be engaged, to be spoiled, to be envied, to be
surrounded by this ever-growing, shining wall of things. The dark
old-fashioned house was bright with the gleam of silver and glass, the
warm glow of china, the cool translucence of jade and agate, the
foam of linen and lace and embroidery.

Anne picked up a card. "That's rather sweet of Mrs. Morehead.
She says, 'I know you have everything, so I send this pretty, useless

thing.' Isn't it divine, Miss Paterson? And it will go beautifully with the clock the Harry Spains gave us." She held up the jade cigarette box. The gold clasp and hinges were set with rubies and diamonds. "I suppose people have always thought so, but I do believe we have more taste nowadays than ever. The most precious materials are used so simply."

The wedding day was near. The shining wall was growing fast. Anne watched it with delight.

Paul was pleased with Anne. "Darling, this was what you wanted." They were on their way to a dinner party.

"The motor?" Anne stroked the smooth, beige upholstery. "Mother was a lamb to give it to us. I know I was right to choose a town car. Your roadster will be fine for trips. And mine will do for just driving around Southampton."

"Not the car, Anne. I mean us. That's what you wanted always, even if you weren't sure for so long."

She moved abruptly. It was stupid of him to go back.

"Don't be ridiculous, Paul. I'm delighted with everything. You, me, and our presents—if you won't think me greedy to mention them."

"I want to be sure it is everything." He stared ahead through the window. He seemed to be studying the uniformed back of the chauffeur. "Do you ever think of that guy, Marco, at all?"

"Heavens, no!"

It was almost true. She never willingly thought of Marco. She never thought of him at all. Only, sometimes, she thought she saw him. There, coming towards her. Over there, turning the corner. There, on the steps of that house. Surely, this time she couldn't be mistaken. She was always mistaken. It was never he.

A street light shone into a taxi beside them. Anne caught a glimpse of the solitary passenger. She leaned forward. Surely this time . . . Funny it should happen at this moment when Paul was speaking of him. The man in the taxi was a stranger.

She turned back to Paul. He took her face in his hands. "I only wanted to be sure." He bent over her.

"No, Paul, please. My face is all fixed pretty for the party."

"I won't kiss you if you don't want me to. I won't marry you if you don't want me to."

"Why, Paul, this is a fine time to start being the one who isn't sure."

"I'm sure. Only, sometimes, I wonder if one of us being sure is enough."

"It's enough." Anne spoke steadily.

"I was just talking. I want you on any terms. Talking's no good between us."

He kissed her.

The car stopped. Anne smoothed her hair and recolored her lips.

The chauffeur switched on the light inside the car. As Paul got out, Anne looked at her ring. It was the symbol of her good fortune. She put her hand on Paul's black sleeve. This is what I want. Being young, I hoped . . . I thought. Now, grown up, I know.

The last week went by. It was the last day, the day before Anne's wedding. The end. The beginning. The eve.

Anne looked about her at the house. The furniture was pushed aside.

The familiar rooms were strange. The caterers and the florists were in possession.

It's the way it was three years ago when I came out. There will be white flowers everywhere. They'll be nice against the dark walls. White is a better background for white than people think. I shall stand here against the flowers. Here where I stood three years ago. I knew then that this day would come.

"Anne! Anne!" Mrs. Brooke was calling anxiously. "It's time for the rehearsal. We've got to get down to St. Matthew's."

Anne stood at the back of the church and watched. That was her wedding. Mary was taking her place in the rehearsal. It is strange to stand with Paul and watch our wedding. I have seen it before. All the weddings—all the beginnings.

Miss Paterson rustled her list. "This, of course, is the bride's side. Now, Mr. Winton——"

"If you wouldn't mind going through it just once more," Mrs. Brooke pleaded.

"There, that was right, don't you think, Anne? Goodness, you look tired, child. An early supper for you in bed."

Anne lay in bed and listened to the cars passing in the street. There were lots of cars now in the once quiet street. There had been so few when she was a child. She had used them for a sign. She couldn't remember her wishes. She could remember wishing and praying. If a car comes before I count ten, let it be true. She remembered counting slowly.

This night is the end of growing up. This is where the fairy stories end—happily ever after. As ever, Anne. As ever. As ever.

She pressed her head into the pillow to shut out the noise of the street.

There were too many flowers. Great white chrysanthemums, pale, faceless heads. "There'll be no room to stand," Anne said. No one listened. There were too many flowers. Their scent was heavy. That shouldn't be. Chrysanthemums have no scent. "It's the lilies I smell, Mother. Lilies should be for a funeral, for the end. Not for the beginning—not for the beginning." No one listened. Anne tried to find her mother. These strangers wouldn't listen. "Not lilies, Mother. These chrysanthemums smell like sad, pale lilies. Lilies that fester. Lilies that fester—I can't remember. Not for the beginning—not for the beginning." Her words were a pattern. They ringed her with sound but no one would listen. "Listen," she tried to call. "Listen." She heard the word but she knew it had not escaped from her tight throat. Her voice tried to press against the band of silence that held her throat. It was hard to breathe the heavy, scented air. She pushed against the stupid, faceless flowers. They were too tall. They were too big for the room. "Listen." Her mind heard the word which her throat could not utter. She pushed the white flowers. They were too tall. She could not see over them. They held her back. She tried to push them aside. It was hard to breathe. She raised her head, she lifted her eyes, trying to see above the flowers. They were all about her. They would not let her escape. Their featureless faces were too big, too close. She could almost see their features in the whiteness. When she saw them, they would be evil. With all her strength she screamed.

Anne moaned and opened her eyes. The pale morning sun of her wedding day was in the room. A yellow bar of light stretched across her bed. Her mother was standing in the doorway. "Happy the bride the sun shines on, darling. Good morning and—more packages. Miss Paterson is doing the last few downstairs. But I brought this."

Anne broke the dark wax seals and unwrapped the thick white paper. She read the card and opened the rosy leather case.

"Mother, look." Anne held out the shining diamond band. "Did you ever see such a bracelet? It's from Bruce Craven. He says he wants to be represented in the wedding-gift display with something prettier and less practical than a check. It matches Paul's clips."

Anne fastened the heavy bracelet on her wrist. She leaned forward to hold her arm in the sunshine. "This is handsomer than anything I have—even Paul's clips. But, of course, clips are newer."

"And Paul gave them to you."

"Yes, of course." Anne twisted her wrist in the sunshine. She watched the light dance on the moving stones.

Norman Brooke was to give his niece away. He drove with Anne to the church. "The family's proud of you, my dear. Paul's a nice feller and his people are the right sort. Good blood. And money, too. That's important. The right sort of money. Bruce Craven is a representative member of the community. A solid citizen. Not one of these Johnny-come-latelys. Hope you'll be happy and all that." He patted Anne's gloved hand. "You deserve it. You've approached this marriage business in the proper spirit. Romance is all very well, but it's an extra. Marriage is a way of life."

Anne smiled at him. "I think Paul and I will be happy, Uncle Normie."

" 'Course you will, my dear. Bound to be. Same breed. Same traditions."

Anne stood at the back of the church. She waited for the procession to arrange itself. There was rustling and whispering in the crowded pews, and around them the hush of the church. St. Matthew's hadn't seemed like a church yesterday. Not with the florists and Miss Paterson rattling the guest lists. But today it was a church. Waiting like this was like something. Anne recognized it. It was like waiting for the choir procession to form in the little church in Southampton. At the head of the long aisle Anne could see St. Matthew's great altar, banked with white flowers, and above it, the tall stained-glass window. She remembered the other smaller altar. The gold cross gleaming. She remembered the Sunday feeling, the rainbow-colored dust dancing in a narrow column of sunshine, the faded red cushions on which she knelt, the grain of the oak pew. To pass the long times of boredom, she had tried to make a pattern of the grain of the wood. She had read the other services in the prayer book—baptism, burial, marriage. Sermons had bored her mind. And sitting had irked her body. To stand, to sing, to kneel were a relief. But, with the boredom and the discomfort, there had been a feeling of security, of being sure. Sometimes she had known quite clearly that this stiff time apart was the only real time. She remembered the sweet safety of the Sunday world. "There is a green hill far away, Without a city wall . . ."

She remembered it so clearly that it startled her when her hand slid across her satin dress. Almost she had believed she would touch the soft white linen and the dull black silk of her long-ago choir robes.

She smoothed her flowers and held them the way she had practiced. Being young was thinking you could be sure. The long-ago Sundays were just one part of being young. The waves of sound from the organ beat against her ears. How many times had she walked to that music! Now it was her music. This was her procession. She walked slowly up the aisle between the white ribbons. Paul was waiting. She stood beside him.

"Dearly beloved, we are gathered together here in the sight of God, and in the face of this company . . ."

The words she had read, the words she had heard were now for her. She must pay attention. She wanted her voice to be just right for her responses. "I, Anne, take thee, Paul . . ."

I mean it. This is not exaltation. This is marriage and that is better. It is not the moment of choice. It is the confirmation of the choice I have always made.

Anne turned with Paul. The triumphant recessional swelled. She looked at the crowded church. She could distinguish the faces in only the first few pews. Anne walked with Paul. She was pale. She held her head high. They went through the wide church doors. The bright lights of Park Avenue pricked the darkness of the late afternoon.

Anne was content. This was her city, her life, her choice.

BOOK II

The End

I

NINETEEN TWENTY-NINE was the best year. Anne was always to remember it that way. To wish for 1927 or 1926 was timid. To be
timid in regretful remembering was as foolish as to be timid in
window-shopping. Economy in fantasy was pointless. The bubble was
bound to burst. So said the wise men after the fact. Anne liked the
bubble best at its biggest and shiniest moment—just before the end.

July 1929. Anne did not know that she was almost at the end of
a time she would regret. The noonday sun was hot. From under her
big hat Anne watched the beach, the gentle Adriatic, the fishing
boats with colored sails. She saw only the Lido shore, but she enjoyed
the knowledge that behind her, beyond her sight, was Venice, floating on still water. Picture-post-card beauty, they said. And told you
to admire an austere little hill town. But this obvious loveliness is
to my taste, Anne thought. To everybody's taste. That's why it isn't
fashionable to admire it. It's too easy. So for fear of being thought
to admire for the wrong reasons, you mustn't admire at all. Silly.

"Silly, isn't it, Paul, not to think Venice is beautiful?"

"Crazy. Any fool can see that."

"That's the point. Well, I can do a pretty mean monologue on
San Gimignano, myself."

Paul sat up. "You don't want to go back there, do you? Hottest
damn place I ever was in and nothing to do. Venice is better than
that."

"Poor Paul. You hate sight-seeing."

"Don't give me that, young lady. Who got tired in the Doges'
Palace? Not I. Well, I think I'll swim."

Paul stood and scowled at the water. "This damn sluggish water. No breakers, and shallow for miles. You can practically walk to Greece or whatever they keep over there."

"But it's worth it, Paul. Even if all the change isn't for the better. It's fun to be away from Southampton. It's different."

"A lot the same, too." Paul looked towards the Princess San Martino's cabin. "Princess Cora's American voice is like home. Brooklyn— that's practically Long Island."

"But she wouldn't look like that in Brooklyn." Anne smiled at the Princess. Her face was unashamedly old, framed in her white hair that was dressed in high Edwardian fashion. Her clothes were so carefully made that one did not at first realize that they, too, were old-fashioned, of an epoch earlier than Edward's. Long, simple lines. Medieval, perhaps, Anne thought vaguely. They were right for her. The Princess looked as every old lady should look. Her age became her and made her beautiful. She was unbecoming to her contemporaries. Beside her dignity they looked cheap, painted, and half naked.

"You bastard. You should have known he had a spade left." The Princess threw down her cards and waved at Anne.

"She wouldn't talk like that in Brooklyn, either," Paul said. "Well, I'm for a swim."

Princess San Martino came towards Anne. Her dress flowed around her as she moved. Veiled in drapery, her walk was smooth. There's a lot to be said for long skirts, Anne thought. She jumped up. "Good morning, Princess Cora."

"Hello, child. Find me a chair. I got so damn mad at Chico I thought I wouldn't play another rubber: I'd see my little Americans. I like honeymooners." The Princess grinned. "Remind me of my youth. But you're too young to hear my memoirs. Americans are so innocent. Perhaps that's why I like them. Not many people can make me feel wicked at my age."

"You like all Americans, don't you, Princess?" Anne glanced at the bridge players. "I mean all of you do. You don't seem to know that there are Americans and Americans."

"Now, my dear. Don't look down your pretty nose at Judy Mason. It's not her fault that men keep marrying her."

"Not Mr. Jones. He just keeps her."

"Oh well, J.C.'s so rich. Sin in such a big way is respectable. All those maids and secretaries and things. It's really a ménage. And they give lovely parties and lose so willingly at bridge. Don't be provincial, my child."

Anne didn't wish to appear provincial. But it wasn't a triumph to be asked to all the great houses of Venice if Judy Mason was invited, too.

"Remember, my dear," the Princess continued, "to us, all Americans are wops and some of the wops are amusing."

"And some are rich."

"All right. But that's how we are. Accept us as we are. You've come a long way to have a good time. Have it."

"You're American, too, Princess Cora. Don't you mind?"

"They don't include me—at least not to my face. I'm too old to care if they did. I'm sorry if I hurt your feelings, child. I suppose I don't remember young feelings very well."

"Who is Chico, Princess Cora?"

"Oh, you must know. He's engaged to Nina."

"But she's married."

"Yes, my dear. Times have changed. All the young girls have lovers and all the married women have fiancés. So unlike my youth. This engagement business does away with the secrecy which made even a dull lover exciting."

"But I thought Italians couldn't divorce."

"They shouldn't. And there's always a fuss. But in the end people like Nina are accepted again. If they're rich and agreeable. Not by everyone, but by everyone amusing. Where's that husband of yours? Americans are the best-looking men in the world. Better teeth than the English and taller than the Italians."

Two small boys staggered by, carrying a pail filled with water. They spilled a little of the water on the feet of their slim, dark-haired mother. She wiped her scarlet toenails.

"Margharita di Stigliano. She's lovely. You know her, of course?"

"Yes," Anne said.

"She adores her husband. I think you can tell by the children. Although, they say, it doesn't make them better-looking. How about you?" The Princess looked inquiringly at Anne's flat stomach. "Nothing yet, I see. Don't waste time. You might as well get it over with.

American children are sweet. But not as sweet as our Italian babies. Look at those two of Margharita's. Those big, dark, pleading eyes. Even when they're being as wicked as they can, their eyes make you love them. The tiny one's hair is bleached by the sun, but it will be black as sin when he grows up."

"Yes." Anne turned the other way. "I think I'll get this shoulder brown now."

"Here's my dear Paul. Your wife and I have been yearning over Donna Margharita's babies. Well, I shall get back to my cards. Talleyrand was right. Old age would take much longer without them."

Anne lay still. Behind her the small Stiglianos shouted as they stirred the muddy sand in their pail.

"Paul, I had a letter from Mary. She and Jim are in Baden-Baden. How about taking our beautiful new Bugatti and driving there? I'm suddenly tired of this place."

"Baden-Baden? What on earth would we do there?"

"I don't know. Have fun. It'll be different, and then we can go to Cannes. We promised Uncle Bruce we'd meet him. They say it's a lovely drive into Germany from here."

"Okay, if you want to. And we may as well see all we can. We won't get over here every year."

"Paul, you're homesick for Southampton."

"Oh, foreign countries are all right, but the people we meet aren't real. At least, not with us. They're fun and all that, and their parties are okay. But I feel as though we took our Italian friends by the day as we do our rooms at the hotel. Americans are on a cash-and-carry basis." Paul stood up. "Hey, look who's here! There's old Phil Sinclair."

Anne smiled at Paul's pleasure in finding a fellow countryman. Europe offered him no sight as pleasing as a familiar American face.

"Well, Mrs. Craven. You're looking very lovely. Having fun?"

"Swell fun, Phil. Paul will tell you about it. I'm too lazy." She twisted her body slowly under the sun. The sand was smooth and pleasantly warm against her skin.

"They're crazy about Anne," Paul said proudly. "And that means something in Venice. They've got a few blondes of their own here. But not like Anne."

"What's doing?" Phil asked. "I'm supposed to be taking notes."

"Parties, you mean? Well, there was a swell treasure hunt last night. The natives got kind of sore, but . . ."

Anne thought of the party. The great dark square and the women's bright jewels and pale dresses against the tall wide doors of San Marco. The treasure hunters had blown through Venice like golden leaves. No, not like that. Like strolling players moving noisily through the ancient, still shadows of the city. Anne shook her head. Because it's Venice I want it to sound romantic. Actually it was like the treasure hunt we had in New York last spring. The same clothes, the same sort of faces, the same prizes. Cigarette cases from Cartier's. She held out the thin gold envelope.

"Look what I won, Phil."

"Smart girl. My money's always on you. How long are you staying?"

"We're leaving tomorrow. Anne's tired of it. And I am, too, as a matter of fact. We're going to meet up with Jim and Mary in Baden-Baden."

"Gets you down after a while, doesn't it—the atmosphere? Not being able to speak out, even if you don't know you want to."

Anne looked at Phil blankly.

"I'm talking about the government. As though Al Capone really took over at home—Teapot Dome with guns. It's a little terrifying as a successful precedent."

"Oh no." Anne lowered her voice. "It doesn't bother us. Their government isn't our business. And anyway, people like us don't have to start worrying about politics, for heaven's sake."

"Besides," Paul put in, "this isn't a bad system. These people can't run themselves or their country. They need a strong man at the head. Why, from what they tell me, the place was in a mess. The Reds were moving in. Of course Fascism wouldn't suit us."

"But you think it suits Italians," Phil said, "like having babies is said to suit peasant women. The happy theory that it doesn't hurt them."

"Well, it doesn't, Phil. Hurt the peasant women, I mean. Not the way it hurts women like me." Anne glanced secretly and fearfully at her slim body.

"You bet it doesn't hurt you as it hurts them. The difference is you get ether and all the trimmings."

"But about Fascism," Paul said. "I don't know much about it, but it's certainly better than Communism."

"Less frightening, maybe," Phil said. "I think that's because Italians are less frightening than Russians. There are fewer of them, for one thing. But if anyone ever went to town with Fascism the way they've done with Communism in Russia, I don't believe that you could choose." He smiled at Anne. "That would be the dagger or the bowl, Fair Rosamond."

"Not to me," Anne said firmly. "Look around you. The Fascists keep a nice luxurious Indian reservation for the rich. That's what I'd choose. I'm practical."

"One hardly notices it, you're so pretty, Anne. Isn't she, Paul? This is too good a day to waste talking politics. Boy, feel that sun."

"Why don't you come to Germany with us, Phil? After that we're going to Cannes."

"I'll see you on the Riviera," Phil said. "Germany isn't fashionable enough for my itinerary. I'm blowing myself to this trip on stock-market winnings, but I keep expenses down with dispatches home."

Anne looked up to see a small Stigliano stealthily approaching her with a handful of sand. It was hard to imagine him grown tall, with hair black as sin. His mother called him. He dropped the wet sand beside Anne and ran.

Anne sat up. "Come on, Paul, let's go. I'm fed to the teeth with noise and glare. Let's get lunch and plan our trip tomorrow over the mountains."

The road wound up the mountains through the early morning mist. Then they were above the clouds. Anne looked down at the white floor of clouds that moved and changed with the light and yet seemed still and solid. It was something she had dreamed long ago, the shining floor of heaven, but she had never really imagined it. There were two kinds of beauty that startled your heart. Of one you said, "So it really is like this," and of the other, "But this isn't what I expected. This is——" And you stopped because you couldn't find the words.

In the evening they stayed at a big empty hotel in a little town once Austrian, now reluctantly Italian.

The hotel manager was friendly but sad. "The Germans don't come any more and only a few Italians." The empty hotel was hollow. Anne felt like a ghost of summer come to winter. She was glad to leave in the morning.

"Do they mind being Italians, Paul, do you think?" Paul was driving slowly behind a market wagon that blocked the street. "To people like this, it can't matter. Is it any worse to be a poor Italian than a poor Austrian?"

"I think they mind." Paul spoke slowly. "Even for us, the worst part of being poor would be not being used to it. Having everything different. Now these people have the burden of strangeness added to their load. Pretty tough to carry, I guess. The kids won't mind." He leaned out of the motor and handed his last lire to a little girl with golden braids. "You'll be all right. You'll make a swell Italian. An odd-looking one, but you'll never know." She waved to him with the hand that clutched the money. "Kids are lucky."

He reached for Anne's hand. "If you had a girl, she'd be like that. Don't you think it would be nice to have a kid? I've sort of planned on a couple."

Anne moved her hand in his. "Please, Paul."

"Everything's swell, Anne, between us. And when Uncle Bruce offered us this trip, I was glad you weren't having a baby. But pretty soon . . ." He pressed her hand against his knee. "You want to, don't you?"

"Yes, Paul, but not yet. Not just yet."

"Not yet. That's what you always say, and then in the end you're glad, as I am. Are you scared, Anne, to have a baby?"

"Oh no, Paul. It's not that. But it would change things between us. It's pretty swell as it is."

The road wound downhill. In a few hours they were driving in the pleasant land of Germany. Anne thought gratefully of Paul's efficiency with the customs. Paul made her life agreeable and smooth. It was a pleasant life on the soft green surface of the earth on smooth roads.

She liked driving with Paul. He drove expertly. Nothing startled him. His broad shoulders never moved.

"What are you thinking, Anne?"

"About you and how I admire you. You do things well. I like that."

"Wish you'd convince Uncle Bruce of that."

"Why, Paul, he says you're doing wonderfully. He said the trip was a reward."

"Oh yes, I know. But I thought last summer that he meant to give me more responsibility. The money's fine. But I'm still a super errand boy."

"Darling, don't belittle my husband's importance. I don't like it. You're going to be the head of Craven and Company one fine day."

"That's my plan, young lady. Don't worry. I intend to live up to your expectations."

"I know. Paul, drive slowly. Look at those little topheavy houses leaning over to see themselves in the stream. It's a lovely world you've endowed me with."

"I aim to please. The moon and the stars, too, if I could. But we've got to get on. We can make Munich sometime tonight and start in the morning for Baden-Baden."

Anne liked Baden-Baden. "It's something left over from King Edward's time. Pretty, pompous villas and victorias and gardens. How clever of you to think of it, Mary."

"We didn't. The Borodinos persuaded us to come. They amuse Jim. And fortunately, the food at the Stephanie is peerless. So I think I can keep him here a week longer. I don't feel very well. I've started a baby."

"That's grand." Anne forced her voice to enthusiasm. "Aren't you terribly pleased?"

"Pleased? That's not enough. That's a little thin word. Anne, this means—this means . . . Like everything that means too much, you can't say it. You know how it is when you fish for a word—when all the old words seem secondhand and you wish you could make one up."

"That must be grand." Anne looked at Mary. Her dark hair no longer curled crisply. It hung limply against her sallow cheeks. Her eyes were tired, ringed in shadow. The beauty of approaching mother-hood was certainly a figment of masculine imaginations.

"I know I look a sight."

"Oh no, just tired, but that's natural."

"No, I look a sight and I feel worse. But I've never been so happy and excited." Mary's lips trembled. "It's as though everything was beginning to make sense for me at last. Everything's different, Anne. Not yet, but it will be. Just a little further down the crooked lane into the green field. I guess I sound pretty silly."

"No, you sound pretty happy."

Anne met the Count and Countess de Borodino at dinner. Ruby Borodino was a slender, sunburned creature. Her short, light brown hair was a simple frame for her small oval face. Anne felt suddenly that her golden curls were too elaborate. Ruby's clothes were simple in the way most difficult to achieve. Anne felt too dressed up, too young. Ruby Black had come a long way from Paterson, New Jersey, and yet not too far. Her French was flawless, but when she spoke English her flat American accent was unchanged. She had been too clever to acquire the international Ritz Hotel voice. Americans liked her because she was American, and Europeans liked her for the same reason. It's smart of her to keep "Ruby," Anne thought, to make her ridiculous name as chic as that great stone on her hand. I wonder if it's real. One never thinks of French counts as rich. Perhaps the Blacks . . . No, Ruby Black, born rich, would not have bothered to learn so quickly. The rich are lazy.

"Borodino? No, it's not Italian." Ruby was answering Paul. "Pierre will delight in telling you about his ancestor who wangled the title from Napoleon."

"Not wangled, *chérie.*"

"Oh, Pierre, everyone knows he was frightfully brave. One doesn't have to keep on saying it. Well then, the old boy and his children made very *ancien régime* marriages. That's what gives Pierre that nice chiseled look. The Bonapartists are apt to be dumpy. They've kept the common touch."

"*Enfin, chérie.*"

"No, darling. Americans want to know. I'm still American enough to remember that. I like to know about everyone. Well, as I say, there were all these splendid marriages, so that I call everyone in France, practically, *ma tante* or *ma cousine.*"

"*A la mode de Bretagne.*"

"No, Pierre. It's no longer chic to understate. So, as I say, that was very convenient. And also makes me feel very grand and Faubourg St.-Germain. Or right out of Proust. That depends on my audience. But Pierre's father made the match of my choice. My mother-in-law was Mlle. Charmant."

Charmant perfumes were sold in every department store in America. But Anne noticed that Ruby used Chanel No. 5.

"I think that old M. Charmant must have changed his name before he went into the perfume business. It's too pat. But Pierre says not. That wouldn't have been respectable. And God knows the Charmants are respectable, for which I'm grateful. In these divorcing days it's a good thing to have a husband with a bit of the bourgeois in him."

"*Enfin, chérie,* it is enough, I think. Tell me, Mr. Craven, you are perhaps the son of Mr. Bruce Craven?"

"His nephew," Paul said.

"Uncle Bruce isn't married," Anne added. She wanted Paul's position to be quite clear.

Before she went to bed Anne stood before the mirror and brushed her curls. She brushed them hard to make her head small and smooth. I'll go to Antoine, she thought. It's time I outgrew the young-girl-graduate look.

"How did you like la Borodino, Paul?"

"She has style. And she's gay and natural. Most of these women look as though they'd crack. Their faces are pasted on or hooked behind their ears."

"Ruby Black has learned a lot. Born in America, remade to order in Europe. They're the most attractive women in the world."

"Not to me." He lifted her curls and kissed the back of her neck.

"No, but, Paul, it's my job to be attractive. I'm learning a lot this trip. The time with Mother, it was museums and the Eiffel Tower and clothes from Marindaz which seemed just like Hollander's until you wore them at Miss Robinson's dancing class and felt you looked a little peculiar. But this time we're really meeting Europeans and being with them."

"Too much being with people and too much talk. When are you going to learn, my darling, that talk isn't for you and me? Other things are much better between us."

It was Ruby Borodino who suggested that they motor across the border to see the new Dornier plane. "The Germans are so proud of her, poor things. They aren't allowed to build them here—that's why she's in Switzerland."

The night in the little Swiss hotel was uncomfortable.

"Why we let ourselves be dragged here," Paul grumbled. But in the morning he stood silent with Anne.

Like a silver bird, the great plane floated on the lake. "It's like something out of H. G. Wells," Anne said. "Only more beautiful and not frightening."

The day was fair. The morning sun shone on the wings of the Dornier. The lake was bright. The plane floated in the light. The water and the air seemed to be interchangeable elements.

"Glad we came," Paul said. "I get a real kick out of this. These are the masterpieces of our time. Not paintings and such. You can bet that this is what old Leonardo would have wanted to see."

When they returned to Baden-Baden, they were greeted by the hotel manager. "It was worth it, was it not? They will see—they will realize they cannot keep down a great, creative people. You will tell them in America how well we are doing?"

"He was pathetic, didn't you think?" Anne asked Paul. "I should think Pierre Borodino would feel ashamed of how they've treated these poor things."

"Yeah. Poor devils. All they ask is a chance like everyone else. Well, they've got it. We've seen to that, we and the British. I know a little about it because Uncle Bruce helped float that loan last winter. The trouble with the French is they're hysterical."

The manager had given Mary a telephone message. She brought it to Anne. "Lisa Blessing wants us to lunch with her tomorrow. You remember her, Anne?"

"Yes," Anne said. "She's lovely. But I'm sort of exhausted after today."

Lisa Blessing was part of the past. You couldn't take one thread from the past; the threads were tangled. If you pulled one thread, the others tightened around your heart. The room at Tony's was small and hot. Lisa Blessing's hair was red-gold under the dark brim of her helmetlike hat. The band played. No, not at Tony's. That was later at the Montparnasse—later again at Mary's wedding. She didn't want to go back, to be reminded, to feel herself dancing again to painfully forgotten music.

"You do look tired, dear." Paul's voice was anxious. "But you turn in early tonight and you'll be fine."

"Don't make her come, Paul, if she doesn't want to," Mary said quickly.

"I'll be all right in the morning. Thanks just the same, Mary. And I'd love to go." It won't be an escape if anyone recognizes it. Mary's knowledge and protection will give substance to the shadow. That's all the past is, a shadow that is shrinking as shadows do at noon.

II

LISA BLESSING was as Anne remembered her. Her beauty was calm. She made Ruby seem meager and shrill. Mary was unaltered. Mary's not pretty, Anne thought; less than ever now, but she's herself. That's really having style, being yourself. People change me.

Frau Blessing liked the American guests. They used different words but their voices were the voices she had known. Their clothes were different but their faces were the same. She remembered the young Americans of thirty years ago: pompadours and stiff shirtwaists above spreading skirts. But the same faces. The fashions had changed but the young faces and the young long-legged bodies had remained the same. The Americans had come every year. The last June of all, in 1914, they had come in hobble skirts that could not hide their grace, with shepherdess hats tilted over their pretty, eager faces. That June had been fair and rich with promise. Frau Blessing remembered saying to her husband:

> "No price is set on the lavish summer.
> June may be had by the poorest comer.
> And what is so rare as a day in June?
> Then, if ever, come perfect days;
> Then Heaven tries earth if it be in tune,
> And over it softly her warm ear lays."

She had tried to make him understand the gentle provincial voice of old-fashioned American poetry, the music of plain wooden churches and small, prim white villages. "Not a cataract of sound, Wilhelm, but if you listen, it's like the beginning of summer."

"Ach, poetry. This is poetry." And he declaimed:

> *"I am called*
> *The richest monarch in the Christian world;*
> *The sun in my dominions never sets.*
> *All this another hath possessed before,*
> *And many another will possess hereafter*
> *That is mine own."*

Frau Blessing remembered American summers. The piazza of the big yellow hotel beside the lake where she had stayed with her father for a long-ago Fourth of July. The girls' pink and white and blue dresses. The fireworks streaking the summer sky with light, darkening the stars. Americans celebrated with noise and amateur parades, ice cream and peanuts and popcorn. A children's holiday. She remembered the sweet taste of vanilla ice cream and the sound of the brass band blaring and the smell of the dust of the parade through the village street.

Now they were back, the Americans. And they were still young and confident. You could hurt them but you could not shake them. That was the thing about Americans—they were a young people. Young and unafraid.

Frau Blessing smiled at Anne. That little one, she thought, looking so admiringly at Pierre Borodino's wife. Doesn't she know, the little idiot, that one can be chic like that forever but only young for a while? Pierre is like his father. It is nice that they come and go again. At least for people like us there are once more no frontiers. In the end for all the people.

"You were saying, Mme. Borodino, that you went to Munich to see *Dantons Tod?*"

"Yes, Mary Forrest and I motored over. It was worth it just to hear the 'Marseillaise' in a German theater. German voices singing it, German feet marching to its time."

"And the applause. That was loud, too, and generous," Mary added.

"Don't worry, my dear," Frau Blessing said to Mary. "I'm glad that they can sing and hear the 'Marseillaise' in Germany. It's a good sign. I'm an old woman. It's not natural for me to hope. And yet, against my years, I think at last today one can hope again."

"I, too, madame," Pierre said. "I, too, have hope. And to have hope is to begin to have faith."

"Lisa was in Munich. But you didn't see your friends, my child?"

"I was not there that night, I think," Lisa said quickly. "But tell me, Mary, you like Baden-Baden? You will stay for a while?"

"Gosh, Lisa, we'd love to stay," Jim said, "but we want to take advantage of our trip—see everything. We want to get a look at the Riviera. They say it's something."

"When I was young," Frau Blessing said, "we went there in the winter. It was very gay and very pretty. We used to pretend it was as warm as it looked. Palms and orange trees and winter flowers warmed our northern hearts. Your country is very beautiful, monsieur."

Pierre bowed. "To the truly civilized like you and your late great husband, madame, France is the second homeland—the homeland of the mind and the imagination."

"This whole conversation is awfully Delmonico, don't you think?" Ruby murmured to Jim. She turned to Pierre. "Come on, *enfant de la patrie,* we've got to be on our way. It's a long drive back to the Stephanie."

Frau Blessing and Lisa watched the cars drive away. Anne and Paul were in the low gray-and-crimson Bugatti. The others followed in the high, swaying Mercedes Benz that Jim had hired. Frau Blessing remembered prewar Europe seen from the windows of just such limousines.

"Once, Lisa, when your father was a boy——"

"Granny. Do you mind? I want to be alone for a while. I'll come in to you later."

"Very well, my child. I shall be upstairs in my sitting room."

Lisa walked toward the pines behind the house. Beyond their high wide branches was the sunset sky. She did not see it. She saw a dark narrow street near the theater in Munich. For two days she had seen only that street, heard only those voices.

Lisa stood beneath the pines and remembered the night she had stood with Franz in the narrow Munich street. A shabby little man walked quickly by then. The swift walk of terror that dares not run.

He broke into a run as his pursuers came around the corner. There were eight of them.

"There he goes, the Red spy!" their leader shouted.

"No, no, gentlemen, I did not know you were meeting there." The little man's explanations cost him his escape. His pursuers caught up with him and swept him around the corner out of Lisa's sight but not out of hearing. She heard him scream once and then again. The second scream broke in the middle.

Lisa ran to the corner. She moved too suddenly and quickly for Franz to stop her. In the next street, in the shadow beyond a street lamp, the men were standing. They were laughing. "Once more, Hans, for good measure."

Lisa stood in the pool of light. "Stop, stop!" Her voice had lost the depth it had learned in the theater. She was shrill with anger and fear.

Franz joined her as the men turned. Their leader spoke. " 'Stop,' you say. Do you know what you are trying to stop, you——" He paused. "But I know you. I have seen you. You are Lisa Blessing, the daughter of Siegfried Blessing."

"Yes, and because I am his daughter I say to you, such things as this shall not be. Listen." From the shadows came a moan. "Listen to pain and fear. Listen to what was a man."

"A man!" The leader laughed and stretched out his arm to bar her way. "You, Fräulein, are the daughter of a man. How can you speak in defense of this scum? On such a night as this did Siegfried Blessing die. On such a dark street. He the hero, they the Red scum." He touched with his boot the crumpled body. "Siegfried Blessing's daughter cannot plead for that. Rather rejoice that thus is your father revenged."

The men in the shadows moved. The figure on the pavement stirred. The moans rose to a high thread of sound. Then they stopped.

"Stop!" Lisa cried. "Not again in the dark street, not pain and terror in my father's name. You cannot do this in his name."

"I regret, Fräulein, it is not possible to allow you to interfere. The man is a Jew. A Communist spy. He must be dealt with. He shall be returned to his friends presently. This one will be more useful to us alive than dead." He spoke an order. Two men lifted the huddled figure from the pavement and disappeared.

"Franz, do something. You can't let them——"

"My dear, do not interfere when you do not understand." Franz spoke to the leader. "You owe an apology to my wife. Fräulein Blessing is also the Countess Erlencamp. You have frightened her."

The leader saluted. His arm rose stiffly. "You do well to explain to the Countess that interference is ill advised. We do not tolerate meddling even from Siegfried Blessing's daughter."

"You have frightened her. Women are sensitive."

The leader cut Franz short. "You would be wise, Count, to keep your wife out of our way. We respect her name. But there is no longer room in Germany for female squeamishness." He saluted again and turned away. The men followed him down the street. As they walked, they sang the *"Heldenlied"*: "From our bright swords the evil blood shall flow."

"Franz, you let them go. You did nothing."

"What would you have had me do, Lisa?"

"We can tell the police."

"Tell the police what? You can't describe the Jew. There are too many like him."

"We can describe the leader. That flat, fat face. We can identify him. We can identify his uniform."

"That would not be safe for you."

"I'm not afraid."

"I am for you. Besides, we have no proof. We have seen nothing really."

She looked up at him as he stood straight and tall beside her. The one against the many, that was the pattern of the nightmare.

Franz took Lisa back to the hotel. He sat beside her on the wide bed in their room.

"My darling, you don't understand. The man was a Jew. A *Schieber*, or a Red."

"They have no different voice to cry their pain. Their flesh . . . Franz . . . 'If you prick us, do we not bleed?' "

"That is the theater, Lisa darling. You don't understand these boys. They are rough, they are cruel if you will, but they are trying to serve Germany. The law leaves them no weapon but their cruelty. The end justifies the means."

"Franz, I'm afraid. Not you, Franz? You aren't one of them?"

"No, my darling. But they are not as bad as you think. They punish crimes that the law will not touch."

"The crime of being born. The crime of being poor. Or not poor. A *Schieber,* you said."

"They work together, those profiteers and the Reds. Between them they squeeze us, the true Germans, so that I, even I, Franz von Erlen-camp, come empty-handed to my bride."

"No, Franz. Brave hands are never empty. You are my strength. But I am afraid. My nightmare has come alive again. I thought it was over. Is nothing ever over?"

"Don't be afraid of those young men. There are not many of them. Just enough for the purpose—to get power for those who will use it more wisely."

"Is it never over? Does it always begin again?"

"Be still, Lisa, my darling. You have seen an ugly thing, even if it was a necessary thing. The real world is ugly. Stay safe behind your footlights until the world is better. It will be better, Lisa. I promise you."

He drew her cold, trembling body close to him. He held her against his warmth and his strength.

Now Lisa stood beneath the pines. They stretched their branches before her. She looked up. The branches stretched wide like the arms of the Cross. She remembered the crooked cross. She shuddered and turned away. She walked into the house and upstairs to her grandmother.

Frau Blessing was sitting beside the window. The flames of the setting sun were reflected in the glass of the picture frames.

"Granny, I haven't told you. The night before I left Munich. It was one of the nights they sang the 'Marseillaise.' Another song was sung that night." Lisa looked at her grandfather's photograph—the last photograph—with the white hair and beard, the tired brow. "Your song. Did you know when you wrote it? Did you know that over and over in dark streets you would have your revenge? Pain and terror, the many against the one. Is that what you wanted?"

"Hush, Lisa. What happened?"

Lisa told her grandmother. "This time I saw it. I need no longer imagine the narrow street and the rush of heavy feet."

"Lisa, what you saw was horrible. It happens everywhere in the world, when men hate and are afraid. Particularly when they are afraid. The many against the one. That is how frightened men make themselves feel strong. They think they can deal with all their fear as they deal with the scapegoat. They destroy him because they want to destroy fear and hunger and cold and failure."

"But today, Granny. There is nothing to fear in Germany. Things are well with us again. The theaters and the restaurants and the shops are full. The factories, the new ships. Of course, Franz says the wrong people have the money. Speculators and foreigners."

"My dear, it always seems like that. The new poor always hate the new rich."

"It is natural that Franz should despise the parvenus."

"Yes, I know. The Junker remembering when Prussia was Germany —when it might have been the world. That Prussian pride with nothing now on which to feed." Frau Blessing thought of the leisure which her wealth provided for Franz's discontent.

"You're prejudiced against Prussians, Granny."

"Prussia is a state of mind. I have seen it take over Germany. I am happy that his Austrian mother saved Franz from that pale Slavic look of a Prussian."

"Don't say things like that to him. He loves his Junker friends at the Herrenklub. It was hard to make him go to Munich but the *Morgen-presse* gave him a chance to do some articles on Munich."

"On the theater? Because you know Reinhardt?"

"It's an opportunity for him. He'll be home today. Driving here, he will see." Lisa smiled. "He will see, as I did, the farms, solidly prosperous, the fat sleek cattle. He will see that Germany has nothing to fear."

"Yes, and so you have nothing to fear. As things are, you need not be afraid of those bands of men. Their leader is a discredited, comic little man. They have no one of any importance."

"They have General Ludendorff. I heard in Munich——"

"Ludendorff is a fanatic and blind with bitterness. He won't find his way to power. You needn't be afraid. Not as things are. Of course," Frau Blessing spoke slowly, "if the lean years ever come again, if there is misfortune . . . The Germans have no stomach for misfortune."

"Granny, that's not fair."

"It's true. Not of individuals, but of the people. If only one could understand the difference between the individual and the people, then one would begin to understand nations. But I know the Germans a little. They will not accept misfortune. Their imaginations are too young. They cannot encompass justice. You can't be just unless you know mercy. The Germans have not imagination enough to be merciful."

"Granny, you mustn't——"

"Listen to me. You may need to understand them someday. They are like children. Children aren't deliberately cruel, but they feel only their own pain. Germans are like that. They believe only in their own suffering. That's all that has reality for them. They have not the imagination to accept the general lot—to share suffering so that it can be borne with justice and with mercy."

"You've lived here so long. How can you hate us?" Lisa's voice was stern.

Frau Blessing stroked her granddaughter's bright hair. "Forgive me, child. I don't hate Germans. Except for my father, all the people I have loved have been Germans—you and your father and Wilhelm. And even the strangers here are not quite strange to me. I should be lonely anywhere else. I am at home only in Germany. Perhaps at my age one begins to be not quite at home anywhere on earth. One of God's queer little kindnesses."

"I'm sorry, Granny. It's just that I love Germany. It's in my bones and part of my flesh."

"Love it, my dear. But don't try to interfere with it. Don't try to understand it. I am foolish to do that. Individuals can't understand nations. Even their own."

"Do you really think everything will be all right?"

"I really do. Don't think about it. Think of your work. The theater can be your asylum as the university was your father's."

"And I have Franz."

"Yes, you have Franz."

"Do you know how it is, Granny, with Franz and me? Do you remember?"

"I remember a little. Sometimes I remember quite well. I had no home until I married your grandfather. My father and I traveled a great deal. He had to because of his mining interests. Often he left me

behind in school. There was a convent in California and an Episcopal
school in Massachusetts. It was a queer, jumbled life, but it was fun.
My father was very gay. He made everything fun."

Frau Blessing remembered young Elisabeth Hanauer and her
father. The dark, wood-paneled private car, the elaborate meals, the
small blue flame beneath the ornate silver dishes, the lights of the unknown towns outside the smoky windows.

"Papa was very good to me when I met your grandfather. Wilhelm
had no money, no title. My father was ambitious for me and could
have arranged something better. He knew the old Chancellor. Wilhelm
was not successful then. He was only the young Wilhelm, the dear,
young Wilhelm. He, too, was tall and proud and young. Only now I
see how young he was. I was eighteen when we were married. My
German home was the first home I ever had. Wilhelm worked hard.
Quite soon his poetry made people forget my money. He was very dear.
I loved him all the years. Even when he was foolish, even when he was
wrong. You can hate him for the '*Heldenlied*.' I can't. There are too
many years for me even to be very angry."

"So will it be for Franz and me. All the years."

When Franz came, he found Lisa sitting quietly with her grandmother.

"I kiss your hand, dear lady. You know how to calm this child of
tears and temperament."

"Less and less, Franz," Frau Blessing answered. "She has left my
arms for yours. Be good to her."

"You need not fear." Franz put his hand on Lisa's shoulder. He
bent his lips to her hair.

Frau Blessing sighed as she watched them. If only he is as strong
as his fine young body, as brave as his bright, dark eyes.

III

FROM MONTE CARLO to Cannes, the Riviera was crowded. The rich of
all the nations and their eager little brothers filled the hotels. The villas
were rented, the pensions were full. They were all there, the followers

of fashion and the sun. Their nationalities were forgotten in the international world that was their playground. *Vogue* and *The Tatler* and the Paris *Herald* were their chroniclers. There were bankers and moving-picture stars, wholesale grocers and gentlemen jockeys, dressmakers and dukes and exiled Russian grandees. They danced to the cheerful tune of the stock ticker. The sunny shore of Europe was a bright outpost of Wall Street.

Bruce Craven's yacht, the *Infanta,* floated at anchor in the harbor at Cannes. Anne was hostess to the guests who sat, after dinner, on the deck. The talk eddied around her. "Radio's a terrific buy at 80." "Judy and J. C. have an entire floor at the Negresco. Most elaborate sand pile an ostrich ever found. Wait till Mrs. J. C. Jones hears about it." "She knows. She's bought herself the Kutzenov emeralds. Wait till J. C. gets the bill for that consolation prize." "You're always safe at Molyneux. He won't sell you Seventh Avenue Fords." "The Andersons' moor cost them plenty. It seems Clara bagged two beaters, and the Duke's nephew, Tubby, asked her when he arrived how she'd been shooting and the old girl boomed, 'Nevah bettah, nevah bettah.' " "Harry Spain lost three million francs." "Well, the franc isn't what it used to be." "But in one night. Now he'll have to go back to Jenny."

Ruby Borodino had brought Beryl Sands, a young English actress. Anne had watched with amusement Beryl's attempt to charm Bruce Craven. It was no use her shaking that dark childlike head at him. She wasn't his type. He liked them tall with figures. And he liked them to have low, even voices and to move slowly. Uncle Bruce's women are never very bright, Anne thought, nor very ambitious. They're lazy creatures, which is extremely lucky for me and Paul.

She looked for Paul. Beryl Sands was beside him. Her hair hung childishly against her cheeks. One small white hand was on Paul's sleeve. She was looking up at him and speaking earnestly. Anne could hear Beryl's voice, eagerly emphasized, but she could distinguish only an occasional phrase. "How *too* sweet. . . . I *do* think Americans . . . How clever. I *never* should have thought of that."

Paul couldn't be paying attention to that silly little thing. Anne joined them.

"Hello, honey. You've met Berry——"

"Oh, Mrs. Craven. Paul's been too sweet and said I could play golf with you tomorrow. That is, if you don't mind my being the most fearful player?" She looked up at Anne. Her eyes were blue, fringed with very thick short black lashes. That's Irish, Anne thought, and pretty and perhaps dangerous.

"We'll have a foursome with Jim," Paul said, "now that Mary isn't up to playing."

Anne smiled and nodded. "That will be lovely." She moved away. She was thinking. Around her there was talk, a background to her thoughts.

"You should have seen Tommy's face when he found them." "Well, my dear, he would marry for love." "I got this from the old man himself. Better buy at the opening. Once it starts going up . . ." "I can't bear it if they make us wear long skirts." "J. C. likes American Can." "Poor thing eating her heart out for Larry. He never marries anyone." "Two hundred shares of General Electric and my broker cabled me that Anaconda . . ." "At her age, having a baby." "It's worth it. She got him back that way before."

"What are you doing, Anne, telling your fortune in the bubbles?" Phil Sinclair asked.

Anne looked up from her champagne. "I know my fortune."

"I thought perhaps you were worried by the pretty little trollop who's got hold of Paul."

"No, Phil. Or is that vain of me?"

"I think not. I don't suppose there's any danger. If there were, I'd trust you to cope with it."

When the guests began to leave the yacht, Paul said, "The Borodinos and Berry Sands want us to go to the casino. How about giving it a whirl?"

"Not tonight, Paul." She slipped her hand into his. "Let's stay here. I don't want to leave this moonlight for a stuffy gambling room. Let's not share this lovely night with other people." She felt Paul's fingers tighten around hers. "You see them off. I'll be in my cabin."

The voices from the launch came through the porthole as Anne undressed.

There was nothing to fear. Not now anyway. But perhaps someday. Paul had loved her so long. She couldn't believe he would ever stop. But men did. There were so many other women and they stayed the same age. Wives got older. Even I, Anne thought, and shivered. Until now the years have added. In a little while they will begin to take away. When I am twenty-five, when I am thirty, there will be girls like Beryl Sands with smooth childlike faces and young round bodies. They won't leave Paul alone. Bruce Craven's heir presumptive is too rich a prize. You can't stop the years but you can arm yourself against them. Is there never an end to arranging your life? Must you work to keep security as you worked to attain it?

The launch had gone. The water gently slapped the side of the *Infanta* as she swung slowly in the moonlight. Anne looked through the porthole at the water. It was black outside the moon's bright path. She shivered in the light breeze and drew her thin satin and lace robe around her. I want only to be safe. I want what I have and I want it to last. She turned to the mirror and smiled at herself. We'll manage. She reached out her hand in a sudden affectionate gesture. Her fingers touched the cold glass.

The door of Paul's cabin opened. She walked towards the porthole.

"Turn out the light, Paul. It dims the moon."

"That lacy thing you have on is the color of moonlight, Anne. And your hair is silver."

She turned to him. Her body trembled against his. "Paul, I love you so much. I want us to have everything."

"I know, Anne, when you're like this—so sweet, I know." He drew her close to him. "Everything you want, Anne, that I can give you, the moon and the stars and the kingdoms of the earth." His voice broke. "Gosh, there I go, talking too much."

"I only want you, Paul."

"My darling, never mind the words." He lifted her in his arms and carried her across the room.

IV

By the twenty-third of October, Anne was sure. I've been sure for days, Anne thought, only I didn't want to be. Tomorrow I'll send for

Dr. French. She fingered a cigarette and put it down. There was no use lighting it. It would have that taste of something rotten. She lay huddled on the sofa in her bedroom. The feeling of nausea was an enveloping misery. She did not regret the decision she had made in Cannes. She had been wise to start having a baby. But the consciousness of her wisdom was small comfort against the ugly humiliating sickness.

She had put off telling Paul. He would be so pleased. Then Uncle Bruce would know, and her mother and Uncle Normie. Her body wouldn't be hers any more. It would be theirs. She would belong, not to herself, but to the family, to the future. To the future that would be the baby's.

I must tell Paul, Anne thought. She had meant to tell him last night but he had had to stay downtown. The damn market. It was always doing something—going up or down. In the end it always went up again. But men like to make themselves important, Anne thought irritably.

She rang the bell. "Bring me a bowl of cracked ice, please, Marie."

"Yes, madame. Would Madame like to see the afternoon paper?"

"No, put it over there. Get me a rug and then the ice."

"Yes, madame." Marie gently tucked Anne's feet in the velvet cover.

And the servants will be yearning over me. Everyone getting an obscene vicarious pleasure out of my predicament.

Anne sucked the cracked ice. At least the cold tasted clean, which was more than could be said for anything else she had put in her mouth. She chewed a piece to feel the cold sharp against her teeth. Presently she fell asleep.

When she awoke the room was dark. She didn't know where she was. She recognized the sickness first. It struck at her unexpectedly after her heavy sleep. Is it different, she wondered, in a different marriage? Is there a kind of joy that is so pervasive that it rims with light the edges of misery and drives away apprehension? In a different marriage would I still feel trapped? That is nonsense. When you feel sick you can think of more gloomy nonsense. She sat up and turned on the light. The jeweled clock beside her said half past seven. There was no sound from Paul's room. He was late. Maybe it's high time I started having this baby.

She walked across the room and glanced at the paper. She stared at the big black letters that headed the thick column on the right-hand side of the front page.

NEW DECLINE OF $2 to $5 HITS STOCKS
Favorites Crumble under New Pounding
Bank Rally Failing
Steel Dives Again
AT&T also Down

"Maybe, after all, I started this baby a little too soon." She picked up the telephone. Paul's line was busy. She could not reach the number.

Paul came in at eleven. "I left the message with Parker. He said you were asleep, not feeling well. Sorry, darling." He kissed her absently. "I can do with a drink and some food. What a day. It was a nightmare. Nightmares come at the end of quiet sleep." He raised his eyebrows as though to lift heavy lids. He slumped into a chair.

"I saw the paper, Paul. I——"

"You can't describe it. Even if you were there you can't. A disaster. A sudden disaster. Like a shipwreck. The way it must have been on the *Titanic*. Everything calm and then danger, unexpected danger at the end of a bright, ordinary day. That's how it happened. In the last hour of an ordinary day."

The butler brought him a tall glass. "Thanks, Parker." He gulped his drink. "I'll have another."

"Paul, are we—is everyone—are we ruined?"

"No, I don't think so. I don't know what to think. Thank God there are a few men like Uncle Bruce. And they are men! But whether even they can stop the panic—this is only the beginning. This is the time when only the crew knows. The passengers still think that everything's okay. But tomorrow—no one knows what will happen tomorrow."

Tomorrow was worse. In the days that followed the stock prices tumbled jaggedly, then rose a little, like a fever chart turned upside down.

The worst day was the twenty-ninth of October.

"This is it," Paul said. "Now even the passengers know. Now anything can happen."

Paul talked only to make things clear to himself. He did not try to make Anne see. "Unless you were there—and even if you were . . . I could see only my own small part of the confusion. Each witness saw the disaster from a slightly different angle and thought his was the only angle of vision. Now I know a disaster isn't ever the way you think it will be, nor the way anyone says it was. The worst was the faces of the little guys. Guys you know. Gray faces."

For a week Anne could not discover the exact situation in which the crash had left her and Paul. Norman Brooke telephoned to assure her that her own trust fund was safe. "Legals look pretty good these days. But you needn't worry about you and Paul being reduced to living on just your income. Craven and Company is sound. Sound as a bell."

But no one was completely sure who was sound. Anne's world was shaken. Its Chinese wall of confidence was cracked. It had begun to crumble. Anne could hear the excitement, mixed with panic, in her friends' voices. The same excitement that follows death. The telephone rang as friends called to be the first with violent tidings. "It's too terrible. Have you heard about the Spains? Jenny's lost every penny." "Everything they had in the world." "You'd better come out to lunch, Anne, or people will think Craven and Company is tottering."

"It isn't but I am. The flu of all things, in October."

"Poor darling." And the voices went on. "Jumped out of the fifteenth-story window. Too horrible for her."

Paul came and went like a stranger. He accepted unquestioningly Anne's explanation that she had flu. "The doctor been in? That's right, honey." He was preoccupied and very tired.

On Thursday, the thirty-first, the exchange did not open until noon. On Friday and Saturday it was to remain closed.

That meant that the panic was over, Paul explained. "This'll give us a chance to straighten things out, and after that it's just a question of readjustment. The country is fundamentally sound."

It was the end of the quake. "Are we safe?" Anne asked.

"We are, thanks to Uncle Bruce. A lot of people are safe, thanks to him. And to a few others like him."

On Friday morning Anne told Paul.

"Golly, Anne. I haven't been very bright." He sat on the edge of her bed. "Do you feel lousy?"

"It's not too bad."

"I hate it to be bad at all for you when it's so swell for me." He took her hand and held it carefully. He stroked her wrist. "I hate to leave you."

"But if the market is closed, do you have to go downtown?" His big solid presence was unexpectedly comforting. "I feel safer when you're here."

"Darling, I have to. We've got to go over a lot of things."

Anne dressed wearily. She would take that walk Dr. French had recommended. It might make her feel better.

When she came in Parker said, "Mrs. Wilson is in the library, madam."

"Mrs. Wilson?" Anne looked blank.

"Mrs. Albert Wilson, madam. I had no orders, but Mrs. Wilson said it was important."

Albert Wilson was in the office. He was something quite important or going to be important. The Wilsons had been at one of Uncle Bruce's dinners. A common little woman with brassy marcelled hair and orange rouge. Anne hoped she hadn't decided to make the crash a basis for sudden chumminess. I'll nip that in the bud right now. Her heels clicked on the parquet floor as she walked across the hall into the library.

Mrs. Wilson's hair was still brassy, but her face was different. No mascara. Anne remembered the carefully beaded lashes. Mrs. Wilson's powder was patchy. Her rouge was crooked—one cheek was higher than the other.

"It's nice to see you, Mrs. Wilson. Was there something?"

Mrs. Wilson's hand was cold and damp.

"Mrs. Craven. It's Mr. Wilson. I didn't know where to turn. I—I know this is presumptuous. Mr. Wilson doesn't know I came. Only I had to do something. This is my fault." Tears filled Mrs. Wilson's pink-rimmed eyes. She tried to continue. "I kept making Mr. Wilson—I mean, I kept asking—and he bought this lovely home. And then we sent Joanie—that's my little girl—to St. Agatha's. They have such lovely girls—we wanted the best for her, the finest atmosphere——"

What have I done to deserve this? Anne thought. A perfect stranger weeping on my sofa about her house and her daughter's school.

Mrs. Wilson was sobbing. No words came through.

"Please, Mrs. Wilson. Don't upset yourself so. Can't I get you a drink?"

Mrs. Wilson shook her head. She dabbed at her face with a sodden handkerchief. The lipstick was smeared on her upper lip.

Slowly the story came out. Mr. Wilson had borrowed money from Craven and Company. "Only Mr. Bruce Craven wouldn't call it borrowing. But Mr. Wilson will pay it back. Everything we had was on margin. We were so sure. You see, I kept spending. On Joanie and on me, too. I——"

"Don't cry, Mrs. Wilson. It doesn't matter now why the money went. You must be calm so you can tell me what you want me to do."

"If you could ask Mr. Craven to give Mr. Wilson a chance. He'll pay every penny back. Mr. Craven can't send Albert to prison. He can't——"

"You want me to talk to Uncle Bruce?"

"If you could. I thought I could make a woman see. It was my fault. All the spending. I kept after Mr. Wilson. He was quite content with our home, but I wanted—I didn't think I wanted much."

"I'll try. I can't promise but I'll try. Is it a lot of money?"

"Twenty-five thousand dollars."

Anne smiled. "Don't worry too much. I'll do my best."

She would manage Uncle Bruce. That was one thing about power. It enabled her to help wretched little people like this woman, to share safely a part of her security.

"I'll never forget, dear. Never."

Anne withdrew from the clammy hands that clung to hers. "I can't promise—but I think it will be all right. Now you go home and let me get started."

Twenty-five thousand dollars wasn't a lot of money to Bruce Craven. It wasn't enough to send a man to jail. Anne leaned back in the motor. She took the gilt mirror from the shagreen case beside her and smoothed on her lipstick. I'll have to take to rouging my cheeks. My face is getting to be a grim color.

Bruce Craven refused to be managed. He spoke gently but clearly. "I'm sorry, my dear. It isn't the money. It's the principle. It's the example. I am in a position of trust. I can't let a thing like this go unpunished. You must see that, Anne."

Anne saw Mrs. Wilson's crumpled face. "You'll destroy these people, Uncle Bruce. Do you have to? Wouldn't he pay you back?"

"He would. I think, fundamentally, he's honest. Funny thing to say about a thief. But a lot of men behaved abnormally under last week's pressure."

"Well then, couldn't you?"

"No, my dear, I could not. In my position I cannot countenance dishonesty. There are standards I must uphold. Albert Wilson will have to take his medicine."

"Please, Uncle Bruce."

"Good God! We have enough of our own friends to take care of. We can't worry about strangers. What can these people possibly mean to you?" Bruce Craven asked sharply.

"Nothing. I only thought——"

"You're not thinking straight. This isn't like you, Anne."

"I'm sorry. Of course, you know best, Uncle Bruce." She didn't want to displease him. She had done all she could.

Paul came in. "Darling, what are you doing here? You ought to be in bed."

"And where have you been?" Bruce Craven asked.

"Shopping, Uncle Bruce. Celebrating."

"Celebrating! Celebrating what, for God's sake? Have you gone crazy, too?"

"No sir. Shall we tell him, Anne? The fact is——"

Anne felt her cheeks flushing.

"Well, my dear, I am pleased." The chill had gone out of Bruce Craven's voice. His light eyes were friendly again. "No wonder you've been behaving sentimentally."

"What has she been up to, sir?"

"About Albert Wilson. His wife went to see her."

"Poor guy." Paul sighed. "Poor guy. If there was any way to help him, Uncle Bruce would."

"These sad things happen now and then. It seems a pretty rotten world when they do. Well, my boy, let's see this celebration."

Paul pulled an oblong case from his pocket. "I know you wanted one, darling."

He fastened around Anne's wrist a bracelet of jeweled flowers. "It was the prettiest one they had."

"It's the prettiest one I ever saw. Oh, Paul, it's beautiful. Look, Uncle Bruce." Anne held out her wrist to show him the bright stones, intricately carved and set.

"Congratulations to you both." Bruce Craven put an arm around each of them. "You take the rest of the day off, Paul. And by the way —the youngster can count on a welcome from me when he arrives. Something practical."

"Uncle Bruce, you are a darling. You spoil us." Anne lifted her cheek for his kiss.

"It's all right, my dear. You deserve it." Bruce Craven watched them go. Then he sent for Albert Wilson.

After the interview Albert Wilson went back to his office. He wrote a short note to his wife. He tried to write one to his daughter. He tore it up. He took his revolver from the desk drawer and shot himself.

The next day Paul kept the morning paper from Anne, but she found the item in the evening paper. She was reading it when Paul came in.

"Poor devil. Maybe it was the best way out for him."

Anne clung to Paul. She was shaking. "Paul, I'm afraid. She was here, sitting on that sofa. It makes it real. You can't think of people like that as different when they've sat and talked to you. She sat right there——"

"Don't be afraid, my darling. You have nothing to be afraid of."

"But before, none of us had. People like the Wilsons were all right. Everyone was. Now it's all started to crumble. I thought you could be sure, but you can't—you can't."

"You can be pretty sure, Anne. Don't worry. I'll look after you." He held her. His arm was strong and steady around her trembling body.

"I thought—I thought . . ." She had thought she could look after herself, and so she could in the world she knew. But if there was a new world—an unfriendly, unsafe world . . .

"We're all right, Anne. It's awful for poor guys like Albert Wilson, but people like us are all right. What's happened is readjustment—a healthy readjustment. But there's no fundamental change."

Anne looked around the room. She remembered choosing the furniture, fussing about the colors. She felt her new bracelet on her wrist. Everything seemed the same. It was only fear that made it seem different. Fear had crept through an unseen crack in the wall around her world. This fear was new. It could remake her world.

Anne pressed her head against Paul's shoulder. Let him be right. Let things be the same. Don't let this new fear be true.

She looked out of the west window and saw the lights across the park. Beyond was the Hudson and beyond that the suburb where the Wilsons lived.

Mrs. Wilson sat in her living room. It had just been done over in fashionable light colors. The angular blond wood of the furniture was the latest thing. She slid the note back in the envelope. She knew it by heart. "Dear Adele: The only thing to do . . . Not your fault . . . The best little wife a man ever had . . ." She touched the revolver that lay heavily between her knees. She moved slowly. She carried the note and the revolver upstairs. Her tired feet puffed over the edges of her tight patent leather pumps. I'd better put these things away before Joanie gets home.

She closed the drawer and locked it. The gun and the note. She hadn't expected them to be the last things. But there they were with all the other things—her wedding invitation and the bridal group and Albert in his uniform and the bronze cast of Joanie's baby shoes. The decorator had banished the shoes from the living room. Joanie would be home soon.

Mrs. Wilson stood before her bureau. With her left hand she steadied her right arm while she carefully applied powder and lipstick and combed her hair.

The bedroom windows faced east over the front door. Mrs. Wilson watched for Joan. The windowpane was cold against her hot forehead. Her breath blurred the glass. "Make it all right for Joanie. Somehow, make it all right."

Across the New Jersey marshes, across the Hudson, across the bright city, Anne trembled in Paul's arms. "You think it's safe. I tell you the fear is here. The walls can't keep it out. There isn't a high enough wall any more."

"Anne darling. You're hysterical. You're just not well."

She clung to his arm. Let him be right. It's only because I'm sick that I'm frightened. Let him be right. Let me be safe. Please let me be safe.

V

As 1929 ENDED and 1930 began, Anne felt less frightened. The sickness of her early pregnancy was over and she was able to believe that the financial sickness would be over, too. Paul had reassured her. "You'll see, Anne. Business is still feeling the shock of the crash, but the panic is over. Things will begin to pick up again. Slowly, of course, but Uncle Bruce thinks that by summer . . ."

Anne's figure thickened. It gave her no pleasure to see herself in the glass. There was no fun in buying clothes only to conceal her body. A horrid foretaste of middle age, she thought.

I have changed, but nothing else has. Anne looked around Mrs. Reginald Voorhees' dining room. No unemployment among footmen, anyway.

She sat next to Phil Sinclair. "After all our fears, February of this year is just like February of last year. The only change I see is that Mrs. V. is using the silver service instead of the gold. Half mourning for Mr. Hoover's prosperity."

"I don't know, Anne. Finance isn't my racket. I got taken, of course, but the boys tell me if I buy in now I can make it all back. What to buy in with is my only problem."

"You should get a raise just for being here. I thought Mrs. V. barred you."

"She used to. Nothing for the press except her personal court circular to the *Times* and the *Herald Tribune*. My being here is an indication, perhaps, of something."

"She wants you to write her up so that there'll be no doubt in the public mind as to who is to be Marie Antoinette. Comes the Revolution, she'll let no one else occupy the first tumbrel."

"Still, it shows uncertainty. There are a few more straws in the wind. There are other peculiar guests. J. C. Jones, for instance."

"Good Lord, yes. He's impossible."

"Yes, but the interesting thing is that he's a bear in the market. Mrs. V. isn't a fool. You don't get to run anything, New York society included, if you're a fool. And if it's smart to have bears to dinner—maybe the future isn't so rosy."

"You're just gloomy because you like to feel like Gibbon."

"Hope you're right. All the same, I may be writing footnotes to a new *Decline and Fall.*"

Tom Webb claimed Anne's attention. "Good thing, parties like this. If there were more people like Mrs. Reggy, you really would see an improvement. It's all a question of confidence. Put money in circulation. Business as usual. That's the ticket. I can't complain. I'm building Rita Brent's house."

He described the plans. "She wants it to be simple. Normandy farmhouse sort of thing but, of course, on a big scale."

Beyond Tom, and from across the table, Anne heard snatches of conversation. "An upturn by May at the latest, you mark my words." "Lucky we haven't a college professor like Wilson in the White House. Hoover's a practical man." "I had a letter from Marjorie. She says Palm Beach couldn't be more gay. Bradley's, the Bath and Tennis . . ." "It's just a question of confidence." "They may be broke, but they're certainly doing it in style. She's still absolutely ablaze with jewelry." "Well, he sees ahead. He knows the recession is temporary. I said to him very frankly, 'Mr. President . . .'" "I thought we might try California this winter." "Last I heard, they were together. I don't think they can afford a divorce. He was hit pretty hard."

"And a swimming pool!" Anne said. "Mrs. Brent is certainly doing herself proud."

"She has taste, you know, Anne. Natural taste, as I told her. I just interpret for her. That's why I want her to get Diane to do the decorating. She can work with her the same way."

Mrs. Voorhees' table was uneven. Anne turned back to Phil. "With all your gloom, you're more fun than Tom. He's a conversational snail. He carries his current house with him. At the moment it's Mrs. Brent's. What threw Mrs. V.'s table out?"

"The Ambassador. She confided to me that she hadn't known he was coming. I gathered that the better ambassadors make this their New York headquarters and drop in unexpectedly."

"And the maddening part is that they do! Can't blame them. It's pretty de luxe living."

"If you like it on a massive and pompous scale. Coming here is like being tapped for the Captain's table."

"It isn't unlike a ship's dining room. Prewar vintage, rampant with gilt."

"Definitely prewar. The Captain's table on the *Titanic*."

"This isn't what you say in print, Phil."

"Hardly. There's no market for my private speculations. Read my column tomorrow evening. I'll describe all this the way you want it to be. The way my readers want it to be. God knows, I hope you're right and I'm wrong. No one with any sense wants to be witness to his own time's decline and fall."

Anne read Phil's column. Not only what I want, but the way it is.

. . . the Ambassador, whose cousin, it will be remembered, made Harriet Voorhees his duchess. Harriet's father was the second cousin of . . . J. C. Jones, accompanied by neither Mrs. Jones nor the beauteous, much-married blonde who . . . Old New York mixed with the best of the new . . . Standards . . . traditions . . . terrapin . . . the grand manner . . . Bruce Craven's nephew and his lovely young wife, who are so happy over the approach of the long-legged bird in May . . . New York's First Lady carrying on through what Colonel Clarkson told an interested few is only a temporary recession. The Colonel, who is continually in Washington, comes naturally by his interest in government. The older generation will remember that his mother, the beautiful Mrs. James Clarkson, was the daughter . . . Good news for Southamptonites that Mrs. Brent's new house is near completion. Rita is not yet on Mrs. Voorhees' guest list but I confidently predict . . . Society is hoping that the Harry Spains have not added marital difficulties to their financial tribulations. However, I must report that the chain-store heiress is . . .

Anne put down the paper. No matter what Phil says for his private amusement, this is what he writes. This is still the way things are.

Mary Forrest's son was born early in April. Anne went to see her.

Mary's hospital room was full of flowers: tall roses, sprays of pale orchids, big baskets and little blue cradles of flowers.

"Mary darling. I saw your aunt downstairs. She said to come right up."

Mary looked anxious. Funny, Anne thought. This is what she wants. Anne turned to reach for a chair. Marco Ghiberti was standing beside the window. Anne steadied herself against the chair and held out her hand.

"Hello there," she said.

She sat down. This had to happen sometime. But why now—now when I look like this? He, unchanged, and I, grotesque. It isn't fair. She felt her heart pounding. Her head felt hot, the skin drawn tight against her skull. Just seeing him can't destroy the time I have so carefully put together. I was free of him. I pictured him a little fat, a little shabby. Different, so I wouldn't care. He hasn't changed.

Mary was speaking. "We're waiting for Jim. Marco has some papers for us to sign—on account of the baby, you know."

"Are you still with Danforth and Kane?" Anne asked.

"He's their white-haired boy."

"I'm so glad."

"Thank you."

It was like the first stiff conversation. There were flowers then for Mary's engagement; there were flowers now for her son. But this wasn't the beginning of anything. This wasn't even the end. That was long, long ago.

"It's not good for you to see more than one person, Mary. I'll come back later."

"No, Marco. Father's coming, too. He'll be furious if he misses you."

Anne felt as though she could not move. But she must move. "Ring for your nurse, Mary, and she can take me to get a peek at the baby. Then I'll go. You oughtn't to have too many people."

She rose and kissed Mary. She did not look at Marco as she spoke. "Good-by. It's swell you're doing so well with Danforth and Kane." She stood in the doorway. "There's the nurse." Against her will she turned and looked at Marco. The line of his brows, the curve of his mouth . . . Not to remember him—just to see him. Just this once to see him again.

"I'm sorry, Marco," Mary said when Anne left.

"It's all right. It had to happen sometime."

"If you'd be sensible. No one remembers that silly performance of Bill's. People would love to see you. Why don't you come around? Seeing Anne was the worst, and that happened anyway."

"No. Your people aren't the people I came to find, Mary. They're the people I left. There is a brave new world here. I'm finding it. It's not your world. You've built a wall. Bill took me once to Tuxedo Park. The wall and the guard at the gate—that is the pattern."

"It was a pleasant pattern. But you're right. We've got to remake it."

"That or have it broken. Your people used to have a hand in things, Mary. The first William Winton. You can again, if you want to."

"Some of us want to. I want to now that it's my son's world. You're right. We have cut ourselves off."

"You're young. You haven't the habit of walls and gates. Your generation can have a share in America. These are new times."

"Bad times, some people say, Marco."

"They needn't be. They can be terrible times or they can be brave times. It's in our hands."

"I'm being happy. Jim—and the baby. But in a little while . . ." She smiled. "But what could I do? I talk so big. What? Charity?"

"I don't know. Each of us must find that out. I mean to find it out for myself. And you will for yourself."

Marco looked out at the gathering darkness. He pulled up the shade. "Is she happy?" he asked.

"I think so. You don't always know with Anne. But I think she knows—knows what she wants."

"I thought I knew her. But one doesn't, of course. One knows one's own heart and imagines the rest. I imagined——"

"I'm sorry, Marco."

"Don't be. I would not have had that summer. And if I had to be Don Marco to have it—why, that's all right, too. I spoke of it only to wish her happiness. I want her to have the life of her choice. I know now that I was foolish to think that my choice could ever have been hers."

Anne went home. Paul was not coming home. He had gone to a business dinner with Bruce Craven. She sat on the edge of the sofa. The past was over. It could not touch you with pain unless you let it. She put her hand against her head. Her fingers were cold against her hot forehead. It was almost two years. Pain couldn't reach through time to hurt you again.

The room grew dark. She had sent Marie away when she came to draw the curtains. Anne looked at the city's lights beyond her window. They were real. They were now.

Presently she was aware of a real pain. A tiny recurrent thread of pain. It coiled around her waist like a snake. It withdrew. She thought she had imagined it. It came again and then again. It was a tiny pain to cause so great a fear. She recognized it. She had never felt it before, but she recognized it. But not yet—not until May. This can't happen now. It was happening now. She could not stop the machinery she had deliberately set in motion. She remembered the yacht floating in the moonlit harbor. She had not imagined, then, the fear. The fear was greater than the pain. But the pain was growing more insistent. Presently it would blot out fear. She rang the bell. Her finger pressed the bell until Marie came. Anne didn't want to be left alone with fear and the pain that was steadily increasing. That slow increase, that slow, recurrent sharpening of the band of pain was terrifying.

"Marie," she said, "Marie, I think you had better telephone Dr. French." Anne's voice was low. There was no use crying out against her time, which was inexorably moving towards her.

The drive in the taxi, the bare hospital halls, the strange room with Paul beside her—none of it was real. She tried to keep it real, not to have pain the only reality. The pain increased. It didn't go away at all now. It blotted out reality and time. It was time and reality.

Anne was moving through a long tunnel ringed with sound. The sound increased. It was within her and around her. No, not again. This was the same corridor and at the end were the bright light and the pain. "No," Anne cried. "No, not again."

"It's all right, Mrs. Craven. It's all right." She wouldn't listen to them. Their voices pretended to be kind but they were the voices that had driven her pitilessly against the pain. "It's all right, Mrs. Craven It's all over."

She opened her eyes. The bright light was gone. There was only an unfamiliar room in a pale gray light. And their faces were not like devils now. Not masked. She closed her eyes. It was really over, unless she woke again. There had been the dream before. It was quiet except for someone crying shrilly, rhythmically, like the pain. "That voice," Anne said, "echoing like—echoing like———"

"It's all right, Mrs. Craven. You have a lovely little girl."

That was the stranger, then—her daughter. "She cries like the pain. It's ugly to cry like that—over and over, over and over."

"It's all right, Mrs. Craven. Try to sleep now."

Anne slept. The nurse pulled down the shade to shut out the rising sun.

VI

ANNE COULDN'T BELIEVE that two years had gone by. Polly had been two in April. Nineteen thirty and 1931 had gone and half of 1932. They were quick, uninteresting years to look back on. There was nothing to mark time. The years before had been punctuated by milestones that loomed high in the flatness of time. Her sixteenth birthday, her eighteenth, her twenty-first. You finished school, you came out, you married, you had a baby. That last experience marked time, all right. Anne shuddered away from even the pale recollection of Polly's birth. Certainly you forgot the pain. But you remembered words that had held horror. Pain was a place. Its time had no relation to other time. Anne shivered. Thank God I haven't forgotten how I felt when I did remember. Never again for me. I won't have to. Paul adores Polly. And even Uncle Bruce has forgiven her for being a girl.

Anne opened the cupboard door and considered what to wear to Rita Brent's party. The depression was Rita's ill wind. She had done well in Southampton. She had been patient and, above all, she had remained rich.

The depression had come in 1929, but they hadn't called it that then. Anne tried to remember when they had stopped saying recession. Anne remembered the lean years. The lean kine devouring the fat— devouring the memory of the fat years. Pharaoh had been lucky to have a prophet. As though anyone would have listened to a Joseph in '28 or '29. But there were prophets now. They knew the way. They would lead you round the corner to where prosperity waited. If only you would listen. Buy now, they said. The White House said it and the tabloids said it. Buy what? Buy furs, buy cars, buy houses. Buy apples from the stands that punctuate the streets with misery. Buy toys, buy radios, buy pencils from the hand thrust into your motorcar. Buy now. Buy stocks and bonds and turn that corner. The corner they say is just ahead. Mr. Hoover's road to prosperity is like the path in *Through the Looking Glass*. It seems to shake itself and here you are back again. The corner as far away as the hilltop Alice tried to reach. Buy farms in case of revolution. Buy food, buy bonds, buy your way to safety.

The white piqué, I think. Anne took the dress from the cupboard. Cotton evening dresses are fun. "It's smart to be thrifty." It's smart but it's boring. The endless talk about the clever little woman who can copy anything. The wholesale house for furs. The mean little economies nibbling at the edges of our lovely luxurious lives. Are all the rest of my young years to be drab ones? And not so young. I'm twenty-five. Anne considered this fact with distaste. Twenty-five was definitely not young. Well, I'll look young in the white piqué. Lucky for me I was wise when I was young. Marrying Paul was a good deal more than moving from one Southampton dune to another. It was finding a rock of safety in the days when all the sands were smooth, before they began to shift. She held the white dress against her and looked in the long mirror.

"Paul," she called, "turn off the radio. You'd better start dressing. We'll be late." I suppose we'll have to listen to politics at Rita's. Only the drunks will dance.

At dinner there was no need of the radio. The coming election was in their midst. On Anne's right, Mr. Winton was solemn. "I don't like it. The feller isn't solid." On her left, Mr. Morehead was angry. "God knows who we'll have running the country if he's elected. Why, I heard—heard from a man who knows him well . . ." All the conversations were the same. Anne could hear bits of them up and down the table. "He's got more half-baked theories . . ." "Oh, if they'd nominated him I might have voted the Democratic ticket myself." "Wish they had nominated him. The trouble with Roosevelt is he may be elected." "Folly to change horses in midstream. If only the public will realize that." "If this weren't an election year, you'd see an upswing. This way, nobody knows." "The trouble with the democratic system . . . You take this feller, Mussolini . . ." "I tell you those people don't want to work, and with Roosevelt, they won't have to." "You're damn right. A new deal, he said—it'll be a new deal with marked cards stacked against us." "Thing this country has to do is tighten its belt—get back to simple Americanism."

Anne was glad when the dinner was over. Rita Brent must get her endless menus from the shade of Ward McAllister. Well, the older generation liked it. Mr. Morehead hadn't missed a course.

Anne was glad when the party was over. "It's no fun, Paul. Politics, the market. No one talks about anything amusing any more. The women discuss economy—some of them practice it. Will we have to?"

"We might go a little slow. My stuff's all well invested, thanks to Uncle Bruce. But the exchange is dead."

"My favorite economy is Mrs. Morehead's. She made a big sacrifice and gave up using Poland water for the depression. I did hear one bit of news. Bill Winton is going to marry Jenny Spain. He was in love with her before, remember—only on account of all that money, he wouldn't——"

"Can't blame him. It's only the heels like Harry Spain——"

"Wait till you hear. Harry's going to marry Rita. She never took her eyes off him all evening."

"Good Lord! She's old enough to be his mother."

"She'll be a nice modern mother. No repressions. She'll give him all the polo ponies his little heart desires. Tom Webb told me. He thinks he'll get to do another house now in Westbury. At least Tom doesn't talk politics. I'm sick of it. I wish Wintergreen was President. Gosh, now they even take candidates for Vice-President seriously. Mr. Winton was talking about Garner."

"Solid feller, they say. Might have a restraining influence."

Nineteen thirty-two became 1933. There were bread lines and there were parties. There was hunger and there was luxury. And everywhere there was fear.

"It looks the same," Anne said to Phil Sinclair. "But the edge is off it." They were dancing at Mrs. Voorhees'. "I used to hate her parties. Stuffy, I said. But now they give me a pleasant sense of continuity— of security. The same orchestra, the same jewels on the same dowagers —or dowagers who look the same."

"You don't look as though you needed to feel safe."

"My necklace?" Anne fingered the smooth, cool pearls. "Uncle Bruce gave it to me. He says it's an investment—if anything is an investment any more."

"Like gold in Switzerland. That's the thing to do this winter, I'm told. Odd for Americans to feel safe because of gold buried in European vaults."

"Uncle Bruce says people don't know what to do."

"He seems to be all right if I can judge by you and Paul."

"He is. I try vaguely to economize. I feel we all should. But I hate economy. It's smart to be thrifty. There's a handy slogan for a depression."

"There's a better one." Phil lifted his glass. "Or haven't you noticed it? It's fun to be fooled. That fits our time nicely."

"Still gloomy?"

"Not at all. I'm an observer. That's why I spend so much time with you. You're a case history of your era."

Anne frowned.

"Don't do that. You're a pretty case history. Very pretty, in fact."

"There you are, my dear." Norman Brooke interrupted. "Want to talk to you. Sorry, young man. Find a place we can be quiet." He led Anne to the dining room, where only a few guests remained after supper.

"Well, the deal's gone through. Good thing, but your mother's upset."

"I don't know what you're talking about."

"The Thirty-eighth Street house. Been trying to sell it for some time. White elephant."

"But Mother's lived there since she was married! Has she lost money? What's happened?"

"What's happened to us all? To most of us, anyway. Fewer dividends. Your mother's all right, but a real estate commitment like that's no good. Sorry, I can see it's a shock to you. Didn't know you were sentimental about things like that."

I'm not sentimental, Anne thought, but no one likes to have the frame of her past removed.

"Point is, my dear—run in and see your mother tomorrow and cheer her up."

Anne looked at the solid grandeur of the Voorhees' house. This one, too, in time. The frames of all our lives removed like scenery. There isn't any program to tell the setting of the next act but I'm not going to like it. I'm not going to like it at all.

The next morning Anne found her mother making a list of her belongings. "Hello, my dear. You've heard, of course. I'm lucky to sell the house, but I feel uprooted. My things just won't fit in an apartment."

Anne shook her head at the massive furniture. "You can take some of it," she consoled her mother.

"If there's anything you and Paul want—just wander around."

Anne walked upstairs. If there's anything I want. I want this to be as it is. Bits of it are no use. She rubbed the dark wood of the banister. She entered her bedroom. She moved her hand against the cane-work doors of the wardrobe. She jerked the doors open. The red velvet lining reminded her of the days when she and Mary had pretended the wardrobe was a castle. The bed matched the wardrobe. The desk was different. It had seemed very elegant and grown-up when it was new. The sofa and chairs had been re-covered when the room was done over for her eighteenth birthday. The old chintz, riotous with large lifelike roses, was more vivid in Anne's memory than the fabric that replaced it. She walked into the day nursery. The piano stood in a corner. It was locked. Anne had forgotten how to play. On the keyboard cover her fingers moved in the pattern of the pieces she used to know. She remembered the feeling of her hand stretching for the octave, the weakness of her fourth finger with which Miss Cunningham vainly struggled. Poor Miss Cunningham, with her raincoat and her sensible shoes and her beads that rattled against her silver and amethyst brooch. The pencil rapping the piano. "One and two and three and one. Hold it."

There is the round, low table where I did my lessons and painted and ate my supper. I always remember it as a big table but now it's no bigger than Polly's.

Anne went down to her mother's room. This, too, holds the slow years, the years when time stretched endlessly ahead, when the years behind you were long and difficult to remember.

"Mother, weren't these walls done in silk once? They were old rose. I remember the color and the feeling of the material."

"Darling, that was years ago. Well, you can imagine, old rose. Silk panels were very smart then. Do you remember the mantel?"

"Yes. There were ornaments on it, and photographs. I remember the clock with the shepherdess. And the lamps. I liked the ones on your bureau best—cupids garlanded with prickly flowers." Anne stretched out her hand to the smooth columns of the new lamps on the bureau. She had had to reach up to touch the old ones. It must have been a long time ago.

"I hate moving, but Norman says it's the sensible thing to do. And he knows."

"Let me help you with the list," Anne said.

The columns were headed Storage, Sell, Take. As Anne wrote, she smiled and hid from her mother her resentment of the tide that was changing their lives. If I understood this tide, I'd know what to do. If you understand the tide, you can be safe, you needn't be swept away.

In March, when the banks closed, Anne thought again about the tides.

"Suppose the banks don't reopen, Paul?"

"Don't be silly. This was a damn sensible thing to do. Even Uncle Bruce admits that."

"I'm afraid. Suppose we none of us had any money. What would we have?"

"Well, I'd have you, Anne, and Polly. That's a lot."

Anne smiled at Polly, who was building a tower of blocks. When the tower fell, the child pushed her straight light hair out of her eyes and slowly began to rebuild.

"Let your daughter be an example to you, Anne. We'd rebuild."

"With what? Suppose they mean to take our blocks away?"

Polly's hair is a lovely color, Anne thought. She remembered, with a pang, that her own hair was getting darker. She had unwillingly noticed it in the mirror that morning. Beside her on the table was her bridal photograph. I was fat then, she thought as she looked at the round young face. No, that wasn't fat, that was youth. All young faces have that full round look.

"How about putting that away, Paul? You have the new Beaton picture. I don't look like this any more."

"I like it," Paul said. "It looks so young."

"Paul!"

"Sorry, darling. But we're none of us getting any younger. Polly couldn't grow up if we did."

Polly stood up proudly. "I am big—I am very big," she said and knocked down the tower and laughed. "I'm a giant." She picked up the blocks and began to rebuild the tower.

Anne watched her. She's so sweet like this. A tiny, lovable accessory to my still young years. We're becoming to each other. I resent the years in which she will grow up and I shall grow old.

"You don't mind them, Paul, do you?"

"Mind what?"

"The years."

"Look who's worrying. This old lady who's almost twenty-six."

Four years to thirty, Anne thought. And the years keep going faster. The Red Queen said "it takes all the running you can do to keep in the same place." You can't stay in the same place. You can't stop time, nor the tide, nor the future. You never could—not even in the old, safe days—but at least then you knew what the future would be. You could plan.

Now there is a new tide, Anne thought. It can sweep me away. Unless I learn to ride it, it can sweep me away into a future that is not of my choosing.

VII

THE SUMMER OF 1933 in Southampton was like other summers. The pattern of the depression was set now and familiar. Some of the old people had gone. Many who were left were shabby. But there were new people who spent their money in the accustomed ways. President Roosevelt did his part to make the summer agreeable. He united the heterogeneous community as an unpopular guest unites a house party.

At the end of August the J. C. Joneses' new house was finished. Anne and Paul went to the housewarming. Anne listened to the talk as music played and supper was served in the J. C. Joneses' elaborate and ugly house.

"A lot of strangers running the country. Even Harding's gang was easier to cope with than this. Better a knave than a fool." "I was in

Washington in the spring and I assure you I didn't know a soul. The cliff dwellers were a relief—dear stodgy souls. At least one knows them." "He says no one has the key to the White House. This new crowd doesn't need a key. They use a set of burglar's tools." "Never earned a dollar in his life. How can you expect him to understand business?" "There can't be any confidence while he's in the White House—take U. S. Steel . . ."

Anne complained to Paul. "Business was dull enough as a topic when it was good. Now that it's bad, it's unbearable. To think I complained about smug stockbrokers. They may have been dull but at least in those days they were cheerful. Let's go dance."

They danced. Harry Spain cut in. Then Tom Webb. It's like all the parties, Anne thought. So, perhaps, was the Duchess of Richmond's ball before Waterloo—like all the other parties.

"Well, what do you think of this whitewashed monstrosity?"

"It's moderne with an *e* all right. Cheer up, Tom, just not to have designed such a house should get you plenty of commissions."

"I don't mean to sound sour-grapish——"

"Tom darling, you don't. We all think J. C. must have used the man who designs his factories. Let's be thankful he only economizes on his architect, not on his chef or his bootlegger."

"J. C. made a smart move when he married Judy. Darn good party she's throwing. Southampton's morale is swell. If only the rest of the country . . ."

The sea air blew through an open window as Tom and Anne danced. She shivered. It's cold out there, or perhaps only stuffy in here.

Paul cut in. "Let's get out of this hot house for a minute, Anne."

"Of course, darling." He looks tired, she thought as they walked through the long window.

Beyond the dunes the waves pounded a heavy bass to the light music that came from the bright room. This is far from New York's misery in time and space, Anne thought. If only I could stay. If only the New York winter needn't begin again. "The poor always ye have with you." But when they were out of sight you could forget their increasing army. Forget the fear of their becoming a conquering army.

"I wish we needn't go back to New York, Paul."

"Why, darling?"

"It reminds me of the change. I get scared."

"You may be right at that." Paul's voice was heavy. "Even Uncle Bruce seems sort of down. He's sure of one thing: Roosevelt's little blue eagle is no bird of victory."

"You're not scared, Paul?" She touched his shoulder. Her fingers tightened on the sleeve of his dinner jacket.

"Guess I'm just sunk. Matter of fact, we don't have to go back to New York. Uncle Bruce is sending me abroad in the autumn."

"How divine! Where? Why?"

"Paris—London. He says it's to check up on the European offices and boost their morale by having a partner over there. A pretty silent partner, but they won't know that." Anne saw the flame tremble as Paul lit a cigarette. "I think he's just letting me down easy. Uncle Bruce hardly tells me anything any more. Remember when I told you he was going to give me responsibility? Remember all I promised? Looks like I was talking too big."

"But, Paul, Uncle Bruce always seems so pleased. He needn't have made you his partner. And your own investments. You've been clever about them. Your income's been cut awfully little."

"I used to look after my own things. But less and less. Uncle Bruce handles everything now. You need to make instant decisions in these times. I guess I'm a slow sort of fellow. So I'm being sent abroad. And it's pretty clear that I'm like the rest of the educated ballplayers —a good customers' man. Fine thing to be when there aren't any more customers."

"You're just depressed."

"For you, darling. This isn't what you ordered or deserved. You should have got a brilliant guy and, God help me, that's what I thought you were getting."

"You used to know me better than that, Paul. I wanted security, and you give me that. Suppose you don't increase the Craven fortune. It's big enough. When your time comes, you'll conserve what Uncle Bruce and your grandfather made. That's worth doing."

"Darling, you're very sweet. Sure you don't mind having picked a second-rate guy? The kingdoms of the earth, I said. Seems I'm not providing any. But you can have my share of Uncle Bruce's——"

"And you're the one who said we talk too much." She lifted her lips to his. His arms held her firmly and warmly. Five years make a love of their own, she thought. Marriage creates its own emotion. I chose well. Safety, which I knew I had, and a slow, unexpected contentment. More than my bargain.

"I'm lucky, Paul." She kissed him and turned away from the dune towards the bright ballroom. The sound of the wind through the dune grass still took her back to the old summer—the summer of choice. I was right, she thought. You choose only once, and my choice was right. She walked quickly. Paul followed her towards the lighted windows.

As she danced Anne watched the party around her. This is my world, she thought, and Paul has endowed me with it. Even if it's only by inheritance. He'll have Uncle Bruce's money someday. It's the power that matters, not the way you get it.

Anne smiled at her familiar world that danced about her. Some faces were missing. But even in good times there were people who failed. And some chose to withdraw. She thought of Mary in the hot city, working at her day nursery, trying to empty the sea with her silver spoon. She's happy. And Jenny Winton in that horrid village house. She's happy because she has Bill. All you need is to have what you think you want. And I have a right to what I want—to my way of happiness. *Pourvu que ça dure.* I'm haunted by Napoleonic ghosts tonight. She missed a step and smiled apologetically at Paul. Those would have been really frightening times in which to have lived. "I'm lucky, Paul," she said, and her hand tightened on his shoulder.

London in October and November seemed to Anne more cheerful than New York. If there were changes in the social pattern, it didn't matter to her, since the pattern itself was unfamiliar. "It's not 1929, but at least it's outside the depression—our depression, anyway. It's like being in a nice, fat Victorian novel—impressive staircases and decorations and names out of the history book and, once in a while, a place like this. Too much white tie and red carpet would get me down." Anne looked, with satisfaction, around the Savoy Grill. "And even this isn't like home. All the English voices—the beautiful English voices—make me feel as though I were in a play. Don't be so gloomy, Paul. I want to be by Coward, not by Ibsen."

"Sorry, I'm tired."

"Not talking looks so married. Drearily married. The other people don't know you're tired. They just think you're bored."

"I forgot the other people. I don't believe they notice whether or not I'm talking."

"They do. Lots more people know you than you think. They all know who Uncle Bruce is and you're his only nephew. You're important. The English are good at recognizing importance."

"Poor little Anne. It really is a play to you. How about some champagne to lend a festive air? I'll feel better when I get a little food. I'm not used to cocktails and a cracker instead of dinner before the theater."

"We couldn't have had dinner between Sir George Merrian's cocktail party and the play."

"And we had to go to Sir George's."

"We certainly did. You owe it to your position to see people like that."

"Madam Queen, Madam Queen. But if it makes you happy, I hope I can hang on to my position—such as it is."

"Don't talk like that, Paul. It's silly. The directors have been wining and dining you like the King's son."

"But there's nothing for me to do. I don't get it. I've been here almost two months. Don't see what on earth there is for me to do. I don't get it."

"I do. Uncle Bruce wants these people to know you. For the future. And for now, it's a holiday. You did enjoy the play tonight."

"Yes. Lisa Blessing is a good actress."

"And beautiful. Even in the last act when she looked thin and lost —more then. The effect was pinched and plain, as though a lamp had gone out. As, of course, it had for Elsa in the play. But even then you still wanted to look at that pale face. That other pretty little one didn't matter."

"Proportion, I think."

"What is, Paul?"

"Beauty. Not just in faces. In living, too. Take us——" He stopped. Anne wasn't listening; she was looking past him. "Here are the Borodinos now. You can eat at last."

"Anne, my pet. I've brought the Von Erlencamps. Do you mind?"

Anne rose. "Of course not. We're delighted." She stretched out her hand to Lisa Blessing. "We saw *The Troubled Heart* tonight. You were wonderful."

"And this," said Ruby, "is Count Erlencamp. Pretty wonderful, too, I think."

Anne looked up at Franz. Those dark eyes and his hair. How funny, she thought. Von Erlencamp. That must be German. Perhaps his mother was Italian. She asked Pierre Borodino.

"No indeed. Austrian mother, Prussian father. It's a good thing you asked me, not Franz. I don't think Italians are thought very Aryan—nor the French—nor any of us, not even the English. You don't believe me. No one does when I say the Germans are just practicing on their Jews."

"Hush, Pierre. He'll hear you."

"The idea is neither strange nor disagreeable to him. He won't mind. Like me, he has read *Mein Kampf*. But I'm boring you. Forgive me." Pierre lifted his glass. "We may as well enjoy ourselves while the Germans are still only practicing."

"No, but seriously, Pierre, they say the horror stories that come out of Germany are exaggerated. It's only the foreign Jews that they——"

"Perhaps. But might not that Teutonic view of foreigners be worth considering? At least by us who are foreigners."

"Well anyway, Nazis are better than Communists. The Reds really terrify me. With Communism, no one is safe."

"Perhaps no one is safe anyway. Perhaps I am too French to see the Germans as the protectors of European civilization."

"You've been worried about the Germans ever since I first met you in Baden-Baden. And nothing's happened."

"A good deal has happened in Germany."

"What has really happened? Parades and marching. It's just Fascism translated into German by a comic little second-rate Mussolini. It's not new."

"I know it's not new. It's a lot older than Il Duce. That is why I believe it to be dangerous."

"Please, Pierre. This is a party. Look at Ruby. She makes everything a party."

Ruby was talking to Paul. Anne listened to her sudden little laugh. It was always natural, never forced. That was one of the secrets of

Ruby's charm—that spontaneous gaiety that was just for you, just for the moment, the lovely moment which you owed to Ruby.

Pierre smiled. "Ruby keeps me in the present—the agreeable interlude of the present. And that is where I belong, since there is nothing I can do about the future. Nothing I intend to do."

Anne turned from Pierre to Franz von Erlencamp.

"It is a great pleasure to me, Mrs. Craven, to meet Americans. I regret only that it is necessary to go to France or England to find the Americans. You will perhaps come to Germany before you return home?"

"If my husband's business permits. We have not been to Germany since—since Hitler."

"You should come and see for yourself what the Fuehrer has accomplished even in so short a time."

"Are you a"—Anne hesitated. She wondered if Nazi was the polite word—"a member of his party?"

"I am a German—I am a National Socialist. You on the outside hear often ill of the party. If you would come to Germany, you would see a country reborn. Birth is always a violent, painful business. Death is sometimes peaceful, birth never. The blood and pain should not blind you to the miracle of a new life. The Fuehrer has brought life to the Fatherland. But I am boring you. Come, you and Mr. Craven. We ask only that you come and see for yourself. Anyone can see."

Anne watched him as he looked across at Lisa.

"And Lisa, too, is a National Socialist?"

"My wife is an artist. As a German artist, she has a special and separate mission. It is not necessary for her to interest herself in politics."

"Isn't that the German—I mean the German in the play?"

Franz looked up. "Yes. Raimund Hoehlmann." He bowed to the man who stood beside the table.

Against the table, Anne thought, pinning us to the wall. A tall, broad man. He hasn't Franz von Erlencamp's thin, pulled-out elegance. But he has strength.

Raimund Hoehlmann leaned on his big pale hands, spread flat and firm on the white cloth, and the table was his. His bright eyes held the attention of the group. They listened to his slow, musical voice, which caressed his commonplace words and gave them the illusion of importance, the promise of wit. He has great charm, Anne thought, penetrating charm that disarms you by its warm friendliness. Funny how many Germans are dark. Hitler, himself, of course, and that hideous little clubfooted one.

"Well, Lisa. Our last night in England." Raimund Hoehlmann lifted Lisa's glass to his lips. "Let us drink to it. Almost I have thought of remaining here. Gerald Michaels has made me a most tempting offer. A play that will be good for New York next autumn after a season here."

"Why not stay?" Franz asked.

Raimund laughed. "No, my fine fellow. You don't get rid of me so easily." He touched Lisa's cheek with one of his thick white fingers. Then he leaned again on the table and spoke gravely. "I want to go home. Like that old Greek fellow who had to touch the earth, I need my native soil. Or perhaps I'm shrewd. German audiences are loyal. They will last out my time. The English and the Americans can't keep me young, and in my romantic business I need that. An actor's own countrymen are best. They were young with him. Their memories multiply his youth a thousandfold. They keep it alive. Foreign success is pleasant but it is only pleasure. One cannot live by it." He smiled at them. "That reminds me to leave you. A bit of foreign pleasure is waiting for me at my table. A very pretty, fluffy bit. Until tomorrow, my dear." He kissed Lisa's hand. He bowed to the others. He progressed rather than walked across the room to his table.

"Insufferable bounder," Franz said to Anne.

"That's not fair, Franz." Lisa spoke quietly. "At least it's only part of the truth about Raimund. He's a very great actor. His talent is the important thing about him."

"He's handsome in a big coarse way," Ruby giggled. "I kind of like that, but I wouldn't have thought of calling it talent."

"Bounder or actor or both, as is, alas, often the case, he has ruined the evening," Franz said. "He has reminded us that we leave tomorrow and must get home early tonight. Come, Lisa, my dear."

Franz was angry. Lisa recognized the withdrawal, the smile that had no warmth or light behind it. The change in his voice that no stranger could hear.

When they reached their apartment, she followed him into the bedroom.

"Yes, Lisa?"

"Don't be like this, Franz. Not when we're going home tomorrow." The first homecoming to a land grown strange. Franz had been back since the new government but she had been playing in England for a year.

"Like what, my dear?"

"Changed—so that I change, too, and feel a stranger."

"I do not understand your friendliness toward a creature like Hoehlmann."

"I'm not friendly to him. He's a devil to play with. And off the stage, he is common and offensive. Also he thinks himself a divine gift to women. I don't like men who behave as though they were a shower of gold from Mount Olympus. But he is a fine actor and, as Karl, he is superb. And he is a German. You shouldn't run down a German before foreigners, Franz."

"He is hardly German by any decent definition."

"You mean his mother? We don't know she was a Jewess. It's just that people have always said so. And what of it? You and I don't believe in all that. You said yourself that it was only an unimportant part of National Socialism, that it would be dropped, that even the Fuehrer——"

"The thousands of Hoehlmanns make it impossible to drop it. I used not to understand. And your gentle heart cannot see the necessity of eliminating these parasites. Even though there be some unavoidable injustice. You see only the temporary cruelty. I see the end. A Germany reborn. Women can't understand. They don't understand war."

"That, at least, we need not fear. That ultimate evil . . ." Lisa remembered the war years—the years of fear. "But about Raimund. He's not so bad."

"He's presumptuous."

" 'Presumptuous' is the wrong word, Franz. He's arrogant."

"Same thing."

"Not quite. If you call it pride it sounds better. And in the theater, as in any profession, we need pride, a sense of our own value."

"I don't understand. I don't understand anything about the theater. Why, for instance, Lisa, did you permit Michaels to bring Hoehlmann here? It would have been better for you to have been the only German in the cast. It would have made your success more conspicuous."

"We needed a German to play Karl. And Raimund has helped the play. Not just by his performance. Women are attracted to him. They fall a little in love with him."

"And you, too, Lisa—you, too? In that scene with his too handsome mouth pressed on yours?"

Lisa laughed. "Now you are ridiculous. As a matter of fact, in that scene where we kiss Raimund keeps me busy preventing him from up-staging me." She stared at Franz. "You don't mean that, Franz. You don't think that I could love anyone else, even a little. Don't you know, don't you remember? They played our American song tonight? Did you hear it?"

Lisa remembered the first dance and the song that was the beginning.

> *Who stole my heart away?*
> *Who makes me dream all day?*

She smiled at Franz. He had been sulky then. One of the first things she had known about him had been his pride—pride that was the scabbard of fear. For a moment she had forgotten and been angry. She had seen him then and, seeing him, had loved him. She still saw him and loved him.

The thick hangings shut out the sounds of London, and in the still room Lisa heard the American song. She turned away from Franz and stared at the heavy brocade curtains. She saw, not the pale design of the material, but the picture of that first meeting. The Baroness with her incredible red hair. Hair that the Baroness couldn't have expected anyone to believe in. The Baroness's bracelets rattled as she moved and talked, and Franz stood tall and quiet. "Gracious Fräulein, may I have the honor?" She had moved into his arms and known it was forever. And this tune of all possible tunes, these words of all possible words had become their love song. The accompaniment of their beginning.

She touched the tassel on the curtain. It was heavy as though it were stone. It did not move beneath her light touch. She saw another beginning. They stood before the wide doors of Schloss Erlenhof. The doors were flung open. Franz carried her across the threshold, out of the shining afternoon sunlight into the castle hall. The brightness had blinded her so that she could not see the flags and the swords and the shields; she could not see the armorial splendor which Franz offered his bride. She could feel his arms trembling as he held her.

The London room was very quiet. The heavy curtains were like the wall on which, long ago, her grandmother had shown her magic-lantern slides. Lisa remembered the one of a snowball growing bigger and bigger in its calamitous descent of a mountainside. But the slides showed a story. Each picture in its proper place in a sequence—the action of the story frozen for a moment, frozen for you to see. Remembering wasn't like that.

Lisa remembered the first morning of her marriage. She remembered Franz asleep, his dark head framed by the white pillow. That was all the picture. Franz's face asleep. His lids heavy and still over his eyes. She had never seen him asleep before. She had sat quietly, watching him. To see him asleep was to see him outside of time, to see him as he had been as a child—to see him as he would be. The pain of seeing too far ahead had made her move. "No, not that. Don't let me ever see that. Please, God, no. Let me be first. Let me be first." Franz had wakened and heard her and laughed.

"Lisa, my darling, you know you are first. Always first with me."

She had seen him asleep often since then. She had forgotten the sharp sweetness and pain of that first time until now suddenly she remembered. Remembered so that she saw the picture of Franz's dark head heavy on the soft white pillow.

There were many pictures in five years of marriage. They were like the pictures on a child's nest of blocks. You pulled them out and spread them before you or built them into a bright-colored tower, and even then you couldn't see them all. You couldn't see any one picture unless you looked at it and forgot the others. A picture on each side of each bright hollow cube. And the pictures had no relation to each other. They were not even in proportion; little things were made big and big things little. An enormous butterfly here on this side and on the other a tiny church.

"What are you thinking of, Lisa?" Franz's voice was gentle.

He is sorry but he can't say it, Lisa thought. But I know that, I have always known that.

"Children's blocks."

"You want a child, I know." Franz stood beside her. "But there is time. For still a little while your career must come first. People must not be given a chance to forget you. Only now are you being really acclaimed as you deserve. Once you are firmly established, we can begin to have our children. And also, in a little while, Germany will be again fit for our son. He will not know the humiliation, the poverty——"

"My career," Lisa interrupted. "But often I think you hate it. At Erlenhof those ladies in the portraits, with their brocades and their jewels and their smooth faces—they look like sisters in fancy dress, not like wives separated by the centuries. I break the pattern. One small blank bit in the mosaic of quarterings."

"Siegfried Blessing's daughter has no need of quarterings. His sword is the sword of Germany."

In the quiet room Lisa heard the *"Heldenlied"* and the feet marching to its rhythm, the steady feet of soldiers, the hurried, heavy feet of a mob. When soldiers become a mob, when the mob is the military . . . She moved so she would not hear the sound.

"That was not my father. If you could only have known him. The professor in uniform. If you could only have known him before they changed him."

"It is you who don't know him, Lisa. His spirit marches in the vanguard of the heroes of the new Germany."

Lisa did not answer. They shall not change him, she thought. If one person remembers, it is enough, it is true.

"Lisa, not because of your heritage do I love you. Not for anything outside you, your body and your spirit, could I cease to love you. It is you I love, not what you have inherited, not what you believe. You will come to see the Fuehrer and the party as they are, as Germany sees them. The Germany that is yours, Lisa, that you love."

"I will try, Franz. I promise I will try."

"And you will have me. Always, no matter what comes, you will have me. I will keep you safe."

He lifted her in his arms and held her. She remembered the slanting light of the afternoon sun and the wide doors of Erlenhof.

The trip across the Channel was rough. Lisa stepped from the *Golden Arrow,* from the sunny English day, onto the boat. The sea was rough beneath the deceptive sunshine. She had stepped from well-being into misery. She lay in the small, too bright cabin and wished that time would pass. She imagined the French shore, the grinding noise of landing. Soon we shall be there. She tried to push ahead out of this miserable little stretch of time. Franz sat beside her.

"Darling, I'm so sorry."

"I'm sorry, Franz. It's so unattractive to be seasick."

"Not you, Lisa. You look only like a sad, pretty child. You touch my heart."

Lisa shrank against the stiff pillow and tried not to breathe as the heavy smell of a cigar floated towards the door. The door opened and Raimund Hoehlmann entered.

"Been looking all over for you. I missed you at Dover."

"Take that damn cigar and get——"

"Sorry, old man." Raimund smiled amiably at Franz and tossed his cigar through the porthole. "Feeling under the weather, Lisa? Too bad. Don't think about it. It's all mental, you know."

Lisa closed her eyes.

"I wanted a word with you," Raimund continued. "You know the powers that be, Franz. There won't be any trouble about me in Germany, will there? I ran into an old pal last night. You remember him—Koenig. Used to be with UFA. They kicked him out."

"Is there something that should make trouble for you?"

"Well, between ourselves, if someone wanted to dig it up, my mother wasn't what's called Aryan. Pity it wasn't my father. Then I could imitate our best people. I'm told it's quite the fashion in Berlin now to try to prove oneself a bastard rather than a non-Aryan."

"Was your mother a Jewess?" Franz asked.

"Well, partly. There was a Jewish strain there. Not like Koenig, of course. Besides, poor fellow, he has no talent. Even the Nazis must respect talent. What do you think, Franz? You know these fellows. What can I expect?"

"You know the racial laws. You know whether or not they apply to you."

"Well, I don't think they have to." Raimund laughed. "I don't believe they will. The theater's always the last thing to be touched, even if our handsome Adolf prefers the opera."

"I should advise you to watch your tongue."

"Sure, sure. Heil Hitler." Raimund lifted his arm and laughed. "I'm no fool."

Lisa managed to speak. "Why not be on the safe side, Raimund, and not go back, just in case? Why not accept Gerald's offer?"

"Well, it's as I said last night: I prefer to go home. Also I have practical reasons."

"Practical reasons?" Franz asked.

Lisa turned her pillow and buried her face in its stiff coolness. "Sorry, I feel rotten. Please, Franz, you and Raimund——"

Franz led Raimund up on deck. "Practical reasons?" Franz repeated.

"Property. I haven't done badly. And in these changing times, better to get home and keep an eye on things. Well, there you are. What do you advise me to do, old man?"

"I don't know," Franz said. "You know the law. You know the situation. You must decide. I can't take the responsibility. I won't take it."

"No, you won't, will you?" Raimund grinned. "Foolish of me to think you would, even in a small matter. That's the truth about you weary postwar gentlemen. You don't want responsibility or decision. Hence the Fuehrer. Into his hands you commit your spirit." He patted Franz on the back. "Sorry I bothered you. And don't worry about me. Not that you were planning to. I can take care of myself in Adolf's Germany. I'm like him. I came up the hard way, too. I think it may be an advantage not to be a Herrenklub boy in the Third Reich."

VIII

THE DRESS REHEARSAL of *The Golden Bowl* was on the evening of January 15, 1934. Lisa sat in her dressing room waiting for the second-act scene to be set.

She was tired. They had rehearsed late last night and now again it was almost ten o'clock and they still had two more acts to play. Lisa's hand, palm outward, moved across her forehead. The classic gesture for fatigue, she thought. My voice, my hands, even my heart serving the parts I play. Perhaps in time there will be no Lisa left, just gestures and a voice and the emotions of imagined women set down with pen and ink for me to bring alive. It's an escape. It's what Granny meant. "Let the walls of the stage, even the fourth invisible wall, enclose you, Lisa. The stage can be your refuge as the university was your father's."

"You said that before, Granny." Once again, in December, Lisa had been with her grandmother in the small upstairs sitting room. The reflected winter sunlight had danced in the glass of the picture frames.

When she returned to Germany, Lisa had gone home. She had not wanted to stay in Berlin with Franz. "Let me go to Waldenberg. That will not be changed. Then I'll know I'm home. Then I won't be afraid."

But fear had been even there. I should have known, Lisa thought, that fear is no stranger to this little room. It has stood here beside us in the sunlight before. Now in 1933, just as in the summer of 1914 when I was little—so little that my first few years seemed endless behind me. My father pretending. The professor in uniform, making a game for me, making of death a foolish scarecrow. But I guessed. My heart guessed. "Not my father, dear God, not my father."

And then the December day in 1918 when I knew. Fear is always here. Hope comes and goes.

"Hope is the visitor. Fear abides. I should have remembered," Lisa said to her grandmother.

Frau Blessing stroked her hair. "It isn't so bad, my dear. Once you know that that is the way things are, you can live with fear more quietly than with hope."

"Franz says it is for the best. And many besides. Herr Thyssen, for instance. I saw him for a moment at the Adlon and he has so often been right. What do you think, Granny?"

"It's too late to think. Now one must survive. '*J'ai vécu.*' That must have been said first long before the French Revolution. When Rome was falling and, before that, when forgotten cities were crumbling into desert dust." The hand on Lisa's head trembled. "I am old, Lisa. Fear and I are companions of long standing. I know his step. But you are young. You must find yourself a shelter."

Lisa held her grandmother's small, dry hand in hers. "Then I am right to be afraid? I have seen nothing really. Berlin seems the same.

And Herr Thyssen said that, if it weren't for Hitler, the Communists——"

"Oh, that Fritz Thyssen!" Frau Blessing's voice was impatient. "Certainly he's a good businessman, but of politics he knows nothing. I like him and I have found his advice good. Particularly during the inflation, I was grateful for his counsel. But in politics he is stupid."

"Franz says——"

"Dear child. Don't try to find comfort in what any of them say. Stay in the theater. That is your shelter until the storm is over."

"Father is our protection, too. I hate to say it. I hate the '*Heldenlied*.' But perhaps he wouldn't mind. Perhaps he would be amused to think that the professor in uniform could be a shield against these men of blood and iron."

Lisa sat in her room in the noisy theater and remembered her grandmother. She has grown old in the last year, Lisa thought. Perhaps, if times are going to be bad, I should take her to America in the autumn. Gerald Michaels has a play for me. Lisa remembered when Franz had wanted to come to America and she had refused to desert the Fatherland. But that was different. One's own fear is always different. I understood then. Perhaps Franz understands now.

Lisa had promised to try to understand, but it was difficult.

She had returned to Berlin in December. "You have grown used to fear here, Lisa," her grandmother had said. "Now it will not be so bad. Besides, you promised Emil Schwarz that you would start rehearsal next week."

In Berlin, Lisa had gone to see Professor Braun, her father's friend. The house was closed. It had the blank, deserted look that comes so quickly to an empty house. The windowpanes, blinded by dust, stared like dead eyes. A torn newspaper blew against the door.

Lisa walked across the street to the house of Sophie Friedrich, Professor Braun's daughter. A timid, untidy maid scuttled away to find Sophie. Lisa smiled as she stood in the dark entrance hall. Poor Sophie. She has not yet learned to keep house properly. She has never really grown up.

"Lisa, this is unexpected." Sophie took Lisa into the parlor. Poor Sophie, indeed. In the bright light her face was tired and not young at all. It had always seemed strange to see Sophie grown up. But to see Sophie not young, to see time blurring the face of one's own generation . . .

"You find us in disorder." Sophie pointed to the packing cases filled with books. "You are kind to come. I should have known. But one doesn't expect it any more of anyone."

"I went to see your father. The house is closed, and now you— what's happened?"

"Didn't you know? Father's book. The one about Rathenau. It was burned. And then they came for him at the university. They came for him for his protection."

"Where is he?" Lisa asked.

"He has gone. They kept him only a little while."

Lisa tried to read the expression on Sophie's plain, tired face. But it was not the face she remembered. Its expressions were unfamiliar to her.

"Did they—did they do anything to him?"

"No, no indeed." Sophie spoke quickly. "They were most correct. And then the American Embassy was able to arrange a visa. And he went to America. And now Hans and I are going, and the children. Oh, Lisa, only today we heard—so I am packing. Not that there is time. I suppose I shan't be able to take anything. But to get ready makes me feel that already I am gone." For the first time Sophie smiled—the wide childlike grin that the grown-up Sophie had never lost.

"Oh, Sophie, I am glad." Tears pricked at Lisa's eyes. She was not glad. Sophie, little fat Sophie with her china-blue eyes, was escaping from Germany. Sophie was Germany. Sophie had been one of the angels in the last summer festival—the children's festival in 1914. "Now I lay me down to sleep . . ." Sophie had clasped her fat hands and lifted her blue eyes to the matching German sky. "Fourteen angels watch do keep . . ."

"Don't cry, Lisa. I'm all right now."

"Do you remember the festival when we were angels—the last festival?"

"Yes. But I am not remembering any more. Now I look forward." Sophie took Lisa's hand. "Good-by, Lisa. Don't tell anyone I was glad to go. Even now they might stop us. Promise, Lisa, promise not to tell."

"I promise. I won't say even to Franz that I saw you."

Now, in the theater, Lisa remembered the fat little Sophie and the long-ago summer.

Now I lay me down to sleep,
Fourteen angels watch do keep.

That was Germany. Not this. Franz said to wait and she would see again that Germany. She had not told Franz about Sophie. But she had told him about Dr. Meyer.

"He's dead, Franz. They wouldn't let him practice. Hitler promised that the racial laws would not apply to those who served in the last war. Dr. Meyer served although he was over age and he was decorated by the All Highest himself. And now your upstart All Highest has destroyed him. The Iron Cross is no protection against the crooked cross. They found him dead. An overdose, they said. Doctors don't take too much veronal by mistake."

"Who told you this story?"

Lisa started to answer. Then she remained silent. It was safer not to tell Franz. She looked at him with fear and saw fear, like a reflection, looking out of his eyes at her. "I don't remember who told me, Franz." Surely it would be safe to tell him but it would not be fair to burden him. "It doesn't matter where I heard it. It's sad about Dr. Meyer. You must feel that it is sad."

"It doesn't matter about the Jew doctor. If you knew him it must, I suppose, seem sad to you. Individual cases always seem sad to someone. The rule is for the general good. That is what matters. But, Lisa, to speak as you did of the Fuehrer!"

Lisa listened to the change in Franz's voice as he said "the Fuehrer!" So most voices change when the speakers pronounce the names of the rich, of the dead, of the powerful. "Franz, you are afraid," Lisa said. "Is this the new Germany, to be afraid of the leader whom the people of Germany have chosen?"

"I'm afraid for you, Lisa. Even Siegfried Blessing's daughter cannot speak lightly of the Fuehrer."

They were alone but Franz looked over his shoulder as though an evil guardian angel might be listening.

"You mustn't speak so, Lisa. You promised to try to understand. Perhaps this Dr. Meyer was an unfortunate case. We don't know all the circumstances. You mustn't look too closely at one case." His lips smiled, his eyes were still anxious. "You will not see the forest for the trees."

A dark forest if even you, who think you know the way, are afraid. But I will walk with you, Franz, and try to find the sunlight beyond the woods.

"I will try, Franz," Lisa said aloud.

That had been a week ago. And now in her dressing room in the Bühnenhaus, Lisa repeated, "I will try. Perhaps Franz sees more clearly than I."

"Five minutes, Frau Blessing."

Lisa smoothed her hair and looked in the mirror ringed with bright lights. "So. I will do."

She walked through the door into the wings. At least the theater doesn't change, nor its people. Raimund was right when he said they would respect the theater. One thinks of the party as They. The multiple evil gods of wartime—the dark gods who had replaced the God of peace. I had forgotten them, Lisa thought, but they are back. And now they walk by day as well as by night. I must not think like this. I promised I would try. And besides, I am safe from them in the theater. They do not walk here.

". . . afraid to tell her." The words were an echo. Raimund had had to repeat them. Lisa hurried; she had missed her cue.

"All right, Lisa," Emil Schwarz said. "We'll take it over. Go back, Raimund, to '. . . the stakes are not too high.' "

"And so and so and so . . . 'the stakes are not too high.' "

Lisa listened for her cue. The scene went smoothly for a few minutes after her entrance. Then Raimund and Lisa spoke at once.

Emil interrupted. "Sorry, Lisa, you forgot I gave that line to Raimund."

"But, Emil, I told you it was absurd. I thought you understood."

"Lisa, my dear, I don't want the line," Raimund said. "But I do agree with Emil that for me to say it about you gives the whole scene more point, more subtle poignancy than for you to say it."

Lisa turned away from him. "Emil, I won't argue about why I don't want Raimund's part built at the expense of mine. But certainly I thought we agreed that there would be no more changes. We open tomorrow night and after all——"

"Now, children," Emil said soothingly, "let's not quarrel. I thought Raimund's point well taken but I don't want to upset you, Lisa."

"I'm not upset. I'm annoyed. And furthermore, Emil, Raimund may think it is subtle and poignant for me to play this entire scene with my back to the audience———"

"Lisa," Raimund said eagerly, "when you turn away from the audience, you're playing the whole thing down. You keep them wondering, don't you see?"

"No. I want the audience to see. Tell him, Emil, will you, to come downstage. I'm a pretty good actress, but even I can't convey a series of emotions with the back of my neck."

"Lisa is right, Raimund. Come down left to the table. Now you take it, Lisa, from 'But you are afraid, Sigmund.' "

Lisa moved slightly upstage and turned to face the theater and Raimund. " 'But you are afraid, Sigmund, and I can tell you———' "

"Herr Schwarz. Herr Schwarz."

"Now what is it?" Schwarz turned angrily to the frightened stage manager.

The actors on the stage were still.

"They are here, Herr Schwarz."

Schwarz rose. He saluted the black-shirted officer. "Heil Hitler," he said mechanically. "As you see, we are rehearsing."

The officer spoke. "Heil Hitler. Is Raimund Hoehlmann here?"

Lisa watched from the stage. She watched as Raimund slowly walked down into the auditorium. Raimund and Emil and the officer walked up the aisle and disappeared into the shadows.

Just below the footlights, a blond young man stood up. He smiled at Lisa. He was Karl Rintner, Raimund's understudy.

When Emil came back alone, Karl Rintner asked, "Shall I carry on?"

"Yes, we'll run through this act from the beginning. We'll have to do the first act last."

Lisa walked down into the auditorium. "What's happened?"

"Just a moment, Lisa. You're on stage at the opening, Karl. All right, everybody. Heinrich, curtain. We're taking Act II from the beginning."

The curtain fell. Lisa turned to Emil. "There's no use rehearsing without Raimund. When will he be back?"

"He won't be back," Emil answered.

"You mean he won't be back tonight?"

"I mean he won't be back at all. You don't come back when they take you. All right, Heinrich, curtain."

"But, Emil, what did you do? Did you just let them take him?"

"Go on backstage, Lisa. We'll have to work all night to get this into shape with Karl."

"I won't play with him."

"Nice old-fashioned word, 'won't.' It's not used any more. Remember how we got Karl? He was very specially recommended. He's the son of an old friend of Captain Roehm."

" 'Son of an old friend . . .' " Lisa's voice rose scornfully.

"Careful, Lisa. That's what the Captain said in his letter."

"Is that why they took Raimund?"

" 'Why' is another word that isn't used much. You've been away too long, Lisa. But you'll learn to be careful." Emil stood up. "No, Karl. Not like that," he called.

"I won't play opposite him," Lisa said. "Perhaps another captain has a girl friend you can put in my place."

Schwarz put his hand on her arm. "Keep quiet, Lisa. You have to play. For God's sake, appear to do it willingly. For all our sakes. Give Karl all the help you can."

"I think it's time someone thought about helping Raimund."

"Perhaps you can. And the first thing is to do your best with Karl. Now get backstage. You're on in five minutes."

It was almost dawn when Lisa got home. The rehearsal had gone badly. Emil had decided to postpone the opening. Lisa determined to lie awake and wait for Franz. He had gone to Hamburg but he would be back on the early morning train. She lay in bed wide-eyed and watched the lamp grow pale in the gray light. She did not believe that she could sleep, but her body was more exhausted than she realized.

Lisa's maid, Matilde, woke her at noon. "The Count said not to disturb Madam the Countess. He asks that Madam the Countess meet him at the Adlon at one-thirty."

Lisa sat at the round table in the Adlon dining room and wondered at her own fear. It had been easy to believe in nightmares in the darkened auditorium and in the shadowy wings of the theater. In the bright, luxurious restaurant Lisa believed again in the normal world. She smiled at her host. He would help her. He was a big fat man. His face was open and cheerful. He must hate creatures like Roehm. And he had been brave in the war—the bravest, some said. Soldiers, particularly the airmen, would hate the secret police and those who used them. General Goering smiled at her.

"You are kind to spare us time for lunch today. Your play opens tonight, doesn't it?"

"No, it's been put off until next week."

"So? I'm sorry. I had looked forward to a pleasant evening."

"We've lost one of our actors. You must remember him, General. Raimund Hoehlmann."

"Not much loss if he's the fellow I remember." The fat man still smiled.

Lisa tried to continue. "They came for him. I don't know why."

"Of course you don't, my dear." The General reached a fat hand for the bottle of champagne beside him. He filled Lisa's glass. "Since you do not act tonight you may drink at lunch." Still smiling, he lifted his glass to her.

One may smile and smile and be a villain. That can be true in Germany as once in Denmark, Lisa thought.

She looked at the General's typically German face—the blue eyes, the firm, rosy flesh. Your enemy is familiar. "The prince of darkness is a gentleman . . ." And he walks by day. That is the horror. He walks by day.

Lisa tried again. "But we've only just returned from London. Raimund played there with me."

"And you were a success and a great credit to us. An Englishman lunched with me the other day and told me. We're very proud of you in Germany. But you mustn't run away too soon again. We mean to keep you in Germany."

"I mean to stay." Lisa curved her lips in a smile. "I like to play in German. But I don't like to play opposite Karl Rintner. He has taken Raimund's place."

General Goering's pale eyes moved. Lisa saw that he recognized the name. Now he knows, she thought, and he won't like it.

The General laughed. "Poor child. No wonder you are worried. Not too easy to play a love scene with him. But you'll manage. And I shall come and applaud you. Now tell me about London. Did you, by any chance, meet my old friend, Sir George Merrian?"

It's no use, Lisa thought, he won't help. They may hate one another but they don't pity one another's victims.

Nor would Franz help. Lisa spoke to him after lunch as they drove towards the theater.

"I'm sorry, Lisa, for your sake. But I can do nothing. I expected something like this. When we were crossing the Channel, I gathered from Hoehlmann that he had been up to something crooked financially. And after all, darling, you don't really like him."

"I still don't want anything to happen to him. And I'm sure he doesn't deserve it. Raimund boasted about money but he never had much—not enough to be involved in anything very big."

"Then he has nothing to fear. There is justice in the Third Reich."

"Will you find out, Franz? Will you make sure?"

When Lisa came home after the rehearsal, Franz was waiting for her.

"Did you find out about Raimund?" she asked.

"Yes, my darling. He's all right. Now you have your dinner quietly while I tell you. You're all nerves." He touched Lisa's shaking hand.

"One imagines. These are strange times."

"You imagine too much. Nothing is different. Look about you. This is the same."

The candlelight shone on the silver and the pale china. The dark red curtains shut out the sounds of Berlin at night. Perhaps it was nerves to imagine that they shut out strange sounds—sounds of fear and pain that had not been there before.

"We speak of him in English so that she won't understand." Lisa looked at Matilde.

"We often speak in English, darling, to enclose ourselves in our private world. It's still our private world."

"That's all that matters." She looked across her table at Franz. "It's the world I care about, and it's the only world I can make. The other, outside one I must leave to you."

"You can leave it to me, Lisa. Only have patience. Wait and try to understand."

"And Raimund? Is he all right?"

"Quite all right. They have arrested him on a financial charge. It was as I told you: a dishonest deal in foreign exchange. But they won't do anything to him. Just scare him a little and fine him and let him go. He has an American visa and an English one. He can't stay here. Now that he's known to be non-Aryan, he can't play with Germans on the German stage."

"But I thought it was about money that they arrested him, not for being a Jew."

"Well, the whole story is known now. He's lucky to get off so easily. Don't worry—he's all right."

"Poor Raimund. I'm glad. His boastfulness got on my nerves, but I wouldn't want it to get him into real trouble. I'm sure that's what he did—bragged of assets he never possessed."

"I gathered that the officials know that. They'll let him go to America. He'll do well there."

Lisa smiled at Franz's face framed in the bright points of the candles.

"It's good to be safe, Franz, to know one has imagined the nightmare."

"Poor darling. You're tired."

"I'm very tired. Raimund was difficult to play with, but he was an actor. Rintner is nothing. Without influence he might be a chorus boy."

"Influence is not new, Lisa. It existed in the old days, too. There will be less now. We Germans are naturally an honest people. Dishonesty is alien to us. Not like Americans. Did you see about your friends, the Cravens?"

"The Americans?"

"Yes. The ones we saw on our last night in London. The paper is in the other room. Come and read it."

Lisa sat beside Franz on the sofa. She leaned against him and read the paper.

AMERICAN MAGNATE BRUCE CRAVEN ARRESTED
$5,000,000 THEFT

Lisa lowered the paper and watched the fire. She lifted her eyes to the Dresden mantel clock that had measured happy years for her. It was good to be with Franz like this. This quiet moment was part of the pattern of five years. "Pattern" was too static a word to describe marriage.

> *Let me not to the marriage of true minds*
> *Admit impediments. Love is not love*
> *Which alters when it alteration finds,*
> *Or bends with the remover to remove . . .*

"Franz, even though this be the edge of doom, we are together," she said.

Franz tightened the arm that held her. Her heart pressed against his heart. She listened to the beat, and her own heart beat faster in time with his. Not a pattern, but a rhythm. A storm, and we are the heart of the storm. When it's like this, there is no word. "Franz." She could not speak above a whisper. Her body throbbed with the beating of their hearts.

IX

ANNE CRAVEN stood before her dressing table in her room at Claridge's. She combed her hair gingerly. She did not want to disturb the gold lacquer powder that the hairdresser had so carefully applied. It definitely brightens it, she thought. I wonder if I ought to have it bleached. They do it so well now. But you eventually lose your eye and end up looking like Broadway. She gave her hair a last gentle pat and picked up her lipstick. The telephone rang.

"Answer it, darling," Paul called. "I'm on my third white tie."

Anne put down the lipstick and picked up the telephone.

"Yes. Yes." It was New York calling. It must be Uncle Bruce. "Yes, this is Mrs. Craven."

"Hello, Anne. Norman Brooke here. Let me speak to Paul."

"Uncle Norman? What's happened? Is Mother all right?"

"Your mother's fine. So's Polly. It's Bruce Craven. Let me speak to Paul."

"Paul," Anne called, "it's for you. Uncle Norman about Uncle Bruce. He sounds awful. I'm afraid it's serious."

Anne walked across the room and began to tidy the dressing table.

She closed her powder box. She kept her face turned away from Paul. She did not look in the mirror. She did not want to see the triumph shining in her eyes. I mustn't feel this way, she told herself. This is wrong. And yet it must always be like this. There must always be triumph mixed with grief in the heart of the king's son. I liked Uncle Bruce. I never wished him dead. And yet, to be the heir is to hope. To hope that you will mourn. There is no sorrow in the rich or royal house of mourning. It remains the house of mirth. The king is dead. Long live the king. Paul isn't glad. Not even a little.

She listened to Paul's shocked, quiet voice.

"Yes. . . . I see . . . When did it happen? This afternoon? Did anyone have any idea? No, I didn't. It's a terrible shock to me. . . ."

How idiotic of Uncle Norman to suppose sentimentally that Paul, three thousand miles away, would have a presentiment of death.

"Thank you for calling me. Anything I have, you know . . . Oh, I see. . . . I'll find out about boats right away. We may be able to get one tomorrow. I'll cable you."

Paul put down the telephone. "Anne, I don't know how to tell you. It's Uncle Bruce."

"I know, Paul." Anne's voice and her eyes were gentle. "I'm sorry. It's hard to be so far away. And to have it so sudden. The shock." She touched Paul's arm. "He always seemed so well. Was it his heart or——"

"Uncle Bruce isn't dead." Paul sat down on the bed. He twisted the dangling end of his white tie. "He—I really don't know how to tell you. He's failed. Craven and Company has gone down the drain. It's really worse than that."

Anne stood and looked down at him. "Worse? What could be worse?"

"Death, perhaps. No. I suppose not. Uncle Bruce's death would have been part of the pattern. I always knew but I never hoped." He stared at Anne for a moment. "No one's to blame for planning, Anne. Not even for hoping. The heart isn't a civilized organ, I guess."

"Paul." Anne's voice was sharp. She stopped herself and spoke softly. "Paul, what's happened? What more?"

"Uncle Bruce has been arrested. It seems to be pretty clear that he —well, that he——"

"Stole?"

"Yes. Hard to say. Harder to believe. Why, I'd have bet my last dollar on Uncle Bruce. Bet my life."

"Did you? Bet your last dollar?"

"Why, yes. In a way, I guess I did. Now you know, Anne. This is the end—the end of the nice smooth road. This is where we get off. Sorry, darling." His hand moved but he did not reach out to her. He jerked off the white tie and twisted it in his hands.

Anne put her hand on Paul's hands. Instantly his fingers stopped moving. They were quiet under her light touch. His whole body was quiet, waiting. Anne felt his stillness beside her. She was stiff. She had nothing to give. She silently repeated his words. This is where we get off. This is where I came in. But I can't get out. You can close the book or leave the theater. But this isn't a novel or a play. This is the life I chose. This is the life I so carefully chose.

Paul broke the silence. "Poor baby. It's worse for you than for me. What say we have a drink? I could use one."

Anne pressed her hand against Paul's. "I'm sorry, Paul. I don't seem to be behaving very well. I'm kind of stunned, I guess."

"I guess." Paul patted her hand and stood up. "I know. I bet my last dollar on Uncle Bruce but I bet my life on you. It's all right. It was worth it."

"Paul, you don't think——"

"I don't think, darling, I know. But it's okay. You take your time. Pick your spot. In the meantime, let's have that drink. Let's have dinner and do the town. A belated farewell to 1929. Remember? That was our year."

Anne and Paul sailed home on the same ship that had brought them to England in October. They had a cabin for two on E deck.

"Sorry, darling," Paul said as he looked at the small stateroom filled with Vuitton luggage. "But last night was the final ride on the merry-go-round."

It wasn't. It's my merry-go-round. I have the gold ring. Admission for life. That's what I thought. Anne twisted her wedding ring.

She picked up a package that was on top of the pile of suitcases. "I might as well unpack Polly's doll and put it in my suitcase."

"Leave it in the London box. She'll like it better."

"It just makes one more thing. We could just as well have got something from Schwarz instead of your dashing out at crack of dawn for this."

"No. She'd have recognized the bell on the Schwarz paper. I remember once when I was a kid and Uncle Bruce was abroad—he forgot. Anyway, she wanted a wax baby doll, your mother said—the kind you used to have."

"At that age, Paul, they don't know what they want for long."

"Maybe. Anyway, leave it in the box. Let's get out of here now and have lunch and go on deck. It won't be bad. There won't be many people on board this time of year."

There weren't many passengers. There was no one whom Anne knew.

Late in the afternoon she stood with Paul by the rail and watched the passengers get on at Cherbourg. Usually one watched them patronizingly. It had always been easy to become quickly established anywhere, even in the few hours of a Channel crossing, to look at the newcomers from the French shore and think, Poor things, how dull they look. Not like us, the old settlers, the passengers from England. Now Anne watched anxiously. She hoped not to see anyone she knew.

"Hi, Anne. Hi, Paul. Tough luck, old boy." A large figure swathed in a polo coat was moving towards them.

Other passengers turned to look at Paul and Anne. She shrank from the loud voice. It was no longer pleasant to be the center of attention.

"Glad to see you kids." J. C. Jones held out his hand. "Come on, I'll buy you a drink."

"Thanks just the same, J. C., but Anne and I——"

"Come on. Don't need to feel embarrassed with me. I'm not one of the suckers. Besides, I've had my ups and downs, too." He took Anne's elbow and propelled her into the bar. "Glad you're on board. This was a quick trip. Judy couldn't make it."

For the rest of the voyage J. C. Jones adopted Anne and Paul.

"He is kind, Paul. Lots of people wouldn't be."

"I can still afford to buy my own cocktails. And he's so damn patronizing. Assumes we're grateful to dine with him in the restaurant every night and——"

"Ah, there you are." J. C. Jones rounded the deck. "What are you doing freezing out here? Come on in the bar. And then we'll have dinner in the restaurant. Don't tell me you kids were thinking of going down to that stuffy dining room. Not as long as I'm on board."

"Thanks, J. C.," Paul said. "We were just going to have a cocktail. Won't you join us?"

"Don't put on a front for me. I know how things are."

Anne followed J. C. into the bar. Now, on the last night, it was as bad as it had been on the first day. Her skin shrank and tingled under the eyes of strangers. She knew that she held her head too high, that she smiled too eagerly or not enough.

The skin felt tight and hot against her forehead and her temples. She must be scarlet. She opened her vanity case and tipped the mirror in her lap. She looked down at her reflection. Her pale cheeks were not flushed, except faintly by carefully applied rouge. This tight feeling, as though she were caught in an invisible trap—she had known this feeling before. It came in dreams. The invisible danger, the strangling web that no one else could see. In the dream no one knows, none of the bright company can see or hear. Anne looked at J. C. He knows, he's sorry. He smiled at her and gave her a glass.

"Here's your martini. You see, I remember. No olive and a piece of lemon peel."

That night Anne dreamed. She forced herself to wake. With painful, endless effort she forced open her eyelids, heavy as stones. She lay trembling. She tried to ward off the thick drowsiness that threatened to send her back into the dream, back beneath the heavy stones. She sat up and turned on the light. Paul spoke.

"Bad dream, honey? You haven't had one for a long time."

"I was under heavy stones. They weren't stones at first. Flowers, and all the people giving them. They couldn't see there were too many, and then they were stones, heavy white stones, but the others didn't see. They went on talking and the stones were closing down and I couldn't speak or move and I knew it was a dream and I woke finally, but it was hard to wake. My eyelids were like stones, heavy to lift. And now I'm afraid I'll fall asleep again."

"Poor kid. Have a cigarette."

"It doesn't sound awful but it was. All of them so gay and not seeing the stones because of the flowers, the heavy white flowers."

Paul held a match to her cigarette. "It's been tough. I'm afraid it'll be tougher. There'll be the reporters tomorrow."

"Do I have to see them?"

"Can't avoid them, I'm afraid. They're just the beginning. You're in for a bad time and there's no way out for you now. You've just got to take it. Try to make time go by."

"Don't be silly. You can't."

"Yes, you can. Put your mind ahead to a definite time and place. July in Southampton, for instance. See that July day and see yourself looking back from it. Then when you get to July, remember to look back just as you planned. That makes the trick work better the next time."

"The next time! There can't ever be anything like this again."

"You never know, baby. And that's a phrase you ought to accept as a powerful truth."

"Nice comforting motto for the Cravens."

"For everybody, Anne, if they only knew. Now how about a little sleep? We want to handle those guys right in the morning."

Anne did not sleep again. She listened to Paul's quiet breathing and waited for the morning.

She had packed the last suitcase when the reporters knocked on the cabin door.

The crowd of strangers filled the cabin. There were more in the corridor. Anne and Paul were pressed back against the wall beside the berths.

"We'd better go upstairs somewhere, I think," one of the men said. "I'm from the *Express*," he added. "Friend of Phil Sinclair."

"No, please, no," Anne protested.

"Can't do anything here. Better come upstairs, Mrs. Craven." The reporter's voice was friendly but matter-of-fact.

"Come on, honey." Paul took Anne's arm. They went up to the empty restaurant.

As they walked through the corridors the questions began.

"You a partner, Mr. Craven? What, exactly, was your position on the other side? When did you hear the news? How about your personal holdings?"

The halls were filled with passengers. They stared at Anne and Paul. Anne held her shoulders stiffly. She was conscious of every motion of her muscles as she walked beside Paul. The procession to Tyburn, she thought, or the prisoner in the crowded courtroom. The crowd watched her pass with Paul. In the history books and in the newspapers, crowds had always watched. The nameless faces had always turned to see the fortunate or the unfortunate go by. The faces don't change, but in misfortune you are on their plane. You don't look down. You look out. You look out through the invisible strangling web. "Buck up, Mrs. Craven," the reporter from the *Express* murmured. "They only half see you. Their minds are really on the customs and how much to tip the steward."

"I'm not used—I . . ." Anne tried to steady her voice.

"You'll have to go through it today. And then, of course, at the trial. After that people will forget. Remember, newspapers come out every day in the year, and every day there are front-page stories. Yours will be forgotten. Your husband's doing all right. Phil said he was a swell guy. I can see he is. Makes it easy for you to stand by him. You'll want to fix up a statement on those lines."

"Yes. I don't quite know how."

"I'll help you."

"This way, Mrs. Craven. We want some pictures. Look over here." "You look at Mrs. Craven. Mr. Craven, please." "Over here, Mrs. Craven." "This way, please." "Over here, please. Turn this way."

Anne moved her head obediently. The cameras stared at her and blinked as they clicked. The bulbs flashed noisily and fell lightly on the carpet.

"Just one more, please. I didn't get one. This way. Turn this way."

"Do you plan to attend the trial, Mrs. Craven?"

"We just want a short statement, Mrs. Craven. You're standing by Mr. Craven—every confidence in him."

"And in my uncle," Paul put in. "I know Mrs. Craven wants to include Mr. Bruce Craven."

"That right, Mrs. Craven?"

"Yes. Please make it quite clear that Paul's family—well, they're my family."

"Good girl," the reporter from the *Express* murmured.

"It's as my husband says. I have every confidence that Uncle Bruce will be vindicated."

A reporter stepped forward.

"My paper has a story that you know the Assistant D.A. who's handling the case."

"I don't think so." Anne smiled. The reporter from the *Express* had told her to smile.

"Sure you do, Mrs. Craven. You used to anyway. We have quite a little story on it. It's a new Assistant D.A. Marco Ghiberti."

Anne tried to speak. "Why—I—I——"

Paul interrupted smoothly. "You must remember him, dear. Friend of Bill Winton's. He was down in Southampton one summer. We saw quite a lot of him."

The room was quiet. The reporter persisted. "I think it was Mrs. Craven who knew him."

"Of course she did. We both did. Hell of a nice feller, as I remember, I don't think you ought to quote us on him, though. After all, he's got his job to do. We don't want to say anything that would be embarrassing to the guy."

"Can I horn in on this?" J. C. Jones made his way through the crowd of reporters. "These kids are friends of mine."

"Any statement, Mr. Jones? Anything to say on the Craven case?"

"Why, no. I don't know a thing. I've been away."

"Did you invest any money through Craven and Company?"

"Why, no, boys. I handle things for myself."

"You've been in Germany, haven't you, Mr. Jones? How did you find conditions?"

"Well, it was just a flying trip. Didn't get a chance to see much. Of course, you know a lot of things Hitler stands for are distasteful to me. I'm an American. But it's their country and Hitler's the feller they want. I think if we give him a chance he'll straighten things out over there. You gotta remember they had a pretty raw deal."

"Was it a business trip?"

"Well, in a small way. My trips generally are. And as far as business conditions go, things are okay. We can deal with those fellers."

Anne and Paul slipped away, unnoticed.

On the pier Anne stood beside the trunks and waited. Norman Brooke helped Paul to round up the luggage. "Got everything now except one hatbox," he said.

Anne laughed. "That ever-missing piece. There's always one."

Everything is the same, she thought. The icy wind that blows from the river, the longing for a cigarette. Anne wrapped her mink coat around her and stamped her cold feet. Everything is the same except the core of things. J. C. Jones walked by.

"Not through yet? Here, let my man handle it."

"Thanks, J. C.," Paul said. "We're all right."

"Thank you for helping us with the reporters." Anne reached her hand to him. "Hello, Judy. J. C.'s been sweet to us on the trip."

Judy Jones kept a firm hand on her husband's arm. "Anne darling. See you soon. We've got to get away from here. I'm frozen."

Trespassers will be prosecuted to the full extent of the law. Anne smiled at J. C. Jones. " 'By, and thanks again."

He smiled at her over his shoulder but he kept step with Judy. There was no help there. No help anywhere.

"Doing everything we can," Norman Brooke said. "Feller that's handling the prosecution is a very decent chap."

The Assistant D.A., Marco Ghiberti. You knew him, Mrs. Craven. How neatly the plot unwound. Just in case you missed the point.

"It's all right, Anne." Paul brushed the dark fur of her coat. "Just mark time. It goes by, you know." He turned to give his keys to the customs inspector.

Time goes by, Anne thought. And it ties everything up neatly in a package. The fine package you bought for yourself.

She must mention Marco. His name wasn't hard to pronounce. It was just that she hadn't said it for a long time.

"I used to know Marco Ghiberti, Uncle Normie." They were walking away from the customs sheds.

"Smart young chap. Just doing his job. We've got Henry Merrill. He'll do everything possible. Not much anyone can do—wanted Bruce to plead guilty. Might yet."

At the apartment everything was the same—that outward sameness ready to crack like cheap paint.

Mrs. Brooke kissed Anne, and Polly hurled herself into her mother's arms. Mrs. Brooke held out both hands to Paul. "My dear Paul. I'm sorry."

"Here's the prize package." Norman Brooke put the oblong box in Anne's hands.

"Here, Polly. Daddy and I brought you this all the way from London."

"You remembered, dear child. With all you had on your mind." Mrs. Brooke smiled at her daughter and her granddaughter.

"Is it a cooking stove?" Polly asked. "A real little cooking stove?"

"That's a new idea since I wrote you," Mrs. Brooke said apologetically. "At her age, you know . . ."

The paper rattled under Polly's eager fingers. "Oh, it's beautiful. I didn't want the cooking stove—not very much. The baby is beautiful. Is she like yours, Mummy, that Grandma gave you when you were little?"

"Just like her, Polly."

"Thank you, Mummy. Thank you for bringing her."

"And Daddy, too," Anne said.

"Thank you, Daddy." Polly pressed herself and the doll briefly against Paul. Then she pulled the box from her grandmother's hand. "I need that to be a bed for her. A nice English bed for her to be homelike in. And the thin paper, too." She smoothed the tissue paper. "It makes good sheets."

"Can I see Uncle Bruce?" Paul asked. "Is he—is he——"

"He'll be here for lunch," Norman Brooke said. "He's out on bail."

Out on bail, Anne repeated to herself. A new phrase to be attached to Uncle Bruce. Mr. Bruce Craven is at the Pierre for a few days. Mr. Bruce Craven is on his yacht, the *Infanta*. Mr. Bruce Craven is out on bail. How will he look? Anne wondered.

When Bruce Craven came, he looked just the same. He took charge of the luncheon table as he had always taken charge of all tables. Where McTavish sits . . . He spoke of business as though it were still his to discuss.

"I think things are looking up a little in the Street," he said. "Of course, there can't be any real improvement as long as that man's in Washington. If we can just hang on till '36. Then you'll see a change."

"Doesn't he know?" Anne asked her mother after luncheon. Bruce Craven had gone into the library with Paul. "Just a few papers I'd like to go over with you, my boy." Norman Brooke had gone with them.

"Doesn't who know what?" Phil Sinclair entered unannounced. "Thought I'd come around and see if I could be any use. You handled yourselves okay with the boys this morning."

"Doesn't Uncle Bruce know what's happened?" Anne repeated.

"It's like when we were children. I'm the king of the castle and you're the dirty rascal. You said it and it was true. Doesn't Uncle Bruce realize? He doesn't seem to have changed at all."

"It takes imagination to change," Phil said.

"But he must know," Anne said impatiently. "He's intelligent."

"It takes more than intelligence. It takes as much imagination to see the present as to see the past or the future. How are *your* eyes, by the way, Anne? Can you see beyond your still elegant present?" Phil gestured at the pale, expensive room that surrounded them.

"Oh, I'm all right, aren't I, Mother? Financially, I mean."

Mrs. Brooke looked doubtfully at Phil.

"Never mind him," Anne said. "He always knows everything, anyway."

"Well, of course, Norman has taken good care of your trust fund, Anne. But I don't know that it will quite run to this."

"You'll be all right, Anne—within the ordinary definition of the word if not within your own. But that's not the immediate problem." Phil spoke gravely. "Right now Paul's your problem—or is he?"

"Of course he is. Don't be ridiculous, Phil. We can stay with you, Mother, for the summer in Southampton and then take a smaller apartment in the fall." The pale gray walls seemed to shrink closer to Anne as she spoke.

"Your uncle Norman can tell you how you really stand. But it's as Phil says, Paul's your problem. I understand he has nothing left. And Paul hasn't been trained . . ." Mrs. Brooke's voice trailed away.

"I know. Poor Paul. So long as he doesn't drink or anything."

"He hasn't been hitting the bottle, has he?" Phil asked.

"Oh no," Anne said hesitantly. "No. Not really."

They heard Paul's voice as the library door opened into the hall. "How about a quick one, Uncle Bruce?"

"No, thanks, my boy. Normie and I have to get along. Henry Merrill is waiting for us at my apartment."

"Hi, feller." Paul greeted Phil and sank into a chair. He rang the bell. "Good of you to show up. Nice guy from your paper at the boat this morning. He showed us the ropes in a quiet way. Bring some scotch and soda, Parker."

"Oh, Paul, isn't it a little early?" Anne's voice was anxious. "I mean——"

"What on earth do you mean, darling? I need a drink after that conference. Girls and boys, I'm clean. I knew it, of course, but after seeing the cold figures, I definitely can use a drink."

"I ought to be going, darling." Mrs. Brooke stood up. "I'll just run in and see Polly for a minute."

As Paul fixed his drink, Phil spoke softly to Anne. "I don't like your idea, beautiful, so drop it."

"Phil, I don't know what you mean." I shouldn't have said that about Paul drinking, she thought, but I can't help worrying. Suppose he really started drinking badly. It would be awful. I couldn't stay with him.

"It's a pleasure to watch you work, lady"—Phil's voice was still soft—"but not on Paul. I won't stand for that."

X

THE NEXT MORNING the newspapers headlined the name of Craven.

Bruce Craven, whose alleged embezzlements reached the staggering total of $6,500,000, will go on trial in this city on April 2. The news of the alleged shortages was first made public when Harold Cook, of Cook, Cook & Faulkner, representing Mrs. S. L. Sullivan, of Boston, informed the District Attorney's office that . . .

Anne looked at the pictures of her and Paul. "CRAVEN PARTNER AND WIFE. Mr. and Mrs. Paul Craven, Who Returned Yesterday from London." She had seen people she knew displayed like this. Poor things, she had thought as she looked at the printed pillory. But mixed with pity there had been interest, even a mild satisfaction at finding a familiar face and name in the morning news. Now she stood there to divert other breakfasters. She stared at herself. Look at me grinning like a fool. Damn Phil's friend. "Anne doesn't seem to mind, I must say. Poor thing, she'll find out." She could hear the light voices. "In the adversity of our best friends, we often find something"—she groped for the exact quotation—"that is not exactly displeasing." Damn the French. They always think of the apt annoying thing to say. She could see Judy Jones pushing the paper at J. C. "Your little friend is in quite a jam, I'd say." No, Judy was too smart for that.

Anne thrust the papers to one side. They slid noisily to the floor. She rubbed her fingers. They were dark with newsprint. Funny, I never minded before. I never noticed before. She dipped her fingers in the bowl of tepid water on whose surface a flower floated. She dried her hands roughly with the lace-edged napkin. All the little luxuries have ceased to be pleasant. They serve only to remind you that they aren't going to last. This is the end. This is where you start downhill. Unless you can find another road. It's a little late for that, my girl.

Anne pushed her tray to the foot of the bed. She reached down for the newspapers to tidy them. There was no need to leave her anger so plain for the maid to see. To add a fillip to the story that Marie would tell anyway. "Poor Madame." No one who has been envied wants to be pitied.

Marco Ghiberti's face stared at her from the printed page. I might have been happy, Anne thought, instead of being clever. She tried to remember how she had felt. "Marco," she said aloud. She spoke his name easily. There was only the memory of pain and no memory of happiness at all. She stared at the photograph. It was a little blurred, almost unfamiliar. If I were to see him . . . You can't see very well through five years. Almost six years. You don't remember. You only imagine. She didn't want to imagine. Another tag end of her schoolgirl education floated through her mind. All the little phrases had seemed so trite. You thought they would never be true for you. She sat straight and pressed the bell beside her bed. There was no use mooning over what might have been. She would put her mind on what could now be done.

In the weeks that followed Anne found there was nothing she could do. Nothing except wait for that second day of April, which must inevitably come. The day of the trial. Like the day of a funeral. Like the day of a wedding. The day that makes a hitherto unnoticed number on the calendar a date. A date to remember.

Anne awoke on the second day of April. She pushed back the comforter. The air was warm. It was a soft day that promised spring. She stretched her hand lazily into the gentle air. She reached her fingers towards the sunlight that striped with brightness the white carpet below the slanting venetian blinds. Suddenly it's spring, she thought.

The beginning. Then she remembered. It's not the beginning. It's the end.

She rang for her maid.

"Tell Mr. Craven I'm awake, Marie."

"Monsieur has gone to the—— Monsieur has gone out. Monsieur said not to disturb Madame. Mme. Forrest would like Madame to call her."

"Anne, my dear. I didn't want to disturb you, but is there anything I can do?"

"I don't know, Mary. I just woke up to it. That it's today."

"I know. It's awful for you. I'm so sorry."

Mary really is sorry, Anne thought. Sorry all the way through. Her mind is all of one piece about me. No trace of amusement. She misses a lot of fun that way. But it's nice to be her friend.

"You're going to the trial, I suppose. Does Paul want you to?"

"I don't know, Mary, but I think I ought to for his sake."

"Would you like"—Mary hesitated—"would you like me to go with you? If it would be any help to have me, I mean."

"Yes. Please. I'd like that."

The heart of gold, Anne thought. You used to say, "She has a heart of gold but——" Now the "but" was not important. That solid, good heart was an ever present help in time of trouble.

"I'll be over in a few minutes, Anne. We'll drive down in my car."

Anne had not intended to go to the trial. She and Paul had tacitly assumed that she would not go. But now, driving with Mary, she knew it was wise to go. You must see the end clearly before you can search for a new beginning. Before you can deal with it, you must see reality plainly.

"I'll find out where we go," Anne said as they climbed the court-house steps. She left Mary and spoke to an attendant. Her voice was low.

"Third floor, second door to your left," he said.

Anne and Mary stood at the back of the small courtroom.

"Let's sit here a minute," Anne said. Not to be part of it. Just for a moment longer, not to be part of it. She saw neither Paul nor Bruce Craven.

The witness on the stand looked frightened. He was a little, shabby man. He must be an underling thrust into the uncomfortable spot-light of Uncle Bruce's affairs.

"And did you on the evening of the sixth of January place these securities in the safe?"

"Yes sir."

"I put it to you that these securities were in fact . . ."

Anne did not recognize the blond young man who was asking the questions. He must be someone in Mr. Merrill's office.

The questions droned on. The witness asked for a glass of water. While he drank, the lawyer who had been questioning him turned back to the table and spoke casually to one of his colleagues. He returned to the questions. Anne did not follow the questioning. She wondered where Uncle Bruce was.

The questions stopped. "Your witness." The blond young man smiled at the opposing lawyer. He was dark-haired. Nice casting, Anne thought. You can tell the sides apart. It's not like a play. It's like a game. Your honor. Your lead.

"Objection," said the blond young man.

"Objection sustained."

The dark young man vouchsafed a small smile to his opponent. Well played, the smile said.

It's not a game to the frightened little man. But it is to the rest of them, Anne thought. The little man doesn't know the rules and yet he must answer according to them. And he is frightened, terribly frightened. The blond young man is doing his best for him, but it's not enough. Nothing is enough except to share the fear. And that the blond young man can't do. Nor does the dark one hate. Certainly not the witness. Nor his true opponent, the other lawyer. At the opposing lawyer's table there was rivalry masked by politeness, and there was occasional suppressed admiration for an opponent's shot well played, even a look of congratulation that could not be spoken. But there was no fear, nor pity, nor anger. Fear sat behind the railing with the little man who gulped his water and stared from lawyer to judge to jury. His eyes stayed longest with the jury. Perhaps there, in some scrupulous heart, he might find an echo of his fear. The jury, too, was strange to this complicated game that was familiar to the lawyers and the judge.

"To satisfy the counselor, I will rephrase the question," said the dark young man.

The witness looked desperately at the blond young man, who smiled at his dark-haired opponent and said quietly, "I object to this line of questioning unless the counselor can show a connection."

Mary touched Anne's shoulder. Before she spoke Anne knew it was the wrong room. The frightened witness was the defendant here as, in some other room, Uncle Bruce would be the defendant. And, in that other room as here, the lawyers would play their intricate solemn game and the judge would keep score.

Mary questioned the attendant. "You ladies want the room at the end. This is the Haven case. Nothing big."

In the right room the trial had not begun. But the legal game was under way. The jury was being chosen. This reminds me, Anne thought. Analogy was an escape from reality, Anne knew, but she groped for the exact memory. Like choosing sides for prisoner's base. But this is a grown-up game. And the stakes are different. Not for the lawyers, perhaps. Money and reputation are children's counters grown up. But for Uncle Bruce . . . She looked at him sitting with his lawyers. He observed the panel of possible jurors as though he were their prospective employer. Once he corrected his lawyer. Paul sat quiet, unsmiling. Paul knows, Anne thought. He knows Uncle Bruce can't win this game. But Uncle Bruce doesn't know.

At the District Attorney's table, Marco turned and looked out into the courtroom. Anne felt as though her heart leaped. I imagine it, she told herself. I don't remember. This is just the shadow of remembering. It seems to have substance only because there has been so little in between.

Marco challenged a juror. "Marco." Anne's lips moved soundlessly. Surely it wasn't a game to Marco. She remembered the dune grass, bright in the afternoon sun, and Marco's serious young voice speaking of justice. "That is why I chose the law, Anne. It seems tortuous and heartless sometimes, but in your American courts the law seeks justice for men in their dealings one with another." He was still serious but not young. His hair was still black as sin. She remembered the little boy playing in the Italian sun on the Lido beach. She thought of Polly's pale straight hair. She watched Marco. His body was young as it moved. But there was something. He looked tired. Perhaps it was not so easy to light with simple justice these dusty courtrooms. Anne smiled at Marco. He looked gravely at the crowded courtroom. He did not see her.

The day dragged slowly on. As the afternoon passed, Anne wondered at her own boredom. Could you be bored at your own destruction? Perhaps, after all, she was not to be destroyed. Uncle Bruce had seemed so confident at lunch. Paul had sat silent.

While Marco and Mr. Merrill discussed something in an undertone with the judge, Anne looked at Paul, slumped in his chair. He straightened up as Bruce Craven spoke to him. He knows, Anne thought. He knows it isn't any use. Uncle Bruce doesn't know and I can be fooled. At lunch, listening to Uncle Bruce. "It's just a matter of making things clear to these fellers. One reason I didn't want a jury trial. Difficult for the man in the street to take a comprehensive view." Paul knew. Anne shivered. And I'm the clever one. She touched Mary's arm.

"Let's go," she said. "I can't take any more today."

Anne sat waiting for Paul to come home. She stared at her carefully decorated living room. "So right for you, Mrs. Craven," Diane Gordon, the decorator, had said. "It simply is you."

It's not me any more, Anne thought. She moved restlessly. She felt like an intruder in the room that was, she knew, no longer hers—the room that was waiting for its new, rightful occupant. She looked out of the west windows at the city's lights. I knew it would come. I didn't know the day or the year. But I knew and I was afraid. Then I forgot. Now it's here. She stared out of the window. She did not want to look at the pretty room that was no longer hers.

Paul's hand on her shoulder startled her. He put his arm around her. "Darling, I didn't think you would come. I wouldn't even ask you to. But when I saw you there, I thought—it made me think that after all . . . I could be wrong, but if I'm right, it could be pretty swell."

Anne pressed her head against him. "I'm afraid, Paul. I was afraid before. Do you remember when that woman's husband shot himself? I knew then the walls were cracking, the elegant pale walls. They were white that year." She lifted her head but she closed her eyes against the unfriendly room. "I'm afraid, Paul."

"I know, baby." Paul's voice was tired. "You can't help it. That's how you are."

"That's how I am, but not how I always was. Just for a little while, when I was young, I was brave. Do you remember? No, of course you don't. You didn't know. You weren't there."

"I remember, Annie. I knew. It was my fault. I let you build your life on fear. I settled for that. I would have settled for anything. Now I'd like to help. I could, you know, if you'd let me in. Really let me in. After all the years. Now when it's just you and me—and no more grandeur, no more Madam Queen. Just you and me and Polly. We might turn out to be quite a family after all."

"Why, Paul, I don't know what you mean. Just because I'm scared. Anyone would be, being uprooted like this." Anne moved away from Paul's arm. He had nothing now with which to allay her fear. His security was gone. He had nothing left. "I was just upset. The trial and all. Why, we are a family. I don't know what you mean."

"Don't you? Are we? All right, baby, play it your way. Just remember I'm on your side. Always."

"Aren't we a little solemn?" Anne smiled at him. "Let me fix you a drink."

He lifted his glass. "In case of fire choose the nearest exit."

He held out his empty glass to her. "Maybe I imagined you. But I don't think so. That girl's still there. That girl that was brave. Don't do away with her even if I wasn't the feller."

"Why, Paul, you're crazy." She filled his glass.

"Could be," he said. "Could be I am. Okay. I'll play it your way. I don't much care." He smiled at her as he drank.

The trial moved slowly on its intricate, appointed way. The third of April. The fourth. Anne watched Uncle Bruce. This is the reverse of the dream, she thought. All of us can see the net in which he has hopelessly entangled himself. Only Uncle Bruce believes he can be free. Paul did his best. He answered Marco's questions carefully, slowly.

"No, it was my wish that my uncle, Mr. Craven, should do so. Yes, I know the securities to which you refer. The sale was justified. That was the arrangement between us."

"You sailed on the seventeenth of October, and on the nineteenth of October Mr. Craven placed on sale the following securities . . ."

"I don't get it, Anne," Paul had said. "There isn't anything for me to do in England." Now he got it, but as Anne watched him his face betrayed nothing.

"I put it to you, Mr. Craven, that your uncle did, in fact, send you to Europe with the intention of secretly and without your knowledge——"

"Objection. The witness cannot testify of his own knowledge to Mr. Bruce Craven's intention."

"Objection sustained."

Paul did his best. But it was no use. He knows that, Anne thought. But still, he offers what he can of loyalty. Doesn't he see that he's entangling himself, making himself look a fool? And for what? For some useless picture of loyalty that he sees in his own mind.

"You were a partner in Craven and Company?" Marco asked. "I do not wish to imply responsibility for actions of which you could have no knowledge."

"I was a partner. I accept all responsibility."

"Objection." Mr. Merrill was on his feet. "The witness can not be forced to incriminate himself."

"I will sustain the objection." The judge smiled. "The jury will disregard the witness's answer."

The elaborate game, Anne thought. The jury will close its eyes and count ten. The jury will disregard. The jury will be deaf and then the jury will obligingly hear again.

At luncheon Bruce Craven expressed his satisfaction with Paul. "You did well, my boy. Of course it was hard for you, not having all the facts. But things will be cleared up when I go on the stand."

"You still want to?" Mr. Merrill spoke doubtfully. "It's not too late to change your mind. I'm going to put Norman Brooke on, and we have some splendid character witnesses. By the way, J. C. Jones called up yesterday and offered to go on for you."

Bruce Craven frowned. "J. C. Jones is hardly the type of man I would care——"

"It's all right: we have plenty without him."

Bruce Craven continued to frown at the interruption. ". . . would care to have associated in the public mind with me."

"But about your going on the stand, Bruce. I really think—the judge will explain to the jury that they cannot construe your not testifying as——"

"I know all about the law," Bruce Craven said sharply. "I am going on the stand because I am the one person who can make this story clear. Paul, here, has taken a very proper position about his securities—very proper. I wish certain other people had behaved as well. However, I feel sure that if the jury has even ordinary intelligence I can make my position plain. You lawyers confuse them and these fellers in Washington—these professor-politicians have poisoned the public's mind. But I flatter myself that I can place the facts before them in such a light——"

"I think Mr. Merrill is right," Paul said. "My things were yours to do with as you saw fit. That's the way I wanted it. But with the Stevenson trust and Mrs. Sullivan and the rest, I honestly don't think you can explain, Uncle Bruce."

"It's not a question of explaining." Bruce Craven spoke slowly as though he were trying to control his impatience. "It's simply a question of telling the story from a businessman's point of view, and I'm the only one who is competent to do that."

"I think I'll go, if you'll excuse me," Anne said. "The courtroom may be crowded."

As she walked up the steps Anne saw Marco. They were alone in the lunch-hour crowd that moved around them.

This is the way it was, she remembered, long ago, long, long ago. Only the crowd wasn't shabby and dreary like this. Nothing was dreary then.

"Marco."

"Anne, stand here a moment. We are quite alone among all these people."

"Do you still love the people, Marco? Now that you're close to them, not just talking about them?"

"Love them? I'm one of them. But I want to look at you. You've changed, Anne."

"Is that kind?" She tried to smile.

"But not completely, I think. You still have time before you change completely. You're lucky. There aren't many second chances."

"Why, Marco." She put her hand on his arm. How curious after all the years. And this time it will be all right.

"I saw Paul clearly today on the stand. And I was glad for you."

"I thought you meant—I thought you still . . ." She looked up at him.

"No, Anne. You can't go back. But you can go on. And it's a good road if only you can see it. I only imagined you. But Paul didn't. Now, looking back on that summer when we were all young, I think he did not. I couldn't see it then. I was angry, but now I see, Anne."

"I never thought I should hear you plead for Paul." Anne took her hand from his sleeve. He isn't really different, she thought. If he were, this would be easier. He says my name now like any word.

"I'm pleading for you," Marco answered. "I saw him meet you at the courtroom door. I saw him look at you. He loves you without imagining you at all. With him, you might even become the girl that I imagined."

"Is that all you wanted to say to me, Marco?"

"That's all. The rest was a long time ago. Perhaps it wasn't even as true as we thought. Good luck, Anne. Take your second chance."

Marco climbed the steps and was lost in the crowd. Anne stood still. It was true, she thought. He can't destroy it. It was true but it doesn't matter now. It didn't matter then because I wouldn't let it. I let all the years be empty. She fumbled with her bag and wiped her tears and repowdered her streaked face. With a steady hand she rouged her moving lips. Perhaps the years ahead are empty, too. But they can be pleasant. I will make them pleasant. I will have the life of my choice.

Anne continued to go to the trial. It had become the right thing for her to do. "I know it's hard," Mary said, "but you must for Paul's sake. You're all the help he has." And Phil Sinclair had spoken to her approvingly. "So I've been wrong all these years, and you're a nice girl as well as a pretty one."

It was painful to watch Bruce Craven on the stand. He is like the little man I saw the first day, Anne thought, only he doesn't know. That is the nightmare difference.

Bruce Craven sat comfortably in the witness chair. He answered easily his lawyer's direct examination. Occasionally he showed impatience at the limitation that Henry Merrill set to his answers.

"I could go further and explain that, in connection with the Stevenson trust, my old and intimate relationship with the late Mr. Charles Stevenson and——"

"Just answer my question, please."

"But look here, I want to place on record the fact that my high regard for——"

"Will your honor direct the witness to answer the question?"

"The witness will answer the question. Read the question."

As the court stenographer read, Anne watched Bruce Craven glance with annoyance at the judge and then shrug his shoulders and assume a look of patience. He considers the judge an interfering upper servant, she thought. And Mr. Merrill irritates him. " 'I'll be judge, I'll be jury,' said cunning old fury." Now he's smooth and cautious again. This must be the manner he used when investors or directors tried to disregard his advice.

"It will be worse in cross-examination," Paul said.

It was worse.

Anne watched Marco. He was quiet and polite. He concentrated on trying to show the jury the truth. Mr. Merrill did what he could for his client.

"Objection."

"Objection overruled."

"Exception."

Bruce Craven was arrogant and impatient. Marco Ghiberti was quiet and persistent. Doesn't Uncle Bruce know? Anne turned away. Doesn't he know that he is completing his own destruction?

"What has Craven and Company grossed in the last two years?"

"I haven't any idea."

"You have no idea, Mr. Craven?"

"You said 'grossed.' We don't think much of that word in my business." Bruce Craven raised his eyebrows and glanced at the jury.

"Can you give me a net figure?"

"Let's go, Mary," Anne whispered.

"Just wait. They'll adjourn soon. Try not to listen."

Against her will, the damaging testimony beat against Anne's ears.

". . . with the full knowledge of the Stevenson trustees that these funds were in your keeping, Mr. Craven?"

"You seem to forget that these people were old and close friends of mine who, after all, had trust in my integrity."

". . . was, of course, against the law for you to hold these bonds and use them as collateral."

"I think you're being pretty technical, Mr. District Attorney. So far as the trustees were concerned, they thought they were as safe as in their own vault."

"Whereas, in fact, you appropriated to your own use . . ."

Anne heard suppressed contempt sharpen Marco's voice. She looked at Paul and wondered if he were following his own advice, putting his mind ahead to a time and place beyond the dingy courtroom.

". . . and acted without consulting your partner, Mr. Paul Craven?"

"For all practical purposes, the firm of Craven and Company was mine. I have always assumed that I had a right to do as I pleased."

"And in regard to the following securities, I refresh your memory by reading the list: 1200 shares of American Telephone and Telegraph, 1500 shares of Bethlehem Steel, 5000 shares of General Electric, 800 shares of National Biscuit, 4000 shares . . . 1800 . . ."

Anne listened to the list of stocks and bonds that had been Paul's fortune, that had been her life. Steel buildings and canned food, cheap soap and shining telephone wires had bought for her jewels and furs and furniture and motorcars and de luxe staterooms on the fastest ships. They had provided all the perquisites of her agreeable life.

". . . and appropriated the funds so realized to your own use without your nephew's knowledge or consent?"

"Mr. Paul Craven explained that to you. Explained it very well."

". . . and did you not with Mr. Paul Craven as with Mrs. S. L. Sullivan, as with the Stevenson trust, as with . . ."

Bruce Craven's cross-examination was not finished when the court adjourned for the day.

Anne drove uptown with Paul.

"I think we'd better stop in at Uncle Bruce's. He might need us," Paul said.

"He didn't behave as though he needed anyone."

"He may suddenly. You never know."

Anne remembered the courtroom with distaste. "All that rigamarole," she said. "For what? Legal puss-in-the-corner so lawyers can earn a fat living."

"Not quite, Anne. This is an open-and-shut case. That's why Mr. Merrill wanted Uncle Bruce to plead guilty. But the rules give you a fair chance. Even if you're guilty, you have your chance."

"Don't tell me the lawyers impressed you. Justice! It's a game for them. They don't care."

"Seems like that sometimes," Paul said slowly. "But I guess professions always seem like that to outsiders. Doctors don't suffer with every patient. Go crazy if they did. But they do their damnedest to save them. Even ministers probably have their little clerical jokes. Got to keep the light touch. But underneath—justice, healing. They count. And in the law—in America——"

"If you're going to start on democracy——" Anne ground out her cigarette on the floor of the taxi. "That's something new for you."

"Never thought about it much before. Lot of things I never thought about that are pretty important. I never had time."

"Time's the one thing we'll have plenty of."

"And that's not so bad." Paul smiled. "You know, that may not be so bad."

In Bruce Craven's apartment the only cheerful person was Bruce Craven. "Drink, anybody? I think I deserve one." He smiled at Henry Merrill. "Join me. You'll feel better. You, too, Paul. Make yourself a cup of tea, Anne." He leaned back in his armchair and surveyed the silent group. "Yes, I think I handled myself rather well. Of course, that little wop was pretty insufferable. Incredible that a man in my position should have to tolerate a feller like that. Yes, all in all, I think we may consider it a pretty successful day. Yes, Murdock?" He looked up at the butler. "Can't stand it when those fellers hover. Well, what is it?"

"This package, sir. The person who left it—a Mrs. Albert Wilson— she was most insistent that I give it to you personally, sir, but I thought that perhaps Mr. Merrill——"

"Not a bomb, is it? No sound of ticking." Bruce Craven's laugh echoed in the silent room. "Here, give it to me. Wilson—I know that name. Feller used to work for me. Most unfortunate case."

He unwrapped the brown paper. "There seems to be a note." He slid the oblong card from the envelope and, as he did so, he rubbed his thumb across the engraved surface. "Yes, that's right. 'Mrs. Albert Wilson.' She says, 'This is the gun Albert used.' What an extraordinary thing." He lifted the cover of the cardboard box and stared at the revolver.

Anne and Henry Merrill and Paul watched him as he examined it. No one spoke until Bruce Craven said, "One shot's been fired. I had one of these in France. You can see. One shot's been fired." He held out the revolver and stared at them. "Extraordinary thing for her to do." He cleared his throat and repeated, "Extraordinary."

"Poor woman. You can see how she felt. Of course your case is quite—I mean, this is completely——" Paul fumbled with his sentence until Henry Merrill interrupted.

"Crank, of course. But still, as Paul says, poor woman."

Anne said nothing. She watched Bruce Craven. He was staring at them as though they were distorting mirrors in which suddenly he saw his reflection. His eyes moved away from them and then, unwillingly, returned. He stared at them.

"That's how it looks to you. That's not how it is, but that's how it looks. I'm different. But you don't see that. None of you see that. I've been looking at you and at those twelve fools on the jury and I didn't see until that poor crazy woman showed me how it looks. How it looks to every damn one of you." He started towards the door.

Henry Merrill stepped quickly towards him. "If you'll just let me have that, Bruce?"

Bruce Craven's hand limply surrendered the revolver. "Willingly, Henry. That's not what I meant. Just think I'll go to my room. I feel very tired." As Murdock opened the door for him, Bruce Craven lowered his eyes. "Think I'll lie down. I'll ring if I want anything."

"That's done it," Paul said as the door closed.

"Yes, now he knows," Henry Merrill said. "None of us was able to tell him."

"Better here than in a crowded courtroom. Better to learn it from her than from the foreman of the jury," Paul said.

"He didn't learn it from her, poor thing." Anne shivered as she remembered Mrs. Wilson. The streaked, unhappy face under the brassy hair. "He learned it from us. He looked at us and saw it in our faces."

"Poor guy." Paul turned the tall glass round and round in his hands. "He really thought he was different."

The trial, for Bruce Craven, ended that afternoon. The verdict had come on an engraved card with a revolver in a cardboard box.

The case continued in the courtroom for three more days. The game has to be played out, Anne thought, but it is lost. Even Uncle Bruce knows it is lost.

The habit of years was strong in Bruce Craven. His voice still rose imperiously. But his eyes fell before Marco's. He answered briefly.

"And on the fifteenth of November you received that key, Mr. Craven?"

"Yes sir. Of course, Mrs. Sullivan had every reason to feel confident. I mean, yes sir."

"And on the eighteenth you took the key and Mrs. Sullivan's signed order and went to the vaults of the Independent Trust Company at 253 . . ."

Anne remembered the defendant whom she had seen the first day. Uncle Bruce isn't small. He's big. He looks strong and safe but he isn't. He's small with fear inside that big handsome shell. He is afraid. You can't see it, but you can hear it. You can hear it when his voice drops.

On the twenty-fourth of April the jury returned its verdict.

"And how do you find . . . ?"

"We find the defendant guilty."

"Is there anything more, Paul?" Anne asked as they drove home.

"No. There's no use trying to appeal. Even Uncle Bruce sees that. Better to get it over with."

"He's changed," Anne said, and remembered Bruce Craven on his yacht at Cannes, at the head of his table in New York, in his office passing judgment on Albert Wilson. Even in the witness chair during most of the trial. Even there he had dominated the courtroom.

"Yes, he's changed," Paul said slowly. "For now anyway. I don't think for good. Mrs. Wilson held up the mirror just for a minute. Even in prison he'll feel different again, different from the other prisoners. After all, they don't get so many St. John-Princeton boys there. You watch. He'll come to believe again—that he's different."

"Well, of course he is. I mean, people like us just are different."

"No, we're not, Anne. You mustn't say it."

"Why? Is it a crime to face facts? It is a fact that we're different."

"An opinion, not a fact. Dangerous, not a crime. We've been warned on the best authority not to say it. 'God, I thank Thee, that I am not as other men are.'"

Anne clenched her hands with annoyance. "Don't go holy on me. We're in a fine mess. But because we're who we are, because we're different, we just may get out of it."

"Poor little Madam Queen." He unclenched her fingers and kissed them gently. "For me, you're different from everyone. Would you like some music? It's better than me talking my fool head off."

He turned on the cab radio. ". . . a verdict of guilty at three-thirty this afternoon." Paul turned the dial. A dance orchestra played. "There. That's better."

Anne listened to the music. It was smooth and sweet. She leaned back against the leather seat. She was very tired.

XI

IN JULY Anne and Polly moved to Mrs. Brooke's house in Southampton. This is it, Anne thought. This is the fine day on which Paul told me to pin my hopes. It's better than the boat and better than the courtroom, but that's all I can say for it. Anne's bedroom seemed overcrowded with furniture now that it held the extra bed for Paul. She looked out of the window at the waves that rolled gently in the soft evening light. I may as well get used to it. We'll be good and crowded in that little apartment next winter—and nothing like this to look at. The back of a dark Park Avenue building, most likely. She wondered if she should have stayed in town with Paul. Her mother had thought so. But I couldn't. It wouldn't be fair to Polly. You can't leave a child for the whole summer with her grandmother, even the best grandmother. Paul will come down for week ends. He wouldn't want me in town.

"I never did before," Anne had told her mother. "It would worry Paul."

"I only thought he might be lonely. Job-hunting is depressing. But you know best, dear child. You've behaved splendidly."

"It's only what anyone would do."

Anne listened to the soft beat of the quiet surf. What else is there to do? It's my life in which I have carefully imprisoned myself. And besides, I'm fond of Paul. It's almost six years. Six years of kindness, of dependence, bind the heart. You can't easily break that bond. It's like love. Perhaps it is love. You can't destroy it lightly even if you want to. And I don't want to, Anne told herself. This is my life. I'll have to make it do. Besides, no other life is waiting for me. Her shoulders sagged as she stood before the window and listened to the rhythm of the water against the sand.

On Saturday afternoon Paul arrived in Southampton.

"Lucky I have the car. My income would hardly run to the train every week."

"Have you one? An income, I mean."

"It's kind of a fancy name for it. Two hundred dollars a month that my mother left me in an unbreakable trust. But pretty handsome it looks to me with no job."

"Still no luck? I'm sorry, darling. Did you see Mr. Finch?"

"I saw everybody. Seems the name of Craven doesn't sit so well in financial circles. And Wall Street's all I know anything about."

"Well, things aren't desperate. We've got my money. Uncle Normie has laid out a budget for me. Under twenty-three hundred for rent. I suppose we can find something for that. And——"

"That makes it worse in a way. Your money, I mean. We could live on two hundred a month. People do, you know."

"Don't be silly, Paul."

"Yeah, I suppose it is. I didn't mean your clothes. Just——"

"And Polly's clothes. And a decent place for her to live and school for her and dancing class."

"They have pretty good public schools in the country," Paul persisted. "I could commute when I find something."

"Darling, you're mad. We're both mad. Standing here on the front steps talking about money. We never used to talk about it."

"We didn't have to, but now——"

"Now you leave it to me. I'll manage. You'll see. Come on, I'll get Thomas to bring in your bags."

"I'll carry my bags. Tell the estimable Thomas to get me a drink."

"Oh, darling."

Paul stared at her. "Don't look at me as though I were the village drunkard. I'm not. Not yet, anyway." He smiled. "But a little talk like this calls for a bracer. A great deal of scotch and very little soda."

When Paul finished his drink, Anne told him that they were dining at the Wintons'.

"Oh, honey, not tonight. I'm beat."

"It'll do you good. And people want to see you."

"They don't want to see me downtown. And I don't feel like seeing them here."

"But you can't slap their faces. When they're being nice. It isn't kind and, what's more, it isn't smart."

"Dinner parties aren't the way back, Anne. Don't kid yourself."

"Well, they help. Anyway, just this once. We haven't had much fun lately."

"Okay, baby. If it'll make you happy, I guess I can pull myself together."

He poured another drink. "Join me?"

"No, and I wish you wouldn't, Paul."

"Sorry, but I can't pull myself together on tea. I had the devil of a day in town."

Dinner parties might not be the way back but they were familiar ground, Anne thought. She smiled at Mr. Winton. It was kind of Mrs. Winton to put her next to him, and it might help. The Wintons were important.

The talk had changed very little in a year. "If we can just hang on till '36." "They've had to sell the big place in Westbury, poor things. They've rented a tiny house down here on the beach." "All this regulation. Talk about Mussolini—why, the SEC is nothing but . . ." "Don't worry about Harry Spain. This time he's hanging on." "Didn't even get to Palm Beach last winter." "Personally, I think it's a good buy at eighty-two. You're bound to see an upswing." ". . . with four incredible emeralds that J. C. picked up for Judy in Germany." "They can call it a purge. Actually, he's cleaned out the undesirable element. Mark my words, that feller Hitler knows what he's doing." "That's what J. C. says. But of course our newspapers are so biased. What can you expect with their advertisers, my dear— department stores and furriers?" "If Roosevelt would just leave business alone."

But now the talk didn't bore Anne. It frightened her. After dinner she found Phil Sinclair. Phil would know. He listened and took note.

"What do you really think, Phil?"

"Don't you know, Anne? Didn't you read me last Sunday?"

"Yes, I read you."

Anne remembered the article.

Southampton's season is in "full swing." Of all the resorts, Southampton has best adjusted itself to our apparently permanent depression. Southampton has always been more friendly towards newcomers than Newport. And now Southampton reaps the benefit. The J. C. Joneses and the Harry Spains, among others, give vitality to the Long Island resort. And incidentally, the local realtors profit as do the Southamptonites who are able to rent their ocean-front residences for sizable sums. The owners of white elephants in other resorts wish their old guard would let down the bars as has . . .

"I read it," Anne said. "The good old Newport-Southampton feud. A very fine Sunday space filler, but really, Phil, what do you think?"

"Those are the events I chronicle. The season here and abroad. I'm sailing next week. I think I'll take in Salzburg this year. The Lido and the Riviera are old stuff. Definitely, Salzburg. Central Europe's sweet music, lullaby by Brahms—very soothing, the Teuton, when he has a mind to be."

"Be serious, Phil. Everyone moans about conditions and then J. C. buys Judy a necklace. And Mr. Morehead says to buy steel or something. What about it? I've got to know. Paul can't get a job. I'm worried about him."

"About Paul or about his job?"

"Both. Paul's going to go to pieces if he doesn't find something."

"And your money doesn't help. And parties like this don't help. Paul has something, hasn't he, from his mother? Seems to me I remember her will."

"Oh, it's some ridiculous sum. You couldn't live on it."

"People do, you know, Anne. They live all right on ridiculous sums. Bill and Jenny Winton, for instance."

"In a horrid village house. I wouldn't mind, but there's Polly."

"Children do live in villages. And it doesn't have to be Southampton. Find one without summer people. Maybe that would be easier for you. Try it Paul's way."

"Did I hear my name?" Paul stood beside them. He held a glass in his hand. "It's a very delightful party. I feel quite at home. One more of these"—he emptied his glass—"and I won't know I've been away.

Anne doesn't know we've been away. Fact, she thinks we're still here. Bread from the children's table—delightfully nourishing."

"Anne's tired," Phil said. "So'm I. How about going home?"

"No," Paul said. "I like it here. Little drops of liquor, little crumbs of food make the rich man's table—hard to find a rhyme for food—unless you had a Scotch nurse. Scotch—that's a nice word. A really pleasing word." Paul moved uncertainly towards the bar.

"You get the car, Anne," Phil said. "I'll ease Paul out the front door."

Phil drove them home.

"I'm glad you're coming with us, old boy," Paul said. "Mrs. Brooke likes guests. That's why she has me. I'm a guest everywhere. Delightful feeling. No responsibility."

"I'll walk home," Phil said. "I'm staying at the Moreheads' down the road." He watched Paul walk unsteadily up the steps and into the house. "This won't do, Anne. You've got to stop."

"For once you can save the lecture for Paul. Even you, Phil, can't blame me."

"I don't blame people. I have the chronicler's mind if not the talent. But I like Paul, and I won't stand for this. I'm not blaming you, Anne. I'm telling you."

"Telling me what?" Anne blinked back the tears. "Getting drunk in front of all those people when I've tried, when he ought to be trying, to make a good impression."

"He wasn't noticeably drunk. And they're not very noticing people. But you'd better stop it. You'd better play it his way if you want to play it at all."

Phil walked down the gravel drive. Anne listened to his crunching footsteps. After he was gone she sat on the front steps.

She heard someone in the doorway. "Oh, Paul." She turned. It wasn't Paul. It was Mrs. Brooke.

"I heard something. Why, child, what is it?"

"Paul got tight and I'm afraid." Anne's voice shook. "Oh, Mother, I don't know what to do. I'm afraid."

Anne wept in her mother's arms.

Paul went to town Sunday evening. "Sorry about last night, Anne. Maybe I'll find something this week."

He found nothing and, the following Saturday night, Paul wasn't drunk, but he wasn't sober. This is the pattern, Anne thought as she danced at the Meadow Club. I'm to be one of those wives with an anxious heart and an eager smile. Left-over clothes and a left-over smile. Paul was a scream last night, they'll say, until it gets so bad that they don't say anything.

J. C. Jones cut in. "What's wrong, Anne? Come on, tell the old man."

"Nothing. I'm all right."

"Say, I hear Paul needs a job. Send him in to see me."

"Do you mean that? After all, we're at a party. I wouldn't want ——"

"Sure I mean it. Listen, they've said everything about me. I can afford to hire Bruce Craven's nephew. Besides, Paul might be an asset to me. Tell him to call my secretary on Monday and make an appointment. I'll fix him up."

Anne told Paul on Sunday morning. "Isn't that swell, darling? You're set."

"I don't know, Anne." He frowned. "There've been a lot of queer stories about J. C."

"Well, really, Paul," Anne said impatiently, "I don't think you can afford to be choosy."

"No, I can't, can I? I keep forgetting that. All right, baby, I'll try it. I guess even without your reminding me I'd try anything. I'm kind of desperate. As I guess you noticed last night."

"I'm afraid other people noticed, Paul."

"Couldn't we leave other people out, Anne? Couldn't we be just us?"

"Don't start that all over, Paul. If we hadn't gone to the dance last night I wouldn't have seen J. C."

"And I wouldn't have got tight. I was tight, you know, not drunk. Just over the edge. Things seem better when you're just over the edge. Sorry. My nice distinctions bore me, too. Don't worry, I'll take J. C.'s job. I'd take any job."

On Monday J. C. Jones gave Paul a job. He told Anne about it on Saturday. "It isn't much. Not while I'm learning the ropes, anyway. My name on a nice shiny desk and thirty-five dollars a week. But that's another hundred and forty a month. Couldn't we try it my way? Take a little house in——"

"No. You wouldn't be worth even that to J. C. in a suburb. This is the beginning, Paul."

"Okay, Annie. I'll give it a whirl. There's nothing else to do anyway."

The summer slid by. Dull times should be sluggish. They should go slowly but they went quickly, Anne found. She remembered the long summers of childhood that had stretched themselves lazily over the expanse of days. From the Fourth of July to Labor Day had been a long time. Perhaps she should be grateful that this empty time moved quickly. She should be grateful, too, that Paul no longer drank too much. He went docilely through the routine of the Southampton week ends. He went to the beach and to church and to the dinners Anne accepted for them both.

"If you'd just look on the week end as part of your business, Paul."

"I do, honey. On one cocktail I'm not likely to forget it."

Nor was she, Anne thought. She was the charming guest. She was charming to the Moreheads and the Spains, to the Wintons and the Joneses. She looked forward to Labor Day. To go before would be to confess defeat. To move away after Labor Day, even to New York, was within the accepted pattern.

By the first of October Anne and Paul were in their new apartment. It was a small apartment in an old building on Park Avenue. Most of the rooms faced a court. Norman Brooke had found it for Anne. "It's a good building, my dear. Not in bankruptcy like so many of them." Anne accepted his choice. Since she couldn't have what she wanted, anything would do.

Too late, Anne realized that, within her means, she might have made a more distinguished selection than this Park Avenue rabbit warren. She stared resentfully at the door 6C. A metallic rabbit hole exactly like A, B, and D. Well, it would do. She shouldn't have chosen something that would do. It wasn't smart. The fashionable magazines gave you a blueprint. How to live smartly on nothing a year. Be uncomfortable, they said, be out of the way, but be amusing. Anne gloomily considered *Harper's Bazaar* and *Vogue*. She turned the pages. Be gay. Be different. Let it never be said that you're run-of-the-mill. If it can't be a penthouse, find high-ceilinged rooms in a forgotten brownstone front. If it can't be terrapin and pheasant, let it be beans in witty little French pots or stew in your grandmother's chafing dish.

Idiots! Anne closed the magazine in the face of the editor who said, "Old-fashioned mattress ticking is more fun for curtains than the banal chintz you can afford." Don't you read your magazine, lady? Anne asked. Don't you look at the pictures? Don't you know that even with lashings of left-over pearls, a twenty-five-dollar number is still a Ford from Seventh Avenue and not a two-hundred-and-seventy-five-dollar Paris model? It's the same with everything. Thriftiness isn't smart, at least not in our terms, madam. There's no two-dollar substitute for high living and haute couture.

Mrs. Brooke worried about Paul. "He's so quiet, Anne."

"He never talked much, Mother. He's just tired. And it's not easy to be the hired help when you're accustomed to what Paul used to have."

"Perhaps if you didn't go out so much."

"Oh, Mother, our social life is just business in evening clothes. I do the best I can. It isn't easy for me."

"I know, darling. You've been wonderful."

Phil Sinclair was less understanding. He danced with Anne at Judy Jones's birthday party at the Ritz in February.

"Paul looks bad, Anne. Why do you drag him to these things?"

"Same reason you're here, Phil dear. Bread and butter."

J. C. cut in. "You look very beautiful. Can't blame myself for hiring Paul. That new?" He slid his hand along her wrist and twisted her multicolored jeweled bracelet.

"Don't be silly, J. C. You remember these flower bracelets. Mine's an heirloom from the days of '29."

"We'll see those days again."

"Really, J. C.?"

"Not quite the same setup, maybe, but string along with me and you'll see."

Paul did not find it easy to string along. He tried to explain to Anne after the party.

"I can't put my finger on it. My job's all right. But there's a lot goes on in that office that I don't know about. Did you know J. C.'s going to Germany again in the spring?"

"Now don't go all melodramatic and anti-Nazi on me. We've got troubles enough of our own."

"Look, Anne, would you mind terribly if I quit J. C.'s firm?"

"And did what?"

"Well, I'm a pretty good salesman. And I'd like to sell something I know about. Now you take, for instance, sporting goods. I was at college with Max Harrington and he'd give me a job at Harrington and Cox. I could learn the business and maybe——"

"Are you crazy? You'd be a clerk in Harrington and Cox. They'd use you to get your friends."

"No, they have my friends already. But I was talking to Max, and he thought some of my ideas were pretty good."

"You have a future with J. C."

"Not me, Anne. J. C. has. But not me. There are things I don't go for."

"Please, Paul." Anne slid into bed. "For me, stay with J. C. Try it a little longer." She reached her hand to him across the night table. She had forgotten to take off her bracelet. It sparkled on her wrist.

"Darling, do you remember? You couldn't forget the day I gave you this. I couldn't." He moved the bracelet and kissed her wrist where it was marked with the print of the stones.

Anne pressed her wrist against Paul's lips. She remembered J. C.'s thick fingers. That was one thing about Paul. "One thing, darling, about us," she said, and her voice was husky.

His lips moved against her arm. "Remind me that we talk too much." He reached for the light switch. Her hand stopped him.

"But, Paul, about J. C.——"

Paul dropped her wrist. "For God's sake, do we have to take him to bed with us?"

"No, Paul, it's not that. It's that I'm afraid the other job might not work out. And with J. C. we have a chance. Don't you see, Paul? I'm afraid." Her arm stretched towards him. The flowers of the bracelet were bright against her white skin.

Paul took her hand. He sat beside her on her bed. He moved the bracelet slowly on her arm. "Darling, anything you want, only let's not talk." He turned out the light.

After that night Paul did not say anything more about his job. If Anne asked about J. C., he answered briefly, "Let's leave him downtown."

He'll be all right, Anne thought. If he'll just hang on. We're on our way up again. She put out the dress she had bought to wear to Mrs. Reggy Voorhees' dinner and dance. She heard Paul slam the front door. "Lots of time, darling," she called. "Dinner isn't until eight-thirty."

Paul didn't answer. He came in and sat down heavily on the bed. Anne smoothed the full, pale skirt of her dress.

"Look what I blew myself to. Leon just got it in. It's from the spring collections. It's definitely 1935. Maybe this is our year, after all. Uncle Normie's budget's working out and next thing you know J. C. will have you making real money." She kissed Paul lightly.

"Paul, you've been drinking."

"Just a quick one on my way home. But it'll take several more to get me to that party, the way I feel tonight."

"Darling, is anything the matter?"

"No, nothing. Just in the regular line of business. The wife of our representative in Berlin was in. Our late representative, I should say. She got out. She's an American citizen. We could have got him out——"

"Paul, you look awful. You'd better have a drink."

"Let me finish. Maybe then you'll want one, too. We could have got Mr. Wiesner out. But no, we let him go. We couldn't afford to jeopardize certain delicate negotiations. So Mrs. Wiesner has a tin of ashes. It seems they picked up Mr. Wiesner to question him. Maybe he wouldn't answer, maybe he couldn't. Anyway, after six weeks— six weeks in which we did nothing, in which we continued our deli-cate negotiations—they told Mrs. Wiesner to come and pick up the ashes. She came in to tell us what she imagined they'd done to him so that they thought it wiser to have the remains cremated before she saw them. She told us quite a lot before the ambulance took her away. The doctors gave her a jab of something. She stopped screaming before they took her out. But they couldn't get her hands loose from the tin."

"How awful, but could J. C. really have done anything? I mean, it's a foreign country and of course right now everything is so upset in Germany."

"Or, as J. C. puts it, the setup is different, but you can do business if you watch your step. In the process of watching our step we let Mr. Wiesner go. Six weeks. Just about the time these particular negotiations took. Six weeks. Lots of minutes and hours for Mr. Wiesner in six weeks. Mrs. Wiesner had imagined them all. All those minutes of consciousness. The Gestapo have a lot of tricks. She told us about them—about the steel rods and——"

Anne pressed her fingers tightly into her ears. "Stop it, Paul. You know I can't stand torture."

"Neither, it seems, could Mr. Wiesner. Not for more than six weeks. All right, I'll shut up. I'm going to get that drink."

"I'll take one, too." Anne's voice was subdued.

When Paul handed her a drink, she pressed the cold glass against her dry lips. "That's awful, Paul. I won't be able to get those poor people out of my mind all night. Maybe it's a good thing we're going out."

"Are we still going to the Voorhees'?"

"Darling, we can't get out of it. I mean, it isn't as though we had a good reason."

Paul looked at her. He didn't answer.

"You're not angry, Paul?"

"No, I'm not angry. I'll go dress."

She called to him through the bathroom door. "If it weren't the last minute—it's not that I want to go, only we can't get out of it." The noise of the shower drowned her voice.

At dinner Anne watched Paul. He was pale but he seemed to be sober. He talked quietly to his neighbors.

"Worried about Paul?" Jim Forrest asked. "He doesn't look well. J. C. a tough guy to work for?"

"Oh no. Paul likes him a lot. Today was kind of a tough day."

"I'll say it was. They raised hell with utilities."

Anne meant to take Paul home early. But she couldn't find him after dinner, nor at the beginning of the dance. She kept her smile carefully bright. Her beautiful new dress floated around her as she danced. She looked for Paul. He was nowhere to be seen.

Tom Webb cut in.

"Have you seen Paul?" she asked.

"A fine question to greet me with—when you know how I am about you."

"You're tight, my lad."

"Just the least bit. Not like a mink. Not so Mrs. Reggy will notice.

The old boy was giving out with brandy. Better watch out for Paul. He's got a snootful."

Not here—don't let him be drunk here, Anne prayed and looked up at the gilded cupids smirking at her from the ceiling. Don't let him be tight enough for anyone to notice.

She was waltzing with Phil when she saw Paul. He was standing in the doorway beside Mr. Voorhees. Paul was pale. He swayed and clutched his host to steady himself.

"Okay, Anne, easy does it. We'll make it." Phil guided her to the doorway. But they did not make it. They had descended only two steps of the marble stairway before Paul collapsed and was sick. Anne left him with Phil and fled down the stairs, away from the awful retching sounds and the small embarrassed gusts of laughter. This is the end, this is the comic end of everything. Phil will keep him tonight, but tomorrow I'll tell him.

Paul did not come home until the next afternoon. He had spent the night with Phil.

Anne told him after dinner. "I'm through, Paul. After last night I'm through."

"But, Anne, you know how I felt. You know I wasn't responsible."

"Just because a perfect stranger—just because of a horror story that may not even be true——"

"It's true, all right."

"All right, it's true. But it has nothing to do with us. You'd never even seen that man. It's no excuse to disgrace me in front of all New York."

"What do you mean to do?"

"I don't know. But I've got to go away for a while. I might go to Uncle Normie in Palm Beach. It's a little late for Florida and that's appropriate enough. It's a little late for everything. Anyway, I've got to get away."

"For good, Anne? Is that what you mean?"

"I don't know."

"I know, Anne. I've known for a year. But I've hoped. I'm such a damn fool that I still hope."

"That's not fair. That's not what people will think."

"The hell with what people think. I know. But play it out any way you like. I'll let you. I repeat—that's the sort of damn fool I am."

Anne did not go to Palm Beach. J. C. Jones asked her to go abroad with him and Judy.

Anne told Mrs. Brooke about her plans.

"You heard, Mother? About that awful scene at the Voorhees'."

"I thought perhaps something special had happened that night. It wasn't like Paul."

"I've tried to hide it, Mother. But it keeps getting worse. You remember that time last summer at the Wintons'. There were other times that you didn't know about. I didn't want you to know."

"Poor child. Poor child. And poor Paul, too. You feel that, don't you, dear?"

"I do. That's why I've tried so. I don't want to run out on him. But there's Polly. I've got to think of her."

"Of course you do." Mrs. Brooke remembered Anne at Polly's age. She had been young then, younger than Anne was now. It was queer to have your child grow older than you were when she was born. The young Anita Brooke had had to put away her grief for Anne's sake. Perhaps grief wasn't the hardest thing.

"That's what I wanted to ask you about, Mother. Would you keep Polly? I can't leave her with Paul. And I've got to get away."

"Of course I'll take her." Mrs. Brooke tried not to sound too eager. It was hard for her to adjust herself to these elderly years. The young years seemed hard, but at least they weren't empty.

"Of course, dear, but"—Mrs. Brooke hesitated—"won't it be hard on Paul? Are you sure it's all right to leave him alone?"

"I've got to, Mother. He has to face facts. Perhaps if he's left alone he'll realize and pull himself together."

"And the Joneses, dear. Are they quite the people—I know times have changed, but——"

"They're just the people. Don't you see? If I go with them, no one will talk. Everyone will think it's natural, the right thing even, for me to accept an invitation from Paul's boss."

There was not much time between Anne's decision and her departure. She persuaded Paul to behave as though nothing had happened. "We mustn't let Polly notice anything."

"No. Nor any of those important people."

"I'm only trying to make it easy for you. And then, perhaps, after we've been separated for a while . . ." She left the sentence unfinished and smiled at him.

"That thread of hope. I'll hang myself with it one fine day."

"And you won't quit J. C. Jones? It'll make things so complicated."

"I don't want to complicate things, Anne. I guess I'll stay on. My staying or leaving won't make any difference. Things will go on the same."

Anne went to see Judy to make the last arrangements the day before they sailed. J. C. liked arrangements. She walked west towards Judy's apartment. Not yet could you see the thin green of the park between the gray houses. Not yet, but you could imagine it or remember it. She turned up Fifth Avenue. The sun was warm against her cheek. No winter wind blew across the park. The tiny branches of the bushes and of the trees were black against the sun. But they weren't gray and dry. They no longer looked dead and forgotten, never to be green again. It was the promise of spring. Anne remembered that spring day almost a year ago when she had awakened to the beginning of Bruce Craven's trial. From now on, would spring wake her only to laugh in her face? In the twenties and before that, there had been lovely springs. Anne walked slowly and held her face to the sun and remembered. Those springs had always promised and you had believed. Now, in the thirties, it was different. Only the century was in its thirties, not Anne. Not yet, but there isn't much time between twenty-eight and thirty. Anne walked quickly up the avenue to the towering white apartment house in whose tallest pinnacle lived Judy and J. C. Jones.

Anne and Judy talked and waited for J. C. Phil Sinclair came in. Judy waved to him.

"Hi. Fix yourself a drink. We're planning our trip. J. C. has some business in Germany. And you and I, Anne, can go to Garmisch-Partenkirchen. That's where the winter Olympic team is practicing. And are they something! Handsome, blond Siegfrieds. Not amusing, though. They're rather solemn, inspired young men."

"That's all right with me," Anne said. "I'm sick of witty substitutes for success. The Germans seem to be going somewhere. The dear U.S.A. is just turning into a well-upholstered Russia. And the upholstery is not for you and me. Comes the Revolution, we won't eat strawberries and cream."

"That's what J. C. says. He says you have to choose between the Communists and the Fascists. And no one with any sense would choose the Bolsheviks. They're——"

"The sophist's dilemma," Phil interrupted. "It always consists of one horn of a true dilemma split carefully in two. Then there is no choice. But I didn't come here to give a Chautauqua lecture on democracy. I came to take Anne home."

"That's very touching," Anne said, "but I have to wait for J. C."

"No, you don't. You're coming with me. Paul wants to see you."

"Is it important?" Judy asked. "Will it interfere with Anne's sailing?"

"No. But I think she'd better come home."

Judy let them go.

"What is it?" Anne asked when they got in the taxi.

"I picked him up at the club. He's on his way to getting good and drunk. If you come home, for some reason that escapes me, he'll stop. You're set on this trip, I suppose?"

"I've got to get away, Phil. You don't understand."

"I understand, all right. Well, the guy's got to get adjusted sometime. I'll do what I can to help him."

"He ought to resign from that damn club," Anne said angrily. "All anyone ever does there is get drunk."

"He would, if you'd resign from all this nonsense. The poor guy has to go somewhere."

"God knows, it doesn't mean anything any more. They let anyone in nowadays."

"I've been telling you for years, Anne, that this exclusive world you picture doesn't exist. I pretend it does, too. But at least I get paid to pretend. That makes some sense. You get to be upper-class by saying you are and having the money to prove it."

"Well, really, Phil. Take me, for instance. Mother's a Colonial Dame and Uncle Normie's a member of the Society of St. Nicholas."

"Commemorating our forebears who had a vision of equality. So Washington wasn't king and your distinguished ancestors remained commoners."

"But for all practical purposes, Phil, they were the ruling class."

"Ah, yes, the great debunking school. The men who risked their necks for liberty were really Tories. I don't hold with it. You see, I remember that, in their hearts and in their minds, they held on to the ideal. They even wrote it down. 'We hold these truths to be self-evident.' As simple as that, Anne. Equality was an axiom."

When Anne got home, Paul was playing with Polly. Anne stood in the doorway with Phil and watched them.

"That's right, Polly, now another block. Now I'll put one."

"Now I'll put one—very carefully, Daddy."

The tower swayed. Paul steadied it with his hand and picked up a block. "Shall we try one more? That's the idea, you know, Polly. To build it as high as you can. In the end it always falls down, but it's fun while you're building."

Anne walked quickly into the room. The tower fell.

"Polly's too old for blocks, Paul, and a little young for allegory."

"Blocks aren't young, Mummy—not how Daddy plays. He doesn't play babily."

"Say how do you do to Mr. Sinclair, darling."

Polly curtsied to Phil. Then she turned to her mother. "Are you going on the boat tomorrow, Mummy?"

"Yes, darling, but I'll be back soon."

"But, Mummy, can I——"

"No, you'll have a much happier time staying here with Grand-ma."

"No, but, Mummy, what I meant is can I go to the boat with Daddy? Can I, Mummy?"

"It'll be cold, darling."

"No, it won't. Can't I please, Mummy? I like boats and I never see them."

Polly went with Paul and Mrs. Brooke to see Anne off. When they had gone ashore with the other visitors, Anne stood on deck and waved. Her heart was light with the relief of going. Even to leave Polly was a relief. Being a mother pushed you towards middle age. Among strangers in a new land Anne thought she might find, at least for a little while, the young Anne that it had once been fun to be. She shivered and waved her white-gloved hand. To look back tenderly on your young self—that was definitely a middle-aged thing to do. She waved at Polly and Paul and Mrs. Brooke. The other passengers, waving too, crowded beside Anne at the rail. She drew her arms close

to her side. She disliked crowds. She remembered standing with Marco
on the crowded courthouse steps. "Take your second chance, Anne,"
he had said. Paul wasn't a second chance.

The ship was moving away from the dock. Anne pulled out her
handkerchief and waved it. It flutters, she thought, for all its whiteness, like a small flag of freedom, not of surrender. You're not beaten
unless you surrender. You needn't surrender. You can seek and find
your second chance. Anne continued to wave as the ship swung out
into the river. The air was cold but the sun still promised spring.
There is time, Anne thought. There is time in another chance, in
another land, in another spring.

XII

ANNE AND JUDY DID NOT, after all, go to Garmisch-Partenkirchen.

"I can't imagine why I thought there'd still be winter in April
except that New York in March makes you believe that spring's been
given up for good and they're going to have winter the year round
from now on. Anyway Berlin's fun—except this damn hotel."

"Why, I like it," Anne said. She liked the overfurnished expensive
sitting room. She liked her big bedroom, with the high old-fashioned
bed and the red carpet. The bed was soft and the carpet was thick and,
beyond the elaborate triple curtains, there was a strange city.

"You like it!" Judy repeated incredulously. "My poor sweet, you
did need a vacation. Why the Germans can't have hotels like everyone
else, I don't see."

"Judy, it's rather fun not to have that same old hotel room in re-
strained good taste, the eternal lifeless imitation of Elsie de Wolfe."

"That pale room is more becoming than this upheaval of color.
You certainly can't dress for the apoplectic sofa we're sitting on."

"Still, it's fun not to have the same room as the one in London or
New York or the Lido. That international room. You liked the Crillon,
Judy, and that's furnished incredibly."

"Oh well, Paris is different. The French can do up a place in pure
Louis Philippe or straight Galeries Lafayette and it has charm. Why,

they even kid you into liking that Napoleonic stuff. However, I can't complain about this place. We've gone out so much. This is the first good look I've taken at our fine parlor."

J. C. came in. "Well, girls, all set for the big doings? Where are Pierre and Ruby?"

"They're meeting us downstairs with Franz von Erlencamp."

As Judy and Anne preceded J. C. through the hall, other hotel guests turned to look at them. Judy's emeralds and diamonds, Anne's less brilliant jewels, and J. C.'s white tie proclaimed to the onlookers that here were three guests invited by Minister-President General Goering to witness the special prenuptial performance of *Die Aegyptische Helena* at the State Opera House.

We are more than an audience, Anne thought as she sat in Franz von Erlencamp's box. We are witnesses. We are part of a pageant that is more dramatic than the musical story of love and forgetfulness and remembrance on the stage.

The curtain fell in heavy folds. The lights blazed in the crimson and gold opera house. Anne looked about her. Curious, she thought, how quickly people adapt themselves to power. The members of the ruling class look alike. They look more like one another, more like their foreign counterparts, than like their lowlier compatriots. That's always been true. In old portraits you can see the resemblance in the royal and noble families of Europe. It is more than a family likeness. It is the look of the master class. The rich and fashionable and powerful world in Berlin is not so different from the same world in New York. There are the uniforms, of course. The real difference may be that, here, people like us have the power still—or again—the Nazis aren't all new. Franz, for instance, and Von Papen and Prince August Wilhelm and Fritz Thyssen and Goering himself. Hohenzollern and Junker and industrialist, saved by an Austrian house painter, saved from the mob, saved from the army of the dispossessed.

"Quite a sight, isn't it, Anne?" J. C. asked. "Our newspapers never give us this side of the German picture. I hold no brief for Nazism. It wouldn't do for America. But you have to give the devil his due. Hitler's straightened things out over here. He's put down the Reds. Of course it wouldn't do for us. At least not without a lot of modification."

The boxes about them were emptying. Anne and J. C. followed Judy and the Borodinos into the wide, brilliantly lighted foyer.

"What does Franz do exactly?" Anne asked. "He's definitely of the old order, isn't he, and yet he seems to fit in. So many of them seem to."

"Sure. This is what they want. Even if a lot of our hysterical New York newspapers try to tell you different. The Germans wanted Hitler, and, as far as I can see, he's doing a pretty damned efficient job for them."

"And Franz?"

"Oh, he's quite a smart guy behind that pale poetic forehead. He's the big man on the *Morgenpresse*. He stands well with Goebbels, though he hasn't any official job with the Propaganda Ministry— and then, through his army connections, he's in with General Goering." J. C. laughed. "And don't make any mistake about the General. He's got a sound business head in spite of that military front. Franz was very useful to me last winter. We had the wrong man representing us here. Franz helped us find just the person to replace him. This is a much more realistic government than the folks at home realize. There's almost no unemployment—no strikes."

Anne fingered her pearls and remembered how she had hidden them with her hands one winter night outside a New York theater. Striking taxi drivers had marched by in a solid column. "Poor devils," Paul had said. Anne had shivered and covered her jewels. There had been too many of them to pity. They had filled the street. They had lost their individual insignificance and taken on strength. Anne had been afraid.

Her fingers trembled now against her pearls as she remembered. She looked up at Franz, who walked beside her.

"J. C. has been telling me fine things about your country."

"He's one of the Americans who understands. And you, too—you begin to see. Tonight, for instance. Here to honor the General Minister-President is the best of the old Germany and the best of the new. I shall present you to him and to Frau Sonnemann."

At the close of the performance Franz introduced his guests to the General. Anne stood beside Pierre Borodino in the group at the head of the grand staircase.

"Even you, Pierre, must admit this is magnificent."

The torches flared as the soldiers from the Regiment Hermann Goering presented arms. The bands formed a square. The music blared.

"What's that they're playing?" Pierre asked.

"The 'Prussian March.' In honor of General Goering's office," Ruby whispered.

"And that, too," Pierre said, "has no significance unless you choose to hear it. To remember Prussia in spite of the Nazi pageantry. Or was it never Prussia? Was Prussia only the symbol, as now the Nazis, of the German spirit? Siegfried alone is bright and glorious—the world a forest for him to conquer, the rest of us Mimes, hideous little people whom he must destroy to take his rightful inheritance by the sword."

"Now, Pierre darling, don't have a rush of French blood to the head. This is fun to watch." Ruby curled her slim sunburned hand in the crook of Pierre's elbow. "Listen to the band as music, not as a challenge. Don't get angry. Europeans get so angry at each other's anthems. You ought to be like Americans. North, east, and west—we all sing 'Dixie.'"

"Ruby, it isn't funny. Though you would charm me into thinking so." Pierre covered her hand with his. "Fit the words to the music they are playing now. '*Deutschland, Deutschland über alles, über alles in der Welt.*' The world, mind you, Ruby. Siegfried on the march against the world."

"Don't be so literal, darling. The 'Marseillaise' is pretty bloodthirsty, too. How about those *sillons* you threaten to water with impure blood?" She rubbed her silky head against his shoulder. She smiled at Franz. "Don't take Pierre too seriously."

They listened silently. The crowd stood motionless in the square before the opera house. The flickering torchlight gave the illusion of movement to the stolid bodies, the illusion of expression to the blank faces. The music changed.

"What's that they're playing?" Ruby asked.

"That is the '*Heldenlied,*'" Franz answered proudly.

"Oh yes, it's about Lisa's father. I know he was a terrific hero. What did he do exactly?"

"He died that Germany might live. 'With his bright sword shall we avenge the shame.'"

"Oh dear. You and Pierre. You do put a grim period to a conversation."

"Perhaps we feel deeply, even grimly, my dear Ruby." Franz stretched his arm in salute.

The torchlit scene changed the luxurious, fashionable evening into something ancient and frightening. The General stood quietly, but his black shadow moved menacingly. Anne wondered if the truth lay in the shadow of the man, not in his handsome amiable face. Was there fear even here at the heart of power?

No other part of the wedding festivities had that threatening quality. Anne forgot her fear. The Germans enjoyed a touch of the *Nibelungenlied*. And if there had to be fear, it was best to be among those to whom it was a weapon, not a threat.

At the afternoon reception Ruby whispered to Anne and Judy, "Come and see the presents. They are something."

"Wedding presents always are."

"How about that silver boat?" Ruby leaned over to read the label. "From the city of Hamburg, no less. Every detail perfect and all adding up to a monster of painstaking ugliness."

"It'll fit in all right in Karin Hall," Judy said. "J. C. dragged me down there. You have to see that place to believe it. *Ivanhoe* and North German Lloyd in equal parts, blown up to heroic size."

"How about this bronze number?" Ruby asked. "Frederick the Great, large as life. You inherit things like that. But imagine having them given to you."

There were massive silver candelabra and epergnes. There was bronze and gold. There were dark, heavy wooden chests and tables, intricately carved. There were huge crystal vases and a bowl of agate as big as a baptismal font. There were paintings and lamps and china and military souvenirs and illuminated scrolls.

Around them the guests moved and talked. Anne listened. Her mind grew accustomed to the task of instant translation. The "Heil Hitlers" were like punctuation marks. A matter-of-fact, unfrightening tribute to the god of things as they are.

"So handsome, the General. And a clever man. We were lucky enough to obtain a few shares in his steelworks." "Heil Hitler, Frau Counselor." "They certainly spread themselves on a present. Solid silver and such carving. She must have hated to give it. After all, she was official hostess before the marriage." "Heil Hitler, General." "He won't change the name. Emmi Hall would sound foolish." "Two dozen of them, and solid gold. How they could afford it!" "They had to. They say her grandmother——" "Heil Hitler." "Like the old days. But better." "I never thought to see him here. I didn't think he was even in the Army any more." "He's all right. Fortunately, he has proof that his mother's husband was not his father." "Heil Hitler." "How pleasant to see, once again, the true German hospitality. And people of one's own class. When I think of those wretched professors and scientists with whom one was forced to put up." "You always seemed very amiable about it. Don't I remember that the former Chancellor——" "Ah, my dear, what a joy it is no longer to have to pretend. But your young cousin, the Baron. I understand he has been mixing in religious matters. So painful for you. You were such friends." "Not at all. The Catholic branch of our family is very distant." "Heil Hitler." "If only the old Field Marshal could have lived to see these times. He worked so long, so patiently." "And so secretly." "One had to be secret." "Have you seen the jewels? There is one necklace . . ." "Emmi has the figure to display such . . ." "Ah, Baroness, Heil Hitler. We were saying that the jewels . . ."

"Let's see the jewels, too," Ruby suggested. "I love it when the Teuton spreads himself. It even makes Pierre laugh. I must find him, poor darling. He's having rather a thin time. But I think it's just good sense to have friends in Germany."

"You sound like J. C.," Judy said.

"No. Americans may still have a choice. I don't think we have. So, if you can't lick 'em, join 'em."

"Do you agree with Pierre?" Anne asked. "Do you think there'll be a war?"

"Heavens, nothing as old-fashioned as that." Ruby's small square teeth gleamed as she grinned. "You don't have to fight wars nowadays to win them. There are other means. And, believe me, the little Fuehrer knows them all."

"Aren't you afraid?" Anne asked.

"Not me. I pick the winner and place my bet." Ruby laughed and popped a piece of gum into her mouth. "That was vulgar in Paterson, New Jersey, but in Europe it's thought a charming Americanism.

And of course I make it absolutely chic by carrying my *bischen Gummi* in a special case. See." She snapped the diamond clasp and slipped the gold oblong into her purse.

"Let's look at the rest of the lavish display. I like it," Anne said, "after the meager years of the depression." She smiled at Franz. "I hear there's to be a twelve-course dinner. You certainly do things well."

"We are glad to show you the true German hospitality."

"Twelve courses! J. C. will like that," Judy said. "He's a happy child of Mammon. I am myself. I have a weakness for grandeur. And this. Boy! This is Mrs. Reggy Voorhees' in spades."

"Have you seen Lisa?" Franz asked. "We were together at the cathedral."

"I thought she was playing in *Romeo and Juliet.*"

"This evening's performance has been canceled. It is necessary that Lisa attend such functions." He looked anxious. "If you will excuse me for a moment."

Lisa was standing beside a slim, black-shirted man.

"There you are, my dear." Franz took her hand and turned to her companion. "Heil Hitler. I did not know that you were acquainted with my good friend Herr Kraussmann."

"Heil Hitler. I did myself the honor of presenting myself to the Countess. Since I know both you and Frau Wilhelm Blessing, I presumed on the privilege of a family friend." Herr Kraussmann smiled at Franz. His eyes, surprisingly blue in his sallow face, did not smile. They were round eyes, bright but expressionless like the eyes of a bird. "Besides, as an officer of the state, it is my duty as well as my privilege to know one who is so much a part of National Socialism as the Countess. We have a very special duty to cherish and protect the daughter of Siegfried Blessing." He kissed Lisa's hand. He saluted briefly. "Heil Hitler."

"Heil Hitler," Franz repeated to Kraussmann's back. "What have you been saying to him, Lisa?"

"Nothing much. I said that we close next week and that I was thinking of going to America."

"You can't do that, Lisa."

"Why not? Isn't this a free country?"

"Of course. In the highest sense of freedom. But for you, Lisa, as for all of us, your duty to the state comes first. The Fuehrer is much interested in developing our national theater."

"I don't want to go right away. But sometime. And I think Granny would like one last voyage to America."

"That's impossible."

"Surely they don't need her."

"No. But I don't think she would want to go. At her age . . . The trip . . ."

"You may be right. It's only an idea."

"Have you paid your respects to Frau Goering?"

"No, but I will. See how she beams with pleasure at her great day. And there is one of our Americans."

Lisa looked at Anne, who stood near Frau Goering. She wondered what the slender young American thought of the Hausfrau decked out in her bridal finery.

Anne looked at the bride and thought, She is older than I. She must be forty. Much older than I. And, for her, the world begins today. So can it for me if I watch and bide my time. She touched her slim body. Her breasts were small and firm under her hand. So can it begin for me.

"Come, Lisa, we must pay our respects." Franz stood a moment and looked about him. "Isn't it fine, Lisa, to see this? So, I imagine, it used to be. It is good to see pomp and circumstance. To know the lean years are almost over. To know that, thanks to the Fuehrer, Germany shall, as once ancient Egypt—that for Germany the fat years——"

"Don't struggle with that analogy, Franz," Lisa laughed. "I'm sure it's in doubtful taste to mention the Egyptian emperor's Jewish overseer."

"Lisa, you mustn't joke about such matters."

"I'm sorry, Franz. I forget. One forgets in the theater. But the people joke. The one about the Aryan as tall as Goebbels, as manly as——"

"Lisa, be quiet."

"I'm sorry. But they do joke. Perhaps they won't, after a while. Don't you know that, Franz? Are you too high up to hear the jokes? You are high up in their councils, aren't you, Franz?"

"Please, Lisa. I do what I can. I serve my country as best I can."

Lisa looked at him without smiling. "Very high up?" she asked.

"You look at me as though you hate me, Lisa. I didn't hate you when you came home from America. When you chose, then, as I choose now, the better part."

"I'm sorry, Franz." She spoke gently and put her hand on his. "I mean to try. But sometimes it's hard. There is much that I don't understand. Perhaps if I could go away for a little while."

"That might be best if it can be managed."

"If what can be managed, Countess?" Herr Kraussmann asked. He was standing beside them.

"To arrange a little rest for my wife when *Romeo and Juliet* closes."

"But of course, we must arrange what the Countess wishes. After her play closes the Countess should rest. Not too long. Our German theater needs her. But a little rest. Perhaps at her grandmother's. Frau Blessing is no longer young. Naturally the Countess wishes to visit her. She feels a natural anxiety for one so advanced in years. I can understand that. Now we must join the General Minister-President. Soon it will be our privilege to welcome the Fuehrer and dine in his company."

After the dinner Franz took Lisa home. "I must leave you, dear. I have an appointment with the Minister of Propaganda."

"At this hour?"

"It's the question of the new flags which we wish to present to the foreign press."

"Ah, yes. The new flags. The crooked cross irrevocably the symbol of Germany."

"Lisa. You don't try to understand. Did you try tonight? At dinner you saw the gentle, the intimate side of the Fuehrer."

"I thought he spoke charmingly."

"You see, Lisa. Even you must admit," Franz said eagerly, "when he spoke so affectionately, so simply of General Goering, his old comrade in arms——"

"I remembered that Captain Roehm was also his dear comrade in arms."

"Hush, Lisa. It isn't safe to talk so. From some things, neither I nor your dead father can protect you."

"Poor Franz. I make it hard for you. I will try."

He stood beside her at the door. She touched his anxious face. "Don't worry, darling. I'll try to do better. Perhaps I'm wrong."

"You are, Lisa. And you mustn't speak of your wrong thoughts. It makes me afraid for you."

Only for me? Or are you still afraid? Is the sword of your life still unsafe in your grasp that seems so strong? she asked. But she did not ask aloud.

Lisa slipped off her coat and stood in the hall of the apartment. She could hear Matilde moving in the kitchen. The maid was waiting to be called. She must be longing to hear about the wedding. Lisa did not call. She stood before the mirror. Her face was white and tired below the golden crown of her hair. She wondered if every woman searched her mirror as anxiously for the mark of the years as an actress must. That was nonsense. The footlights would be kind for many years. She lifted her hands to her head. Her braids were heavy.

The handle of the front door moved. There was a sound from outside as though a child were moving its hand lightly against the door. She opened the door. A man entered. His hat was pulled down over his face. He closed the door and leaned against it. She did not recognize him.

"Lisa, will you help me?" he asked in a barely audible whisper. He lifted his face and shaded his eyes with a gloved hand against the bright light of the chandelier. She stared at him. She did not want to recognize him. His lips were sunken, and his cheeks. He wasn't tall. He was bent over. He was a thin, stooped old man.

"Don't you know me, Lisa?" he mumbled. "It's I, Raimund Hoehlmann."

She stared at him. This couldn't be Raimund. There was not time enough in a year to do this. Not days enough. Not pain enough. This was a crippled, toothless old man who stood muttering of Raimund Hoehlmann. Unwillingly she recognized him. Unwillingly she stretched out her hand. His hand in its glove shrank from her touch. Horror left no room for pity. She remembered Raimund, tall and strong. She could see him gesturing, managing in every scene to display his white hands, grinning to show off his gleaming teeth. There had not been enough time for such a change. There were no men with hands evil enough to work such a change in a meager year of time.

He crouched against the corner of the wall. Unheeded tears, like the tears of an untidy old man, ran down his unshaven cheeks. His tongue licked away the salt drops that came near his mouth. He trembled. He held his arms against his sides, his bent shoulders were hunched about his neck. He tried to keep still but his body trembled.

"You must be cold, Raimund. Come in by the fire and Matilde will get you something to eat."

Cold, illness, hunger—those are natural evils. Let it be one of those. Let him be cold. Let him be ill.

With his back to the wall, Raimund dragged himself toward the door. "I thought you were alone. I saw Franz leave. I forgot the maid. I forget so much of before."

He reached behind him to open the door.

"You mustn't go. You are safe here. Don't be afraid of Matilde. She has been with me since I was married. She is faithful and kind."

Matilde had heard their quiet voices. She came into the hall. "Did Madam the Countess call?"

"Here is an old friend of mine, Matilde. Bring some brandy to the library. And then prepare food."

Raimund moved a chair against the wall near the fire. He gulped his brandy and watched the door into the hall. Lisa moved towards the door to close it.

"Don't, Lisa. Leave it open. When doors are closed, they can be opened. At least like this, you can see. They cannot suddenly open."

"You are safe here, Raimund. When you have eaten, we can plan. Let me take your things."

"No. I keep my gloves. It is not good to look at my hands. I don't like to see them. And my hat. I would see my head reflected in your eyes."

"You are safe now. You have got away."

"Yes. I was helped. I was to have been moved to another—to another . . . It was made easy. Someone helped. Someone arranged that the door be left unlocked, that I be left alone in the car. I think it was——" He made a sound that was meant to be a laugh. A small hissing sound. The spit dribbled over his chin. "I don't tell—even you. I knew Emmi well once. But I don't tell. So much I have been asked to tell. When there was nothing. There's nothing. I have nothing, I tell you." His hands jerked up to cover his face. Then he turned and looked sharply at the wall behind him. He pushed his chair tight against the wall. He crouched in the chair and stared past Lisa, at the door into the hall.

"I will get you away," Lisa promised. Her voice sounded confident as her mind groped uncertainly for ways. "As soon as you have eaten I will get my car and drive you to Granny's. She will hide you. And we'll investigate, we'll find out who———"

"You can't go to them. You must get me away."

"But if you've done nothing wrong, Raimund———"

"Wrong, right—right, wrong. Words. A confusion of words.

> *I have done no harm. But I remember now*
> *I am in this earthly world; when to do harm*
> *Is often laudable . . ."*

The words came misshapen from his slack lips. He stared past Lisa. She wondered if his clouded eyes saw the stage and the shining arc of the footlights.

> *". . . to do good, sometime*
> *Accounted dangerous folly: why then, alas,*
> *Do I put up that womanly defence,*
> *To say I have done no harm?*

"Womanly defense! It was Emmi who said that, not I. I stood in the wings and listened. And now I say her part, not mine. All the parts are mixed. I can't remember. They wanted me to remember so much that wasn't. And now I can't remember what was."

He rubbed his gloved hands lightly together. The room was silent around the small sounds: the crackling of a spark, the rubbing of the dry leather, the ticking of the Dresden clock.

Lisa looked up at the round white dial. "I'll go and help Matilde. She's awfully slow."

"You said you could trust her. I didn't trust her. I watched the door so she couldn't go for them."

Lisa remembered the back door. But not Matilde. Others change. The world changes, but not us. We aren't the world. Not us. Not Matilde.

Lisa listened for the clink of dishes and Matilde's step. Everything was silent except the clock and the fire and the creaking of Raimund's chair as he pushed it against the wall.

Then, beyond the kitchen, were sounds, the quick, heavy feet. They had come with Matilde through the back door.

Matilde pointed at Raimund. "There he is. Creeping in the night. I would not help him. I am not a fine lady, but I would not help him." She spat on the flowered carpet.

Lisa stared at her. That was their weapon. The black hate, unleashed. In the hearts of the dispossessed as in the hearts of the powerful. The hidden hate of fear and greed.

Lisa stood before Raimund. She stretched out her arms and held her head high. Even now she could find only the dramatic gesture. But perhaps the authority of the theater would help her. The appearance of power might stop the men whom Matilde had brought. They could not be very high in the pyramid of authority which was the Third Reich.

"How dare you break in here? Do you know who I am?" she demanded.

"Heil Hitler." The leader of the Storm Troopers raised his arm stiffly. "We regret that we must disturb the gracious Countess."

"I am Lisa Blessing, the daughter of Siegfried Blessing."

"We regret, gracious lady, but we must act on information received. Inadvertently, I am sure, you are sheltering an enemy of the Reich." He had the smooth voice and the slight build of a clerk, perhaps of a former civil servant. What they called a March violet, Lisa supposed. But he was swollen with the dignity of boots and uniform. He was strong with the strength of the two men who stood behind him.

"Here is no enemy," Lisa said. "This man is a former servant of my grandmother, Frau Wilhelm Blessing. He has been ill. My maid did not recognize him, or perhaps there was jealousy. You know how it is among servants." She was trying to make a bond between her and the Storm Trooper. To raise him above Matilde, to turn him to contempt for her.

Almost she succeeded. "The daughter of Siegfried Blessing. If we have made a mistake, gracious lady," he said uneasily, "we regret——"

"Better take a look at the fellow," interrupted one of the troopers. "Making a mistake the other way is worse. Remember what happened to Heinrich."

"If the gracious lady permits." The leader pushed Lisa to one side. He looked at Raimund. "Illness! I know that sort of illness." He laughed. "Let me see your hands, my man. Take off his gloves."

The troopers obeyed. Raimund whimpered. It was a thin whimper, long drawn out on one wavering note. The small sound grew loud in Lisa's ears. The white face of the clock grew as large as the red faces of the troopers. They moved about her in a slow circle. And Raimund's head, hatless, and his hands without the gloves. She stood still as the circle moved around her to the sound of the shrill whimper, loud now because it was no longer outside but crying in her brain. The circle moved faster and tilted. The flowered carpet rose towards her as the circle tilted. Her eyes closed against the faces and the sound was still.

When Lisa opened her eyes, she was lying on the floor. Matilde had put a pillow under her head and was standing beside her with a glass of water.

Lisa sat up. The room swung slowly about her. Then gradually it stood still. She looked at Matilde, who had become once more the correct maidservant.

"If Madam the Countess will permit . . ." Matilde helped her to rise. "Better Madam goes to bed."

"No. I will wait for the Count. You may go now, Matilde. I will speak to you in the morning."

"There is nothing to speak about. I did only my duty." Matilde replaced the cushion on the sofa. She put the glass of water on a table beside Lisa. "If there is nothing else . . ."

Lisa looked at her. The mask was back in place. This was the pleasant face she knew. Or was the other, the spite and hatred, the mask? Lisa did not know. That was the horror. That you did not know. Not with Matilde. Not with anyone. All the faces were masks.

Lisa waited for Franz. Only the slow movement of the hands across the white face of the clock marked the passage of time. How stupid to think that time is absolute, that it can be measured.

She heard the click of the key in the lock. She did not speak until Franz stood beside her.

"Lisa. You look as though you had seen a ghost."

"And so I did. I saw Raimund Hoehlmann. I saw him but I did not recognize him. You said he was safe. You said he had gone away."

"Raimund Hoehlmann is here! How did he get here? Lisa, you were mad to let him——"

"So you knew. Of course you knew. I have been mad indeed."

"Where is he? This is dangerous."

"He's gone. They've taken him. So you knew."

"Darling, I could do nothing. There was no use to tell you, to hurt you." He put his hand on her shoulder. She lowered her shoulder from his touch.

"And you won't help now?" She searched his face. His dark eyes were troubled. It was useless to search in any of the masks for the eyes of mercy.

"Don't look like that, Lisa. It is I. Franz. You love me."

"Yes, I love you." She was astonished to know her words were true. "Love is not love which alters . . ." So this was the edge of doom. This was doom—to be alone. To know that you had always been alone, that there had not been two together, two against the world as you had believed.

"Lisa, believe me. We cannot help Raimund. We can only endanger ourselves. His coming here does not look well. Fortunately Kraussmann, of the secret police, is friendly. How did they know Raimund was here?"

"Matilde. Matilde brought them. Did you know Matilde hated us? I'll get someone in her place. Matilde and I were friends."

"You can't dismiss her. It would make matters worse."

"She can't stay, Franz. I can't have her near me, touching me. I can't bear it."

"You will have to bear it. I'm sorry, Lisa."

"We are all sorry. We are all sorry, pitiful creatures. It doesn't matter. As well Matilde as another."

"Lisa, I'm sorry." He stretched out his hands to her. "These are difficult times. But you will see. Out of these present evils, good will come."

" 'And the corrupt tree shall bring forth good fruit——' "

"You won't try to understand. But you must. You must see as I see."

His words didn't matter. His hands were trembling as they reached towards her. Men made too much of words. She took his hands in hers. "I know, Franz. My poor Franz."

He knelt beside her. She cradled his head against her. "It's all right, Franz. It's not your fault. It's not your fault about Raimund—about anything. You, too, are caught in the chains."

"No, Lisa."

She pressed his head against her to silence his muffled voice. He was caught in the chains he had helped to forge. But he didn't know. He still believed the chains were a coat of mail, the safety for which she had watched him seeking during all their years together. His fear had been between them. Fear divided more sharply than a sword. She had known that. But she had hoped. Now she ceased to hope. She smoothed his dark hair. Without hope and without faith, there is still love. How strange, she thought, it's true. Love is the greatest of these. It does not alter.

The next morning Lisa determined to see Herr Kraussmann. He was connected with the secret police. He was friendly. He had offered to help her. "Not that there is likely to be anything that I can ever do for Lisa Blessing." She remembered the address.

Kraussmann stood beside his desk when Lisa entered.

"So, Countess, I did not expect so soon to have the pleasure."

His voice was friendly. Except for his bright eyes, his face was ordinary. She looked away from him, at his desk. It was the desk of any businessman. There were family photographs in a leather frame. There was an elaborate bronze inkwell and a tray of unused pens and sharpened pencils. The cigarette box and the ash tray matched the inkwell. There was a neat pile of papers on the wide spotless blotter. There was a small silver vase of daffodils to show that either Herr Kraussmann or his efficient secretary was fond of flowers. He was an ordinary man, a civil servant such as you would find in any government office. It should not be hard to speak. But the words came haltingly from her dry throat.

"You haven't heard about last night?"

"Was there something I should have heard? If the Countess will be so good as to seat herself, we can talk."

Lisa sat down. She thought carefully of what she must say. All the way here she had planned the words that would save Raimund. Once again the morning light had revealed a reasonable world. All around her she had seen the familiar, friendly, busy city. The traffic policemen had reminded her that Berlin was still a city of law and order. And now she was sitting in an ordinary sunlit office, not in the dark chamber of an inquisitor. The secret police was an arm of the law. The laws had changed but not the law. It still worked according to the rules. Justice could not be a random thing. It must be reasonable. You had only to present your case clearly. She licked her lips and tried to think of the exact reasonable words that would save Raimund.

"It is difficult, is it not, Countess?" Herr Kraussmann asked.

"I don't quite know how to begin."

"Let me begin then, at the beginning. I will admit to you that I have some knowledge of the matter in hand." He touched the papers on his desk.

"In the case of the Jew, Raimund Hoehlmann—you know that he is a Jew, Countess?"

"I had heard it rumored, but——"

"It's true. He concealed it as, of course, they do when they can. He was also guilty of concealing from the state properties to which he had no right. For this he was punished."

"Have you seen him, Herr Kraussmann?"

"I have seen others. Hoehlmann was stubborn. We do not tolerate stubbornness."

"He has suffered enough. Herr Kraussmann, I beg of you. You said if there was ever anything——"

"One says these things, Countess. But the case of Hoehlmann is out of my hands."

"His hands, Herr Kraussmann. Just for a moment I saw—I saw his hands."

"Do not distress yourself—or perhaps you should, Countess. Perhaps it's as well that every German, even you, Lisa Blessing, should see a little of what we can do."

"If my name means anything to the party, let me use it to help Raimund."

"The name of Blessing means a great deal, Countess, but it is we who use it." He turned over the pages. "Now about the case of the criminal Hoehlmann. As I said, it is out of my hands. It would have been interesting to know how his escape was managed. We should have learned. With patience and ingenuity one can learn anything from a man. But, unfortunately, Hoehlmann hanged himself in his cell last night. Now we shall never know the details of his escape. Too bad. I regret that he was allowed to die. But there are those more highly placed than I . . ." He smiled and placed the papers in a folder.

Lisa watched him. The folder was only a small part of the paraphernalia of law and order. Outside were other neat offices. When she went out she would hear the typewriters clicking merrily. Murder and torture on a business basis. Savagery is not finally unbearable until it wears the mask of civilization, until it smiles behind the blind face of justice. The ultimate nightmare does not peer from the shadows, it smiles at you in daylight.

"Poor Raimund," Lisa said. Now for him the horror was done and she could weep for the big man so ingenuously broken. "He has found the only sanctuary that is left in the Third Reich."

"Be careful, Countess." Kraussmann's thin lips still smiled. "You may not be afraid for yourself but it is not always the guilty individual alone who suffers. We do not believe in individualism. There is the Count. There is your beloved grandmother."

"You wouldn't dare."

"Do you say that when you know all we have dared? Don't be foolish, Countess. After your play closes, go to Waldenberg to Frau Wilhelm Blessing. She will give you good counsel."

"She would not wish me to be a coward."

"And for whom are you brave, Countess? Hoehlmann is dead. Come, go back to the theater, to the land of make-believe which you understand. Leave Germany to us who understand her. I will forget your misguided sympathy for Hoehlmann. Much can be forgiven to the daughter of Siegfried Blessing. But not too much, Countess, not too much."

He held open the door for her and saluted. "Heil Hitler."

"Heil Hitler," she answered mechanically and walked away through the busy outer offices.

At the street door she passed a young Catholic priest. His lips were moving silently. She wondered if he, too, were rehearsing useless words, if he, too, thought that where there is duly constituted authority there must be justice. It is hard to recognize anarchy under the semblance of law and order.

When Lisa had gone, Herr Kraussmann rang for his secretary. "Send for Count Erlencamp. I wish to see him immediately. He's either at the *Morgenpresse* or at the Ministry of Propaganda."

While he waited, Herr Kraussmann straightened the photographs on his desk. With his handkerchief he wiped a speck of dust from the glass-covered face of a flower-crowned little girl. He put the Hoehlmann folder to one side. He unlocked a drawer of the desk and took out another folder. He opened it and studied the papers that it contained.

His secretary announced Count Erlencamp.

"You wished to see me, Herr Kraussmann?"

"Yes. Sit down, my dear Count, sit down. It's about the Countess. You know of her interference in the matter of Raimund Hoehlmann."

"He came to her for help. She was at fault in not turning him away immediately."

"Yes. I know. I know how his escape was arranged. It had nothing to do with the Countess. But the way in which the Countess spoke—she does not see things as she should. It isn't healthy to have unorthodox views."

"She is very tired, Herr Kraussmann. She needs a rest. Perhaps, after all, she should go to America."

"Leaving the grandmother here, of course." Kraussmann rubbed his chin and looked at the papers before him. "Yes, that might do. You could be useful to us in America. We have for some time considered sending you there. Americans like you. You would have to see to it that the Countess was also useful in America."

"It would be easier there than here."

"Yes, even if she is thought to be a little against us, that is not bad. That will help you in tasks that may be assigned. I suggest that you go immediately to see Frau Blessing. The Countess does not know about her grandmother?"

"No, Herr Kraussmann."

"The old woman had better know that we know. Don't tell her that her old friend betrayed her so he may continue to keep an eye on her fortune. It's a wretched business. That old fool, Wilhelm Blessing, tricking us into making a hero of his mongrel son." Kraussmann frowned.

"It would not be good for the party that the truth about Lisa's father should be known. Otherwise, Herr Kraussmann——"

"Otherwise, my dear Count, you would surrender her."

"I did not say that, Herr Kraussmann."

"Keep your hands off my desk. You didn't say it but I know. As things are, you like the Jew money and the false glory. And the Countess is beautiful. One would never know by looking at her."

"If the Countess knew, Herr Kraussmann, she could make it awkward for us all and she would not be afraid."

"Fortunately you are afraid and you will see that she does not know.

Take her to America and see if you can make her more useful there than she is inclined to be here. That is all. I will help you to make the necessary arrangement. Good day, Count. Heil Hitler." Herr Kraussmann stood up.

"Heil Hitler."

Herr Kraussmann closed the door behind Franz. He returned to his desk. He took a fountain pen from his pocket and wrote briefly on the papers. He returned them to the folder and locked the folder in the drawer of his desk.

XIII

FRAU BLESSING received Franz in her drawing room. She sat on the satin-upholstered gilt sofa below the tall portrait of the young Frau Blessing.

"Had I known you were coming, Franz, I should gladly have delayed dinner. At my age one dines too often alone to mind waiting a little for company. Shall I send for something? Coffee? Brandy?"

"No. Nothing. I have come to tell you that—— Yes, a little brandy, if I may."

Frau Blessing pressed the enameled and jeweled bell. "Poor Franz. It is something you wish to put off. Haven't you yet learned not to be afraid of me?"

"It's not that. After the servant has gone."

"Some brandy, Karl, please." Frau Blessing smiled. "If it's money again, Franz, I don't mind. Lisa would want me to give it to you and she would want me not to tell her. But I thought that, since the new regime, things were well with you."

"Yes, they are. If you want me to, I can get you all the money I owe you."

"You are angry, Franz. That makes me think you are steeling yourself to hurt me. It's not Lisa? Lisa is all right?"

"Yes, Lisa is all right. No fault of hers. She has been foolish."

"Politically foolish? No, wait. Here comes Karl."

Franz sipped brandy from the big thin glass.

Frau Blessing cupped her glass in her hands. "My father gave me these glasses. In those days most people had tiny cut-glass ones. The glass was thick and cold between the brandy and one's hand."

"That's it. Your father."

"My father, Franz?"

"And your mother, too, I suppose. I should have guessed it, looking at that raven-haired beauty."

"My portrait? What should you have guessed? Suppose you speak plainly, Franz."

"Certainly. If you want me to. It is known that you are a—that you are not Aryan."

"Well, Franz." Frau Blessing laughed. "Is that so awful? And in view of the '*Heldenlied*,' isn't it rather funny? My poor Wilhelm never thought of that. He had the knack of not thinking of things that displeased him."

"It's not funny. They know in Berlin."

"How did they ever find out? Someone in business who was told long ago. And saved the secret for the useful moment. Who was it? No, of course you can't tell me. How odd that it should be important again."

"It has never been unimportant or you would not have concealed it."

"It was not quite like that."

"I will listen to your explanation."

Frau Blessing held her glass of brandy against the light. "And I think, Franz, that I will not explain. Not to you, at least. Lisa is different."

"You can't tell Lisa. She mustn't know. Things are bad enough. She almost got into trouble trying to help the Jew, Raimund Hoehlmann. He escaped and came to Lisa. Luckily Matilde called the Storm Troopers and no irreparable harm was done. I have seen Kraussmann. I have permission to take Lisa to America. She'll be safer there. But they won't let you go."

"I see." Frau Blessing turned the glass in her hands. "And if Lisa knew, she wouldn't leave me. I won't tell her. I will persuade her to go. I'm rather old to be a hostage but as I'm all they have, I'll have to do."

"She will want you to go. Even without knowing, she will not want to leave you in Germany. Lisa has grown afraid of Germany. How can we persuade her?"

"*We* cannot persuade her. *I* can. Don't come back here with Lisa. You will betray your feelings. Lisa is no fool. She will see that something is wrong. Leave it to me. We will part tonight. But you will sleep here. Your room has been made ready. And nothing must seem strange to the servants. You can leave in the morning. And you can easily make an excuse not to return with Lisa next week."

"I have not liked telling you this, Frau Blessing."

"Don't look so embarrassed. You told me nothing I did not know."

"I had always felt respect. Now I——"

"Don't bother about your feelings for me, Franz. They are of no importance. Keep Lisa safe. That's all that matters."

"You can trust her to me, Frau Blessing."

"I have to trust her to you. And, Franz, remember, only as long as Lisa is safe are you safe."

"I don't know what you mean."

"Think about it and you will. Listen to your fear, not to your false pride. Now good night. I shall remain here. And I prefer to be alone."

Frau Blessing rose to dismiss Franz. She watched him walk across the room and through the tall door. She turned and looked up at her portrait. The young Frau Blessing. The beautiful young Elisabeth Blessing.

She remembered the young Elisabeth Hanauer. The eighteen American years that had seemed long were now a brief time in the span of her remembrance. She looked at the proud young woman. A beautiful young Jewess. She hadn't thought of herself as that. Nor as a beautiful young American. She had been Elisabeth. Elisabeth, not a Jewess, not an American girl, not a German wife, but herself, Elisabeth. Even now, when to all the world she was Frau Blessing, when no one was left to call her Elisabeth, she was still in her mind Elisabeth.

She remembered her father. He was a proud man. But proud only of what he had made himself. He was proud of being an American because America was in the making and he was part of that making. He was not proud of being a Jew. He was indifferent to it. He had given his daughter no religious training. "You are the only human being I love, Elisabeth. How can I tell you a fairy tale and laugh at you for believing it?"

She remembered his liking for cats. There was always an elegant pale Angora or Persian creature picking its way aloofly through the hotel apartments in which Dan Hanauer and his daughter lived. "They're pretty creatures with a proper self-respect. No superstitious doglike nonsense about believing in man. If man can like cats, maybe God can like atheists."

Elizabeth Hanauer hadn't needed a religion. There were no injustices for a distant heavenly Father to right, no hopes for Him to promise. Dan Hanauer ruled her world with justice and kindness. When she was left with a governess or at school, it was to letter writing she turned, not to prayers. "My father won't let you. My father will say I may." Unlike less obedient gods, he never disappointed her.

"If your mother had lived," Dan Hanauer had said, "it would have been different. She would have taught you to pray, to light the Sabbath candles, to prepare all the gentle, homely beauty of the Sabbath."

"I don't need to pray. I have you, Father."

"Yes. You have me. And later you will have yourself. You are like me. To have yourself will be enough."

Frau Blessing sighed and looked at her portrait. It had been painted the year of her marriage. Perhaps Franz was right. Perhaps Wilhelm should have seen Queen Esther's ancient beauty. But Wilhelm had seen, at first, one of the imperious young American heiresses who were becoming the European fashion, the brides of English nobles and German princelings. And then, because Wilhelm had loved her, he had seen only Elisabeth.

She remembered the day her father had told him that they were Jews. "It's never been important to me but you ought to know all about us. We're German Jews. At least so my parents were born. But I've grown up an American freethinker."

Wilhelm had minded. But he had loved Elisabeth more than he had minded. "I see, Mr. Hanauer. That could be of importance here. It would perhaps be wiser if it were not known. Is it generally known in America?"

"Upon my word, I don't know," Dan Hanauer had laughed, "and I've cared less. But from now on, it shall be a secret. You young people must please yourselves. You don't owe anything to the past. Forget the patriarchal forebears, Wilhelm, if they don't suit you."

And Wilhelm had forgotten. He had a gift for forgetting anything that did not fit his pattern of life.

Frau Blessing smiled. She saw not the white-bearded poet whom Germany honored. She saw the young Wilhelm. He was young and fair and slender. He had kept a small boy's burning ambition to be a great man. Fortunately he had had enough talent and perseverance to become *"der Dichter."* Frau Blessing smiled across time and the intervening memories. She smiled at the young Wilhelm. He would have admired his handiwork; he would have liked to know he was to become, as he stubbornly intended, the great Wilhelm Blessing.

She was the only one who remembered the young Wilhelm. Lisa remembered only *"der Dichter"* and hated him for the *"Heldenlied."* Lisa did not understand that the song was Wilhelm's last despairing attempt to set his world right, to make a glory of the unbearable grief, to change to immortality the death of his only son.

And for Lisa's own sake her grandmother must also be misunderstood. If Lisa found out, she would not understand. Frau Blessing wondered if she could leave a letter. That was impossible. A childish idea. It could be dangerous to Lisa. She smiled, pityingly, at her desire to be known, the lonely human desire. To Lisa, she was the grandmother. She was loved by Lisa but she was seen only through a few of her years, not in the roundness of time. So it had been with them all. She had been a girl to some, an old lady to others. A daughter, a wife, a mother. An American to Germans and, for long, a German to Americans. Only to herself had she ever been, would she ever be, Elisabeth.

Frau Blessing turned out the lights and walked slowly upstairs. She had a few days in which to plan her words to Lisa, the words that would set Lisa free.

Lisa came to Waldenberg on the following Saturday night. On Sunday morning she sat with her grandmother beneath the pines and listened to the church bells.

"I might have gone if I weren't so tired. A Protestant church is, at least, less embarrassing to look at than a Catholic one. One does not face the image of the crucified Jew."

"Do you care so much about Jews?" Frau Blessing asked.

"No, I care about Germans. Germans changing. Our whole people growing dark in the shadow of the crooked cross. The cross that crucifies again, and this time a thousandfold. It is the Germans who are being destroyed, not the Jews. Pain and death aren't destruction. But to wield them with pleasure, to live willingly in shadow . . ."

"Lisa, you have had a bad time. You have seen something."

"I have seen what I knew was there. I knew when Sophie left. I knew, but I tried not to know. I tried to stay in the theater as you told me. Our fine, living German theater. Trivialities or Shakespeare. You take your choice. Fortunately, Emil Schwarz takes Shakespeare."

"Be grateful that the government has not turned Shakespeare out of Germany. He has been here long enough to belong to us."

"I know and I have wrapped myself in the beautiful words. I have loved and died in beauty with Juliet. Raimund Hoehlmann did not die beautifully. He crept along a slow degrading path of pain."

"Franz told me that you——"

"That I had endangered myself? I have let him keep me blind. But not any more. I let Sophie go. I wept for Dr. Meyer. Poor Dr. Meyer. I wept for him. And I wondered about young Kurt Reisner. He disappeared after Mass one Sunday. His parents hid their fear. They have a daughter, too. Our cheerful world closed over Kurt's disappearance. And I wondered and then forgot. I have seen only stage settings and not just in the theater."

"Lisa, why don't you go to America? Franz says it can be arranged. Why stay here and watch what you are powerless to change?"

"Would you come, Granny?"

"My dear, if you don't mind, I am better here. I should see nothing I remembered of America. And here I am at home. I have my little accustomed way of life. I like the small familiar days as I live them here. Routine is important at my age."

"I don't want to leave you alone in this Germany that has become a strange land."

"All lands are strange, Lisa, when one grows old. And one is alone. I have outlived too much of what I have loved. It is my pleasure that you shall outlive me."

"Granny, don't."

"Sorry, my dear." Frau Blessing laughed. "I was rather dramatizing the obvious. This is my small stage, you know. But I don't want to go to America. I should hate to uproot myself. I'd like you to go. I'd like my little Lisa to live in America, the land of my youth. The land of liberty. I didn't know it then. Liberty seems an ordinary thing when one is young. The young always think they are free. But you, Lisa, can still be free."

"I thought of a visit, not of living there. No, that's not true. I thought of escape. But I can't live there. I no longer love Germany. At least, I no longer wish to love Germany, but I can't love another land."

"Yes, you can, my dear. It isn't Germany you love, it's your youth you love, it's the frame of your life. You love these trees and the way the sun will set beyond them. And, just as much, you love my little sitting room, although, in your eyes, it should be hideously out of fashion. You love the white birches of Whitsuntide and the increasing candles of Advent, and the foolish-faced wax doll who has had always the place of honor on the tree. You love me and Franz and Wilhelm, whom you think you hate, and Sophie, and Kurt Reisner's sister."

"There is nothing for me in America."

"I think there is, Lisa. I know there is nothing for you here except the memories that hide the face of Germany. The face that you never would see."

"You don't like Germany, Granny. Why do you want to stay in a country you hate? We can find you pines and a hilltop in America."

"Whether I like or dislike Germany, I am tied to it. This is where I have lived my life. Wilhelm was young here with me. And Siegfried was a little boy. A little German boy. All my memories of them are tied to this country. If I left it, I should leave them. I should leave all the years I have made. It doesn't matter whether or not I like Germany."

"But, Granny, if things get worse."

"I have seen one war, Lisa."

"There won't be another war. There can't. But if you think so, how can I leave you?"

"I promise you, Lisa, that if there is war or any other real danger, I will try to arrange to come."

"Try, Granny?" Lisa asked anxiously.

"That is a silly word for me to use, isn't it? As though I could have any difficulty. I have many friends. It hardly seems likely that the government would refuse anything to the mother of Siegfried Blessing."

"Nothing for yourself, certainly. Well, since I have your promise, perhaps I shall go." Lisa looked up at the sky. She shaded her eyes against the noonday sun. "I don't mean perhaps. I mean to go."

"Keep to that intention." Frau Blessing laid her hand on Lisa's head. "Follow the sun, my dear. It lights your way to freedom."

Lisa put her head on her grandmother's knee. "Those are just words. You can't live with fine words. You can't love words." Her voice broke with ugly, hard sobs. "I love you. I love this place where I was born. They can't take it from me."

"They have taken it, Lisa. And you must go."

XIV

At the end of July Lisa and Franz reached America.

Lisa stood beside Franz on the deck of the *Europa*. She looked at the harbor of New York. The buildings seemed higher and more numerous. This city was a taller, brighter, more densely armored outpost to a strange land than Lisa had remembered. Around her on the deck the stewards spoke German. They were her people. The English-speaking passengers were strangers. Lisa touched the shining brass fitting of the rail, scrubbed bright by German hands. How can I leave? How can I put my life into the hands of strangers even if the hands are kind?

Their room steward came up to Franz. Franz had warned her to be careful in speaking before him.

"Bruno is the party chief on board."

"Higher than the Captain?" Lisa had asked.

"The party discipline controls all. Thus is old and new welded into one hierarchy of strength. The Captain understands. He is an intelligent man."

"But I needn't try to understand since I am leaving all that behind."

"But, Lisa, you will——"

"I will be careful not to speak before the room steward."

Now, on deck, Lisa looked at Bruno, the enemy. He was an earnest, rosy-cheeked young man. He did not look like an enemy. He looks like Sophie Friedrich, Lisa thought. He might be her brother, he might be mine. That is it, the German enemy is still my brother. How can I find my brother, my father, my life among strangers? Even though they are kind, the Americans, even though they are free, they are foreigners.

> *I had long since a lovely Fatherland.*
> *The oaks would gleam*
> *And touch the skies . . .*

She remembered her grandmother's words: "It's your youth you love, Lisa." The birches shining white in the dark halls at Whitsuntide. The Advent candles in the December night. Only my youth. But I am my youth.

Lisa looked at Franz. He had turned to speak to the American beside him. All around Lisa were the foreign voices, the foreign faces. Only Franz was not a stranger. But he is a stranger, Lisa thought. The stranger, perhaps the enemy. Her fingers trembled against the smooth brass. They touched his arm. He smiled at her. She looked at him gravely. All the faces are masks. But this is the mask I love. The mind and the will are not as strong as the heart. Lisa looked at the stone-covered steel towers of the foreign city. "Westward, . . . the land is bright." Perhaps under this western sun Franz and I together—not alone, dear God. Surely You see that I cannot do it alone. Those others, my great-great-grandparents and all the others before and since, they came together. Surely You see, dear God, it is too hard to do alone. Lisa stopped herself. Remembering had taken her back a long way, to the birch trees of spring, to the Advent candles of winter, back to the days when she had reasoned gently with the dear God. Not my father. You see, he is not really a soldier, only the professor pretending.

The *Europa* was swinging into the pier from the river. On the dock the people were small, their voices subdued by distance. They are not strangers. They are people like Granny, like my father. Franz and I are the strangers, but we need not be. We need not be strangers in this land of adoption whose people have come from all the foreign shores, have come hoping, fearing, praying. But let it be Franz and me. Let it be together, dear God, not alone.

Lisa felt alone at first. It was Franz who found a world into which he fitted.

He found a house on Long Island. "It's lovely and cool, Lisa, with a breeze from the Sound. And near enough for you to commute."

In August *The Mirror* went into rehearsal. Lisa's days were spent in New York.

The theater was her familiar world. It was natural she should be at home in it. But with Franz and his acquaintances Lisa was a stranger. Franz was at ease with the Americans whom he had selected to be their friends. On Long Island Lisa was the stranger. Perhaps later she and Franz would find friends together. Perhaps after all they were to be together.

"You seem more at home than I, Franz," she said to him. "But perhaps when the play settles down to its New York run—please God, it's a long run. We are spending a good deal——"

"I have money, Lisa. You were too preoccupied to notice in the last year in Germany."

"But I thought you were not supposed to bring money out of Germany."

"There are ways. Particularly for one who has been as useful to the Fatherland as I."

"But you like America, Franz."

"I like this, if this be America. To me it seems like all the easy places of the world. Denationalized like the Lido, which is no more Italian than Deauville is French."

"And the Adlon in Berlin and the Stephanie in Baden-Baden."

"But in Germany one feels always the heartbeat of the people, the national spirit."

"You haven't tried to find it here, Franz."

"Perhaps we shall find it together, my dear. Meantime, if this comfortable little colony be America, I like it very much."

"Together, Franz. If we could be together again, not afraid, not doubting."

"I have never doubted you, Lisa. I have loved you with all my strength." His dark eyes were anxious. Lisa followed the curve of his brow with her hand.

"I know, Franz. No one can give more than all."

This comfortable corner of America was not what Lisa had come to find. But perhaps that other America was only her grandmother's dream of youth. Perhaps it had existed before that only in the words of poets no longer read and in the deeds of brave men no longer living. Perhaps that America was the flower of a time that had passed away here as everywhere on the earth. The good time had been destroyed with violence in Germany. Perhaps here it was dying, too, only more quietly, more respectably.

"Franz, do you remember Mary Forrest? I think if we could see more people like her——"

"She's a nice woman, but a little heavily virtuous."

"That isn't fair. At least she is not like those people whom we see. She wants to belong to her country and she does."

"You can find in Germany many plain women who devote themselves to good works. Frau Counselor Rieber, the Princess Rodenstein . . ."

"It's not just her day nurseries, but she interests herself in politics."

"I hear she's a Red."

"Oh, Franz, that's just an elastic hate word. And on Long Island it means you voted for Roosevelt."

"If you want to see her, Lisa darling, you can quite easily. We are invited by her to a party, Thursday of next week, to welcome home Anne Craven."

"I can't. We open in Boston the following Monday."

"I could fetch you after your rehearsal. The party's at Anton's, only a block from your theater. It would please Mary, and since you like her . . ."

On Thursday night Lisa sat in the theater and watched Gerald Michaels direct a scene in which she did not appear.

"Coke, Lisa?" Pat Lee asked.

Lisa drank the sweet liquid and smiled at the young girl who sat beside her. These are my people. They were my people in Germany.

"No—God, no, not like that." Gerald's voice rose. "Sorry. I guess we're all tired, but we've got to get this right. Take it over from Hugh's entrance."

Lisa looked at the stage. She looked at the empty seats shrouded in white. Here and there the dust covers were turned back.

This is home. Lisa remembered the German theater as it had been.

As it had been until the end. The end had been when they came for Raimund Hoehlmann.

She remembered the heavy feet that echoed in the silent theater. The silence had been fear. The fear that was everywhere in Germany. The cardboard walls could not stand against the fear.

"Okay. Let's knock off for fifteen minutes. Then we'll run through it again and take Lisa's scene with Hugh." Gerald sat down in front of Lisa. He stretched his long legs into the aisle. He rubbed his thin gray hair. "Actors, actors, actors," he muttered. "And I suppose you repeat just as angrily managers, managers, managers."

"No, I'm quite happy," Lisa said, "with managers, with actors, with writers, with directors—with everybody in the theater."

"So'm I, really. God knows no one would choose this lousy profession if he liked anything else."

"That's the point, isn't it? That one does choose it."

"I sometimes wonder why. Get me a coke, Pat, will you? God, I'm tired and I could eat. We'll all go across the street later and get something."

"I'm sorry, I can't. Franz is coming for me."

"Out with your gaudy fashionable friends again, Lisa?" Gerald asked. "You see a lot of fancy folk, don't you?"

"Franz has a lot of friends."

"You'd get more laughs sticking around with us. Of course, their food is good. And their liquor. The rich have their good points. And their inverted snobbishness is flattering."

"As though any snobbishness were straightforward or reasonable."

"Some of it's practical. Be impressed by the right people and you get asked to Palm Beach and maybe even get a sound tip on the market, though that's rarer nowadays. But what do they get from us? Something they think is glamour. It's not worth the effort they make. Does the Count know about all that?"

"You mean Franz?"

"Yeah, I mean the Count." Gerald took the paper cup from Pat Lee. "He doesn't want Broadway for you except in working hours. He doesn't know that Broadway's a short cut to Fifth Avenue."

"It isn't that," Lisa said slowly. "It's any husband and any wife. He wants to shut out the alien world to which she alone belongs."

"Okay. Sorry, Lisa." Gerald patted her shoulder. "I was just inviting you to stick around with us. And I was trying to word it so as to appeal to the Count."

"Franz."

"To me he's right out of Molnar. The Count in person." Gerald stood up. "I can't blame you for blowing yourself to him. He's a handsome guy and, for all I know, a nice one. Tell him to stick around."

"It's hard . . ." Lisa hesitated.

Gerald wasn't listening. "Okay, everybody," he called. "Act II. Round 'em up, will you, Charlie?"

Any husband and any wife, Lisa repeated to herself. There is no room for Franz in the world of the theater. There is no room for an outsider in any profession. But somewhere here Franz and I can make our world. Our private world. The world I once believed we had.

Lisa looked at Gerald's tall figure at the foot of the aisle. She watched the actors. She remembered *The Newcomers* in 1928. Then she had been at the beginning. This, at least, hasn't changed. The American theater hasn't changed. Here all the walls are safe. Here the theater thrives. The profession of choice in the land of choice.

Lisa stood up and walked backstage. This is my place. Here I am at home. This is the America that I remember. The theater is part of the America I came to find. The America that Franz has not seen.

"Five minutes, Miss Blessing."

"Okay, Charlie." Lisa listened for her cue.

After the rehearsal Lisa walked with Franz to Anton's. The elaborate glass and wrought-iron doors of the restaurant swung heavily open. The soft September air blew dustily through the opening as Lisa and Franz entered.

"It should make one sad. Summer's shabby end," Lisa said.

"Please, Lisa, let's be gay tonight. You are overtired from rehearsing, so everything seems sad."

"But that's just it. It isn't sad. It ought to be but it isn't."

Jim and Mary Forrest's party was gathered around a big corner table. Lisa sat beside her host. Beyond him was Anne Craven.

Lisa was tired. The theater had been hot. Here in the damp, cool room she sat quietly. It was like a dream. Little Kay's dream of a snow palace. No, it was not the coolness that was the dream, it was the feeling of recognition in a strange place. I have been here before.

"Drink, Lisa?" Jim Forrest asked. "You look tired."

"I am a little. And the air conditioning after the heat outside . . . I feel rather odd. As though I had been here before."

"You have been here before," Anne said. "Don't you remember? It was long, long ago. Seven years, to be exact. This was Tony's then. Not swell at all. Red-and-white checked tablecloths, but good food. And the rest followed."

"And good liquor," Jim said. "I remember that party. It was just before Mary and I were married."

Lisa stared at the enlarged and elegant Tony's, now Anton's. The dusty summer air blowing into the hall, the weight of the doors, the feeling of the steps beneath her feet, the shape of the room—these things had reminded her. They had reminded her of that other summer, of that happy end of summer, which had been a beginning.

This, too, this coming to America, should be a beginning. A return and a beginning. It was not like that. Not yet. Lisa remembered the evening when Anton's had been Tony's. She looked at Anne. She is pretty, she thought, very pretty and slim. But there was a light that had gone out. I have tried to find my way to a time, not to a country. To youth, not to America. Not just my youth but Granny's. And her parents before that. America was their youth, their hope. Was. Is all the hope and youth in the past?

Lisa watched Franz as he listened deferentially to J. C. Jones. Franz, too, recognized something. Had Franz recognized the present while she dreamed of the past? Did the world everywhere belong to the greedy? J. C. Jones, here as in Berlin, another fat man with his uniform and his steelworks.

"Dear Lisa, you look sad."

"Only tired." Lisa smiled at Woolie von Elsfeldt, who stood beside her. She turned to her host. "May I present the Baron von Elsfeldt?"

"Sit down, Woolie, right here by Lisa and me. The Baron indeed. Why, Lisa, Woolie's practically an American. His cousin, Harry Johnson, was in my class at Yale."

"I'd like not to be 'Baron,' but it's fun for Daphne. Women like the small grandeurs. Crowns on their pocket handkerchiefs. Don't they, Lisa?"

Lisa nodded. She remembered the small proud pleasure of being the Countess Erlencamp.

"Where is Daphne?" Lisa asked.

"At her bridge club. I had to work late."

"Atta boy," Jim laughed. "Gotta keep the old German Lloyd afloat."

"North German Lloyd?" J. C. asked. "Great boats. Never travel on any other. My wife and I just got back on the *Bremen*. You connected with them?"

"Not very importantly, sir."

"Say, Woolie," Jim said, "it's silly for you to be a German. Ever think of dropping the whole business?"

"Often. Unfortunately I inherit a sentimental streak from my German forebears. And from my mother, an American feeling for the underdog. Can't very well quit a country when she's down. At least a man can't. It's different for a woman." Woolie looked apologetically at Lisa. "Well, anyway, far as I'm concerned. There it is. First everyone remembered the war. And now the present regime. Hell, Jim, you know how a lot of people feel."

"I know how you feel, Woolie. And you're a right guy," Jim said emphatically. "Wish there were more Germans like you."

"There are. Only they don't get a chance to say much." Woolie turned to Lisa. His blue eyes were still anxious. "You know I don't mean you, Lisa. I gather that you intend to become an American eventually. Everyone's got to do things his own way."

"It's all right, Woolie. I'm not very clear about things myself. But I know I couldn't stay in Germany. You haven't seen. You haven't heard."

"Don't think about it, Lisa. I know from Franz that you saw some ugly things."

"You haven't seen it, Woolie. Today in Germany 'Earth and Heaven crumple. And night resumes its dark and ancient rule.' You haven't seen it."

"No. When I was over last year, I just saw the family. What's left of them. Two old aunts who live in Dresden. It's different there from Berlin or even Munich. And then I was at Garmisch with my sister's boy. He'll be on the Olympic ski team. Those youngsters are the real Germany. The real Germany that you and I and all the world will see again."

Lisa touched his hand gently. Dear Woolie. His pasty, good-natured face looked quite solemn for a moment. Poor Woolie. He believed in the Germany that was gone. Gone with Sophie and the children's festivals. Gone with the smoke and ashes of the burning books. "Dear Woolie," she said, "I'm glad you remember. I remember, too. My father. The professor in uniform."

"What a queer way to speak of Siegfried Blessing."

"I don't usually. Only you understand."

"I understand a little, Lisa. And you understand. I mean about my working for the North German Lloyd."

"Of course. It's your job."

"It's more than that. It's my link with Germany. With Germany which now it's better not to see. It keeps me from being too homesick. And for my son's sake. He's going to be a hundred per cent American, is young Rupprecht."

Lisa laughed. "That's not a very American name for a start."

Woolie flushed. "Daphne chose it. It was my father's name. And the old boy was pretty wonderful. He and his name rather took Daphne's fancy. He died right after the war, but I have his medals. And the portrait."

"I remember the General Baron von Elsfeldt," Lisa said. "Once he came with my father. Almost at the end."

Lisa remembered the sun's last rays that slanted through the long windows of the drawing room. One did not receive the General Baron von Elsfeldt upstairs. The logs had crackled all day to warm the cold room. The flames had danced on the gilt arms of the pale upholstered chairs.

"The Baron is a real General. He must not know our game," her father had whispered. "He thinks I am a soldier."

She had watched the straight back bow over her grandmother's hand. Lisa remembered the little cakes and the chocolate and the crystal decanters gleaming gold in the setting sun and the firelight. Such good things they had not had for long. Not even for Father when he came. They were offerings, the child Lisa had known, like the old times in the Bible. Granny to the General as Lisa to the dear God. What shall the Lord thy God require of thee? Not my father, dear God. But with generals it might be different. Will the Lord General Baron be pleased with thousands of rams or with tens of thousands

of rivers of oil? With warmth and sweetmeats and treasured wine from
the Blessing cellar? Not my son, dear General. Not my son.

"I remember the General Baron von Elsfeldt," Lisa said to Woolie.
She wondered how the tall, splendid old man had come to have so
plump and undistinguished a son. Poor Woolie. Probably he minded
his commonplace appearance.

Woolie asked again, "You do understand, Lisa? I mean about my
working for a German firm. I mean when there are so many things
about the present regime that one can't—that even I can't——"

"Of course, Woolie. I know. It's difficult for us all. Even for Franz,
though he seems so sure and brave."

"Even Franz?"

"Even Franz." Lisa smiled at Woolie's soft sigh.

"And another thing, Lisa." Woolie lowered his voice. "And don't
say this even to Franz. Through my position with the line sometimes I
can help——"

"I don't understand."

"If you ever need to, you will. I can facilitate a passage." His voice
trailed into silence. Franz was watching them. Woolie lifted his glass.
"To Lisa Blessing. May she repeat here the success that she has had in
London and Berlin."

Anne lifted her glass with the others. She smiled at Woolie amiably,
although she found him tiresome. A typical American businessman
who thought it romantic to be a German baron. Or perhaps he really
believed that Germany was the lost cause, the lost nation.

"He doesn't know," she said to Franz.

"About Lisa?" Franz asked.

"No, I didn't mean the toast. Of course Lisa will have the most
enormous success. I was speaking of the Baron's sentimental notions
about Germany. Judy and I saw a lot, thanks to J. C. Hitler's doing
a good job."

Anne remembered the spring and summer days in Germany. There
were new roads across the fields and hills. Wide straight roads on
which she had driven in the big foreign cars of the party leaders.
Anne and Judy and Ruby had driven in the motorcars. They had
danced in Munich and across the border in Salzburg. They had even

dined on the mountain crest of Berchtesgaden. All the kingdoms of the earth, Anne had thought as she looked down through the huge panel of glass at the land of Germany that lay at the feet of its leader and his chosen, fortunate few. She had looked with envy at plump Emmi Goering. At Edda Ciano, thin and elegant. They, like Judy Mason Jones, like Ruby Black Borodino, were the new aristocracy. They had the power. They had the power because they had known how to choose and when.

"It's a question of timing," Ruby had said. "First come, first served."

"And Pierre?" Anne had asked.

"Oh, Pierre's a sentimentalist. He's at home, dreaming of a France that never was, at least in my time, or looking to Geneva for a future that won't be. Meantime I'm having fun. And doing a little business for Charmant perfumes on the side. Though you wouldn't guess it to look at me."

Anne remembered Ruby's slim tan body, expertly but scantily covered in clinging white silk jersey. She could hear her chuckle as she tossed her smooth, light brown hair, and turned her light laughing eyes up to the handsome, heavy-set man beside her. "The Minister-President and I are becoming to one another. The General and the lady. Who could guess to look at us that we are both good business-men?"

Anne could still hear the General and the lady laughing as she spoke to Franz. "Your Leader and the men who surround him have done great things for Germany. I wish there were men like that here in America."

"You feel that?" Franz spoke eagerly. "So few Americans under-stand."

"Too many Americans are squeamish. But J. C. understands. He's practical. And there are lots of Americans like him. Me, for instance."

"You, Anne? You are too pretty to be practical."

"Don't let her fool you, Count," Phil Sinclair whispered. "There's a nice little brain ticking away under that slick coiffure."

Anne lifted her glass. "Thanks, Phil, if that's a compliment."

They had had champagne long ago when this was Tony's. She looked at Franz. His dark head was bright under the light. When I first saw him, he reminded me. She twisted her glass. I don't want to be reminded. I want to start again, to have it new.

"Careful, Anne, glass breaks." Phil took her glass. "I see an acquisitive gleam in your eyes. Is it Franz? I rather thought that J. C.——"

"Then you rather thought wrong," Anne said sharply. "Judy and I are friends."

"And well matched at forty paces or less."

"Besides, there's my husband." She looked across the table at Paul. "Or did you forget him?"

"No, I didn't forget. But I thought you had."

"Paul is the one who forgot. He promised to stay with J. C. But I hadn't been gone very long when he left to go to work for Harrington and Cox."

"He's doing well, you know. I saw Max Harrington the other day."

"Getting his friends in to buy. Like a girl working in a dress shop."

"Careful, beautiful. Don't let the spite show. It's not becoming."

"It's not spite, Phil, it's humiliation. Not for me, really not. I'm thinking of Polly. Her father a clerk in a shop. Drinking too much. But you don't understand."

"I understand. Let's not discuss it. Unless you want to tell me your plans. You have plans, is my guess."

"I haven't any plans, only a job to do. Polly's my job. And Paul's part of that job. The trip was a vacation."

"You liked what you saw in Germany?"

"Certainly. It's lovely to look at. Orderly, clean, and beautiful."

"And the people?"

"They're on their way and they know where they're going. I find that refreshing."

"They know where they're going, all right. I'm not sure that the rest of us have a clear picture of the itinerary."

"Oh, Phil, don't be tiresome and political. I had fun. I had fun because I felt safe. There aren't many places where people like us can feel safe."

"Poor Anne, still seeking safety in unlikely places."

"Anne, I wonder." Paul leaned across the table. "I know Mary won't mind. I've got an early start to make."

Anne rose. "Of course. Vacation's over."

Vacation is over indeed, Anne thought. She stood in her small hot bedroom. She had unpacked only a little. At the edges of the suitcases the tissue paper rattled in the hot dry breeze.

"You don't want to, do you?" Paul said. "Unpack, I mean."

"Not tonight, if you don't mind the mess."

"Not tonight, and not ever, Anne. And that's the truth. That was the truth that night at Claridge's long before my unfortunate performances at the Voorhees' party. I knew then. I've known ever since. Only I've hoped once in a while. I'm a hoping sort of guy."

Anne did not look up. She was staring at the bright German and Italian labels that covered the suitcases. They're all that's left of it, she thought, the soiled, bright pieces of paper. Like the crumpled paper favors that Polly brings home from her parties.

Paul left the room and came back with a drink. "I haven't been doing much of this but tonight . . ."

"So you tell me."

"Look, Anne. Don't sound like that. Hate the poky apartment after the Adlon and the Excelsior." He read the labels, "And the Stephanie. Hate this and the breaks we've had. I hate them for you."

"Then do something about it." Anne sat on a suitcase and carefully tore off the narrow edge of tissue paper.

"I plan to do something. I should have done it a long time ago. But I thought maybe you'd come back. I thought you were back. This morning, just for a minute, when I met the *Bremen*. While I could still only see you. That was before we were together."

"But what are you going to do? Just say the word and J. C.——"

"No, not that. Even if it wasn't J. C. That's not for me. I can't get Claridge's, and Cartier, and the Blue Train back for you. I can't grab off a kingdom for you."

"Look, Paul. Couldn't we skip this tonight? I'm very tired."

Paul stood up. Anne's head was bent over the Vuitton suitcase. He put his hand gently on her hair. Her head bowed a little farther away from his touch.

"You see, I'm a hoping sort of guy, but not articulate. Not even with this." He drained his glass. "Remember when we didn't need the words? They never were any good."

Anne did not look up. "Not tonight, Paul. I'm very tired."

"Not tonight. Not ever. That's what I thought. Not what I hoped. But what I thought, what I knew. Not ever."

Paul walked out and closed the door quietly behind him.

Anne sat still. She scraped the Hotel Excelsior label from the suitcase.

I should unpack, she thought. This is the end. And I might as well unpack and throw the labels away. The months with Judy and J. C. were only an interlude, not a beginning. The labels tell the spring and summer story. Damn Phil for a good guesser.

Princess Cora had guessed, too. She had sat beside Anne on the Lido beach.

"I like you, my dear." The Princess smiled benignly. "But look out for Judy. She means to hold on to J. C."

"But, Princess Cora, I don't want——"

"That's as may be. It doesn't matter what you want. Amateurs can't compete with professionals. And Judy's a professional. She's a sharp, smart bitch twenty-four hours a day. Same like Ruby Borodino. You're in fast company, child. Better go back to that nice husband of yours. Or find an easier way of starting over."

"Princess Cora, I—I——" Anne was angry to feel tears strangling her voice. It was the contrast. It was remembering the summer when the Lido, like all the surface of the earth, had been hers. When everything had been easy.

"You're scared. I know. And times are hard in America. And obviously different. While the Lido is unchanged, or seems so. All the same"—the Princess's strident voice dropped to a whisper—"I wouldn't try for J. C. and I wouldn't get tied up with one of Il Duce's bright young men either. That's not security."

"But here as in Germany——"

"Two very different places, my dear. Don't let the patter fool you. Two different countries. And neither one is for you. Go back to your American husband. Settle down in one of those little houses full of ice boxes and shiny gadgets. I've lived here all my life and I get lonesome. It's a funny thing to have an Italian son, born to a foreign name, to a foreign tongue."

Anne looked across the sand at Prince Ascagnio San Martino.

"Princess Cora, you're just talking. You love Europe. You've been such a success."

"Yes, I'm a success. I'm a landmark, even, one of the sights of Venice. And I shined up the San Martino name for Ascagnio. And made it important. Even with dollars, not everyone could do that for a Neapolitan title. I've done well. But you go back to America."

"You don't want to go, Princess Cora."

"No, but I wish I did. One gets tired of being a carefully thought out landmark. The effect is good, but actually it's ersatz. White hair and widow's weeds to match." The Princess touched her snowy draperies. "And even the unexpected blasphemy. Americans are expected to be rich or amusing. And I've been both."

"But Ascagnio."

"Ah, to Ascagnio it has all been useful. It's helped him with Agnelli at Fiat."

"He's very handsome. You love him very much in spite of all you say."

"What did I say? Not a damn thing. His foreignness doesn't stop my love. Only makes it ache sometimes. But don't you yearn over Ascagnio, young lady," the Princess said sharply. "He's not for you. I intend that Ascagnio shall marry a rich young virgin. I suppose she'll have to be an American."

Not Ascagnio. Anne pulled her thoughts away from the shining Lido sands. She was back for good. Back in her stuffy little Park Avenue apartment. She began slowly to undress.

Not Ascagnio. Not that I wanted him. For all his handsome strength he's more ersatz than his mother. And not Lieutenant von Eigen, one of Hitler's strong young men. But from someone the strength. Not J. C., but from someone the power.

The power and the glory. I'm more blasphemous than the Princess. And I'm not as clever.

Anne thought of Paul as he had stood beside her with a glass in his hand. Though she hadn't looked up, she could see him standing beside her. She heard his voice.

She turned down the bed. You couldn't expect that service of a maid by the day. She remembered the soft beds that had stood ready in the high-ceilinged rooms in the hotels of Europe.

She folded the spread unevenly and clumsily. She turned back the corner of the sheet. It is all in the copybooks, my girl, she thought, only Miss Seton's was too swell to go in much for copybook maxims. This is the fine bed you so carefully made for yourself. She laid herself down to wait for tomorrow, the tomorrow that she had forgotten during the interlude of vacation.

The next morning Anne woke to find Paul sitting beside her bed.

"Why, Paul, I thought you'd be down at the shop. Isn't it late?"

"It is, rather, but I thought we'd better get this over. It is over, isn't it? Between you and me, I mean."

"If you want it to be. Do you want it to be?" Anne asked.

"That, too? All right, baby. Yes, I want it. This is no good for me. I'm bowing out. Only thing we've got to settle is about Polly."

"But, Paul, I thought last night you were just talking. You've said things like that before." Her voice broke. Her throat felt thick. The words wouldn't come. She wanted to be free of the meager life in which she had trapped herself. No, in which Paul had trapped her. She had been sure she wanted to be free.

"Paul, I don't know." She looked at him through the tears that fell blindingly, unexpectedly. "Seven years are long. I can't—I guess after all—I love you."

"I guess you do, Annie, and more than you think. But not enough. It's not your fault. It's just the breaks. We won't talk about it. Only thing we've got to settle about is Polly."

"But I'll have to take her." Anne wiped her eyes. "That's the natural thing. Girls always go with the mother."

"Don't worry. We won't do anything that looks queer. I just want to be sure I can always see her. Have her to visit when I get a little place of my own."

"You've planned it all out."

"And I'd like her to be brought up in America."

"Of course."

"I guess we'll have to draw up some sort of an agreement. Uncle Normie can fix us up with a lawyer."

"Paul, I——" Anne's mouth twisted into ugly sobs that broke her sentences into unintelligible words. "When you talk . . . lawyers . . . papers . . . so final . . ."

"It is final. And it hurts, baby. You didn't think it would. I knew.

That makes it easier for me. Like you said, you love me. Not a lot, maybe. But long. And you're scared. A fresh start sounds fine but when it's right there it's frightening. Once you make the break, you'll be all right."

"But what about you, Paul? I'll feel like a heel. I'll look like——"

"No, you won't, honey. This hasn't been any good for me. I've wanted it, but it hasn't been any good."

"You mean my having some money of my own and all like that?"

"I mean all like that."

"Well, if it's for you . . ." Her voice broke again.

To imagine a fresh start, to want it to be new—that was different. That was like young daydreaming, when courage and good fortune were easy, as flying was easy in a real dream. But to start over in fact, not in imagination, to begin again seven years late . . .

"I'm afraid, Paul."

"I know, Annie. That's your trouble. But you needn't be scared. You're smart. And you're pretty—the prettiest there is."

"Am I really? Am I really still?"

"Yep. The prettiest there is. And that's my trouble. So let's call it a day, but quick. You go down to Southampton to your mother. You were planning to go to see her and Polly anyway. It'll be easy. You're not unpacked."

"I was going to——"

"Were you, honey? Well, anyway, you go down to Southampton and stay there—and I'll stay here until we get things worked out."

"Oh, Paul, what will people say?"

"Whatever you want them to. They've got to start saying it sometime. It might as well be now." He touched the top of her bent head with his lips and walked quickly out of the room.

Anne heard the front door close behind him.

She sat with her knees drawn up under her chin and wept. Her tears were for her and for Paul and for their misfortune and for the seven years that were gone—for all the years that had gone that made the past long as once the future had been.

Anne lifted her eyes and looked around the room. Suppose it's like this, she thought, suppose it's narrow and dreary like this only without Paul.

She looked at the bright-colored labels. I can find these places here. I can find the life I want. I can find my way back. It will be easier without Paul. He wouldn't even look for the way.

She picked up the telephone and dialed Mary's number.

"Mary. Mary, is that you? Paul has left me."

"Paul has left you? Why, I thought——"

"I know. Everyone did. They thought I'd be the one. But I never would have left him. Really I tried, Mary. Maybe I nagged him too much about drinking. I was only trying——"

"But he wasn't drinking last night. I haven't seen him tight for ages."

"Not at the party, Mary. But when we came home. But that's not it. And anyway, I don't want to talk about it. But I'm frightened."

"Poor Anne. But are you sure he meant it? If he had too much to drink——"

"No, he said it this morning. He was cold sober. And he meant it. And I'm frightened. I'm going down to Mother's. If I could see you first. I'm so frightened, Mary."

"Of course, Anne. I'll come right over."

Anne put down the telephone. I'm frightened, but tomorrow it'll be different. I'll see it clear. Mary will help me, and J. C. and all the others. Mother and Uncle Normie. I'll start again. Somehow I'll start again. It will be different tomorrow.

XV

MRS. BROOKE had not come to New York to meet Anne because she had a cold. By the time Anne reached Southampton the cold had turned into pneumonia.

"Is it really bad, Uncle Normie? She hardly spoke to me and she looked so little. Mother never looked little."

"Pretty bad, Anne. Dr. Phillips is doing all he can."

Polly was sent to stay at Mrs. Winton's.

"But you just came home, Mummy. Must I go? And, Mummy, did you? Grandma said for me not to ask, but now she can't, so I have to. Did you bring me a present?"

"It's in New York." I can buy her something in the village, Anne thought. "I left so quickly on account of Grandma that I forgot it in New York."

"I knew you didn't really forget. You and Daddy always bring me a present when you've been away. Can't I wait for Daddy to bring it down? Do I have to go to Mrs. Winton's, Mummy?"

"Yes, darling. We have to keep the house quiet for Grandma so she'll get better."

It was strange to Anne to keep the house quiet for her mother. It had always been Anne who slept late in the morning while Mrs. Brooke hushed the servants. It had been natural for her mother to lie awake at night until Anne came home from parties.

"She always was the one, Uncle Normie. She looked after me."

The library was airless. It was quiet. It had the stiff Sunday feeling that Anne remembered in the parlor at boarding school. The parlor at Miss Seton's had been stiffly quiet like this when you sat and waited for visitors.

"It's not like the house at all without her, Uncle Normie." It was like Miss Seton's. Without her mother everything would be like that. Anne remembered that when her mother came to Miss Seton's she was no longer just one of a group of girls. She was special, she belonged. Anne had not thought of it then. But now she remembered. And in the grown-up years since Miss Seton's, in her mother's mind as in her own, Anne had been special.

"Now I'll be alone," Anne said. "Because of her I wasn't. I didn't know."

"She knew, Anne," Norman Brooke said. "Someday Polly will know. That's how you'll repay Anita. How she'd want it."

Anne didn't want to be thrust into the inevitable sequence of child to mother to age to death. Now, according to Uncle Normie, she was Polly's barricade against the last frontier.

"Not yet," Anne said. "It's too soon."

"I know, my dear. Anita's a comparatively young woman. We can only hope."

Anne did not really hope as she stood beside her mother's bed and listened to the heavy, tired breathing. She's too little to fight anything as big as this, Anne thought. How queer that in all my grown-up years, as I have stood beside her, I never thought of her as little.

On the third day after Anne came Mrs. Brooke died.

The mechanics of mourning occupied Anne. Mary Forrest and Norman Brooke helped her. Mary brought her black stockings and a veil and black-edged note paper. "You'll need it for your letters. There are so many flowers." Mary sorted the cards from the flowers. Anne stared at the packages. For this, everything is black except the flowers. For a wedding, they are white.

Norman Brooke made the funeral arrangements. "If you'll just say what Psalms you'd like, Anne. And the hymns. Any that you particularly associate with Anita."

Uncle Normie kept saying "Anita" instead of "your mother," as though he, too, were remembering.

Anne turned the pages of the hymnal. It had always been on the corner of the nursery piano.

"I don't know, Uncle Normie. 'Now the Day Is Over' and 'Jesus, Tender Shepherd, Hear Me.' But those were the ones she sang with me. And what she liked for herself I don't know."

Anne's memory of her mother was like a mirror. It reflected Anne's life, Anne's hopes, Anne's fears. It held nothing of Anita Brooke.

Paul went to the funeral.

"He must be there," Norman Brooke said, "if only on Polly's account. I didn't like to ask any questions when you didn't send for him. But he must be at the funeral. You owe that to public opinion."

After the funeral Paul came back to the house with Norman Brooke.

"I haven't liked to ask Anne, but you can tell me, my boy. Is there a definite break between you?"

"We're separated. It happened the morning Anne came down here. I didn't know Mrs. Brooke was so ill until after she died. I wish Anne had——"

"Poor child. She was so upset."

"I know. I'd have liked to say good-by to Mrs. Brooke, that's all. She was always very nice to me—always."

"Well, if that's how things are, I suppose there's no point in your staying here."

"No, I guess not. I'd like to see Polly, though."

"She's at Mrs. Winton's. We felt it was the best thing to keep her away from all this. She doesn't know."

"No? Kids guess a lot. Worst thing is they have to hide it. I'll stop by and see her."

The next day Norman Brooke spoke to Anne about her mother's will.

"Do we have to talk about it, Uncle Normie? Couldn't you just fix everything?"

"Better to get things settled. It's all very simple. Everything goes to you, of course. And, not to add worry to grief, even with the depression, things aren't too bad. Anita very wisely cut her losses in '33. And we got a lot of tax-exempts. Anita wanted to keep the principal safe for you. You'll be all right."

Anne stared at him.

"She never lived extravagantly. Wanted to save it for you. It's not what it might once have been. And with these outrageous taxes . . . But still you ought to have——"

"Please, Uncle Normie. It seems so awful talking about money. So heartless."

"As though you could seem heartless. You're as thin as a rail in that little black dress. And where are the roses in those cheeks of yours?"

"I've been buying my pink cheeks for a long time," Anne said. "Things haven't been easy. Paul and I, you know. Paul——"

"Yes, he told me. Sorry to hear it. Always seemed a nice feller. But weak, I suppose. Bad stock. That's the trouble. Bad stock. They had us all fooled. We were talking at the club the other day about Bruce Craven. He seemed the soundest feller imaginable, but there you are. Bad blood somewhere. You shouldn't trust these Johnny-come-latelys. Bruce's grandfather was a grocer. 'Pon my word, that's true. And in a very small way. I'd forgotten it till they were speaking of it at the club. But where were we?"

"Paul and I——"

"Oh, that, yes. Well, we'll get around to that. Get the separation papers drawn up. But not for a while. Wouldn't look well to do anything about it so soon after Anita . . ." Norman Brooke paused. "You don't remember, of course. But Anita Howard was the prettiest girl I ever saw. She and your father. I can remember standing beside them at the Church of the Incarnation. Don't seem long, but it's thirty years. I remember it better than if it was last week. She came up the aisle behind all those pretty girls, Mamie Winton and Sally Morehead and the rest of 'em. And Anita was the prettiest of the lot. I stood beside Tom at the altar. Not a big church, but the Howards had always gone to it. Lived round the corner on Murray Hill. Poor old Murray Hill. Anita was the prettiest of the lot."

Norman Brooke blew his nose.

"Well, no use harking back. Yes, Anita—and very properly, of course—left you everything. And as nearly as I can figure, young lady, after we pay the Government, you can count on about twenty-five thousand a year."

"Why, Uncle Normie, Mother hasn't spent that much for a long time."

"I know. She saved so you can spend."

Anne closed her eyes for fear her pleasure shone bright in them. It can't be wrong to be pleased. She meant me to be. This is her last present to me. With this I can escape.

"It's not a lot, of course," Norman Brooke continued. "And the Lord only knows what those fools in Washington will do to our taxes. But I'll do the best I can for you. Now about this other thing. Want me to see Paul? I'll get a lawyer for you when the proper time comes. Jim Alexander will handle it. Good firm, Hale, Alexander. You'll keep Polly. Goes without saying."

"It's better for her. And Paul wants me to——"

"Well, you never know till the papers are signed. I've seen husbands kick up an awful fuss. Even if they don't care sixpence for the child. It's a question of pride. But you leave it to me."

Anne left it to Norman Brooke. In November he came to see her in New York to report his progress.

"Nice place you have here." He looked admiringly around the pale blue living room. The tall white curtains framed a view of Central Park. "Blue's your color, my dear."

"I had to move. The other place had so many awful associations. Poor Paul. He used to drink. I don't like to talk about it."

"Quite proper. Especially on Polly's account. But of course I knew. I was at Mrs. Reggy's that night when he disgraced himself. I hoped at the time it was an exception."

"If only it had been."

"Well, as I say, it's quite proper for you not to speak of it. And we won't use it unless we have to. But Paul's being a little unreasonable.

Jim Alexander saw him on your behalf. You'll probably have to talk this over with Jim. But here's the trouble. Access to the child at all times convenient to you. Polly to visit him at your convenience and if Paul can provide the proper surroundings. Those are both all right. They leave us the whip hand. But Paul insists on a clause forbidding you to take Polly out of the country. And should you take up your residence outside the United States, he is to have full custody."

"But that's ridiculous, Uncle Normie."

"Jim Alexander told him it was out of the question. I know you have no idea of settling abroad. But you never know. And there's no reason why you shouldn't."

"What'll I do, Uncle Normie? This isn't like Paul."

"Leave him to me and Jim Alexander. We'll take care of it. I'll give you a ring tomorrow."

The next afternoon Phil Sinclair telephoned Anne. "How about giving me a cocktail, Anne, if I come round?"

"Oh, Phil, I have an early dinner and——"

"And your side of the story, I should have added. Mustn't antagonize the press, you know."

"Well, not for that, Phil. But if you can come right away."

As Norman Brooke had done, Phil admired Anne's apartment.

"I think it's pretty," Anne said.

"Very pretty." Phil moved a pale bowl filled with flaming roses and placed an ash tray within easy reach of his chair.

"Now about that drink, Phil. What'll it be? Martini, scotch and soda——"

"Nothing, thanks. I didn't really come for a drink. And not to hear your story, either. I didn't come to listen. I came to talk. About you."

"About Paul, you mean."

"And about Paul and about Polly. You've got to give in and sign those papers that will keep her in this country."

"But I'm not going to give in."

"You haven't in the past. You've done more taking than giving with those lovely little hands of yours."

"I know you don't like me, Phil, but that really has nothing to do——"

"As a matter of fact, I've always liked you. And I've been sorry for you. I'm sorry for the frightened people, and you're one of 'em,

Anne. Fear and greed. They go naturally together and they make for evil."

"What is this all about?"

"You. You've destroyed yourself. Perhaps you couldn't help it. You very nearly destroyed Paul. I'm not going to let you finish the job."

"You've never known anything about Paul and me. I——"

"You married him," Phil interrupted, "for security. Well-upholstered security. And ever since that disappeared you've been looking for an out. You even created one: Paul's drinking."

"You're crazy."

"Look, Paul stayed sober during the twenties. Anyone who didn't drink then is no real souse."

"But it was because of Bruce Craven. Paul couldn't take it."

"It was because of you. Paul couldn't take that."

"Well, whatever the cause"—Anne crushed her cigarette firmly in the deep crystal ash tray—"he does drink and he isn't fit to have Polly."

"He hasn't been drinking since you went abroad, Anne. Your mother could have told you. He used to go and see Polly every evening. He loves that kid, you know."

"Look, Phil, I'm not planning to take Polly abroad, but Uncle Normie won't let me sign the papers with that clause in. Can't Paul trust me?"

"I shouldn't think so, not even Paul, though he's a trustful sort of guy. Anyway, he's not signing. And you can't get a divorce unless he lets you."

"I can get a separation. I don't want to use drunkenness. But if I have to . . . Everyone knows, Phil. Everyone was at the Voorhees' party that night."

"Yes, that seems to be your strong point. Well, I hate to tell you, Anne, but it's no good."

"At least two hundred people could swear to it."

"Yes, and two doctors from Bellevue and several clerks could testify to the incident in J. C. Jones's office that set Paul to drinking that night. And if you bring out the drinking, why, Paul's lawyer will bring that out. I really came to tell you to tell that to Jim Alexander. Hale, Alexander get quite a lot of business from J. C. Jones. J. C.'s not a squeamish feller but I don't think he'd care about having that story in evidence. It has too many interesting ramifications."

"That's blackmail, Phil."

"Yeah. Not pretty. Neither is what you've done to Paul. And I don't intend that you shall take Polly where he can't see her. Now I've said my say. You figure it out any way you like. Tell Jim Alexander or not as you like. But the separation agreement stays as is. Now how about that drink? May I fix myself one?" Phil rose.

"Why don't you go?" Anne asked, and her voice trembled. "You've had your little triumph. Or would you rather enjoy it here while you drink my liquor?"

"As a matter of fact, Anne, I don't enjoy it. You were nice to me when a lot of people were down on me. And you're pretty. And I like you."

"Why, if you despise me?"

"I don't like all the people I admire. And I'm not sure that I despise you. I'm sorry for you because you're one of the frightened people. With you, I think greed has been a weapon against fear. I'll stop your harming Paul. But I'm fond of you, Anne. I'm fond of a lot of people like you. Only thing, I hope there're not too many of you. If there are, the way I see it, the world's destroyed."

"Mix me a drink and stop this fancy talk. All right, you've won Paul's battle for him."

She lifted her glass and smiled. It was wise to be on friendly terms with Phil. "Let's remember old times and be friends, Phil. Even if you don't approve of me."

"Okay, Anne. Here's to you and your safety, just so you don't destroy the rest of us."

When Phil had gone, Anne stood alone by one of the tall windows and looked across the park at the lights that were beginning to glow in the dark buildings against the bright western sky. In the dim light the walls around her were drained of color. This pale room was like the rooms in which she had lived with Paul. Paul had won about Polly. What had Uncle Normie said? It's pride even if they don't care sixpence for the child. What about my pride? How will it look? I can explain to Uncle Normie that I'd rather give in to Paul on this. That it isn't important enough for an ugly quarrel, since I don't ever mean to live abroad. And if ever I do go abroad, it will seem all right to leave Polly behind for a little while. It will be the right thing to do.

She pulled a silver thread in the braid that edged the smooth silk curtains. She would not have to go abroad. She would find what she wanted here in the security of her familiar world. There were enough people like J. C. to make America safe again. Safe for her and the frightened people.

Why must we be frightened? Anne asked, and her lips moved. Why shouldn't we be safe again? Why shouldn't I be safe again? Why shouldn't I begin again? Like Judy Jones when she was the age I am now. Like Emmi Goering, already middle-aged. Not Ascagnio. Not Lieutenant von Eigen. Not J. C. But from someone, somewhere, for me, too, the power and the glory.

XVI

ANNE READ THE INVITATION that was in the edge of the mirror over her dressing table.

Mr. and Mrs. Reginald Voorhees
request the pleasure of
Mrs. Brooke Craven's
company at a dance in honor of
Miss Clara Voorhees
at half past ten o'clock
on Thursday, October fifteenth

Clara was the Voorhees debutante of the autumn of 1936. Anne tried to remember if she was Reggy Voorhees' great-niece or grand-daughter. It was difficult to disentangle the branches of that enormous clan. They had married well and often and for the last thirty years they had dominated New York. The depression seemed not to have tarnished their vast and complicated pyramid of riches. Anne thought how pleasant it must be to belong to a big, continuously successful family like that.

There were other invitations against the glass. Anne replaced one that had fallen. She hadn't put up her invitations that way since she was a debutante. She liked to look at them. They were tangible evidence that she was wanted.

She had felt unwanted in Reno and after that in Southampton. Southampton hadn't really counted. There never were enough men in Southampton unless you were sixteen or sixty.

She considered herself in the mirror and smiled at the reflected image. She held her head back and brushed mascara on her upturned lashes. Twenty-nine was a good age to be if you had any looks at all. But a year from now, ten years from now . . . She shivered. She remembered the high-school student who had done the chores in the ugly little rented house in Reno. He was tall and angular. He grinned and said, "Sorry, ma'am," as he shied away from one piece of furniture only to crash into another. He ducked his head nervously when he walked through a door. It was really being young not to be used to the size of your body, to the feel of your grown-up proportions. The kids on the beach at Southampton were like that. Their voices were loud from classrooms and assembly halls and gymnasiums. They played tennis and danced with perfect grace. But they stumbled over the umbrellas on the beach and knocked over the back rests. They were really young. They were really at the beginning. They still had all the time there was. And when you noticed that they were different, then you weren't young any more. No matter what the mirror said. Mirror, mirror on the wall, am I the fairest one of all? There needn't be Snow White beyond the seven hills. There need only be a whole new generation.

The dance at Mrs. Voorhees' was like the dance she gave every year. Only this one was earlier in the season.

"It would have to be," J. C. Jones said. "They really have to make an effort for that poor little bucktoothed kid."

"Or maybe," Anne suggested, "she's afraid Roosevelt will be re-elected next month. Four more years of the New Deal might stop even Mrs. Reggy."

"No fear of that. Of his being re-elected or of anything stopping her," Woolie von Elsfeldt said. "At least I'm sure about Mrs. Reggy. I don't know anything about politics except what everyone says."

Anne looked around the supper room. The old lady was certainly letting down the bars. But then she always had. She followed the times at a dignified pace. Tonight there were even a few New Dealers. The men said Roosevelt couldn't be re-elected, but Mrs. Reggy had a fashionable feeling for the future. You had to be three parts fortune-teller to be a successful social leader.

"What do you think, J. C.?"

"About the election? 'Fraid it's in the bag for the long-haired boys."

"But everyone says . . . Listen to them."

"The American way. Great slogan."

"Why, I was talking to a feller on the *Tribune* and he said . . ."

"Only eighteen days to save the American way. That's good stuff."

"And the *Digest* Poll." "Of course these damn New Dealers are spending money like water." "And it's our money. The taxpayers' money. That's what burns me up." "Don't let it get you down. The big boys are coming through. Why, we just got a check from . . ." "Do you really think it'll be all right?" The feminine voice was plaintive. "Robert says if he gets in we can't open the house in Palm Beach. We'll probably go and live abroad."

"Well, J. C.?" Anne asked.

"Don't listen to 'em talk. Look at their bets. The odds in Wall Street tell the story. I offered four to one and no takers for any decent amount."

"You bet on Roosevelt?" Woolie asked. "I wouldn't have taken you for a New Dealer, sir, although I think I see one or two here. Isn't that Sam Pierson over there with Lisa Blessing?"

"Yeah, Pierson's a brain truster from away back. Came from some jerkwater college. No, I'm not a New Dealer, but I'm certainly not a sentimentalist about gambling," J. C. said. "Anyway, he isn't getting in forever. A lot of things can happen between now and 1940. A lot of things can change more than you think. Me, I take the long view. And it doesn't look so bad." J. C. chuckled. "The world isn't so big any more. You can't stop the future no matter where it starts. And you don't want to, if you know how to play it."

Anne looked across the room at Lisa's table. There were two men whom she didn't know. One of them must be Sam Pierson. There was Mary. And beside her Marco Ghiberti. Anne looked at him and felt nothing. How curious to look at him across a room and to feel nothing at all. If you looked across enough time there was nothing left but the memory of a memory. There was something to be said for time. Once in a while it worked in your favor.

"Let's get Lisa away from that crowd," Woolie suggested. "Franz wouldn't like it. And even I—well, everyone knows how I stand on most of the things Hitler's done, but when you see these Reds slyly creeping in . . . That Ghiberti, for instance. He's anti-Fascist. Anti-Nazi, too, I guess. And that's all right in theory. But the fact is that most of these anti-Nazis are Communists."

"Then why are you against Hitler?" Anne asked. "Hasn't he stopped the Reds in Germany?"

"Yes, that he has done," Woolie said reluctantly. "And I suppose that by stopping them in Germany he has, in a way, stopped them everywhere. But there are things about his regime that I can't——"

"Oh, Woolie, you're too sentimental."

"I am. And it's a silly thing for a man to be. For anyone to be in these times. Just the same, I'm going to stick my neck out and get Lisa away from those people. She's an actress. All artists are just children. She doesn't understand. She——"

"Perhaps she does," Anne interrupted him. "Perhaps she agrees with them. I recognize that fat man with the glasses. He's a writer, a refugee, Gottfried Lieber. And Lisa's absolutely drinking in his words."

"Please come, Anne." Woolie's face was troubled. "That's no good for Lisa. Franz wouldn't like it. He's of the old regime. He saw the suffering in Germany during and after the war. And somehow the Nazis seem to have given him hope. It's patriotism, in a way."

"Certainly it is," Anne said sharply. "It wouldn't hurt you to be like Franz. A little more loyal to your father's country."

"It's hard sometimes to figure out where loyalty lies. I'd be just as mixed up if I decided to become an American. Lucky thing for me, there's no real problem. Americans are more like Germans than any European people. Even though a few snobs would like it to be the English."

"Not me, Woolie. I like the English but they're tired. The Germans are young. Hitler's given them back youth and hope. Even you must admit that."

"I suppose so," Woolie said slowly. "Only I wish it might have been done in some other way. But we ought to get Lisa. You don't know Franz von Erlencamp——"

As Woolie spoke, Franz approached the table. "That's where you are wrong, Woolie. I have the honor to know Anne and indeed to have shown her some of the glories of the Third Reich. Now what is this so solemn conversation about?"

"I've been trying to convert Woolie, but he's stubborn."

"Well, come and dance with me. No." Franz frowned. "First I must speak to Lisa. However did she get with that *galère?*"

"I was worried about it," Woolie said. "It's none of my business. Except that in a way I'm a foreigner, too. And I know we have to be careful. You really should explain to her, Franz."

"I will. Come with me, Anne."

Anne smiled at the relieved expression with which Woolie returned to his champagne.

When they reached Lisa's table, Marco was speaking. ". . . as you told me long ago, Lisa. You'll find it here."

"Did you lose something, my dear?" Franz asked.

"We were talking about America," Lisa answered.

"And about Germany," Sam Pierson said. "When one meets a German like Miss Blessing, it restores one's faith in the people of Goethe. Though they have now become the silent people."

"How can they help their silence?" Lisa cried. "You don't know. You haven't seen."

"But you have, Lisa," Franz interrupted, "so you understand why it is wise to be silent."

"Your husband is right, Lisa, at least for you," Gottfried Lieber said. "Do you remember me, Count Erlencamp? I used to see you sometimes in the old days at the *Morgenpresse*. I remember how right you were, how wrong I was. It was not the children of light, the children of Goethe, who were to inherit the land of Germany, but the children of Bismarck."

Franz bowed stiffly.

Gottfried Lieber rose. "Will you dance, Lisa? We have all talked too much."

Anne looked across the narrow table at Marco. He was watching her. There was pity in his eyes.

The pity should be for him, in my eyes, she thought. That's the way it would be if the world hadn't turned upside down. She turned to Franz.

"Shall we, too, dance?" Franz asked gravely.

"If you really want to." Anne put her hand on his arm as they walked away from the table. "I'm sorry, Franz. That was hard for you."

"It's of Lisa that I am thinking."

"Lisa is very beautiful." Anne didn't want to say it. But she wanted to hear his answer.

"And she's good. But, unfortunately, in others she mistakes weakness for goodness. She cannot see the beauty in strength."

"Poor Franz."

He bent his head to look into her upturned face. "You, a stranger, look at me with such kindness, Anne. Sometimes Lisa looks at me as though she hates me. As though she knew——" He stopped himself. "I shouldn't talk like this to you."

"Please feel that you can talk to me. I'm alone too."

"Yes, I read of your divorce. I'm sorry, unless it's what you wanted to do."

"It's what I had to do for my little girl's sake. But be sorry just the same, Franz. It's not always easy to do what you have to do. Now let's dance. We've talked too much."

Franz took her in his arms as they entered the ballroom. Most of the guests were still at supper. There were not many couples. The orchestra played the "Blue Danube."

"Do you like our German music?" Franz asked.

"Yes. Music is better than talking."

Franz held her closer.

Anne felt her heart pounding, almost, it seemed, in time with the music. A pulse in her throat throbbed in a way she had forgotten. This, too, was to be young, to feel your blood pounding and throbbing, to be aware of your body.

The music stopped. Anne stepped backward, away from Franz's encircling arm. He kept her hand in his. "That was good, Anne." He paused. "You are right. Music is better than words."

"But if you need words, Franz, if you ever want to talk, come and see me."

"That is kind of you, Anne. Lisa is going away. The tour of *The Mirror* begins in ten days. I shall be lonely."

"Then come to see me. Since we are both lonely."

"You are kind, Anne, and I am in need of kindness." His eyes looked beyond her. She turned and saw Lisa standing at the other end of the long room with Gottfried Lieber. Franz hesitated. "Perhaps I should. Woolie is right."

"Take me downstairs, Franz. I'm going home. I'd like the evening to end with the 'Blue Danube.'"

"But you can't go alone."

"She can go with me." Woolie had quietly joined them.

"But Daphne?" Anne asked.

"Daphne will stay for hours. I'm a workingman. I don't worry about Daphne. And I'm not going to worry any more about Lisa. Franz will take care of her."

Anne watched Franz walk across the gilded ballroom towards Liza. Pity from him she didn't mind. In a well-ordered world those who, like Franz, were born to inherit would come into their own. And perhaps pity was not quite the word. Perhaps this evening was a beginning. Or was she looking for a beginning, seeing it where it was not because she was hurried, frightened by the really young who were stepping on her heels?

The dancing couples hid Franz and Lisa. Anne turned and followed Woolie down the marble stairs.

"If you will permit me." Franz touched Gottfried Lieber's shoulder. "Would you like to dance, Lisa? Or will you let me take you home?"

"As you like, Franz. Dancing should be fun."

"A party should be fun. It was you who forgot party behavior at the table with Lieber and those others."

"We were only talking. In this country one is free to talk."

"You and I are not free, Lisa, even here."

"If I thought that, if I believed you . . ." Lisa's voice rose. She stopped herself and laughed. "But it's not so. You know it's not so. Take Woolie, for instance. He's a German citizen still and he says what he pleases. Just look at Woolie."

"Even so, Lisa, it's better not to talk. Let's go home. I will try once more to explain. You see only the surface."

"And you, too, Franz. The shadow that you fear and remember is only a surface thing."

When they reached their apartment Lisa lit the fire in the living room.

"Let's sit and talk, Franz. We haven't seen each other. Not really.

All these months. These months that are more than a year. I have been so busy. But now in these days before I go, let's talk. Let's tell each other what we have found in America. I have not found much." Lisa's voice was sad.

"Lisa, those were the wrong sort of Americans to whom you were talking tonight. It's the wrong sort of Americans who listen to you. And for them, for expatriates like Lieber, you endanger not only yourself but your grandmother. Have you forgotten that she lives under the regime that you feel free to criticize?"

"You can't frighten me for her, Franz. If all Germany were to go up in the flames of self-destruction, she would be safe. There is some value in the 'Heldenlied.' "

"You are foolish, Lisa. Now no one is safe. No one anywhere."

"No one ever has been safe. There has always been danger and fear, but also there has always been courage. Above all, here in these United States, born of a courage that must have seemed insane to contemporary observers. Those men knew the danger, but they had the courage. 'And . . . we mutually pledge to each other our lives, our fortunes, and our sacred honour.' "

"And do you still see it here, that courage, Lisa?" Franz's voice was tired. "Can you honestly say you see it? You must live in the world according to your own time. Not in the forgotten times of history."

"No, I haven't seen it. At least not much. How could I see it among the friends you have chosen, the little frightened people who try to build a wall of safety out of the fortunes their fathers left them, or the fortunes that they themselves made in an easier time?"

"Lisa, you sound like one of the Reds whose company you chose so conspicuously tonight. So conspicuously that Woolie noticed it and——"

"Poor Woolie. But you know he'd be one of the good ones if he weren't so mixed up. I suppose he's afraid, too, poor Woolie. I have met only a few who are what I imagined all Americans to be. But now on this tour I shall have the chance to find what I seek. One cannot find America, one cannot find any country in the denationalized playgrounds of the idle. In these playgrounds are the little, frightened people. These are the little people. And those others whom they call little are big, in numbers and in heart and in mind. And I shall find the big people of America when I go into the country. Into the towns and the villages, the flat farm lands, and the mountains." Lisa's eyes were bright as she looked past Franz at the flames. "It's no use looking back. Although there are beautiful words in which to look back. Do you remember, Franz?

> *"I had long since a lovely Fatherland.*
> *The oaks would gleam*
> *And touch the skies; the violets would nod.*
> *It was a dream—"*

"Yes, I remember." Franz pressed his face to hers. "I remember the end of that poem.

> *"You'd kiss me and in German you would say . . .*
> *I love you*
> *It was a dream."*

Presently he withdrew his lips from hers. "It was a dream, wasn't it, Lisa? And now you are going to leave me for a new dream, a new Fatherland, a new love."

"Never a new love. Never a new love, neither in joy nor in sorrow. 'My darkened heart still loves you.'"

"Your darkened heart, Lisa?" He drew her close to him. "Is there such a shadow between us?"

"Shadows are only surface things, Franz. I think we shall find the sunlight together. But in darkness or light, whether I wish it or not, for my heart there can be no new love."

She lifted her lips to his and spoke the German words, *"Ich liebe dich."*

XVII

IN JANUARY 1937 *The Mirror* played for two weeks in the Midwestern city that was near the college town where Hans and Sophie Friedrich lived.

Sophie fetched Lisa on Sunday morning. "It's not far, Lisa. I'll get you back in plenty of time for tomorrow night. We're only two hours by motor."

"Sophie, you sound so American. Miles are now minutes to you."

"I am American, Lisa. Soon I shall have my first papers—and the children, Wilhelm and Johann. Now they are Billy and Johnny. We are all American. And you, Lisa?"

"I don't know. I have seen America. At least I have seen it a little. The fair Eastern rivers. The little towns with only the wooden bars of a crossing gate to separate you from Main Street and the shops and the houses. And I am seeing it today. The wide heart of America." Lisa looked through the car window at the winter pattern of the flat fields. The furrows were caked with irregular strips of snow. Close to the road was a white house, set tall on a narrow high-stepped porch. Beside it was a big red barn and the thick red tower of the silo.

"I like American houses," Lisa said. "They have been built to fit a particular need or to please a special taste. We traveled through the Mohawk Valley by daylight. I remember a green house with a lawn that sloped to the river's edge. Just a plain middle-sized house. And on each side of the door on the sloping lawn was a bright gold lion. I cannot tell you how charming they were, those gold lions."

"And the people, Lisa?" Sophie asked. "Not just the places but the people. Do you like them?"

"I do, Sophie. On the trains I have talked with them, and in the shops, and to ask my way. 'Sister,' they call me, and 'dear.' I like it. They are so friendly. It's part of the bigness of their country. They have room to welcome the stranger. I like America, Sophie, I like it very much. Only——"

"Only?"

"I am lonely. Not often, you understand, Sophie. Not in the theater. But the theater is different. It's my small familiar world. The world I knew in Germany before the fear came. Then the theater was only part of my life. Now it's all I have. Then home waited. Granny's house. And our flat in Berlin with the Dresden clock on the mantel above my hearth that waited for me."

"You're homesick, Lisa."

"I didn't think I should be. I had seen too much to hate there. I wanted to come here." Lisa's eyes followed the broad fields until they met the horizon. In the clear winter air the horizon was plain to see, definite as the sharp line in a child's drawing. "I want not to remember. But Heine's lonely verses keep running through my head: 'I had long since a lovely Fatherland,' and 'The German heart is sick within this breast, is sick I can't conceal it.' Or do you hate to be reminded of Germany, Sophie, even by a poet?"

"No, Lisa. He is, after all, exiled, as we are."

"And I, too, am exiled, Sophie. I was slow to see but, having seen, I came here. I hoped."

"At first Hans and I were lonely. We felt like strangers. But we had each other and the children. And then we learned that all here are strangers, or were, and that none need be——"

"I know that, Sophie."

"You know it only with your mind. The heart learns slowly. But your heart will learn, Lisa. All the people are here. And all the people are your people. When you feel that all the people are yours, then you understand America. You must join the human race to be an American." Sophie's round blue eyes were bright. She was pink-cheeked and breathless. She took one hand from the steering wheel and pushed a wisp of hair out of her eyes. She looked at Lisa, who was staring ahead at the straight wide road that seemed narrow between the broad fields. "I know it's been easier for me, Lisa. I have Hans and the boys. But perhaps Franz, perhaps, after all, Franz . . ." Sophie stammered and was silent.

"I think not," Lisa said. "And that is what really troubles my heart. Not homesickness. Granny said it was my youth I loved in Germany. You, Sophie, and the children's festivals—that was my youth. But you are here and there are no more children's festivals. It was my youth I loved in Germany, but above all it was Franz. It is for his German heart that mine grows weary."

"Perhaps Franz will change," Sophie said doubtfully. "But I heard —that is, they said——"

"That he is a party member, even high up in the party. That's true, Sophie. But it was because he was afraid. He has not the cruelty and the greed. The cruelty . . ." Lisa pressed her hands against her eyes. "I don't want to remember it. I want to begin again here. Long ago I knew this was a land in which was the beginning. In which might be the hope of the world. In which, at least, the world could see a pattern. But then I thought it my duty to return to Germany, to be part of the German pattern like my father and yours and Dr. Meyer. The children of light, Gottfried Lieber called them. But it is the children of darkness who have inherited Germany. They had always the power. They took my father and made him a soldier. Now they have burned the books. But all the books, the poems, and the plays were never more to them than scraps of paper. Frederick the Great, Bismarck, Hitler. That was the pattern which I would not see. The pattern of darkness. And I want to live in the light. I want to live among these friendly people in the light in the wide free air."

"You will, Lisa." Sophie lifted her hand again from the wheel to touch Lisa's clenched fingers. "The homesickness will pass. And you, like the others before you, will cease to be a stranger."

Billy and Johnny Friedrich hurled themselves at the car as Sophie and Lisa arrived. "Hi, Mom. Hello, Miss Blessing." They were two little American boys. One was eight and one was six. They tugged at their mother. "You know what, Mom? You know what?" Billy hitched up the slacks under his leather jacket. "The 'lectric freezer broke, but Hank next door lent us their ol' hand one and we can have ice cream anyway. Me and Johnny turned it and turned it. We got kind of dirty. so it was a good thing we had these ol' slacks on. Hey, Dad, Mom and the lady are here. Hey, Dad."

"Well, Lisa, it is good to see you. Only I don't. I have the wrong glasses." Hans removed his spectacles. "So. It is better."

Lisa held out her hands to him. She stood between him and Sophie. Sophie took off her round blue hat and stood beside him. Her hair was pulled back into a tight knot on the nape of her neck. "He looks well, the Herr Professor, doesn't he? Only we are both too fat." Sophie smiled at Hans. Lisa smiled at them both. The German professor and his German wife.

Johnny and Billy capered around them. "Come on, Mom. Can we take the lady in? We got the spare room fixed up real nice." Billy took Lisa's suitcase. Johnny steered her by the elbow.

"You'll like our house, Miss—uh—Miss . . . ," Johnny said. "Dad built that sun porch last summer and we helped. We'll show you everything. We're glad you could come."

"Thank you," Lisa said. "Thank you both very much."

The boys, like their house, like their town, like their country, were American.

In February Lisa traveled with the company of *The Mirror* through the Southwest to Los Angeles. She looked from the map in her hand to the unknown land beyond the double glass of the train window. At the edge of her vision, at the edge of the flat, tan plains, jutted suddenly the snowy tops of mountains. The distant mountains seemed near in the clear dry air. It was as though an invisible property man had made a mistake. The mountaintops must be left over from another set. They did not belong on the flat desert plain. But they did. The train moved on. Nearer at hand the mountains sprang from the plain. This was a painter's world, not nature's. Here there were not streams and deep, green forests, the gradual, expected height of mountains and the white peak that was natural like the fall of snow on the crest of a pine tree. Pine-green and snow—that was the natural beauty. Not sand-color and snow. The landscape you have seen, the view you long remember—that is the natural thing. Lisa watched the strange land as the tracks curved. Presently the snowy mountaintops could no longer be seen. The landscape was sepia like a picture in the rotogravure. The hills and the flat plains and the adobe houses all were one color.

Lisa wondered if this was the road her great-great-grandparents had taken. How curious it must have seemed to their German eyes. Their eyes were German as no eyes could be in today's small world. After the sea voyage from home they must have looked refreshed at the noble valley of the Hudson that was like their own beloved Rhineland. But the prairies of Kansas and then these desert plains. How had it seemed to them? Lisa smiled at herself. Perhaps they hadn't seen it. She knew so little of those remote great-great-grandparents. Perhaps they sailed from the East Coast of America to the West, and saw many foreign sights on that long journey, so that their eyes expected strangeness when they saw California. Perhaps for them California lay beyond the distant tip of South America.

On the last morning Lisa awoke to the shock of sudden summer. She tried to remember her first trip to the Riviera with her grandmother. She could remember Frau Blessing singing Mignon's song, "Know'st Thou the Land?" And the song had reminded the child Lisa of warmth and perfume. Her earliest memory of the southland was the song, not the Mediterranean shores whose first sight she had forgotten. In the cold winters of wartime she had asked her grandmother to sing the song.

Lisa stared from the train. If she could recapture that lost memory it would not be like this. In Europe the south was near. It was not like this. Here there were days of flat fields and prairies and desert plains and then the cold in the high mountain barrier. Lisa had felt the height as she traveled through the darkness. And here was the end. She had dropped swiftly onto the green and golden coast. The orange trees were near. She could see the bright fruit. Beyond the groves, two-dimensional, like a backdrop, were the dusty, painted hills of southern California.

San Francisco was the final stop for *The Mirror*. This was Dan Hanauer's place. The proud hilled city was the last outpost of the West. The gaudy city of Los Angeles, with its palm-lined, flowered suburbs and its sandy, crumbling hills, was not of Dan Hanauer's time. San Francisco, held close among its hills, looking westward to the Orient, was his city. Earthquake and fire had not altered the spirit of San Francisco, the spirit that had thrust boldly onward to face the western sea.

On Thursday night of the last week of the San Francisco run Lisa drove up the steep hill to her hotel. Beneath her were the bright lights. Even at night this city was the Golden Gate. The names of the hotels recalled Dan Hanauer's time. The Mark Hopkins. The Fairmont. Lisa smiled at herself as she tried to forge out of his past time a link with the present in which she wished not to be a stranger.

Lisa stopped at the hotel desk for her key.

"A lady called, Miss Blessing," the night clerk said. "It's rather late but I allowed her to go up and wait. I hope it's all right. I was not sure if you expected her."

"Quite all right."

As she walked to the elevator Lisa wondered who the visitor could be. How pleasant to have no fear mixed with the wondering. In America even an unknown midnight caller could present no threat.

As Lisa opened the door of her sitting room an old lady rose to greet her. She was small and thin. Only the black eyes were alive in her wrinkled face.

"I hope you forgive that I come so late." The old lady held out her hand. It was light and dry as paper. Lisa felt it tremble in her own. The bright dark eyes peered into Lisa's. They were bright, but they were wary like those of a wild animal that has learned to fear man.

"I am Mrs. Abraham Stern. You do not know the name? I was born Sarah Klein. Elisabeth has never—you have never heard Elisabeth speak of my family?"

"Elisabeth?" Lisa's voice was puzzled.

"I thought perhaps—my father was Jacob Klein. Dan Hanauer and he—I thought perhaps your grandmother . . ."

Lisa stared at her. Since her grandfather's death she had not heard anyone call her grandmother Elisabeth. But once to everyone, as now to this old lady, Frau Blessing had been Elisabeth. Then Sarah Klein's dark eyes had sparkled in a young, perhaps a pretty face. Lisa tried to imagine her, to find beneath the mask of age the face of the girl, Sarah Stern, Sarah Klein.

"She never spoke of us?" Mrs. Stern asked anxiously. "Of course, Mr. Hanauer came more often than she. But I thought perhaps—you see, old Mrs. Hanauer was my mother's cousin. They came together from Germany." She paused and looked closely at Lisa. "I don't wish to presume, only it is a matter of life and death. My nephew's boy, little Max Klein, went back to Germany. We haven't heard." Mrs. Stern paused. The wrinkled lids closed over her eyes. Her hands turned slowly outward in a tired gesture. "Perhaps you don't wish to help us."

"I do. Only I didn't know. You see, I didn't know——"

Mrs. Stern continued. "Maxie went back. There was an opening for him with our cousin Felix in Hamburg. But we have not heard. For a year now we have heard nothing. The letters are returned. And when I read in the paper that you were here, I hoped that because of your grandmother—Elisabeth would remember. And she would want to help Max because of the old days, because of the old folks."

"I will try, but there is so little. I've tried for others."

"You don't believe me. Perhaps many people come to you because your grandmother is Jewish."

"No one has come before."

"But we are truly cousins. I can show you the grave where Rachel Hanauer lies buried. In the plot next to my parents. Or perhaps you would not want to be seen going to the burial place. I purposely did not come to the theater. I suppose that because of your grandfather Blessing and your father you are an honorary Aryan. Hitler promised to reward the war veterans. At least in your case, for your father's sake, he kept his word."

"He couldn't help himself. He didn't know."

"Felix thought the veterans would be safe. But for Felix it is over. He is dead. It's little Max. If only we knew."

"I can give you no hope," Lisa said.

"Perhaps if you wrote to Elisabeth. Since she is safe."

"But is she?" Lisa knew that the fear in Mrs. Stern's eyes must be reflected in her own. "The *'Heldenlied'* should be a weapon." Her fingers curled around an invisible sword. "It shall be a weapon to save us all."

"If God wills. Just so you try."

"And will you take me tomorrow? I should like to see my great-grandmother's grave. She was young like my mother. Forever young, forever free."

Mrs. Stern shook her head. "It is better I do not go. We must not be seen together. The Nazis are everywhere. My son laughs at me and says I see them under my bed. But I know." Her hands moved again in the tired gesture of resignation. "For our people it begins again."

"But you will take me?"

"No. For Maxie's sake it is better not. I haven't told even my son that there is a connection between us."

"But you will tell me how to go?"

"I will tell you, my child." The dark, restless eyes were quiet, their brightness was misty. "It is good for the poor dead to be a little remembered."

When Mrs. Stern had gone Lisa stood still. Across the strange room her image looked at her from a mirror on the wall. Only her reflection in the glass was familiar. The rest of the room was strange. One of a succession of rooms through which she had traveled —all the hotel rooms seen briefly and forgotten. Not this room. This room she would remember. How curious to learn about yourself in a strange room.

Lisa looked at her reflected image. It, too, should be unfamiliar, changed by the new knowledge. Lisa looked at herself with detachment. Just so had she looked in dressing-room mirrors rimmed with glaring lights. Just so had she studied her face before a dress rehearsal. This I must do, and this, to become the stranger whose part I play. Lisa touched the cold glass. Now I have become a stranger. Mrs. Stern has transformed me into the stranger that I always was. The face is not changed nor am I changed. Nothing about yourself deeply astonishes the heart. It's as though you had always known.

I should have known, Lisa thought. I should have seen that my father was a Jew. He did not know. But it is my business to see people, to study their faces as I study my own. Looking back, I should have known. I should have recognized the scholar, tireless in his desire to learn, and equally tireless in his desire to share his knowledge. I should have recognized the gentleness, the patience—the patience that, over and over through evil times, has hardened into endurance that nothing can destroy.

Lisa lifted her head. She repeated the words aloud: "That nothing can destroy." I belong to the people who are not destroyed. The crucified are not destroyed. The Germans are destroyed, but not the Jews. I knew that before I knew that I belonged to them. I belong to the only German people who are not destroyed, who are not part of the pattern of darkness. My German heritage is not part of that pattern. My people did not destroy the Fatherland, the lovely Fatherland I saw through Jewish eyes and praised in Jewish verse. My father would have liked to know he had a special kinship with the poet he loved so well.

Lisa looked away from the mirror. She closed her eyes the better to see his face, the professor in uniform. He did not know. But I should have known. Looking back, I should have known. I should have recognized the Jewish gift for finding comedy in tragedy. The joke between us that was a comfort against my terror. I should have known it for a Jewish joke, the mockery of the oppressed. They have had time in which to practice it. They have learned to sing by the rivers of Babylon, and even to laugh a little in captivity, to laugh at those who wasted them.

My father never belonged in that bloodstained pagan heaven. But his song shall save her.

Lisa felt the stab of fear. The song is not much of a weapon, and I am so far from her. If only she had told me. That last Sunday when we listened to the church bells, she might have told me.

Lisa shook her head. Her reflection moved and she saw the fear rising in her eyes. Granny would not tell me then, not when there was danger. She would not let me see the danger. She has always stood between me and the danger, between me and the fear in my heart. When my father died . . .

The distant December day was for an instant close in time and space. Lisa remembered her grandmother sitting by the fire. Her hands had moved. They had moved in the weary gesture of resignation, of patient acceptance of mortal evil. I should have seen, Lisa thought, but I took blindly the comfort she gave me.

Lisa's hands trembled. She clasped them to steady them. Now my strength is all she has. Now I stand between her and the danger. Let me find the ancient strength, the ancient wisdom.

A clock stood on the table. Lisa counted the hours. In Germany it is morning. The sun has risen on her fear. I no longer stand outside the fear as I stood when I pitied Dr. Meyer, even when I saw Raimund. Lisa shivered and raised her clasped hands to her eyes to shut out the memory of Raimund, to shut out the picture of the sunlight on the pines at Waldenberg where her grandmother was alone with the danger.

"You are not alone," Lisa said aloud. "Soon I will help you. Not soon. Today and tomorrow must pass before I can begin."

Lisa sat on the bed and thought of the time that must pass before she could do anything for her grandmother. She could only wait for time to pass. So little of today was gone.

Lisa turned away the face of the clock. She did not want to watch the slowness of the time in which she could do nothing. Then she remembered there was one thing she could do. One small thing. She could visit Rachel Hanauer's grave. As Rosa was to Lisa, so was Rachel to Lisa's grandmother. The young, unremembered mother, loved as a nursery legend, imagined tenderly. For her daughter's sake Rachel Hanauer should be today a little remembered.

The cemetery was on a hillside. The midmorning sun was hot. The stone beneath Lisa's hand was warm.

RACHEL HANAUER
Beloved Wife of Dan Hanauer

Young and beloved. Lisa knelt beside the stone. Her finger traced the carved lettering. Rachel had not thought to lie forever alone. Nor had Dan Hanauer meant to leave her so. But he had died at sea. It had been so long ago, the loss of the *Titanic,* that rehearsal for tragedy in a prewar world. Lisa remembered the old sad tale from her childhood. The ship sinking as the voices rose in song: " 'Nearer, my God to Thee, nearer to Thee.' " Dan Hanauer had been like God, old and indistinct. In that cloudless, so young world Lisa had had no need of God. He, too, might have died. In that early time only the very old had died, except Lisa's young mother. And that had puzzled Lisa's childish mind, but it had not frightened her. Lisa's mother, for some mysterious reason, had turned into an angel.

> *Now I lay me down to sleep,*
> *Fourteen angels watch do keep. . . .*

Prayer then had been not a crying need, but a peaceful close of every day. It had been the quiet of evening time. Dan Hanauer's death had not disturbed that quiet.

Lisa stood among the graves. There was a handsome monument to mark the tomb of Jacob Klein and his wife Leah. But for Rachel there was only the gray stone. Even that must have seemed too heavy for her light, young body. And beside her was the empty place that had waited in vain for Dan Hanauer.

This was an old cemetery. It belonged to the dead. Few were left to mourn. A car drove slowly by on the road outside, but no visitors came.

The sunny hillside was far from Waldenberg. It was strange to think that these poor, quiet dead could threaten that distant German hillside.

But the threat is mine. Lisa's lips moved. Forgive me, Rachel, that the threat is mine. I can bring Granny home. Now that I know, I can bring Granny home. I can destroy the *"Heldenlied."* No longer will Siegfried Blessing be a name of fear. He need no longer seem a son of darkness.

Lisa looked down at Rachel's grave. Rachel was young as Rosa was young. My young German mother. Will I then reject her heritage? Will I accept nothing from her? She left me my childhood, my German childhood which is part of me. The songs and the stories, the bright pictures and the words that rhyme. The candles of Advent and the carols that herald Christmas, the silent night, the holy night of which I sang. The pious, lowly couple, the humble Jewish family of whom I sang in the silent night. That, too, is my heritage.

Lisa walked slowly between the graves to the gate. These are my people. But the Germans, too, are my people. My poor people. My poor people, who, in destroying, are destroyed. I am my father's people and my mother's. Jew and German and American. In America are all the people, and I am one of them.

XVIII

IN NEW YORK the sun was setting. Franz stood beside Anne and looked out over the park.

"I don't like to see the days grow long," Anne said. "It's the end of our winter."

"Need it end?" Franz asked.

"That's up to you. Or is it up to Lisa? When is she coming back?"

"What you and I have is apart from Lisa. It belongs to us."

"I've never been a girl to think well of half a loaf."

"And that's all we've had." Franz turned Anne's lips towards his. "Stop looking away from me." He kissed her. "It's been half a loaf. It's been no bread at all. Dances, people. An occasional hour alone. An occasional kiss. That's for children, Anne."

"You see, I have a child." Anne moved away from the window. She sat on a low stool before the fire. "I can't please myself. I have to think of her."

"But, Anne, we can't go on like this. Why can't we have our separate happiness? Tonight, for instance. Polly isn't here."

"No, she's spending the week end with Paul. But you and I are going to meet at the Joneses'—quite respectably."

"This damnable American respectability."

"I have a native taste for it." Her mouth was set in a stubborn line. She looked into the fire. "It's for you to choose, Franz. When Lisa returns, you can make your choice."

He has made it, she thought. I have won against her beauty and all their years together. Her lips curved and parted in a soft smile.

He bent his mouth to hers. She clung to him for a moment. Then she pushed him away and stood up. "You must go, Franz. I must dress. I have to make myself beautiful to please you at the Joneses' party."

"To torment me." Franz laughed. "One can't be angry with you. You are too pretty. You are like a flower. One of your own flowers."

He took a rose from a crystal bowl and put it in his buttonhole.

After he had gone Anne stood before the fire. She took a flower and rubbed it against her lips. I had forgotten, she thought. Until Franz came I had forgotten. This winter I have been alive again.

Franz was whistling as he entered his apartment. He picked up a telegram on the hall table. He paused on the threshold of the living room. Woolie von Elsfeldt was sitting before the fire.

"Woolie! Is this wise? I thought that you preferred that our acquaintance should appear to be of the most superficial."

"It is necessary that I see you. And no one knows I am here except your servant, who is not interested. It is necessary that I see you about Lisa. One of our people in San Francisco telephoned me a little while ago. It seems that Lisa went on a sentimental pilgrimage this morning. She was seen visiting the Jew cemetery where Frau Blessing's mother is buried."

"But how . . . ? I did not know. How did Lisa know?"

"The important thing is that we did not know the grave existed. All the records of the Hanauer family were destroyed in the fire after the earthquake. We checked very carefully on that. Now we shall see that the gravestone is removed. I have already given the orders." Woolie laughed at Franz's puzzled expression. "Don't worry. It will be done very discreetly. Several stones will be removed at the same time. And several monuments will be defaced, possibly with swastikas. But we shall not appear in it. It will be attributed to native American vandalism. We might even arrange to have a fiery cross. The Ku Klux touch is always authentic."

"How did you find out?"

"Naturally, we've kept an eye on Lisa. Now it might be wise for you to go out to her. It would be unfortunate if she acted impulsively."

"The tour ends tomorrow night," Franz said. "This wire may be from Lisa." His long fingers tore at the yellow envelope. "Yes, she arrives by plane on Monday."

"Is that all she says?"

"Just that." Franz gave the telegram to Woolie. "And her love."

"Ah, her love. That is a useful factor. Well, perhaps we can wait then until Monday. This changes matters, Franz. I was never in favor of coddling Lisa. But in Berlin they thought she might be useful to us in spite of herself."

"Lisa is liked and admired here, Woolie. She is successful. That is useful."

"Possibly. But there is another way in which she can be even more useful. It will now, I think, be simple for you to persuade her to be reasonable about the money."

"I shall do my best," Franz said. "I have already tried."

"So you tell me. But now it will be easier for you to make Lisa see the necessity for co-operation."

Woolie rose. "I shall hear from you, then, on Tuesday. Tonight you'll be at the Joneses', of course?"

"I was going," Franz said hesitantly.

"And why not? Nothing has changed. And Anne Craven will be there. A very pretty second string to your bow, Franz. But just remember that for the present it is a second string. Lisa is still of some importance to us."

Woolie paused in the doorway. "I shall hear from you Tuesday, then, at the latest. It might be well to give Lisa a hint, just a hint, that the old woman has not had too easy a winter."

"I have heard nothing. Frau Blessing's letters are cheerful."

"But you have guessed, Franz. You're not stupid." Woolie balanced his fat body on the balls of his feet and swayed slightly on the threshold of the open door. He laughed. "Really, my friend, innocence becomes your poetic appearance, but one does not rise, even in these troubled times, as you have risen in Germany, if one is stupid."

Lisa arrived in New York on Monday. As the maid served lunch Lisa managed to talk quietly of indifferent things. "Yes, they loved us in San Francisco. More than in Los Angeles, I think. Los Angeles is not much of a theater town. Gerald is pleased."

"He telephoned this morning. I left the message in your room."

"I know. He sent on a play for me to read. But I can't do anything just now. Something has come up. Coffee, Franz? Or shall we have it in the other room?"

"No. Stay here. It's so long since I have had you at my table. I have been lonely, Lisa. Tell me—you wrote of Hans Friedrich? He is doing well? Extraordinary how grateful Americans are even for second-rate German scholarship."

"Hans isn't second-rate," Lisa answered. "He has only been overshadowed by his father-in-law's world-wide reputation."

Lisa watched Franz as he slowly drank his coffee.

"A little more, if I may, Lisa? It is good to be with you like this. Like the other happy times when you have come home to me."

Lisa's hand trembled as she tilted the silver coffeepot. Franz dropped his eyes before hers as he took the cup. It was as though he knew. As though he were trying to put off the hour which he knew would be an evil one.

"Please come, Franz. I must talk to you." Lisa led the way into the living room. She closed the door. She fumbled in her pocketbook. She withdrew a clipping from a San Francisco paper. She gave it to Franz. "This is as good a way as any for me to begin to tell you."

Franz looked at the printed words.

JEWISH CEMETERY DESECRATED

Gravestones Removed
Monuments Defaced

"Well, Lisa?"

"Poor Rachel. This final indignity in some way was my doing. In some way that I don't understand, it was my doing. The poor, lonely dead, whose hillside I visited. You see, Franz, Mrs.——" Lisa stopped herself. "Someone came to see me and told me."

"Someone, Lisa? You are afraid to say the name to me."

"I'm afraid of your fear, Franz. Not of you."

"My fear is for you, Lisa. It has always been for you. That is why I didn't tell you about your grandmother. She and I. We both knew it was better for your sake not to tell you that her parents were Jews."

"You knew, Franz." Lisa stared at him. "You knew, and, knowing, you left her in Germany."

"It was for you."

"You left her to the danger. Because you were afraid. But I am not afraid. There is the '*Heldenlied*,' Franz. Between us, my father and I will save her."

"You can do nothing, Lisa."

"If I tell—Siegfried Blessing, the Nazi hero, is a Jew."

"Siegfried Blessing is dead. Germany has many dead heroes. You have only one living grandmother. You cannot tell."

"I can bring her safely out with the threat to tell."

"They won't let her go."

"Then I will go back."

"No, Lisa." Franz reached out his hand to her. She moved away from his touch. "Lisa, you are safe here. If you are quiet, you are safe. If you go back, you will not lessen her danger. You will break her heart."

"Do they know?" Lisa asked. "Of course they must, if you know."

"Yes, it's known. It's known to a few."

"And knowing that they knew, you left her——"

"It was her wish, Lisa."

"And what news have you of her?" Lisa forced herself close to Franz. She put her hands on his shoulders and looked into his eyes. She searched for his knowledge. She looked at the beautiful curve of his mouth as he spoke.

"You know yourself from her letters that she is well. Why should they molest her?"

"She wouldn't tell me. And you won't. And I can't see in your face." All the faces were masks. This beloved face, too. The beautiful mask that hid the stranger, the enemy. Her beloved was her mortal enemy.

"I know no more than you, Lisa. But if all was not well with her, I think I should know. Leave things as they are. That is safest for us all."

"There is no safety for any of us. Haven't you told me that?" Lisa asked. "Haven't you told me that often? You knew and I didn't. But I will make her safe, Franz. I have the weapon. Grandfather did not know for whose hand he was forging that sword. Will you help me, Franz?"

"I cannot, Lisa." He took her hand and held it against her will. His dark eyes looked sadly into hers. "I cannot help you, Lisa. And you cannot help her. You can only destroy us all."

"But we are destroyed, Franz. If we leave her, we are destroyed and there is no health in us."

She wrenched her hand free from him and walked out of the room. She heard him call, "Lisa!" . . . His voice, his face. She had loved them. Her heart still yearned to love them. Even though they had become the voice and the face of the enemy. She took her coat and hurried out of the apartment.

For a long time Lisa walked blindly through the streets. She turned into Central Park. The sun shone from the west. It was growing late. The procession of baby carriages and children and nurses passed Lisa on their way home. She stood uncertainly beside a small, deserted lake. She looked up at a tall apartment house. Woolie and Daphne lived there. Woolie would help her. She remembered his words. "I can facilitate a passage." She slowly climbed the steps out of the park. She waited for the traffic light to change. She looked above the line of cars that crowded Fifth Avenue. She looked up at the building where Woolie lived. He would help her.

At the Von Elsfeldt apartment the butler showed Lisa into the library. Daphne was curled up on a sofa. She shook herself like a kitten and jumped lightly to her feet. "Lisa, how nice. I was very bored with myself." She patted her dark curls and held out her hand.

As she took it, Lisa thought, How curious, she seems to have no bones at all. Not in her soft hand any more than in her body. Daphne's face, in its frame of childish ringlets, was like a kitten's. No, not like a kitten's. It was the face of a doll, the merry, impertinent face of a modern doll.

"I came, really, to speak to Woolie about a business matter."

"My dear, he'll be delighted. Woolie adores business. He's on the telephone now about something dull. I'll go and call him." Daphne ran out of the room. "Woolie, Woolie, Lisa Blessing is here."

Lisa listened to Daphne's light voice and the small clatter of her heelless sandals as she disappeared across the hall.

She took a cigarette from a silver box. Daphne did indeed like crowns. The box, the ash tray, the lighter—all were conspicuously engraved. Poor Woolie would never be allowed to become an American citizen. Daphne enjoyed too much being the Baroness von Elsfeldt. The pretty, luxurious little Baroness.

"Well, Lisa." Lisa had not heard Woolie enter. "Daphne says this is business, so I sent her along to have her tea. Now tell me, how can I help you? You look upset."

Lisa put up her hand to her hair. "I'm sorry, Woolie, I must look a perfect sight. I've been walking in the wind. I didn't notice."

"That's all right, Lisa." He touched her hand. "But you're cold. Let me get you some tea, or would you rather talk first?"

"I must talk. Dear Woolie, you will help me, won't you? You won't be afraid? There's no need for us to be afraid. We have the weapon. The *'Heldenlied.'* But Franz said——"

"Just a minute, Lisa." Woolie settled a cushion behind his back. "You know I'm your friend. That I want to help you. Now tell me the story clearly. Begin at the beginning."

"I don't know the beginning, Woolie. I don't know how it happened that my grandmother kept her birth a secret. But the fact is that she is a Jewess and I have only just discovered it."

"Are you sure, Lisa? Have you proof?"

"Yes. Someone told me in San Francisco. And I went to the Jewish cemetery. I saw my great-grandmother's grave. 'Rachel Hanauer, beloved wife of Dan Hanauer.' "

"Yes, the grave is evidence. And you have papers, perhaps, family pictures, letters——"

"No. There was nothing but the grave."

"But surely your informant—who did you say told you?"

"I didn't say, Woolie. Not even to you. There have been too many inadvertent betrayals."

"I see. Well, what do you mean to do about this awkward bit of information? I mean, it must be rather a jolt for you, Lisa."

"No, it wasn't a jolt." She tried to explain to him. "Although I hadn't known, it seems now—it seemed instantly as if I had always been waiting to know. But I felt fear—fear for her, and admiration for her courage. She came rightly by it, the courage that has prevailed against cruelty in all the generations of her people, of my people. That courage sent me to safety and did not let me see that she was brave."

"Still, it must have astonished you that your father, a National Socialist hero——"

"The astonishment was that I had not recognized that he belonged to the people of the Book. I knew well enough that he did not belong in the latter-day *Nibelungenlied* which my grandfather created for him."

"Look, Lisa——"

"I am looking. Now I see, as I always should have seen, my father, the professor, the Jewish professor. I should have seen that he and Heine were the same sort of Germans."

"Of Germans?"

"Oh, I know, Woolie. Not according to the current definition, but in the other Germany. Or was that other Germany, that lovely Fatherland, always a dream? The light was the dream. And the darkness was the reality. Now I see the reality. I am grateful that my father's people were part of the dream."

"Well, one reality, Lisa, is that Siegfried Blessing, heretofore a German hero, was, according to you, a Jew."

"And that's it. Don't you see, Woolie, that is a jolt for them—the Nazis, I mean. Oh, a few of them know. But they would hardly like it to be public property that Siegfried Blessing was a Jew. Don't you think it might be a jolt, Woolie? Isn't it a threat for me to use to get Granny out safely?"

"Hardly that, Lisa. It would be awkward, but the Third Reich has survived more than awkwardness. After all, Roehm and Gregor Strasser were once National Socialist heroes. It's not good enough, Lisa. Not good enough to save Frau Blessing."

Lisa stared at Woolie. He still smiled good-naturedly. His voice was slow and pleasant.

"You have played your card, Lisa: the truth about Siegfried Blessing. It's not much of a card. The truth about one dead hero of the Reich. It's not much against a life you hold dear. A life that is, you must realize, rather frail."

Lisa stared at him silently. She twisted an unlighted cigarette in her fingers. It was again the nightmare. The nightmare that walked by day. Here in New York as in Berlin. Woolie, that ordinary, friendly businessman. Herr Kraussmann was an ordinary civil servant. His sunny office was as commonplace as this comfortable Fifth Avenue apartment.

"I'm sorry to startle you, Lisa. You look quite white. Surely you didn't believe that Wolfgang von Elsfeldt could be anything but a German? And it's not only patriotism. Did you really think I was fool enough in these times to throw in my lot with this soft, helpless democracy? And you, Lisa, are you stupid enough to choose America when you might remain a German?"

"I have no choice."

"But you have, Lisa. You are considered an Aryan. You can continue so all your days. I am authorized to tell you this. After all, you have beauty, talent . . . Lisa Blessing is an asset to the Reich."

"You don't understand, Woolie. I mean that only one choice is possible to me. I choose liberty and the light. I do not wish to return to the prison darkness."

"You're a fool, Lisa. However, that's your affair. Now to continue. We were talking about cards. A card is worth only the skill of the player. We have a card in the health of your grandmother. And we are skillful players. She has perhaps been too considerate to tell you that this past winter has not been easy for her. There has been difficulty about provisions—about her coal supply. Matilde, your former maid, is now in charge. We persuaded Frau Blessing that, at her age, she requires the services of a housekeeper."

The cigarette dropped from Lisa's fingers. She pressed her nails into the palm of her hand. The small pain kept her attention. It helped her to listen. She must listen. She must think.

"Yes, Matilde has been useful," Woolie continued. "We know how to manage people like that. We turn to our purpose the old envy, the small, sharp malice."

"The *'Heldenlied,'*" Lisa said. Her voice was loud in her ears. "That bright sword, it——"

"Lisa, don't talk sentimental nonsense. We would, of course, like to preserve the legend of Siegfried Blessing. And I think that, for your grandmother's sake, you will help us to preserve it. But that is a small matter compared to the money."

"The money?"

"Really, Lisa, the Jewish strain must be strong in you if you can so easily contemplate keeping the money which would buy your grandmother's safety."

Lisa's lips formed her words with difficulty. "Tell me what you know."

"I know that your grandmother managed to put a million and a half dollars in New York in your name. That money belongs in the

Reich. It is not permitted to remove German resources from Germany.
Franz would, of course, give us the money, or at least so one assumes
of a good party member. But it seems your signature is necessary. Until
now, so Franz tells me, you have refused to sign, to transfer the
money."

"And if I agree?"

"If you agree, my dear Lisa, everything can be arranged. After all,
we Germans are practical people. And not particularly cruel, except
where cruelty has a value. Here the value is a million and a half dollars. And dollars in America can be useful. Is it a bargain, Lisa, a
sensible bargain? In making your arrangements, you will, of course,
not permit my name to appear."

Lisa spoke slowly, carefully. "I will see, Woolie. I will talk it over
with Franz. I will see what can be done."

She must speak and act carefully. Woolie was right. No card was
worth more than the skill of the player. For her grandmother's sake
she must play her hand skillfully.

It was dark when Lisa walked home. The wind blew more coldly.

Franz was waiting for her. "Lisa, where have you been? I have been
almost crazy."

"Have you, Franz? I have been walking. And I have been to see
Woolie von Elsfeldt. He told me about the money. Don't look so
frightened. You are quite safe. I pretended that I knew. He still thinks
that you told me."

"Lisa, I would have told you. Only I promised Frau Blessing. And
besides, it wouldn't have been any use."

"Suppose you tell me now. I can find it all out from Woolie. But for
your own sake, Franz, suppose you tell me yourself."

"Your grandmother arranged that this money be placed in your
name in New York. It's in what I think they call a custodian account.
No one can touch it but you. Your grandmother didn't want you to
know about it unless you needed it or unless she died."

"I do need it now. How can I get it? Will you tell me or must I ask
Woolie?"

"It's in the care of James Hudson, of the City and Country Bank.
His father and your grandmother were friends. Hudson has handled
certain business matters for your grandmother before. How this was
arranged, and at what cost, I don't know."

"Then tomorrow I will arrange to see Mr. Hudson. He must plan a method whereby this money can be used for ransom. What an ancient thing it is, this new National Socialism. Hostages and ransom. The rack and the screw."

"Lisa, be sensible. There is no effective way to pay ransom. You will not save her. You will only lose the money. Don't be a fool, Lisa."

"It can be done, Franz, and it shall be done. Only there is so little time. Did you know that Matilde was there with Granny? I never saw Matilde until the night Raimund Hoehlmann came. You didn't see Raimund, did you, Franz?"

"Lisa, don't torture yourself."

"It is not I who am tortured, Franz. It was never I. I have been quite safe. While all around me those I love, the known and the unknown——"

"Lisa, please. You upset yourself."

"Yes, so I do. And that's foolish. I need to stay calm to see clearly."

Lisa held her hand against the door to steady herself. The room turned slowly around her. Everywhere in the world there was darkness beyond the safe lighted rooms. Because of the darkness none of the lights were safe. She closed her eyes until the swinging walls were still again. She walked slowly into her room. After she was in bed she reached out her hand to turn off the lamp. She did not touch the switch. She would sleep in the light. She could not lie alone in the darkness.

The next day Lisa made an appointment with James Hudson. He received her in his office. The windows behind his desk overlooked the harbor.

"This is a pleasure, Miss Blessing, or should I say Countess Erlencamp?"

"I come as Lisa Blessing."

"Of course. I've known your family for many years. Dan Hanauer saved my father in the panic of 1907. Sit down, my dear, you're trembling."

Lisa studied his grave face. It was a kind, middle-aged face. The gray eyes behind the shell-rimmed spectacles were shrewd.

"It's about the money, Mr. Hudson. I have just learned about it."

"Hm, yes. I was very pleased to be entrusted with it. Grieved, of course, by the necessity. And the cost to your grandmother. The money represents only a small part of the cost to her. However, we should be grateful for saving that much. It's a lucky thing that German officials are venal. Pity they're so greedy."

"Mr. Hudson, I need the money."

"Well, it's yours, of course. We have it conservatively invested. There's a nice little income. I hope you don't mean to touch the principal."

"Don't you see? I need it for my grandmother. To save her. You know that she is a Jewess?"

"Why, yes, as a matter of fact, I do. My father told me that Dan Hanauer never made any bones about it until your grandmother's marriage. And then he thought it would be better for her. I never knew Wilhelm Blessing."

"It was he, of course," Lisa said. "I should have known. It wouldn't have seemed important to my grandmother. She loved Wilhelm Blessing. I used not to understand so clearly. But when you love someone dearly and for long, you give up many things. One by one. They seem unimportant. And you give them up."

"Yes—er—quite so." James Hudson moved uncomfortably in his chair. "But now, of course, this matter of your grandmother's origin becomes important. Grave, even, if it's known. We certainly should take steps to persuade her to come over here."

"They know. They won't let her come."

"Surely they wouldn't harm an old lady."

"Unless you have seen it, Mr. Hudson, you cannot imagine what they would do. I had hoped to force them to free her through the *'Heldenlied.'* "

"The what? Oh yes, the song about your father. Awkward for them, that. Your Teuton doesn't like to be laughed at."

"But it's not enough. They want the money. If I give it up, they will release my grandmother."

"But will they? My dear young lady, will they? This is blackmail, you know. And that's a bad game for the one who pays."

"But if I promise that the day she lands——"

"Well, I know. Just looking at you, I know that your word is good."

James Hudson looked at Lisa. Under the braided golden crown of her hair her brow was drawn into a troubled frown. Her wide-set eyes looked anxiously into his.

"Yes, I know, my dear," James Hudson continued. "I've had experience in judging faces. You can't last in my business unless you learn when to trust as well as when to doubt. But those birds don't trust anyone. Oh, they're businessmen all right. We had a lot of businessmen like them in prohibition days. Gangsters don't trust anyone."

"Well, then if I paid part of the money in advance?"

"You might do that; it might expedite matters—though I doubt it. They'd try to squeeze it all out of you and give nothing in return. They'd take the down payment just as a starter."

"If you will arrange for me to have the money, I'll sign whatever is necessary so I can draw it out."

"No, you send the feller to me. It's a dirty business. I'll handle it."

"But they won't see you. They know that only my signature is necessary."

The gray eyes behind the spectacles twinkled. "That's the impression I gave your husband. You see, he thought he could draw on the money. I guess Mrs. Blessing gave him that idea. She's a smart old lady. Well, I explained that his signature was no good. We had to have yours. There was no reason to tell him that they have to have mine, too."

"But you will sign? You will bring her home?"

"Yes, I'll pay every dollar to get her out—though she wouldn't want me to. If you believe she's in any danger, I will arrange the payment."

"She's being badly treated. They told me. Don't you see? The money doesn't matter."

"It matters to them. And we've got to use it as best we can to save Frau Blessing. They know you're desperate. But I think they can be persuaded that I'm more cold-blooded—that I'd like to keep this account for the bank. You need an old Wall Street horse trader like me. And I'll do my best for you. Send the feller along."

"I don't know if he'll be willing to see you."

"He'll see me, all right, when he knows he has to. And he'll try to put the whole transaction on a very high-minded basis. He'll be a patriotic German trying to get back some money that was illegally removed from his country. Your grandmother's exit permit will be something else, a matter on which he'll be anxious to help us. He'll talk about red tape, official delays, and the rest of it. I'll do my best. I can't promise you more than that, and I don't know if it'll be good enough."

Lisa left James Hudson's office with very little hope. She knew that that was what the old man had intended. The old knew how difficult it was to live with hope deferred. She realized now that he was old. It was curious how long Americans managed to keep the look of middle age. Mr. Hudson was old and he was wise. She must trust to his knowledge, to his experience. And she must wait. That would be the hardest part, to wait.

She could no longer see the harbor that had been spread before her eyes beneath the windows of the tall office building. An ocean liner had passed as she sat with Mr. Hudson. Into freedom's harbor came ships from all the world. From Cherbourg, from Bremerhaven. In Germany the sun would have set behind the tall pines. The lamps were lit now in Frau Blessing's sitting room. Lisa remembered the lamps and the firelight. In March the evenings were still cold. Perhaps there was no fire burning in the little room. Lisa shivered. The hardest part was to wait.

XIX

THE SPRING became summer. Franz insisted that they take again the house at Port Washington. "It is better, Lisa, that everything should seem the same between us."

Lisa and Franz lived as strangers in the pretty rented house.

In April, on Lisa's insistence, Mr. Hudson had reluctantly made a payment of five hundred thousand dollars.

"This isn't the way to do it, my dear," he had said. "The money should be put in escrow to be paid on Frau Blessing's arrival. This payment is useless. Nothing will happen."

Nothing had happened. In two months nothing had happened.

In June Mr. Hudson sent for Lisa. "I have put the money in escrow with Adams, of the County Loan and Trust. Upon your grandmother's arrival in New York he is to transfer the funds to Baron von Elsfeldt. I set a time limit of two months."

"But suppose they don't let her come? Two months are long. Suppose something happens to her?"

"Nothing will happen if they want the money badly enough. We must hope they do. That is our only hope. And, above all, we must make them feel that the time limit is ours—that we are not driven by fear."

In the evening Lisa drove slowly back to Long Island. It was hard to hold on. Hard to wait. She tried to think of her own affairs. She must decide about the play. Mr. Hudson had pointed out to her that she had her living to earn. "I understand that your husband is not without funds, but even so . . ."

Lisa tried to think about the play. It was a better part than she had had in *The Mirror*. Hilda, in *Before Dawn*, was the whole play. But I can't be Hilda, Lisa cried. Hilda is young and merry and brave. She can't have a heart broken with anxiety. I can't leave my heart backstage. "The show must go on" was a slogan for other, easier times. Woolie is right to count on my nerve breaking. It has broken.

She closed her lips tightly. Her soft mouth was a thin anxious line. She looked at the clock on the dashboard. It was late. Guests were coming to dinner.

Everything must be as it had always been, Franz had said. And Woolie had agreed. "It is good from our point of view that there should be a popular young German couple like you and Franz. And during these rather delicate negotiations you will do well, Lisa, to act according to our point of view."

Lisa looked at the house. Its lights were bright in the summer twilight.

> *They're having a party this evening*
> *And the house is gay with light.*

But my darkened heart is now alone, Lisa thought.

> *I move alone, apart;*
> *How little can you see, then,*
> *Into my darkened heart.*

To the edge of doom, she had thought, love must last. But not this. This was an alteration that love could not survive.

Franz was standing in the hall when she opened the door. "Well, Lisa, any news?"

"Mr. Hudson has put the funds in escrow, to be paid when Granny comes."

"That's the businesslike way to handle it. Mr. Hudson is doing his best for you. Perhaps he can save your fortune."

Lisa turned away. "I'm sorry, Franz. Forgive me now. I must hurry to dress. Our guests will be here." She smiled at him and walked up the stairs.

With smiles and friendly phrases it was possible to live with a stranger. But Franz was not a stranger. And this was not alteration. She should always have seen the fear and the greed. But she had refused to see anything but the beloved mask. That first time eight years ago on the dark Munich street she had closed her eyes and refused to see. Through all the years with Franz she had refused to see. Lisa caught the sob in her throat. "My darkened heart still loves you." But love is a habit the heart can outgrow.

Lisa thought of Sophie and Hans and their children. It is so hard to live alone. Dear God, You see it is too hard to live alone.

Lisa sat before her mirror and stared at her moving lips, at her eyes dark with fear. This is what I mustn't do. Mr. Hudson is right. They must not see the terror for her that drives me. And Franz is one of them. He must not see.

In the mirror the reflection of her bedroom door moved.

"Is that you, Franz?" She managed a smile.

"I only wanted to say that, about the money, I am not thinking of myself but of you and of what Frau Blessing herself would wish. One must be practical in this harsh world."

"I understand how you feel, Franz." She smiled at his reflection. She did not turn her head. She wanted to keep the mirror between them.

He put his hand on her shoulder. She felt the pressure of his fingers through the thin silk of her dressing gown. In the mirror her eyes met his, the eyes of a stranger.

His hand on her shoulder was the hand of a stranger. Not only her heart but her body must learn. It must learn not to need that dear, familiar touch.

Lisa and Franz drove with their guests to the Harry Spains'. The Spain house blazed with lights. The grounds were gay with colored lanterns. Lisa walked with Franz towards the wide door, towards the sound of dance music. Woolie separated them. "An attractive young couple, Lisa, should not be conspicuous in their connubial devotion. That verges on eccentricity. Suppose you dance with me."

"As you like, Woolie."

For the present, for the long, slow present, everything must be as Woolie liked.

"Quite a party." Woolie held out his hand to his hostess. " 'Lo, Rita. Lisa and I were saying this looks like quite a party." He guided Lisa into the ballroom.

Gerald Michaels cut in. "The girl I wanted to see. What about my play? You've stalled long enough. God knows why; it's a swell part."

"It's a great part, Gerald. But I'm tired. I played in *The Mirror* for a year and a half."

"On you, Lisa, tiredness is becoming. You look like a million dollars. But if you really don't want to go to rehearsal right away, I'll tell you what I'll do. I'll put off *Before Dawn* and do *Summer Week End* first. It's been running in London for six months and I'm scared to death of these English hits. But I can put this one on for buttons. Then I've got that damn revue on my hands. Why any manager in his right mind ever does a musical——"

"I take it you haven't the man yet for *Before Dawn*."

"Well, I have a couple of possibilities lined up."

"Then I can wait, Gerald? I'm tired, I need time."

"Just so you're not deserting me for good. I don't want these people to do away with Lisa Blessing and just leave the Countess. She's pretty, the Countess, but no talent, I bet."

"I notice you're here, Gerald."

"Sure, I like a little plush once in a while. Besides, Rita's an old friend of mine. And I like to see her at her Journey's End. Even if, to me, it seems a long and expensive trip to make to a siding—even such an elegant siding." Gerald avoided a collision with J. C. Jones. "Bad casting. If Society was my production, I wouldn't cast it like this. And not just J. C. None of 'em look very Charles Dana Gibson."

"Plush and elegance are hard to combine. And the Spains' little group is definitely plushy."

"All of 'em are, Lisa. All I've seen. The limited, elegant few—they're only in the books, I guess. Or did you have 'em in Europe?"

"We had these. And, talking of bad casting, did you ever see a Hohenzollern, Gerald?"

"Now the Count I'd hire. He looks the part."

Franz and Anne Craven danced by. Lisa looked at them with indifferent eyes.

Anne looked at Lisa's dark-fringed gray eyes below the bright coronet of her braids. Lisa is beautiful, Anne thought. After all the years, still Undine. And I am only pretty. But I have taken Franz away from her. For all her golden beauty, I have taken him away from her.

"Let's go outside." Franz guided Anne towards an open french window.

"But Lisa's right there. She'll notice."

"She'll notice nothing. An actress talking to her manager hasn't eyes for anything else." Franz took Anne's hand and led her out onto the lawn.

"Does Lisa know about us, Franz?"

"No, she doesn't. The little there is to know." His hand tightened on her wrist.

"No, Franz." She moved away from him. "Not until you're free. I thought you meant to be free."

Anne looked back to the winter, to the evenings when they had been alone. She remembered the parties where his presence had made her feel young. Parties were for the young. And when you were desired, then you were young.

"You've made me feel like a debutante all winter, Franz," Anne said. "It was fun. But you aren't free. You were alone only for a little while. Now that Lisa is back——"

"Lisa isn't back," Franz said. "She and I—I can't explain, Anne. But this is a crucial time in Lisa's career. At this point she needs my help. It's just for a little while. If only you will be patient. If only you will be kind—kind as you are lovely." His fingers moved against her arm.

"No, Franz. I'm not getting myself into a jam. When you're free, as I am——"

"Anne, you know how I feel about you. If I were free——"

"I hoped you were." Anne looked at him. The dark head. The curve of his brow. Had she fallen in love with a ghost from the past? She had been falling in love with him, falling slowly, lightly in love with him. Her desire for him was an ache in her body. But she would not permit her body to betray her. She would rule her body as at twenty-one she had ruled her heart.

She turned and walked towards the house. "When you are free, Franz, come back."

"You will wait, Anne?"

"I will wait, if you're not too long."

Anne was glad to leave the soft light of the lanterns, to be back in the safe brightness of the ballroom.

Phil Sinclair cut in. "How about a drink, Anne? And a little food. The Spains always do well by one in the food and drink department. . . . Rather conspicuous with Franz, weren't you?" Phil asked as he helped himself to champagne. "Don't hold out on me and my readers."

"There's nothing to tell, Phil. After all, Franz is married."

"He didn't act very married when he was with you last winter."

"Poor soul, he was lonely."

"And you consoled him. Okay." He stopped her protest. "You don't have to convince me. I'm quite sure that nothing went on. You were never a girl to take risks. But tonight, with Lisa back—I just wondered."

"Franz is absolutely loyal to Lisa."

"Loyal to her, but also rather taken with you. And he can't make up his mind in which direction his best future lies. He ought to look out or he'll starve to death like the donkey between the two bales of hay."

"You draw a pretty picture." Anne pushed back her chair.

"Sorry, Anne. Stick around. You saw the beginning of my career. I'd like you to be in on the end. I'm quitting my job on the paper."

"But why? How can you?"

"Call it a leave of absence. I've put a little away here and there, so Mother's all right, and I thought I'd like to go abroad and take a look-see. I don't know if anyone would accept a war correspondent whose sole training was on the Newport-Southampton front, but I can try. I'd like to get into Spain. That's the curtain raiser before the big show."

"A curtain raiser before the Revolution. The Revolution that won't come off, please God. Didn't you see those movies that J. C. showed last winter? Those ragged, badly disciplined Red soldiers. But so many of them. The mob, armed."

"Yes, I saw the movies. Pro-Franco propaganda and not bad. But those ragged soldiers didn't frighten me. They reminded me of other ragged, ill-equipped troops that won a war for you and me. Remember them: the Continental Army?"

"I'm not going to argue with you, Phil, about a foreign civil war. It's too silly. No one really knows the rights and the wrongs of it. I'm just instinctively on the side of order against the mob."

"I'm not equipped to argue, but I'd like to be." Phil sipped his drink reflectively. "So I'm off. I'm sick of reporting our little gilded ant heap."

"Don't tell me you're developing a conscience after all these years."

"Maybe that's it. Maybe my conscience is the chill I feel. Or maybe someone's walking on my grave. There's a chill wind blowing from somewhere, Anne. I want to know from where. Perhaps the future is always cold, like an early morning wind."

"Cold or not"—Anne stood up—"it's a certainty that the future isn't here in America. And, please God, it's not Russia. And that leaves Germany."

"Yes, those boys are on their way." Phil sat still and looked up at Anne. "They're on their way and it looks like a bandwagon, so you call it the future and climb aboard. Me, I think different. I think the future is everywhere. And I think it belongs to all the people."

"How about leaving this guy on his soapbox"—J. C. touched Anne's arm—"and dancing with the old man?"

"Can you imagine that guy Sinclair?" J. C. asked. "I hear he's quitting his job. He's not like you and me. Doesn't know when he's sitting pretty."

"Are we sitting pretty?" Anne asked anxiously.

"Surest thing you know. String along with me."

Anne moved into his arms as they entered the ballroom.

"What's with you and Franz?" J. C. asked.

"Nothing much. He's married."

"Well, so were you, once. And so was I once before Judy. As your father confessor, let me tell you that Franz is all right. I know all about him. He's got a good head on his shoulders. The boys over there think very well of him. If things work out between you, you've got my blessing."

The dance floor grew crowded. The party moved around Anne. This was like old times. The old, safe, pleasant times. Her heart was in her throat as she saw Franz. He was looking for her. He cut in.

"Let's not talk, Anne. Let's just belong to the music. They're playing our tune."

They moved swiftly to the rhythm of the "Blue Danube."

"It will be all right, Anne, you will see."

Her fingers clung to his. All the yesterdays had once been tomorrow. But perhaps this tomorrow would be different.

The music played faster. As Anne whirled in Franz's arms, the room spun around them. It made a pattern, like the gay patterns in a child's kaleidoscope, a familiar, luxurious pattern of color and gaiety and brightness.

XX

THE SUMMER DAYS dragged by. All the days were alike to Lisa. Their sunniness was darkened by her silent fear. Mr. Hudson had no news for her. He said in July what he had said in June. "The money is there waiting for them. Now it's up to them."

"Is there nothing I can do?"

"Nothing but wait. And don't show your fear. Don't let them think that anything would persuade you to break the escrow."

Lisa's house was full of guests. She carried out Woolie's instructions. The Erlencamps were a popular couple.

"People believe what they see," Woolie said, "and you and Franz are a charming, living contradiction of the newspaper lies about Germans."

Phil Sinclair came to say good-by to Lisa.

"Where's everybody?" he asked. "This is a pretty house, but it's as incomplete without people as a Gerald Michaels set without actors."

"At a luncheon at the Spains'." Lisa touched the manuscript on

the low glass table beside her. "The final draft of *Before Dawn*. I said
I had to read it and came home early."

"What's on your mind, Lisa? You've been giving a superb performance as the fashionable Countess Erlencamp. But it is a performance, isn't it?"

"I'm afraid all actresses seem rather stagy by daylight. When do
you go, Phil?"

"Next week. Look, Lisa, I may go to Germany. That's one way of
getting to Spain. Can I do anything for you?"

Lisa shook her head silently. Then she said: "Yes, there is one
thing."

Mrs. Stern's fear had been Lisa's warning. And yet she had done
nothing for her. She had been able to do nothing except to keep all
knowledge of Mrs. Stern from Woolie. Now Lisa looked at Phil. Could
this ordinary man be a savior as other ordinary men had been be-
trayers? He might be able to help. Through his newspaper connections
he might be able to learn what had become of Max Klein.

She told him the little she knew. "Felix Klein's office was in Hamburg—Gebrüder Klein. He is dead. The boy, Max Klein, has disappeared. He has relatives here who asked me to help. No one can help,
but if you could find out—it's not knowing that's unbearable. When
you don't know, there's no limit to the imagined horror."

Phil looked around the cool shaded terrace. Beyond the bright
awnings the water of the Sound danced in the sunlight.

"You seem remote from terror here," he said. "The handsome
young Erlencamps make the horror seem incredible. I wonder why you
want it that way?"

"If you could find out about Max Klein. Not do anything, just find
out."

"And may I go to see your grandmother? I met her several years
ago when I was in Germany."

Lisa kept her voice steady. "You are very kind, Phil, but Granny
has not been well. She sees very few people."

"Okay, Lisa. Maybe you're giving a command performance and a
better one than I thought. You can trust me."

"Thank you, Phil. I believe I can trust you. I have known you so
long, and——"

"And besides, you have to trust someone. Look, Lisa, I came

through the garden. I didn't go into the house. Wouldn't it be a good idea if I left the same way, and left now? I guess I sound pretty melodramatic for this peaceful setting, but it might be as well if no one knows I've been here."

"And have you been giving a performance, too, Phil?" she asked. "You look rather soldierly. Not at all like Peter Pierpont of the *Express*. Was that an act?"

"It was my living, and a good one. But now I've made enough. I'm giving Peter up. I'm tired of him. Not that I'm cut out to be a soldier."

"You never know. You might be." Lisa held out her hand to him. "Good luck, Phil, and thank you."

She watched him as he walked between the trees into the garden. She had known him long, but he was a stranger. There were only strangers and one must trust them. She picked up the play. It was heavy in her hands. She did not see the typewritten words. She saw the sad, bright eyes of Mrs. Stern, whose confidence she had entrusted to a stranger. Dear God, let it be that I have done right. She smoothed the thin page. She forced her eyes to read: "Act I, Scene I. The living room of Mrs. Booth's house. An open door on the left discloses . . ."

When Franz came home he found Lisa sitting on the terrace. He looked over her shoulder. "Act I, Scene I," he read. "You haven't got very far."

"I'm sorry. I am perhaps too occupied with the role that Woolie requires of me to concentrate on Gerald's play."

"Lisa, you have become a stranger."

"And it's hard to live with a stranger. I know, my poor Franz, I know." She stood up. "I know. But my pity and my knowledge can't help you. We have no help for each other. But perhaps we can together help her. We can only try. We can only try to play our parts in Woolie's summer comedy. The charming Count and Countess. The popular young Erlencamps."

Through the summer days and nights Lisa acted her part to Woolie's satisfaction. It was like last summer and the summer before that.

This luxurious little colony was remote from the wide country through which Lisa had traveled. She was back in the world that

Franz had chosen. Back with the Spains and the Joneses, the rich and their greedy little playmates.

It is not because they are rich, Lisa thought. It is not money but the love of money that is the root of all evil. The Joneses and their kind have made of wealth a beloved burden that they carry as a snail its house. Without that golden shell they would feel naked, stripped of their only armor. And they would rather keep that golden burden than pass through the narrow gate of the kingdom of Heaven. There is still truth—wise and witty truth—in the ancient metaphor of the camel and the needle's eye.

A maid knocked on Lisa's door. "The Baron von Elsfeldt asks to see the Countess. He says it is urgent."

Lisa glanced at the clock beside her bed. It was nine o'clock. She had put off getting up. She had not wanted to begin this August day. This day that would be like all the other summer days, without hope, without change.

"Tell the Baron I shall be down directly."

When Lisa went downstairs she found Woolie with Franz on the terrace.

"There is bad news," Franz said. "I sent for Woolie as soon as the message came for you." He gave Lisa a cable.

AM WELL BUT CIRCUMSTANCES FORCE ME TO CHANGE ADDRESS AFTER TODAY. IMPORTANT TO ME THAT YOU MAKE IMMEDIATE PAYMENT. LOVE.
                                                                    GRANNY.

Lisa stared at the carefully worded cry for help. She looked from Franz to Woolie. "What does this mean?" she asked.

"It's pretty obvious," Woolie said. "The wonder is that she was left, even with Matilde, at home so long. Now she is being taken elsewhere."

"Where will they take her, Woolie?"

"I have no means of knowing. Probably to a concentration camp. I cabled at once to Kraussmann asking him to delay action until tomorrow." He looked at his watch. "It is now afternoon in Germany."

"We'll go to see Mr. Hudson right away," Lisa said. "Franz can telephone him while we drive into town."

"And you had best persuade Mr. Hudson to act quickly. Berlin has been patient, Lisa." Woolie rose and walked towards the front door. "But even German patience is not inexhaustible. And now it is at an end. We are almost in September. We do not propose to wait forever for you to make what is, after all, only restitution."

"But you agreed to the arrangement, Woolie."

"It was a temporary agreement as far as we were concerned, and your Mr. Hudson might have found a way to wriggle out of it. Now you force us to put pressure on you. You might have spared yourself that, and her."

When Lisa and Woolie reached New York, James Hudson was waiting for them in his office. He studied the cable. "You'll forgive me, Baron, if I check with Western Union."

"Of course, Mr. Hudson. Although any delay . . ." Woolie left his sentence unfinished and looked at Lisa.

"You are a businessman, Baron. You understand that once Mrs. Blessing arrives in New York Mr. Adams will transfer the funds to you. Even if this cable is authentic, it does not affect the situation. You see, Lisa——"

"Excuse me, sir," Woolie interrupted, "but Lisa sees certain things that are difficult for an American businessman to understand. If Frau Blessing's were an ordinary case this would be a simple matter. But she is the mother of Siegfried Blessing. Most of the members of the party are businessmen like you and me, Mr. Hudson. They are practical men. They prefer a million dollars to revenge, but there are other less reasonable men who would prefer to punish Frau Blessing for the gross deception that she practiced."

"You wouldn't get away with it," Mr. Hudson said. "I can make inquiries through our embassy."

"You have already done so, Mr. Hudson. Do you think we did not know of the young man who visited Waldenberg? But he found everything in order, did he not?" Woolie asked.

"You didn't tell me," Lisa said.

"Mr. Hudson didn't want you to know that he is worried, too. He did not wish to add his fear to yours, Lisa. But now, Mr. Hudson, now that there is a question of a concentration camp——"

"If you did that the embassy would certainly act, Baron."

"But even if your embassy were willing to act officially, which is unlikely since Frau Blessing is not an American citizen . . ." Woolie paused. "After all, embassies never move very quickly, and Frau Blessing is not strong. Even a few days at Dachau——"

"You can't let them, Mr. Hudson!" Lisa's voice broke. She could not hide the fear. "You don't know—you haven't seen."

"But, my dear," Mr. Hudson said gently, "even if we take the money out of escrow, even if we pay, we have no guarantee that your grandmother will be set free. Can you guarantee it, Baron?"

"You know I can't." Woolie smiled apologetically. "I can't even guarantee that she will be left at Waldenberg. I can say only that it is possible that, if the payment is made, she will be let go. It seems to me worth trying. Once the money is paid the practical men will be satisfied, and Frau Blessing is not without friends in Germany. There is a chance that her departure can be arranged. The question is whether this slim chance is worth a million dollars to Lisa."

"Suppose you wait in the outer office, Baron, while I confirm this cable and have a talk with Miss Blessing."

"Certainly, sir." Woolie rose. "But I must emphasize that speed is of the essence."

Lisa looked beyond Mr. Hudson at the tall windows behind him. If only the ship might come. She watched the harbor while Mr. Hudson telephoned.

"That's right, to Port Washington, Long Island. Received at eight-fifteen this morning. You'll call me back? Thank you."

Mr. Hudson removed his spectacles. He frowned at them. He took his handkerchief and carefully wiped the spotless lenses.

"Look here, my child," he said. "I don't think you ought to give up this money. If you do, they will have no reason to release your grandmother."

"And if I don't . . ." Lisa pressed her hands to her eyes. "If I don't . . . You haven't seen, Mr. Hudson. You don't know."

"I still believe it to be only a threat."

"A threat in which she believes, so that for the first time she has asked me for help. In her letters there has been no hint."

"Once you have paid, there is no guarantee that they will let her go. Elsfeldt himself admitted it."

"I cannot refuse her."

The telephone rang. Mr. Hudson picked it up. "Western Union? Put them on. . . . Yes, speaking. . . . From Waldenberg at 7:30

A.M. German time today? Thank you very much." He turned to Lisa. "The cable was sent from Waldenberg. It may be authentic, although we have no proof that it was sent by your grandmother."

"They need not have waited all these weeks to forge a cable."

"No, and there is no reason for them to risk a million dollars by confining her. Let me get in touch with the embassy, my dear. There's something fishy about this."

Lisa shook her head. "Because you can't imagine you will not believe. But I have seen. I know."

"You think they would lose a fortune for the pleasure of revenging themselves upon an old lady? It's not reasonable, my child."

"They don't live in a reasonable world. They live in the nightmare. It's what Woolie said—'a slim chance.' But it's all we have and she has asked me to take the chance. I can't refuse, Mr. Hudson."

"You don't even know that she has asked."

"I know nothing. But if this was her cry for help and I did not answer—she has never asked before. She has never let me see the fear. The authority is mine, and I must take the responsibility."

"I can't let you do this. It seems to me useless."

"But you can do it?" Lisa asked. "You can tell Mr. Adams that the conditions have been met satisfactorily?"

"It can be arranged. It will take time, but——"

"There isn't time!" Lisa cried. "We have time, but she hasn't. There is only a little of today left in Germany."

"I think you imperil Mrs. Blessing by giving up the money."

"She's in peril anyway, and she has asked for my help, and she has told me how to save her."

"You aren't even sure of that. Let me have the embassy send someone to see her."

"There isn't time. She would be gone before anyone could come. Her only chance is that we act at once."

"Can nothing persuade you to listen to my advice?"

"Nothing. You see, you don't know."

Mr. Hudson sighed and rang for his secretary to admit Woolie.

"While you were talking, I took the liberty of calling my office," Woolie said. "I have received a cable from Herr Kraussmann in Berlin, whom Lisa knows. It says: 'Assure client that if payment is

made today goods will be shipped from Bremerhaven the day after
tomorrow.' You can verify that cable, too, Mr. Hudson."

"I don't doubt that the cable was sent, but unfortunately, I have
no way of verifying the assurance. Miss Blessing and I have no reason
to have faith in your promises, Baron."

"It's all right, Woolie," Lisa said wearily. "You win. I'm going to
pay."

"You are wise, Lisa."

"I don't know that I am. I know only that what she asks I must
do."

"If you will be here tomorrow at ten-thirty, Baron," Mr. Hudson
said, "that will give me time to complete the arrangements."

"Right. Coming, Lisa?"

Lisa did not answer. Woolie left the room. Lisa looked from the
window at the harbor. Perhaps now, at last, a ship would come from
Bremerhaven; perhaps the practical men would be satisfied with the
money. Perhaps they would let her grandmother go. "Perhaps" was
the slim chance. It was the only chance in all the possible ones in which
Lisa must believe, if she was to endure the hours before the news
came. And what of her, Lisa wondered, what of the hours at Waldenberg? Is she there, or have they taken her? Lisa turned from the
window. She held out her trembling hands to Mr. Hudson.

"My dear," he said, "let us hope yours is the wise decision. There
is nothing I can say to alter it?"

"Nothing. I cannot do otherwise. You have been kind and you have
tried to help."

"You haven't let me help you. Good-by, my dear, until tomorrow
at ten-thirty."

The next morning the transaction was completed. Lisa watched
Woolie seal the envelope which Mr. Hudson gave him.

"After I have deposited this, Lisa, I will drive you to the country."

"And you will cable them, Woolie? You will cable immediately?"

"Certainly, my dear Lisa."

It was just two o'clock when Lisa and Woolie reached Long Island.
Franz invited Woolie to stay for lunch.

"I should like you to stay, Woolie, until we have news from
Germany," Lisa said.

"We may not hear today. I might as well go back to the Spains', where Daphne and I are staying."

"I should like you to stay," Lisa repeated. "We can put you up overnight, if the news does not come until tomorrow."

Lisa walked slowly upstairs. She looked at her watch. The minute hand was only a little past the hour. This American day is long, Lisa thought. Dear God, let it be long enough. It is already evening in Germany. The evening star is bright beyond the pines. Perhaps that peaceful star is even now watching over the beginning of her journey. Let it be her journey to safety.

Lisa looked from her watch to the bedside clock. The slow measure of time. The sunlight lay in bright squares on the carpet below the windows. In Germany time had already left the daylight behind. There the clocks were measuring the hours of darkness.

Woolie had cabled. Soon there must be an answer. Lisa picked up the telephone. Perhaps they had not told her grandmother. Perhaps she did not know. Lisa called the telegraph office and dictated a cable: "Complete payment made. All love. Lisa."

"How do you wish the message sent?"

"By the quickest method. It's urgent. And can you let me know if the message is delivered?"

"Yes, we can do that. I will repeat the prepaid full-rate cablegram from Port Washington to Frau Wilhelm Blessing, Waldenberg. . . ."

Lisa listened. "And you will confirm delivery?"

"Yes, madam, we'll have it confirmed."

Lisa put down the telephone. She thought of her message traveling along the wires. It will go quickly, like light. How many kilometers a second? I knew once. Faster than sound. Faster than time. It will travel beneath the ocean into the darkness of Germany.

The hours went by slowly. Lisa went downstairs. She sat on the terrace and watched the sun sink beyond the trees. Slowly the sky was emptied of light. In America, too, there was darkness.

Lisa sat with Franz and Woolie at the table. It was strange to dine with your enemy, to watch his face between the candles in their tall silver holders.

"We won't hear tonight, Lisa," Woolie said. "It is foolish for me to stay here."

"I wish you to stay."

Franz put out the backgammon board. "Will you play, Lisa? It will pass the time."

"I will watch you."

Lisa watched their hands. She watched them move the black and crimson counters as the dice rattled on the board. She tried to keep her eyes from the clock. Soon it would be dawn in Germany.

Woolie pushed the doubler towards Franz. "Sixty-four, my boy. How do you like that?"

Franz refused the double.

"This is silly, you know, Lisa." Woolie stood up and mixed a drink. "It's much too late for us to hear tonight."

"I would rather wait."

"As you like. I'm doing very well," Woolie chuckled. "Franz hasn't his mind on his game."

Lisa watched the black and crimson counters. She listened to the rattle of the dice.

The telephone rang. Lisa answered it before Woolie could move.

"It's for me," she said. "Western Union. Yes, this is Countess Erlencamp."

"I'm sorry to call so late. I'm sorry, Countess. About your cable— the one that was sent urgent to Frau Wilhelm Blessing. It couldn't be delivered. I'm sorry, Countess." The girl's voice sounded young. It trembled.

"You couldn't deliver it?"

"No. The party it was addressed to—the report is—I better read it to you. 'Cable to Frau Wilhelm Blessing, Waldenberg, undelivered. Addressee dead.' "

Lisa put down the telephone. She leaned her hand on the table to steady herself. "She's dead, Franz. Granny is dead." She stared at Woolie's damp, sallow face.

Franz spoke. "You shouldn't have learned it like this."

"So you knew!" Lisa cried. "This, too, Franz, you knew."

"We both knew," Woolie said. "But it was our duty as Germans to obtain for the Reich the funds that——"

"Never mind the money," Lisa interrupted. "She is dead. When did she die? What day? What hour? How did she die? Do you know, Woolie?"

"I haven't any details. She has not been well for some time. I know that she died two days ago."

"But her cable?"

"The cable was sent from Waldenberg by my orders. It was the only way to force you to pay—to restore——"

"And you knew, Franz. This, too, you knew."

"He knew, Lisa. You would have known tomorrow. A newspaperman has the story. It has been held up this long only with difficulty."

"She died two days ago," Lisa said. She steadied herself against the table. "You knew. While I who should have mourned still hoped. You knew, while I imagined the peaceful evening star, the journey to Bremerhaven."

"Lisa." Franz touched her arm.

She slowly lifted her head and looked at him. "Though you were not there, others like you were there. You left her to them."

"Lisa, I tried."

"You tried!" She stared at him. "You tried only to save——" She stopped herself. What good was it to betray the betrayer?

"To save her fortune," Woolie completed Lisa's sentence. "Don't worry about giving Franz away. I have realized for some time that he wasn't co-operative about the money. Even if he had been, I doubt if it would have gone easier with Frau Blessing. And since we have the money, Franz has nothing to fear. From his point of view he was practical. It's an excellent thing to be a practical man. The important members of the party are all practical men."

While Woolie spoke, Lisa walked towards the doorway. She heard Franz behind her and turned. "Don't come, Franz. I'm going now. The comedy of the Erlencamps is finished."

"Lisa, where are you going?" Franz asked. "What are you going to do?"

"I am going to mourn for her as once I mourned for her son. For her, too, the end was in darkness."

"But you can't go like this—in the middle of the night."

"It is day there. A day she never knew. Now all her days and nights are counted."

Franz did not follow Lisa. He stood before the door she had closed. He listened to her footsteps. Presently he heard the sound of her car as she drove away.

"I could do with a fresh, stiff drink," Woolie said. "We've had a narrow shave. Why Berlin ever let an American reporter near the place when they knew she was dying! And the dolts in charge, to let a stranger into the house. They swear they never saw him. Bribed, probably." He helped himself generously to whisky. "Then Berlin informs me that they can hold the story for three days and I have just that much time to get the money. They should have sent the cable a week ago, as I advised. They knew the old woman couldn't last. And we'd strung the suspense out long enough. Lisa has been ready to break for some time." He gulped his drink. "We'd have been blamed, you know, if anything had gone wrong. When it would have been their own stupid fault. They should have kept her alive until we had the money. Certainly they should have concealed her death."

"Lisa has gone." Franz stared at the closed door.

"Well, you expected that, didn't you?"

"I expected it. But I didn't imagine it."

"You'll get over it." Woolie stirred the ice in his glass. "Little Mrs. Craven will be delighted to help you get over it. They approve of her in Berlin, by the way. She's financially sound and an Aryan. As Aryan as any American."

Franz did not answer. His eyes were fixed on the closed door.

"Look here," Woolie asked impatiently. "You're not still mooning over Lisa? Berlin will be much better pleased with Anne. The '*Heldenlied*' was all very well in the early days. Here, take this." Woolie handed Franz a glass. "And pull yourself together. They expect you back, by the way. And soon."

Franz was silent. Woolie spoke sharply.

"You mean to go back, don't you?"

"I have to go back. That is where the future is."

"And, like a practical boy, you mean to be part of it. You can get your divorce there. And I suggest that you fix things up with Anne before you leave. As I say, Berlin approves. She has a nice little fortune and she has the right sort of friends—friends who will be useful to us when the time comes."

"And she is pretty and she understands as Lisa never did. Only ——"

"Only Lisa is beautiful. Beautiful as the Lorelei and as dangerous to you. 'Boat and boatman are gone. . . . This, with her singing, the Lorelei has done.' Get on with your career, man, and forget the non-Aryan dream."

"You say they really approve of Anne?"

"They do," Woolie said impatiently. "Now get on with it. Time moves fast, you know. Lingering in America won't forward your career in the Reich."

Franz put out his hand. "Tomorrow," he said, "I'll get on with my career. I'll go down to Southampton. Good night, Woolie." He hesitated a moment. Then he opened the door that Lisa had closed.

XXI

ANNE CRAVEN was in Southampton. She looked back on the summer that now was drifting to its golden close. It had been a summer of waiting. She had thought in June that this summer would be a beginning. Perhaps tomorrow, before it ended, it would begin. Enough tomorrows added up to all the yesterdays of your life. *La belle trentaine.* To translate it into flattering French did not alter the fact that she had slipped into the last decade. The last decade that could in anyone's imagination be considered young. Perhaps time's passage was easier to endure if you could count your children's years as another beginning. That was what Mary Forrest did, and Jenny Winton and the others. They were content to be links in the chain of time. Anne wanted her future, not Polly's. She found no comfort in vicarious youth.

Anne decided to drive over to Judy Jones's house. It was curious to be more at home with Judy than with Mary. Judy had improved, of course. Time and fashion had toned down the brassy, cut-rate beauty. Anne remembered their first meeting at the Lido. She had been too smug then, too young to see Judy's qualities: energy and shrewdness and determination. The last was the most important. You had to care desperately about success to achieve it.

Judy was sunning herself on her terrace beside the pool. She was dressed in white shorts, topped by a scarlet handkerchief. She wore all her pearls. "The man at Cartier's told me the sun was good for

them. And, besides, I sometimes get fed to the teeth with good taste."
She stretched out a jeweled hand to Anne. "God, I'm bored with this
midweek manless desert. J. C.'s in Detroit or I'd be in town. He's a
little stuffy about my being in New York alone. And quite rightly, I
guess." Judy laughed. "But I don't know why you don't go up to
town."

"The apartment's closed," Anne said. "Actually, I like New York
in summer. I only keep the house here going on Polly's account."

"You know, Anne, that's one of the things I find attractive about
you. You have a lovely, well-brought-up child but you don't talk
about her endlessly."

"It's not always an advantage. Sometimes I think I ought to send
Mademoiselle to the hen parties. She's better equipped than I am to
cope with them conversationally."

"Darling, those hen parties! And then their week ends. Starting
at the station on Friday afternoon in a Buick crammed with children.
Tennis or golf and a little decorous dancing on Saturday and dinner
again *en famille* on Sunday. It's something out of the *Ladies' Home
Journal*. I'd take a drink if it weren't for my figure." Judy stretched
out her slim tanned legs and looked at them admiringly. "You know,
Anne, I can remember when I used to read in the papers about
Southampton. It sounded wonderful. But now I'm here, it's an awful
lot like Jackson Heights."

"I'm a little bogged down in stodginess myself," Anne said. "If
Uncle Normie doesn't scream too loud about taxes, I might blow
myself to a trip to Europe."

"Ah, now we're on interesting ground. How about you and Franz?"

"That wasn't anything." Anne smiled to hide her sharp fear that
her words might be true.

"It looked like something to me last winter, all right. What more
do you want? He's handsome, smart, and on the right side. J. C. says
it's the winning side. And he says that, if the right people here and in
England can be made to see it, why, the victory can be quick and comfortable for all of us."

"But suppose they don't see."

"They see it in Spain. They're not giving the Reds any help there.
That's the tip-off."

Anne shivered as she remembered the moving pictures that J. C.

had shown. The ragged soldiers, the fierce, dark faces. "But there are so many of them, and they don't surrender. They have nothing to lose. And Franco looks like such an ineffectual, pudgy little man."

"There's nothing ineffectual about his allies. Those babies will see to it that he doesn't lose. You're just depressed. What you need is for me to get Franz down here."

"No, please."

"I guess you're right. Better wait for him to show up under his own steam. I bet you he will, and my advice to you is: grab him. He's got a future, J. C. says."

"And Franz is a gentleman." Anne hesitated. "I mean in a foreigner that's something you've got to have."

Judy laughed. "Sometimes you sound a little stodgy yourself. And you're mistaking the trimmings for the essential. Though, at that, I guess Franz's Junker background has been useful. Everything's useful if you're smart." Judy stretched and shook her bracelets so that they sparkled in the sunshine. "I heard on the radio that Lisa's grandmother died. She must have been a hundred and two. Did you ever know the old lady? She was quite remarkable."

"No—yes. I met her years ago."

Anne hoped that her voice sounded natural. Suppose Lisa used her grief to hold Franz. Beauty drenched in tears had an appeal. But surely even, as great an actress as Lisa could not make tragedy of the quiet, inevitable death of an old lady. This natural grief could not bind Franz to Lisa. But it could delay him. It could once more postpone tomorrow. Anne looked at the western sun. In a little while it would slip over the edge of the horizon. At the end of the day you could see time move.

Franz was waiting in the library when Anne went home.

"I have come, Anne. I am free and I have come."

"Franz, I didn't expect you. I——" She felt her hand tremble against his. He lifted her fingers to his lips.

"I have left my bags at the Irving House. I have taken a room there."

"A hotel is so dreary. I can put you up."

"No, my dear, it is best that I do not stay here, so long as I am technically still married." He smiled. "My little tribute to your American respectability—and I, too, have certain old-fashioned standards."

"Your standards are part of what I like in you, Franz. But what has happened? Come outside and tell me."

They sat on the steps that led down to the beach. The surf was quiet. The foam of the small waves faintly reflected the brilliant color of the evening sky.

"It's very simple," Franz said, "and a little sad as endings must always be. The summer's end, the day's end. Even though one knows that the spring will come again and the sun will rise. Because of you, I know."

"But what's happened?"

"It's over between Lisa and me. She's left me. She wishes to go on alone. And I am willing that she shall. She is successful. She doesn't need me. It's part of her talent to be able to be alone, even to prefer it. And perhaps I have been to blame." He hesitated. "You see, I have never been able to make Lisa understand her heritage. Her grandfather and her father were Germans. Her father was a German hero. But Lisa—it has almost been as though she identified herself with the enemy. With Siegfried Blessing's enemy. Lisa's German mother died when she was an infant and Lisa was brought up by her grandmother, an American who in her heart never became a German. It was not a good influence for Lisa. I don't like to speak against Frau Blessing. It is only that I try to explain Lisa."

"You don't have to explain to me. I know you've done your best."

"It wasn't good enough. But at least I have the satisfaction of knowing that I have helped to make her successful here, that now she is safe without me and I am free—free to return to Germany. While I am there I shall obtain my freedom legally. And then, Anne, and then—Anne, will you be my wife—my German wife?"

He drew her close to him. She lifted her lips to his. There was no sound except the faint rustle of the breeze through the dune grass and the gentle ripple of the water against the sand.

"You do love me, Anne?" Franz asked. "I may hope? Because of you I can hope, I can know."

"But let's not go too quickly."

"We cannot go slowly, Anne. I have only ten days. I am ordered to return. And I wish to return. My future is there. But I don't want to return without the knowledge that you will come. It is easy, Anne.

You have only to say a few small words to make my future whole."

She looked into his eyes, which were close to hers.

"Let me say the German words then. *Ich liebe dich.*"

His eyes slid away. He looked beyond her.

"Franz. It's as though you saw a ghost—a beautiful water-borne ghost beyond my shoulder."

"The Lorelei? She is only a legend from an ancient time. There is no one but you. And for you?" He smiled at her. "And for you, too, there are no echoes, no ghosts of the past?"

She traced with her finger the beautiful curve of his mouth. "No, Franz. No echoes. No ghosts." She stood up. "All the same, it's growing cold." She shivered. The breeze was louder in the dune grass, and the waves were growing bigger and swifter.

"We'll go in. But first, Franz, do you know you haven't told me you love me?"

"There should be new words for you. I would like to find them. To tell you."

"The old words will do, Franz. I'd like to hear them."

"I love you, Anne."

"Say it in German, Franz. That must be the language of your heart."

"As you like, Anne." He fixed his eyes on hers. "For you the language of my heart. *Ich liebe dich.*"

He kissed her. They walked across the dune into the house.

The ten· days of Franz's visit held all the summer for which Anne had waited.

On the last Saturday night the Joneses gave a dinner and dance.

"You look very fine, Anne," Judy said. "So fine that I suspect you and Franz of being up to no good."

"That just happens not to be true." Anne sat before Judy's mirror and carefully rouged her lips.

"Holding out for the old gold band? I guess you're smart at that."

"It's not smartness. It's——"

" 'Never explain. Never complain.' You don't need to do either. This virginal interlude is definitely becoming. It makes you look like a debutante. Why shouldn't you act like one if you like? Me, I always was a more earthy type. But yours is certainly the safer method. And as long as you enjoy it . . ."

Anne stood back and looked at herself in the mirror. Her reflection pleased her. Her honey-colored chiffon dress was artfully cut to show the curve of her small breasts. But the skirt swirled wide when she danced. It was like the skirt of a debutante's dress. And why not, since she, too, was beginning? The music downstairs was gay and new. This summer's songs would be an accompaniment. And one old song. She would ask for the "Blue Danube." That waltz was older than her memory. So it, too, was new.

Franz was waiting at the foot of the stairs. She danced with him. The music was loud. It drowned the noise of the surf beyond the french windows.

Between her dances with Franz there were other partners: Johnny Payne, Tom Webb, Pete Smithers. The same faces. And because Franz was new, because she herself felt new, the faces seemed suddenly old, like those of actors made up for the last act of a play with too long a time span. It was almost ten years since they had all been young. Time had blurred the features and thickened the bodies. "You don't change, Anne. You look so young." The compliment of middle age. The young never said that. They did not prize youth. They took it for granted.

Anne was dancing with J. C. Jones when Woolie von Elsfeldt cut in.

"You're very lovely tonight, Anne. You even look graceful dancing with J. C. His partner usually reminds me of a trainer out with a dancing bear."

"Is that a respectful way for one American businessman to speak of another?"

"Still teasing me for my disregard of my baronial splendor."

Beside the noisy orchestra, cool air streamed through the window. Woolie mopped his face. "Come out on the terrace. It's hot as blazes in here."

Anne sat beside Woolie at a small table. "And shall we renew our argument about Germany, Woolie?"

"You make a very appealing advocate for the Reich. And I'm not so difficult to convince. After all, I have remained German. They seem to be doing well over there. Perhaps you've seen the situation more clearly than I."

At the next table voices rose.

". . . up a few points, then down again. Impossible to know where to put your money." "Give me the good old days when there were no politics. Coolidge was smart. He kept his hands off Wall Street." "A mania for power. That's the trouble with him." "You said it. A dictator pure and simple. You mark my words. Until we get him out of the White House, we'll never get back to sound, democratic, American principles." "Thirty-five cents an hour and glad to get it. But now labor has the bit between its teeth. We may live to see the end of private enterprise." "Got to hand that to Hitler. He put a stop to unions." "And in Italy there's no trouble, no strikes. That's what we need here—a Mussolini." "You said it. A strong man who won't stand for any nonsense."

Woolie laughed. "Isn't this where we came in?"

"Let's go in and dance, Woolie. I've listened to them talk in a circle like that for years."

"Why don't you get off the merry-go-round, Anne? Start over with Franz. It's apparent how he feels about you."

"Maybe they wouldn't approve of me in Germany. Maybe they wouldn't let him marry me."

Woolie laughed. "Now you see, you go farther than I. I don't always endorse the political actions of the Reich, but I know they don't interfere with the private lives of German citizens. After all, Anne, Germans are civilized people."

"Maybe they won't think I'm civilized. They probably think of all Americans as red Indians. What's the Nazi policy on red Indians, Woolie?"

"Now you're joking. But in all seriousness, Anne, I think you would be happy in Germany. You have too clear an intelligence to endure this muddled democracy. There is only the bureaucracy of the Administration and the gangsterism of labor. Your own group is caught hopelessly in the middle."

"I think my own group is pretty ineffectual. Perhaps we aren't safe anywhere."

"You would be safe in Germany, Anne. As Countess Erlencamp you would belong to the elite. In Germany the elite is safe."

"Why do you struggle along here, Woolie, if it's all so wonderful in Germany?"

"My mother was American. Daphne is American. I went to college

here. I have many ties. But I plan to visit Germany shortly. It may be
that I've been hasty in judging National Socialism. Why don't you
come over with Daphne and me? We'll chaperone you while Franz
gets his divorce."

Anne shook her head. "Not yet. I'm not yet ready to decide."

Woolie rose. "There's Franz. He must be looking for you. He won't
be patient. You won't have much time in which to decide, but
enough. You see, I know." Woolie smiled. "I know, even if you don't,
that you have already decided. Franz appeals to your heart, and the
German system appeals to your intelligence."

Franz crossed the terrace. "I've been looking for you everywhere.
Forgive us, Woolie. Let's not go in again, Anne. This is our last night.
Tomorrow I go. I have to be in Washington on Monday morning.
Let me take you home now."

Anne and Franz were silent as they drove home. They walked
through the dark house. The tall grass gleamed in the moonlight. The
crests of the waves were silver.

Franz took Anne in his arms. "Tonight, Anne. Let it be tonight,
so that I may take the knowledge of you back with me."

Anne freed herself from his embrace.

"No." That would be the final decision. "Not yet. Not until we can
really be together." She moved away from him and watched the
waves. They were quiet in the ebb tide.

"But why not, Anne? Since you love me, since you are to be my
wife——"

Her mind must decide. Not her body.

"I love you, Franz, but I want to wait until we are sure. After all,
you don't even know that they will want me in Germany. Woolie
says they will. But he can't possibly know."

"There will be no question, Anne."

"When you are sure, come for me or send for me. And I will come."

"You promise? Anne——"

"I promise."

"Then I'll go. And I must go quickly because I have not much
strength against your loveliness in this light. Good-by, Anne."

"Not good-by. I'll see you off on Tuesday."

"But there will be people."

"We're safe with people and daylight."

"At least I have your promise."

She watched him as he walked towards the house. She listened to the sound of the car as he drove away.

She had given him her promise. A promise was a word, not a deed. Only deeds were irrevocable. Because of the promise a new beginning was within her grasp. But the beginning was not yet irrevocable; it was still part of the untouched future.

XXII

LISA HAD TAKEN REFUGE in the hotel where she had stayed in 1928. She had not wanted to go to the fashionable, towering caravansary where she and Franz had stopped two years ago.

The hotel seemed to have shrunk. From its windows Lisa could still look over the low buildings at the towers of New York. But after having perched with Franz on the thirty-fifth story of one of the towers, the fourteenth floor seemed near the ground.

Lisa pulled up the venetian blinds. There had been lace glass curtains before. She gazed at the shining city. So had she gazed nine years ago. She knew that she was seeking refuge in the past. With Rachel, with Siegfried Blessing, with Elisabeth.

Now surely Frau Blessing was Elisabeth again. Safe, outside of time, she was Elisabeth again as she had been in the beginning. The young Elisabeth whom the living did not remember. Lisa wondered what had happened to the portrait. She wished she might have saved the portrait of the young Frau Blessing. The painted likeness of youth had been dear to Elisabeth grown older. Lisa tried to recapture the painted features. She remembered the diamond crescent against the dark cloud of hair. She remembered the smooth white hand that held the heavy fold of the crimson velvet curtain. But the young face of Elisabeth Blessing was lost to Lisa's recollection. Her heart had never learned that face. It had never known nor wanted the young Elisabeth. It had loved and needed only Elisabeth grown old. Frau Blessing. Granny.

Lisa walked away from the window. This room reminded her of that other room nine years ago. But it was not a refuge. The past was not a refuge for the living. She tried to face the future. Her imagination rejected the future as it rejected the past. It rejected all but the small pocket of time that was an August day and night. For four weeks Lisa had lived in that day and night. So, long ago, the child Lisa had lived over and over a December night, but the child Lisa had not been alone. Her grandmother had been there to give her back her future.

Lisa turned once more to the window. She ought to go out. She ought not to stay alone in one room in a day and a night of time. But she clung to the shelter of the four walls which had become familiar to her grief.

Mary Forrest had been kind to her. And Marco Ghiberti and Mr. Hudson. But they had not reached her where she stood alone in a day and a night. A day and a night that would not pass. Now there was no one to lead her out of this blind alley of time. Blind and dark, because she could not see. She could not know what the dark end had been.

"Thank you, Mary."

"I'm quite all right, Marco."

"We did our best, Mr. Hudson."

She had spoken to them. She had smiled at them. She had not heard them. She had not seen them. They could not help her. She was alone in a day and a night of time.

The telephone rang. Lisa picked it up and listened to the clerk's voice.

"John Carver?" She repeated the unfamiliar name.

"He has a letter for you which he must deliver personally."

"Ask him to come up."

John Carver gave her the thick envelope. "I promised Phil Sinclair to give you this myself."

"Thank you. Won't you sit down? Where is Phil?"

"I left him in Paris. I think he's on his way to Spain. I won't keep you. You'll want to read the letter."

When John Carver had gone, Lisa held the letter. Her fingers hesitated to open it. Now she would know. She forced herself to tear the flap to pull out the thin pages.

My sympathy cannot help and yet I cannot resist the human impulse to offer it. Dear Lisa. I saw her. I saw her a few hours after her death.

She was peaceful. It is true what they say of the dead: they are young again. She looked as though she had died of weariness. She had pneumonia in the spring. They wanted her to live, but in spite of their nursing her heart would not recover. Finally on that August afternoon it stopped beating. The old man, her servant, told me.

That would be Karl, Lisa thought.

I met him in the village and he took me to the house. He told me the winter was bad. She was cold and hungry a good deal of the time. I tell you the truth. It is better for you than your imaginings. At the end they sent Matilde away. He told me that you would want to know that at the end Matilde was not there. You must have read the news in the papers. Poor Lisa. And yet I knew you would want to know—not to imagine her still living. I gave the fact of her death to a friend of mine who's with the A.P. and he managed to get the news out. The Nazis held it up for three days. The old man is brave. Luckily, they think him only stupid. Perhaps he is, but he is brave and he loved your grandmother. He gave me this letter from her.

Lisa picked up the enclosure that had fallen on the floor.

"Dear Lisa." The letters shook a little, but only a little. Lisa remembered her grandmother's back held straight against age and grief. Her hand, too, had obeyed that proud determination.

This is the last letter, the letter that they wanted me to write. I would not write it for them. But I leave it for you. I would not make myself pitiful for their purpose. Nor am I pitiful nor afraid. It's not that I am brave, my dear. But at my age death is not so terrible. One has grown used to him. And their only threat is death. Fortunately I am not strong. So they have no other threat.

This, then, is good-by. And there should be a message. They say the old are wise and there should be a message. But I am tired, Lisa. You are not tired. And the future is yours. Don't turn back. It has been written, "Hold thy hand uplifted over hate."

Hate will turn you back to the past. Don't hate these men. They are prisoners of the darkness they have made. Don't hate Franz, though I think you will free yourself from him. Don't hate Wilhelm. I loved Wilhelm. I would not want him to be hated. Free yourself of Germany, but do not hate it. Remember your youth, the children's festival and the Advent candles. The children's stories which we read for your mother's sake. The root children and Hansel and Gretel. The Christmas songs. The angel on the tree. The Christmas tree. How green are thy leaves. The birches of spring and the pines of winter. Remember your youth, Lisa, and take it with you to America. As my grandparents once brought their youth to the strange land. I wish for you a future under the western sun. I wish for you the good things. Freedom and the sunlight. Your American heritage.

God bless you, my child. Don't be afraid for me. For me this is the end of a long day. I am only tired. I only lay me down to sleep.

As Lisa saw her tears drop on the letter, she realized that they were her first tears. In her last extremity Granny had made it possible for Lisa to look up without terror into the face of death. She held Lisa's hand again as she had held it long ago. Now, as then, she gave her back her future. Lisa remembered the songbook with the bright beautiful pictures. She remembered the children beneath the fair summer sky.

> *Now I lay me down to sleep,*
> *Fourteen angels watch do keep.* . . .

Lisa wiped away the tears that eased her heart. She returned to Phil's letter.

I have only bad news for you. I was able to find out about Max Klein. He is dead. At least his people can know. He was shot, trying to escape, they told me. Whether or not that is the exact truth about his end, I do not know. But I do know from independent witnesses that he is dead. It is over for him.

Poor little Max, Lisa thought. It is worse for the young to die. I must write to Mrs. Stern. That is the unbearable grief to be old and to survive the young whom you have loved. That's not true. Lisa stared at the blank paper before her. It's your own grief that is unbearable. What I cannot bear is that Granny was alone. There were only the photographs, the silent photographs of those she loved. And around her the voices of strangers. And outside the wind sighing through the pines. For her a foreign wind blowing beneath a foreign sky. Lisa's tears fell on the white note paper. But Granny has given me back my future. She gave it to me to begin with. She and Wilhelm Blessing, whom I must not hate, and my father, the professor . . . Rosa and Rachel, whom I never knew, and old Dan Hanauer, whom

I don't remember. My future is theirs. Their future which they made but will not see. I am my youth and I am theirs. I am my father's people and my mother's people. Here in America is the heritage. The heritage of all the people.

Lisa took a fresh sheet of paper and began her letter to Mrs. Stern. There was a knock on the door. She put her letter away and went to the door. Woolie entered.

"Sorry, Lisa, not to have myself announced. But I thought this way would save argument. We still keep an eye on you, so I knew your room number."

"But what do you want of me?" Lisa asked. "You have the money. And she is dead. What more do you want?"

"Well, my dear"—Woolie lowered himself into an armchair— "there is still the matter of the *'Heldenlied.'* "

"I had forgotten." Lisa stared at him.

She had forgotten. That still was to be done. "Hold thy hand up-lifted over hate." But this was not for hatred's sake. Granny did not mean this. This she must do for her father. She must remove him from the dark pattern. She must show to the world the true Siegfried Blessing, the gentle Jewish professor in uniform, in whose name no bloody sword should be lifted.

"Come, Lisa, don't pretend with me," Woolie said amiably. "Of course you intend to give out the story. Or were you saving it for your friend, the reporter, who went on your errand to Germany?"

"Yes, Woolie, I mean to tell the story. And now you can't stop me. The weapon is mine and you are helpless."

"It's not much of a weapon, as I told you before. And now, as you say, you are free to use it. You permit me?" Woolie lit a cigarette. "It'll be hard on Franz, but you owe him nothing."

"Has the song helped his career so much?" Lisa asked.

"It was useful to him to be Siegfried Blessing's son-in-law. Though Franz always had other qualities. But that's not quite the point. Certain party members take such things as the *'Heldenlied'* seriously. And they will naturally wish to be revenged on someone. Your grandmother is dead. You are here. But Franz is in Germany." Woolie paused and smiled at Lisa. "The *'Heldenlied'* was a mistake and, if the deception is revealed, someone will pay for the mistake. Franz will pay for it. His friend Goering won't help him. Nor will anyone else. After all, the Fuehrer himself dedicated a monument to your father."

"But Franz is not to blame."

"Someone will be to blame if the world learns the truth about Siegfried Blessing. And Franz will be the scapegoat. The scapegoat is part of our system. I don't know, Lisa, if you have ever seen anyone who has been in a concentration camp. Dachau, for instance. I don't know if you can imagine Franz. After even a few weeks he would be much changed. And there would be many weeks, there would be months, perhaps years. It is part of the treatment not to let the victim die."

Lisa stared at him. She saw, not Woolie, but Raimund Hoehlmann. For a moment she saw Franz. His hands. The dark head that she had loved.

"I have seen," she said. "I cannot let you destroy Franz as I have seen a man destroyed. Not by my words, not in my father's name, can I let you destroy him. You win again."

"We always win. You see, we aren't squeamish. We are willing to play our cards."

"You win the small victories against us. You defeat us singly. You won't defeat us when we stand together. You haven't strength enough to defeat all the people. You can win the little battles. You cannot win the war, the war against the free people."

"Fortunately, my dear Lisa, the free people are lazy and they are blind. We shall continue to win our battles singly. There'll never be a war. Only battles that we shall win one by one. War won't be necessary. That should please you, Lisa. I imagine that you belong to those who consider war the ultimate evil."

"I knew nothing of evil when I thought I could name its limits."

"Now I shall say good-by." Woolie pulled himself slowly out of the chair. "Daphne and I are sailing tomorrow. My usefulness here to the Reich is finished. I have been forced into the open. But for a million and a half dollars, it was worth it. Not good-by. I hope to return someday. America is an agreeable playground."

Lisa closed the door. She thought of Franz and remembered the days and the nights of the years in which she had loved him. She remembered his face on the pillow beside hers, his hands relaxed in sleep. Not through any act of hers would they destroy him. He had returned to their power. He had returned to the prison he had helped to build—to the prison that he believed to be a fortress of safety.

Siegfried Blessing's memory must also remain imprisoned in darkness. I cannot free him, Lisa thought, I cannot destroy the *"Heldenlied."* It is part of the dark pattern. The web of cruelty in which my father and the others like him were caught. To free him, all must be free. The whole pattern, not just a part, must be destroyed.

"Hold thy hand uplifted over hate." Hate is ended for me. All the darkness is ended. And my youth is ended. Only the memory of it is left. The pictures in a child's book. The scent of pines and the white birches gleaming in the sun. The small sweet flowers of spring and the sparkle of silver on a Christmas tree.

Lisa walked over to the window. Below her was the strange city and beyond it the strange land.

"I had long since a lovely Fatherland."

She looked down at the city upon which she had looked nine years before.

That was a beginning. This is the end. In this end there can be another beginning.

Below the windows the city was golden in the light of the setting sun. The western sky was bright.

BOOK III

The Beginning

I

In SEPTEMBER of 1938 Anne was again in Southampton. It was the end of summer. The twenty-first of September marked the end on the calendar. The increasing pace of time, Anne thought. It's as though the earth moves more rapidly, like a globe that spins on its metal axis beneath the impatient touch of a child's hand. But for a child time is slow. The nursery days are long. Beyond nursery windows the seasons slowly ripen and last their full time. Now, in the swift-moving, shortened years, spring and autumn touch one another. In September, May is yesterday.

Anne remembered May. The magic month of May. She remembered the German words that Franz had quoted:

All in the magic month of May
When every bird was singing . . .

After his divorce was granted, Franz had been unable to go to America. His duties at the Ministry of Propaganda kept him in Germany. So in May Anne had gone to him.

She stayed at the Adlon. She went to the opera. It was like that other German spring three years ago. But this time, Anne thought, I need not only watch, I can be part of the power. Now, for me, too, the power and the glory.

Franz persuaded her to go with him to Waldenberg. "I have guests coming at the end of the week, but first you and I can have two days together. I should like you to see the spring at Waldenberg."

"Not at Erlenhof?" Anne asked. Ruby Borodino had mentioned the castle.

"That you must see soon, Anne," Franz had said. "While she lived, my father's sister, the Baroness Billingsloeven, kept the place up, but since her death I have not been able to afford it. Erlenhof is closed. I have not been there"—Franz hesitated—"I have not been there for many years, but perhaps you and I can restore its ancient splendor. In the meantime we have the house at Waldenberg. That, too, is mine. It's strange that I should be the heir of Siegfried Blessing, but so it is. And so he would have wanted it, since I am part of the new Germany for which he died."

> *. . . the magic month of May*
> *When every bird was singing.*

The birds sang at Waldenberg and the buds opened. Beyond the light green of the grass was the dark green of the pines. In the grass were small flowers shaped like stars, pink and blue, the colors of the sunset sky beyond the pines.

Anne stood with Franz beneath the pines. Beyond them, in the valley, was the village of Waldenberg. "The little church," Anne said, "I think I should like to be married in that little church we passed."

"No, not there. We shall be married in Berlin, Anne, so Field Marshal Goering can be present. I want all Berlin to see my lovely bride. You have only to choose the date."

"I'd have to go home again, Franz. I haven't told Uncle Normie. I haven't arranged about Polly. Could you come?"

"I don't know. My duties at the ministry have grown. Perhaps it can be arranged. The important thing is that we be married."

I have decided, Anne thought. I have quite decided. There is only one more step—the step that puts decision in the past and puts beside it, to mark its finality, a date—the date of my wedding.

"Show me your house, Franz."

"Our house."

He took her hand and led her into the house. "This is the drawing room."

The drawn shades dimmed the light. A tall portrait hung on the far wall. Anne stood still. He can't mean me to live with Lisa Blessing's painted likeness. She shall not stand beautiful against the wall of my house.

Franz raised a shade. "I don't use this room much. It's so formal, but you, perhaps, will change that."

Anne saw that the portrait was not Lisa. It was a dark-haired young woman, elegant in the fashion of another time. In the dark hair was a diamond crescent. "Frau Wilhelm Blessing," Franz said. "The Government naturally wishes such relics to be preserved. The portrait is rather valuable, but if you don't want it, we can present it to a museum."

"It doesn't matter," Anne said. It doesn't matter because I have won. I can banish you and yours, Lisa, from this house which now is mine, as Franz is mine, as his future is mine.

Anne followed Franz through the house. There were no pictures of Lisa. In the hall there was a bust of Wilhelm Blessing. In the upstairs sitting room there was a miniature of Siegfried Blessing.

I may not banish them, after all, Anne thought. I may keep them since their glory now belongs to Franz. He is heir to Wilhelm the poet and Siegfried the hero since Lisa has forsaken and denied them.

"These are your rooms, Anne," Franz said, "soon our rooms." He touched her hand.

Anne imagined herself sitting in the armchair beside the fireplace. She and Franz would sit together in the winter firelight. Franz opened the bedroom door. A maid was unpacking Anne's suitcase.

"Matilde will take care of you," he said. "Shall we dine at eight?"

As Matilde unpacked, Anne looked about the square, high-ceilinged room. Through the wide west windows she could see the tall pines dark against the twilight.

At dinner Franz placed Anne beside him. "Sit here since we are alone, so I can imagine our future as it will be."

As it will surely be, Anne thought. This final future will be as I imagined it.

The dining room was lit by candles. The paneled walls gleamed darkly in the soft light. The dark solid walls were a symbol of security.

"I like this room," Anne said. "I like the whole house. It has a solid, unchanged feeling."

"It has been like this since Wilhelm Blessing's time," Franz said. "We Germans are a solid people. We do not like change. But we grow.

You will see the growth, Anne. Today Germany, tomorrow . . ." He lifted his glass. "To tomorrow, Anne."

"To tomorrow." Anne held up her glass. The champagne was golden in the candlelight.

"Shall we have coffee upstairs?" Franz asked. "And I have some rather good brandy left."

The May evening was cool. Franz lit the fire in the little sitting room. Anne sipped brandy from the thin balloon glass. Around them the house was still. Beyond the windows the wind sighed in the pines.

"This is the way it will be, Anne," Franz said. "This is the way it must be."

There is uncertainty in his voice, Anne thought. He doesn't know I have decided. He's not sure of me. His voice betrays the uncertainty. She put down her empty glass and reached out her hand to him. He took her hand and drew her to her feet. He put his arm around her and led her towards the door.

The room was warm from the bright fire. The house was quiet. The thick walls shut out the wind.

Franz fumbled with the handle of the bedroom door. "Come, Anne."

It's still a question. He's not sure of me. Because he's not sure, he sounds uncertain, even afraid. She stumbled against him. He held her close to him. Together they stood in the doorway. The square, high-ceilinged room was dim after the brightness of the sitting room. The only light came from a small rose-shaded lamp beside the canopied bed.

Anne awoke before Franz. She moved carefully so as not to disturb him. I have wanted this so long—his dark head beside mine on the pillow. It was not because of an afternoon in the lovely month of May. It was not because of the warmth of the fire or of brandy in a thin glass. This is what I want. It was not my body that decided, but I, Anne.

Beyond the windows the sky was blue. There were small white clouds in the blue sky of spring, soon the sky of summer. And I have chosen the foreign sky, Anne thought. I have chosen the foreign land where I can be safe. Here I need not belong to the frightened people, the ineffectual, disinherited people. In Germany the world is not turned upside down. The heritage is secure. Franz von Erlencamp is safe. He and his heritage are safe, and they are mine.

The dark head on the pillow beside mine. After all the years the imagined delight . . . Anne moved abruptly. It is Franz I love. His dark head . . .

Franz stirred. As he awoke he sighed. The sigh was a word, "Lisa."

"It is I, Anne." She spoke quickly, not to hear the other name on his lips. In dreaming, you go back into the past in spite of yourself, not because you want to. Franz wants the future, and I am the future. Lisa is only the past.

They breakfasted on the lawn. Franz announced that he must drive to Baden-Baden. "I have to see the local officials. Baden-Baden is important to us. So many foreigners go there. It is necessary that they receive in every detail the correct impression of the Reich. You will come with me? It's a lovely drive."

Anne remembered the drive from Baden-Baden to Waldenberg. That was long, long ago. Then this house belonged to Frau Blessing and to Lisa. Now Lisa is gone, and of Frau Blessing there remains only the youthful portrait which has no reality.

"I'll wait for you here," Anne said.

"Perhaps you are right, since so soon we shall be openly together. But the others come this evening, and Ruby Borodino has sharp eyes."

"I'm not afraid of her," Anne laughed. "I'm not afraid of anything any more."

"Nor am I," Franz said.

Anne smiled at the determination with which he spoke. He wants to reassure me, she thought.

While Franz was gone Anne explored the house. She opened the door of the morning room which Franz had made his office. On the desk was her photograph, the photograph she had sent him from New York.

She sat at the desk. She looked through the sunny east windows at the lawn. On the edge of the lawn birch trees gleamed in the morning sun. Above them was the May sky, the sky that promised summer.

Anne touched the smooth wood of the desk. As she pressed a panel, a drawer moved out to meet her hand. She smiled. A small, secret drawer unused through the years and found now by me. No, not unused. In the drawer she saw a book and a small silver folding clock.

She picked up the book: the poems of Heinrich Heine. The book opened at "The Lorelei."

> *The ghost of an ancient legend*
> *That will not let me be . . .*

How odd to keep hidden a book of verse. Then Anne remembered that Heine was now forbidden, and even Franz must be careful.

She picked up the silver case and opened it. It was not a clock. It was a frame. In it was a picture of Lisa. In the black and white of the photograph Lisa was still beautiful. You did not need to imagine the red-gold hair and the luminous white skin.

Anne closed the frame and put it and the book back in the drawer. The wooden panel clicked shut against her hand. The desk was as it had been before Anne touched it. She stared at the grain of the wood. You could easily forget the panel was there. The book and the frame had been left there forgotten. Anne stood up. Of course they were forgotten. Only I, like a fool, had to discover them where they have lain forgotten for years. The leather-bound poems and the silver frame. But forgotten silver tarnishes. This is shining. Someone has polished it. Someone has kept bright the frame for Lisa's beauty. Not Franz. Matilde, perhaps, or some other overconscientious German servant; certainly not Franz. I will not even ask him.

In the afternoon Franz and Anne waited for the guests. "Who are coming, Franz, besides the Borodinos?"

"Fritz von Eigen; he is now a captain. And the Elsfeldts. And the Princess Rodenstein is dining with us. She is my neighbor. I wish they need not break in on our lovely month of May."

"Our magic month of May. He was a great one for magic, Heine, wasn't he?" Anne asked. "The Lorelei's music beneath all his poems."

> *"A maiden, lost in dreaming,*
> *Who combs her golden hair* [Franz said].
> *Combing her hair with a golden*
> *Comb——"*

He stopped himself. "But the Lorelei and her poet belong to another time. What have they to do with us? This is now, Anne. Our time, yours and mine."

At the day's end the guests arrived. "Now we are separated," Franz murmured. "I can't even have you beside me at dinner. I must put the old Princess on my right, and Ruby on the other side. She's touchy about such things, is Ruby, in spite of her little jokes about the Faubourg St.-Germain."

Anne sat beside Pierre at dinner.

"Do you remember that summer day nine years ago, Anne?" Pierre asked. "We came here right after our expedition to Switzerland to see the Dornier, the beautiful plane which was so admired. And now there are thousands of them—Dorniers, Messerschmitts, Heinkels. I imagine I can hear the beating of their wings as they prepare to fly—to fly to our destruction."

"Oh, Pierre," Ruby laughed, "you haven't changed an atom in nine years."

"Our planes need not fly, monsieur," Captain von Eigen said to Pierre. "We ask so little: only to bring our people home, only to have our own again."

"The bastions of Bohemia," Pierre murmured.

"Not at all, monsieur; we have no interest beyond the Sudetenland. The Fuehrer himself has said it."

"I still hear the wings of war," Pierre said.

"Fortunately for the world," Woolie put in, "there are those who do more than listen. They act. I think you will see that the English Commission in Prague will prevent trouble."

"Will there be trouble?" Anne asked. She had heard talk of the Sudeten problem in Berlin, but she had not been afraid. As long ago as 1935 there might have been trouble, but the question of the Saar had been settled peacefully, and all the questions since. Now she remembered the silver plane. She imagined that she, too, heard the threatening wings.

"Will there be trouble?" she repeated.

"There won't be trouble over anything." Ruby's teeth gleamed in a cocksure grin. "Not for people like us, anyway. We are friends in every country. Allies, one might even say confederates. That's more important than being French or German."

"If only all your friends would see that, madame," Captain von Eigen said.

"They will see," Princess Rodenstein chuckled. "They have seen before and they will be made to see again. I can remember my father-in-law telling me the story of the Chancellor—I mean the old Chancellor Bismarck, of course——"

"How much you must have seen yourself, Princess," Woolie interrupted smoothly. "The prewar court of William II——"

"I remember well." There was a fine spray of bread crumbs as the Princess laughed again. "And I have waited for it to come back, and now it has. Not royalty, of course, but then the Rodensteins taught me to think of the Hohenzollerns as upstarts, rather. And now the grandeur is back, and with it the power. Not so royal but just as German."

The power, Anne thought. That's what matters. If you are on the side of power you needn't be afraid of the threatening wings.

On Sunday evening Franz and his guests were sitting in the drawing room. Ruby glanced at the portrait of Frau Blessing. "I see the Blessings are still with us. Franz certainly wraps himself in the mantel of their glory. Nice and snug for him."

"Siegfried Blessing and his people belong to the Reich," Woolie said, "and Franz is the natural guardian of their greatness."

"I know. Don't get solemn about it. No tokens of Lisa, though." Ruby looked around the room. "But one remembers her."

Anne stood up. She held her glass out to Franz.

"I could do with another drink."

"Certainly, my dear." Franz tipped the silver shaker. "And shall we tell them now?"

"Not now, not here." I was a fool to come here, Anne thought. When we are married, we'll go to Erlenhof, never here. Waldenberg is too near the Rhine. It belongs to the Rhine maiden, to the Lorelei. Waldenberg is ghost-ridden. It belongs to a ghost with golden hair and a golden voice. A golden ghost in a silver frame.

Franz was speaking: "I ask you to share my happiness." He filled his glass. "To drink with me the health of the future Countess Erlencamp."

The others raised their glasses. Anne accepted the good wishes. The talk centered on her. The ghost was forgotten.

In the midst of the talk Franz was called to the telephone. He returned and said gravely, "I regret so much, but I must return to Berlin now, tonight. I must be at the ministry in the morning."

Anne stared at him. So there was trouble.

"It's nothing serious." Franz smiled at her. "The Fuehrer himself has said that the Sudeten question is an internal one to be settled between Beneš and Henlein. But there are those who misinterpret—the evil forces that are the enemies of Germany. Of the world, if the world but knew."

"Come, come, Franz." Woolie spoke cheerfully. "There is no catastrophe, is there? Except that our charming week end ends abruptly. In times like these it is inevitable that the Ministry of Propaganda be overworked. That's it, isn't it, Franz?"

"That's it," Franz said quietly.

"I thought so." Woolie poured himself a drink. "Sorry as I am for you, old boy, it's better, after all, that the propagandists get busy than the generals. Isn't that even your choice, monsieur?" He looked at Pierre.

"I think it is a sequence, not a choice," Pierre said, "but I suppose one should be grateful for time. Perhaps even this anxious time will someday seem pleasant to remember."

Anne flew to Berlin with Franz.

In Berlin the fear grew. It crept through the walls of the Adlon. Anne felt afraid at the parties. The Germans were not afraid. It was like the old nightmare when only Anne could see the danger.

On the twenty-first of May Anne and Franz dined with the Elsfeldts.

"Have you heard?" Daphne asked. "They say our troops are at the border. It's March and Austria all over again."

"It's only a gesture," Woolie said calmly. "You will see. There'll be no trouble."

"Oh, Woolie, it's exciting." Daphne reached for a cigarette. Her dark eyes sparkled in her small rosy face. "A little war would be exciting. Fritz von Eigen and boys like that are simply dying for a small war."

"I'm sorry they have to be disappointed," Woolie said, "but there will be no war."

"Well, I know something else," Daphne laughed. "The English are getting out. Their ambassador has ordered a special train. Is that a gesture, too?"

"That is a rumor." Woolie held a match for Daphne's cigarette. His hand was steady.

Now, in September, in Southampton, Anne remembered that night in Berlin four months before. She saw Woolie's calm face and the match in his hand. Then the room had shaken at the noise of the explosion. Franz had jumped to his feet. "Those damn Czechs. It's begun!" The match had not trembled in Woolie's hand. He had calmly blown out the flame. "I think you'll find you are mistaken, Franz," he had said quietly.

Anne had thought Woolie brave. Now she supposed he had known of the demolition of the near-by hotel that had been scheduled to take place on that evening. Anne had been frightened. In the quiet that followed the explosion she had determined to sail for America.

The next day Franz had begged her to stay since it was a false alarm. "An alarm in which you believed so readily is too real for comfort," Anne had said.

Four months later Anne knew she had been right. She remembered the room that had trembled. She heard the shrill clash of the crystals in the swaying chandelier. She saw Daphne's cigarette on the flowered carpet and Franz on his feet beside it, and Woolie bland and calm, the lighted match in his hand. In that moment fear was concentrated. Anne's present knowledge altered nothing. The explosion had been only a stick of dynamite that had touched off the routine demolition of a small building, but the fear had been real. Until the fear passed Anne would not return to Germany.

Norman Brooke had applauded Anne's decision. "This is no time to tie yourself up with a European even if things aren't so rosy here."

Anne did not want to remember the rest of her talk with Uncle Norman. "Your principal's safe, Anne. Sorry about this cut in your dividends," Uncle Norman had said.

In Germany the principal would buy her a proper income. Woolie had explained it to her. "Where there are no strikes and no unemployment, capital is safe. And, of course, with Franz's connections . . ." Woolie had smiled. "It's something of a feat to have the friendship of both Field Marshal Goering and Dr. Goebbels. Franz will do all right. He's no fool. Your fortune will be in good hands."

In Germany all power is of a piece, Anne thought, political, financial, social.

In his last letter Franz had begged her to return. Anne reaffirmed the answer she had sent him. "Not until the danger is past."

Anne closed her bedroom door. When Mademoiselle came in from the beach she would turn on her radio. For days the radio had threatened war. Anne shivered. She had been right to return to America. She was right to remain until the danger was averted.

Mademoiselle and Polly should come in. Anne looked out at the sky. It is a curious color. Perhaps the edge of the tropical storm will, after all, touch Southampton. I should have gone to New York. The little decisions are as difficult to make as the big ones. All the warnings are Delphic. You never know until afterwards. Then your knowledge doesn't matter.

Beyond the windows the sea was thick and dark. This gray, unquiet day was a long way from the peaceful afternoon in May at Waldenberg. Anne shut the windows and drew the curtains against the threat of the storm.

It grew dark in the room. She moved one of the curtains a little. Against the glass the rain was a second curtain. It blinded the window. The house shook in the wind. This storm would be worse than the one last year. Anne dropped the chintz curtain. She did not want to see the darkness. Darkness by day was frightening. She did not want to see the rising waves. They reminded her of her childhood fear of a tide that had no ebb.

There were books and magazines on the bedside table. Anne looked at them. It was silly to stand and listen to the creaking of the house, to remember forgotten fears. She twisted the dial of her radio. There was only static. That, at least, was a good feature of the storm. Mademoiselle's radio would not work either. Mademoiselle would not be able to come with the news.

The door opened. Mademoiselle stood speechless on the threshold. The wind whined at the windows. The draft from the hall sucked at the door. It seemed to leap from Mademoiselle's hand. It slammed shut.

"Yes, mademoiselle?"

"Oh, madame, we cannot leave the house. We are engulfed. The wave came. The giant wave. It came over the dune. The road is flooded. Poor Polly! The poor little one!"

"Mummy! Mademoiselle!" Polly called from the hall.

Anne dragged the door open. Polly flung herself into the room as if it were an island of safety.

"It is all right, Polly," Mademoiselle said softly. She spoke in English.

"It's all right, Polly," Anne echoed Mademoiselle. "The storm will be over soon."

"Will it, Mummy? I'm frightened."

But she's less frightened, Anne thought, less frightened than we who glibly promise safety. Polly has us and she thinks that in us she has safety.

The storm increased. Anne took Mademoiselle and Polly into the hall. The maids were there. The women and the child huddled in the inner hall. It seemed safer than the outer rooms. They could still hear the roar of the wind and waves, but they were farther from the whining at the windows.

Downstairs a clock struck. The sound had no meaning for Anne. This dark day is outside of time. I thought that once before. Anne could not remember. She could not escape from the present. The present was the noise of wind and water. It was the creaking of the house that was no longer solid. The house was built on sand. The wind and the water devoured the sand.

Presently the wind died down. Anne thought it must be evening. It was still dark. There was no measure of time.

She heard a hammering at the door. They had come for her. There were men and a boat. Anne stared at the Coast Guard and their boat that rocked gently on the water. Water and land had changed places.

Anne sat silent in the boat beside Polly. The men rowed across the water. Anne looked down at the dark water. The land was not safe. Where it had been, there was water. This time the tide had not turned back.

The Coast Guard took Anne and her household to the Wintons'. They walked from the gate to the house. They climbed over a tree that had fallen across the driveway.

"This is exciting, Mummy," Polly said. "It's like a book. Only this afternoon I didn't like it much."

Anne held Polly's hand. I didn't like it at all. The frame of my life changed and destroyed by one storm or another. Aloud she said, "It's all right now, darling, we're quite safe here."

"I know, Mummy." Polly skipped beside her mother. "That's why I like it now. I like it to be exciting when it's safe, too. Then it's really like a book."

Anne picked her way along the muddy drive. Nothing is like a book. The end is not written for you to see. She looked at the lights that moved in the Wintons' windows. There I shall be safe from the storm. Against every storm there is a place of safety. Security is waiting for you if you can find it, if you can reach it in time.

The mud splashed against Anne as she ran towards the moving lights. She slipped on the wet steps. The edge of the step scraped her leg as she fell. Polly pushed open the unlocked front door. Anne dragged herself to her feet and stumbled towards the warmth and the lights. There were voices and hands that reached towards her. No, not towards her, towards Polly.

Anne leaned against the frame of the doorway. Mademoiselle caught up with her. Mademoiselle and Mary Forrest led Polly into the house. Anne could not move; she clung to the wood of the doorway. Her body trembled. Before her waited light and warmth and safety. Behind her waited darkness and water where land should be. In the dark you could not see the water. It might even now be rising. It could rise and blot out these lights. Anne heard her voice. It was pitched too high. She must stop herself. In this moment she could stop the screaming. The moment was past. Anne let herself go into the spiral of sound. "Poor thing." Beyond the shrillness Anne heard the soft voice. She felt someone help her. The shrill screams were loud; they choked her. Anne could not stop the spiral of sound. She could only let it unwind beyond her control. Slowly it grew quieter. Anne sobbed and gasped, and sobbed again. She was lying on Mary's bed.

"It's all right, Anne," Mary said gently. "Mademoiselle said you were wonderful during the storm. This is just reaction. Here, take this."

Anne swallowed the white tablets. She lay still. She was very tired. "Stay here, Mary."

"I'm here. You're all right."

Anne closed her eyes. "I'm all right. I can slip into sleep."

Before she plunged into the dream Anne heard the other voice. "Poor thing!" Or was that the beginning of the dream?

Pity was the beginning. Pity and fear. In the dream Anne could see that they were the same. Two sides of one fabric. Two sides of a wave. Anne could see it clearly in the picture. She put her hand on the golden frame of the picture. It was the painting of a storm. Within the frame the picture moved. No, it was not a storm, it was a tide that did not turn back. A giant wave that would engulf the land. On this side of the frame she was safe. She held the gilded wood and watched the rising tide. The wood was not golden; it was weather-beaten.

Anne clung to the steps. She must climb the steps. Her body was heavy. She could not move quickly enough. Behind her was the wave. She must not turn to look at it. Then she would not be able to move at all. She dragged herself painfully up the steps. Behind her was the wave and the wind crying. She could hear the wind, but she could not distinguish the pitying words. Beyond the steps were the lights. The flickering lights. If they would only come with the lights. The wind was too loud. It blew Anne's words into silence. It held shut the door against which she pushed. Her hands made no sound against the heavy door. She could not move the silent door. She pushed against the darkness. They must come with the lights, even if they were only candles that flickered. She lifted her eyes to see the light. Her eyelids were heavy. They were too heavy for her to see. She struggled against the heaviness of the lids. She tried to speak. Her voice made no sound against the thick quiet. She was sealed in darkness and silence. "Help me," she screamed, "help me." There was no scream, only a tiny thread of sound. She pressed her eyelids against the darkness. There was a thread of light. "Help me." The thread of sound was the thread of light.

Anne opened her eyes. She was alone in Mary's room. The darkness had been a dream. She was awake. She was safe.

Anne got up. She looked out at the morning. The lake reached halfway up the lawn. The storm had not been a dream. From the window she could see the track of the storm. The sea had washed over the dune into the lake. The storm had gone, but its path was plain to see. I will not stay here and look at the destruction. I will go to New York. I will go to New York and wait. The storm was a sign.

Anne remembered the sign she used to demand from the darkness long ago when she had lain awake in the Thirty-eighth Street house. If a car passes before I count ten, let it be true.

The storm is a sign you can't mistake, a sign that there is no safety here.

The bedroom door opened softly. Mary came in. "It's late, Anne, but I didn't want to disturb you."

"Poor Mary, I expect your house is crowded with refugees."

"A little last night, but now we're getting straightened out. There's just you and Polly, and Phil and Lisa. They were staying here anyway."

Anne was not astonished to hear Lisa's name. She had known it was Lisa's voice in the dream.

"I think I'll go to New York, Mary. I'm sure my house isn't habitable."

Polly came in to her mother.

"We're going to New York, darling," Anne said.

"Oh no, Mummy, not in summer. Let's stay here for the rest of the summer."

"There isn't much summer left, Polly."

"There's quite a lot, Mummy; there's two weeks."

Anne looked at her. Polly and I move in our separate sorts of time. Hers is long.

"And I want to see what the storm did, Mummy. Don't let's go away just when it's exciting."

"Well, if Mary wants to keep you."

"Of course I will, Anne."

"And you'll forgive me if I start for town as soon as I'm dressed? I can't bear to see Southampton looking like this."

"Take my car," Mary said. "Jim can drive it back tonight."

Anne dressed quickly. She was determined not to meet Lisa. Not to hear the gentle, pitying voice.

There was no one in the hall when Anne came downstairs. When she reached the front door she heard someone behind her. She did not turn her head. She walked through the open door and down the drive toward the garage. Behind her she heard the voice: "Anne."

She did not look back. She imagined Lisa standing in the doorway. The doorway was a frame. Anne quickened her steps. Lisa was in the past. The frame and the picture would grow dim and be forgotten. The future belonged to Anne.

II

LISA WATCHED Anne walk down the drive. Poor thing. She is tired, and this is her refuge, not mine. I should not be the one to turn her away. How strange to feel pity for her.

Lisa looked at her left hand on which there was no ring. And my heart is free, too, not bound to Franz. I could not pity her if I were still tied to him. Anne has shown me that I am free.

Lisa listened to the motor. Beyond the green barrier of the fallen tree she saw Anne drive away. She remembered the first time she had seen Anne, not knowing her name, only seeing a pretty American girl in a bright blue motorcar with shining fittings.

This September was far from that June day. Lisa looked again at her bare left hand. She remembered the summer sun shining on the crimson stone. It is a long time ago, that June day. Not just in our time, in the world's time. Poor Anne. I should not pity her. Pity is for a sister, not for a stranger whom one has seen but never known. But our paths have been the same, not separate. The beginning and the end interchangeable. It has been one path. And the world's time and our time have been one.

Anne had gone. The drive was empty. Lisa still saw a car, but she did not see Mary's black sedan. She saw a blue open car with bright red wheels driven by a young American girl. Ten years ago we were all at the beginning. All the time was before us. It is not Anne I pity, but all of us. There seems to be so much time. For each of us the untouched future. For Anne and for me and for Franz, as once for my grandmother, as once for my father. It looks like so much, and it is so little. There is so little time to find your way, to make your choice.

Lisa walked past the house towards the lake. All the houses are strange, even this one which I remember a little, but only a little, so that the broken tree is not sad to me. But somewhere I shall find my place. Lisa remembered her own voice saying to her grandmother:

"We can find you pines and a hilltop in America." I shall find that hilltop. I am free and I shall find it.

Behind the house the overflowing lake covered half the lawn. Poor Mary. This was to her what my grandmother's house was to me. These trees were rooted in her memory. It is sad for her to see them uprooted, to see the place of her childhood spoiled. No storm has touched Waldenberg, but it is destroyed and only the memory is left.

Phil Sinclair called Lisa. She walked towards the house.

"Look, Lisa, how about our clearing out after lunch? We're only in Mary's way."

"Of course, Phil."

"And we can drop Polly off at Paul's. He called up and asked for her. Mary's going to get hold of Anne to find out if it's all right with her."

"Will it be?"

"Sure. Anne has other things on her mind besides Polly."

"Poor Anne," Lisa said. "She was terribly frightened last night."

"Poor Anne," Phil repeated. "Poor Anne, indeed. Though it's odd you should pity her."

"It would be even an impertinence, if she knew. One doesn't want pity from a stranger. But I remember her when we were both young, when I first saw her, when I first met her. I thought she had everything. Her path seemed so clear and sunny."

"I wish I could head her off the path she's on now." Phil laughed briefly. "Pretty silly to worry about one person when at Godesberg they're bargaining the world away. It's not Czechoslovakia, it's the world. It was the world in Spain, but the traders won't see."

"They will, Phil."

"Will they? I used to think so, but the months in Spain rather dashed my native optimism. At any rate, let's find a radio and see how old Chamberlain's making out."

The radio in the library faded in and out. It was impossible to hear the news. Phil turned it off.

"No use struggling with that. Tell me about you, Lisa. How was Mexico?"

"It was very beautiful."

Lisa remembered the months in Mexico City. It was like a dream. Not the remembrance. The time itself was like a dream, outside the sequence of her life. The winter sunshine and the thin mountain air. The floating gardens. Only in a dream would you see islands of flowers moving slowly on the surface of a stream. Lisa remembered the pyramid which she could not climb. It was difficult to climb or to move quickly in the unaccustomed altitude. That, too, was like a dream, but most like a dream was to feel again the timelessness of childhood. The long days were so alike that in memory they seemed to be side by side, not to follow one another in the chronology of time.

"I felt very young," Lisa said.

"But you're settled—you came in on the Mexican quota?"

"Yes, I can eventually become an American citizen."

"Good for you."

He doesn't know how good it is, Lisa thought. Here the light is the reality, the promises are true.

"And when do you go to rehearsal?" Phil asked. "I saw you've got the lead in that play of Gottfried Lieber's that Gerald Michaels is putting on."

"Yes, we go to rehearsal on Monday."

"It'll be like old home week. Even without a German author I guess the theater's pretty much the same everywhere."

"That used to be true." Lisa remembered the Schauspielhaus in Munich, and the gay, rococo theater in the crooked street in Budapest, the Bühnenhaus in Berlin, Gerald's theater in London, and the one in New York. There used to be no boundaries between them. For the theaters one had needed no passport, as once for the countries of Europe. Lisa remembered her grandmother's description of prewar Europe. That was long ago. So much of liberty was long ago, so much of peace.

"The theater is only as free as the city in which it is. My last year in Berlin there was no freedom. Emil Schwarz would not touch the modern plays that were permitted, so we did Shakespeare, and censored him ourselves for fear a party member might recognize the underlying theme and banish Shakespeare, too."

"And Shaw? I thought they allowed Shaw?"

"They did, but I wasn't right for him, Emil thought."

"Not *Candida* or *The Doctor's Dilemma?*"

"*Candida* has been played too well. But Jennifer Dubedat is very tempting. Do you remember when she and Louis talk of the burning bush? '. . . we lit the first fire of the winter; and when we looked through the window we saw the flames dancing in a bush in the garden. . . .' At Waldenberg the flames of the sun danced in the glass of the picture frames. The reflected flames lit the darkness of the little room. I could be Jennifer, I think."

"And Lieber's play?"

"It's good. It's the best part I've ever had in America. So I say *Morning Song* is a fine play. But I believe it is. Gerald must think so. He doesn't like vehicles." Lisa smiled. "Poor Phil! What a monologue you let yourself in for when you start a dialogue with an actress! Tell me about yourself. You were still in Spain when I left."

"I wrote my little pieces. I had an idea they were pretty futile, even when I was sending them off. And how right I was. No one listened to what any of us said. So I came back. To talk. No one wants to hear."

"And what will you do?"

"If you mean 'accomplish,' nothing. The paper'll send me abroad again but not to Spain. The two men they have there are enough to cover the inevitable death throes. They'll send me somewhere in Europe. Languages come in handy. The first dividend my expensive education ever paid."

"Where will you be sent?"

"I don't know. Wherever it is, I'll see the same war. But no one will listen, no one will recognize it. I'm sick of words and they're all I'm endowed with, and not too well endowed at that. But the boys who speak with the tongues of angels don't seem to make much of an impression, either."

He turned on the radio and bent his head to listen to the faint words. "Don't know why I'm so anxious for the bad news." He turned the switch. "Only words come out of them, too. All over the world these machines are giving out with words, and nobody hears, nobody believes." He stood up. "I'd better go pack. Hope we can take Miss Polly along with us. She'll be refreshing company. Her world is still ten or fifteen years away. Good or bad, it at least has the merit of not yet existing."

Paul Craven lived twenty miles from New York, in Eastgate. Lisa looked at the small, neat houses, at the small, newly planted shrubs.

"I like it," she said as she watched Polly run towards the back door of Paul's house. "It's like a toy village set on a green carpet. But it's a queer place for a man alone to choose."

"He chose it for Polly. He thought he'd have her for the summer, but Anne got home in June. Well, he'll have two weeks, maybe longer. Anne doesn't approve of Eastgate, of course."

"But why not? There are children for Polly to play with. It's in the country."

"Eastgate's a development. So, of course, is Southampton's summer colony, and Tuxedo, and a dozen other places of which Anne does approve. But they are on a larger scale."

"And does Polly like it?"

"It seems so."

They watched Polly, who stood staring at a little girl advancing slowly from the house next door. Polly moved forward. "Hello," Polly said.

"Hello."

"What you doing?"

"Nothing."

The children walked away together. One gave a little skip, then the other. Then side by side they skipped towards an empty lot. They ran out of sight. Lisa and Phil could hear them laughing as they played.

"Anne hasn't managed to teach Polly that no one lives in Eastgate. Perhaps there won't be any invisible people in the world that's waiting for Polly ten years away."

When Paul came home he found Phil alone. "Polly's gone to have supper with the little girl next door."

"What happened to Lisa Blessing?"

"I drove her to the station. She had a date in town with Marco Ghiberti. He helped arrange things for her with the Mexican Government so she could come in on their quota. What we take for granted is so precious to her."

"Well, you can't blame a European for wanting to get out of that mess. Boy, that little storm we just had wasn't anything compared to the one that's blowing up in Europe. Maybe Chamberlain can straighten things out, though the radio isn't very hopeful."

"Nothing's very hopeful," Phil said, "nothing immediate anyway."

"You sound like Marco."

"I didn't know you knew him, Paul."

"I got to know him through Mary and Jim Forrest last winter. He's a nice guy, but he's got queer ideas. He ought to be in line for the district attorneyship in another four years, but he says no one can plan four or five years ahead. He says there's a war to be won. It's coming in secret or coming in the open. That's how he puts it. And he hopes it's coming in the open so it can be fought. Pretty pessimistic sort of hoping."

"Maybe the only hope left is the hope of being allowed to fight the war. The Spaniards chose not to die on their knees. Maybe Marco's right to hope. Maybe we won't choose to die in our sleep."

Paul shook his head. "Funny sort of optimists, you and Marco. Me, I hope it blows over. Let's go see what Mrs. Thompson has for our dinner. She's a good cook, and Polly likes her. I got her last spring. Lucky thing I kept her, and this place, now that I have Polly for a couple of weeks."

"You'll have Polly for longer than that, unless I miss my guess, or unless Hitler misses his, or Anne decides he's missed it."

"I'd like that," Paul said. "To have Polly, I mean. Do you think I could manage it?"

"I think you could manage fine."

"Maybe it isn't fair to her. Maybe I ought to let Anne keep her, even if she takes her abroad. Anne can do so much more for her. Maybe I ought to let Polly have her chance."

"This is her chance."

"Think so?" Paul asked anxiously.

"Polly thinks so," Phil said. "Listen to her."

The screen door slammed behind Polly. She hurled herself at her father. "Hello, Daddy. I had supper with Alice Williams, and Mrs. Williams says if you say so we can go to Jones Beach with them next week. Can we, Daddy? Can we?"

"Well . . ."

"Please, Daddy. Alice says Jones Beach is beautiful. She says it's the most beautiful beach in the whole world."

"Okay, Polly, we'll——"

"Goody." Polly's voice rose in a shout of triumph in which Alice joined from outside. The door banged as Polly and Alice ran with the news.

"See what I mean?" Phil asked.

"I see." Paul's face creased in a broad, contented grin. "It might work out for Polly and me at that. I can extend the lease on this little place. Might even be able to buy it one day."

"I hope so," Phil said. "I think that here, with you, Polly'll have a chance to grow up into the wide, new world that, please God, is waiting for her."

III

ON SATURDAY, October first, Phil and Lisa dined at Anton's. The restaurant was crowded.

"Listen to them," Phil said. "Their voices sound pretty cheerful. And they're not the only ones. Everywhere people are rejoicing over the impossible promise, 'Peace for our time.' Paul Craven, for instance. He's jubilant—believes peace is all nice and safe on a scrap of paper."

"It's hard not to believe in what you want to have true. Hard not to cling to our time as long as it lasts. You see that time is running out, Phil, because you've been in Spain, and I see it because I remember——"

"The old man who made the bargain for us didn't see. The frightened old man——"

"It's not just the old men, Phil, it's not just the leaders. The people don't see. How can you expect the people of Europe to see? They remember 1914. That was the evil that must not be again. In every European heart that was the ultimate desolation. In America you don't remember it. You were safe."

"We only thought we were safe. In the end we had to fight for our security. We only think we're safe now."

"You don't know what it is to lose a generation. That is the terror. The terror of the flesh, deeper than thought. Even in my heart. Though I know that war isn't the ultimate evil. In Germany I've seen destruction without war, and so, I know, can the world be destroyed. But knowledge doesn't alter the deep fear. Even in my heart war is the fear. Nineteen fourteen to 1918, the dread years. The cold years when the young men died. The fathers, the brothers, the sons. How can you blame the people? They remember. They're afraid."

"And the head guys, too? You think that's the fear that drives them? They're little people, too, I suppose."

"The people are never little, Phil. That's a false expression. But each of us separately is little. Little and afraid."

"And so we let the little men speak for us. And we let them trade our world away, trade with other people's liberty, and we don't see that all liberty is one."

"We will see it. Americans are beginning to see it, else why should Americans feel that Europe's reprieve is theirs? You can tell they feel it; you can hear it in the sound of their voices in this room."

Phil looked around the restaurant. He listened to the cheerful voices.

"Maybe without knowing it we're beginning to see," he said. "Easy enough to blame the British and the French. We haven't been digging trenches in Central Park and fitting our kids with gas masks. America's belief in her separate safety is Hitler's weapon, too. As deadly a weapon as Europe's fear."

"America will see that there's no separate safety, that freedom is indivisible."

"And you think we'll see it in time, Lisa? There was Spain. We let Spain go. It's too late now. And Austria. And now the Czechs. Bit by bit we let our world go, and we watch. Do you really believe that we'll ever do anything except watch and bargain for time? Time in which to die a peaceful death."

"We watched, but it hasn't been easy to see. The issue in Spain was confused and, in a different way, so was it in Austria. Even in the Sudetenland, Phil, do you think it's so easy to see?"

"It's part of the pattern. The pattern was clear in Ethiopia, in China."

"It has to be clear to all the people. It has to come close for the people to see. Then they'll lift up their hearts. They'll find the courage to save their world."

"Maybe you see clearer than I. After I drop you at the theater I think I'll go home and read a little history—American history, English history. Remind myself we've been on the ragged edge before and found the courage and the strength in time."

"Those are the histories the people have made, not the rulers. Pushing westward in a free world. The people will not 'meanly lose the last best hope of earth.'"

"I know you're right. Maybe the trouble with me is the people I see. Not you, Lisa, not Marco, not Paul, but the little gilded group that it used to be my business to see. Whom, from habit, I still see. From habit and from affection, God help me! They're the little people, all right, the little frightened people."

"And you mind for them. At least, you mind for Anne."

"You're right. I do. I don't approve of her, but I mind for her. Affection's a habit. It hasn't much to do with one's judgment."

Phil beckoned a waiter and asked for a telephone. He listened to the sound as the operator rang Anne's number. "No answer," he said. "She's out, maybe celebrating with the J. C. Joneses. There's a guy who hasn't any misgivings. He's so sure and we only hope."

"Our hope is stronger than J. C. Jones' certainty. He looks big but he's only a greedy little man. Don't be afraid, Phil. 'The only thing we have to fear is fear itself.' That's still as true as when it was first bravely said." Lisa rose. "I must go. I'll be late for rehearsal. Don't come with me."

"I think I'll stay," Phil said. "This is as likely a place as any for Anne to come."

Phil waited at Anton's, but Anne did not appear.

On Monday afternoon Phil went to see Anne.

"I don't know why I let you come, Phil. You're never anxious to see me except for something unpleasant. If it's about Polly you needn't have bothered. I'm going to let her stay with Paul. A few middle-class years won't hurt her. Meantime I'll arrange a slightly more glamorous future for us both."

"It's not about Polly. It's about you, Anne. I think I know your plans, but will you tell me what they are?"

"Of course I will. I'll tell the world." Anne laughed. "That expression dates me. Remember when we said that? There was a song the year I came out: 'I'm Sitting on Top of the World.' Remember that? Well, I mean to get to the top of the world. It's pretty clear now where that is."

"It looks like Germany for the moment, but——"

"It is Germany," Anne interrupted, "and that's for me."

"The world spins, so that for the moment Germany is on top, and

that's for you, and you make your bet. You shouldn't make your bet,
Anne, until the wheel has stopped."

"Unfortunately that's against the rules. But I think my bet's pretty
safe. And it wouldn't do to leave Franz too long. I'm going back to
him before he forgets me. I think I made up my mind the night of the
storm. Since we're dealing in metaphors, the storm was a nice meta-
phorical reminder."

"You're going to the heart of a worse storm than any you've ever
seen."

"Think so?" Anne laughed. She remembered Ruby Borodino and
Edda Ciano. Tough and smart beneath the sleek appearance they
presented to the world. They know how to ride the storm and so do I.

"I think I can ride the storm," Anne said.

"With Franz?" Phil asked gently. "My poor Anne, don't you see
Franz? Don't you see him at all? You think he rides the storm when
actually it bears him indifferently like a leaf in the wind."

"For once you're wrong. I know a little something about German
politics, and I know Franz von Erlencamp's position."

Anne smiled at Phil. I don't mind his pity, since he's so completely
wrong. He was wrong before.

"You were wrong before. Do you remember, Phil? You were wrong
about the future. You said it belonged to the people. The ones you
call the people, in Spain, don't seem to have much of a future."

"The wheel's still turning, Anne. This isn't the future, not yet. But
the future's on its way and you can't stop it. You can't escape it."

"This conversation is getting definitely boring. You were more fun
when you were Peter Pierpont. Though even then you had your self-
righteous moments. Have a drink and wish me luck."

"I do. I always have."

"I suppose you have. Though your idea of luck has never been
mine." She stirred the ice in her glass. "Really, Phil, this is a sensible
move for me. I can have a nice life in Germany, and even you must
admit Franz is attractive."

"Yes. He's attractive."

"Well, then! And since now there's no danger of war——"

"And you're willing to leave Polly?"

"That's only for the time being. Besides, I should think you'd be
pleased that Paul's to have her for a while."

"And not just Polly," Phil continued. "You'll leave all you've ever known: the country where you were born, the friends you've always had, not the new overmoneyed friends, but the old ones, the Forrests, the Wintons, and the rest. For a mirage you call the future you'll leave your past, all your years——"

"Pretty unpleasant years, the last ones," Anne said angrily. "Oh, I'm all right now." She looked at the luxurious room in which they were standing. "But I don't know if it'll last. Taxes keep going up, and even Uncle Normie can't always tell about dividends. I've been frightened, Phil." Anne's voice trembled, as she remembered when her fear had begun on an October night in just such a pale, pretty room as this. "In Germany I'll be safe." She turned her mind from the old fear. She remembered the present promise of safety. "Over there I'll be safe. The right people are running Germany. The elite. And Franz is one of them. The Munich pact makes it clear that no one's going to stop them. Don't you see, Phil?" She wanted to drive the pity from his eyes.

"I see, and you don't. Though I shouldn't blame you—I've been frightened, too. But you're wrong, Anne. You think you're headed for the future. A nice safe tomorrow. Actually it's the past. An ancient, ugly past, if you could only see it. I don't think the past is the future, not even in my darkest moments. I think the wheel's still turning. I think it's turning forward, not back. I think the future's waiting, and I think it belongs to the people."

He lifted his glass and held it for a moment in the light of the western sun. Then he drank.

"Sorry, Anne. Once again I've said my piece to you, and once again it's had no effect. Forgive me, and come out and have dinner with me."

"I'd love to, but I can't. I'm dining with the Joneses."

"I thought that was Saturday night."

"Why, no." Anne looked slightly surprised. "No one was in town Saturday. I was at the Spains' over the week end. The Joneses were there, and J. C. decided to give a little party tonight. Everyone's so relieved at there not being a war, and J. C. thought it would be nice to have a celebration. You can see how he feels."

"Yes," said Phil, "I can see."

J. C. Jones's party was at Anton's. Anne looked with pleasure at the group that surrounded her. She was glad she had had the foresight to buy a new dress. She thought gratefully of the French. I'm glad that even on the edge of war they were able to keep their minds on clothes.

The dark brown of Anne's dress made her hair seem lighter. The somber color was becoming to her even, golden tan. The room became the dress as the dress became Anne. The colorless beige of the walls was a perfect background for dresses, for dark dresses and for bright ones. Anton's was a carefully designed showcase for fashion.

As she talked to J. C., Anne watched the fashions dance by—the gay and charming fashions of October 1938. After all, our time is safe. The showcase is still intact. The fragile glass unbroken. The safety made in Munich protects the brittle world. I will go where safety begins, where the power is. I will choose the safe side. The side of power is the safe side.

Anne continued to admire the room, the setting of her farewell. There's just enough pink in the beige to be becoming to faces that are growing tired. The lights gleam in crystal. They seem bright and clear but they, too, are faintly rose. Not like Tony's. The dark cheap wood that reflected the yellow wall lights. Tony's has come a long way.

We've all come a long way. Anne looked at J. C.'s guests: young Mrs. Bertie Voorhees, James Albright, the ex-Ambassador . . . J. C. and Judy have come a long way. And I with them. I've come the long way back. I'll go further. I'll go to the end of the road—to the heart of power, and that's no longer in America.

"I like your party, J. C." Anne smiled at her host. It's my party. It's my farewell. Farewell is when you decide to go, and I have decided.

"You look very pretty, Anne," J. C. said. "What I mean is, you look cheerful. You've seemed kind of peaked lately."

"These last weeks haven't made anyone feel too cheerful."

"I'll say they haven't. Things looked bad to the most optimistic of us, and no matter where you went the damn radio kept blasting you into a nervous breakdown. Well, thank God, it's all behind us. It's going to be plain sailing from now on."

"Do you really think so, J. C.?"

"Think so? I know. Listen to the talk. And remember how people were talking a week ago. People know."

"These aren't the people," Anne said, "at least, not what are usually called the people."

"They're the people who matter. Listen to them. Not to what they say, but to their voices. They know they're all right again."

". . . only sensible thing to do." "They couldn't stand up forty-eight hours against the German air force." "Who wants to die for the Czechs, I'd like to know?" "They'd have us playing Russia's game." "Sure, and I say give him a free hand in the East." "Feels good to get our world back intact. Means I can get to Palm Beach by Thanksgiving, not have to stay here watching the market. You can imagine what a war would have done to what's left of that." "Anyway, it would have been absurd to have a war over this. If these people want to be Germans, why, let them—they are Germans, aren't they?" "Peace for our time's good enough for me, just so they put off the deluge till I'm gone." ". . . talk a lot of idealistic claptrap. It's not practical to have all these little countries." "You bet, and for my money Hitler can run Central Europe." "A lot of his ideas aren't half bad." "I can think of one or two we could use right here, not that you'd get our press to admit it, or those smooth talkers on the radio." "Or that smooth talker in Washington—he's a troublemaker, if you like." "The important thing is you've got to have peace to do business. War would murder us." "As far as we're concerned, I say we can do business with Hitler. Isn't that so, J. C.?"

"I've never had any trouble," J. C. said cheerfully. "The German leaders are practical men. It's easy to come to terms with them."

"Why do you stay here, J. C.?" Anne asked.

"Meaning what?" J. C. asked sharply.

"Why not go to Germany where the terms are made? Why stay here where the best you can do is meet them?"

"Well, it's not quite like that. The Germans do business with us and they know which side their bread's buttered on. For anyone who knows his way around, I figure the terms'll be kind of mutual. My business gives me an international outlook. I don't want to sound like a professional patriot, but it's not a bad thing for the U.S.A. to have a few guys with a really sound international viewpoint."

"You mean big business is a sort of practical League of Nations?" Anne asked.

"You think you're kidding? Big business is a lot more international and does a lot more to hold the world together than those crackpots in Geneva ever did. Listen! I'm an American, and naturally I'm for America first, but that doesn't blind me to the good in other countries, and there's a lot of good in the German setup. Not that our newspapers ever tell us so. We could learn from the Germans, and maybe we will. Times have changed, and the Germans have changed with them. They're the boys who understand our time. And we'll have peace in our time just as long as we play ball with them."

"Do you think there's still a chance of war?"

"No, I don't. Munich settled that."

Rita Spain touched J. C.'s arm. "You and Anne sound very serious. Are you settling the affairs of the world? I thought this was a celebration."

"The affairs of the world are settled, and you bet we're celebrating." J. C. grasped the stem of his glass. "Let's drink to the settlement and to its lasting our time."

Anne lifted her glass. She watched the champagne bubbles dance in the hollow stem. She remembered the color of the wine in the candlelight at Waldenberg. She remembered the toast Franz had given her: "To tomorrow."

She looked at J. C. He rose to dance with Judy. His square body pushed its way through the crowded dance floor. Men like J. C. will keep the peace, Anne thought. There are men like him in every country. There are men like him in Germany, and Germany is the heart of the new power. In Germany the shape of the future is plain to see. There tomorrow is waiting. Not at Waldenberg. Waldenberg with its pines and its flowering May is part of the old time. Franz and I will be married in Berlin.

Anne imagined her wedding. For me, as once for Emmi Goering. She'll be there with the Field Marshal. And the ugly, clever little doctor. They will all be there, the men who run Germany. The men who run the future. And Franz is one of them.

Anne imagined the castle of Erlenhof which she had never seen. The proud towers above the wide courtyard. We will go to Erlenhof. Tomorrow should begin in a place you have never seen.

IV

ON A NOVEMBER MORNING Anne started on her journey. She stepped from the taxi at the crowded entrance of the pier. She watched the porters take her suitcases. She shook her head at the flower seller. She did not need the cheap roses with their stems wrapped in newspaper. Her cabin would be filled with flowers. She watched the line of taxis. She looked for familiar faces among the prospective passengers. She stepped from the street into the shelter of the doorway.

A woman was coming down the steps towards her. It was Lisa Blessing. Anne turned her head. She did not want this meeting. If only the porters would hurry. Lisa couldn't be sailing, too. Anne remembered yesterday's papers with their glowing tributes to *Morning Song,* their tributes to Lisa. It's been easy for her and hard for me. But in spite of her talent, in spite of her beauty, I have won.

Lisa stood before Anne. Her coat was gray, the color of the cold sky. The small hat did not conceal the shining hair. In the harsh light Lisa's hair was bright.

"Anne, forgive me for speaking. There isn't time enough, I know. There isn't quiet enough."

"Then why not say hello and let it go at that?"

"Because I can't let you go. Anne, I saw you first in the sunshine. And now on this gray day I can't let you go into the darkness. You don't know where you're going."

"That's just what I do know. I've always known. But I can't imagine what it is to you."

"It's that you were the girl whom I saw in the sunshine. The girl to whom America belonged. When we were both young. The separate threads of our lives have been part of one pattern."

"The pattern's worked out nicely for me. Though this is hardly the place to discuss it." Anne smiled and beckoned to her porters. All this talk about remembering. She's just jealous. "Don't you remember, Lisa, when you chose the life that now is to be mine?"

"I didn't know then. And today you don't know. You haven't seen the darkness. Your American mind cannot imagine the darkness and the fear."

"I hardly think that the Countess Erlencamp will find much to fear. And things look pretty bright in Germany. Particularly since Munich. I'm afraid you're the one who's guessed wrong, Lisa. It looks as though I've won."

"You don't belong with the children of darkness. Nor does Franz. But it's too late to save him. The children of darkness will not inherit the world. The world will reject them. The people will turn back the dark legions."

"That sounds like something from one of your plays."

"It's in Lieber's play. It's also in the history books. You should read them. Not the frightened daily papers."

"Hi, Anne!" J. C. Jones pushed through the crowd. "Here we are. Judy and I and the Spains. The others went on. Well, for God's sake, Lisa. I never expected to see you two girls together. Congratulations on your play, Lisa. You got swell notices."

"Anne, believe me. Before it's too late, believe me——" J. C.'s booming directions to the porters drowned out Lisa's voice.

Her friends swept Anne towards the stairs. Anne looked back and saw Lisa standing alone in the crowd. *She is alone and a stranger. And she dares to pity me.*

"Come on, Anne. Got to drink to the bride."

"Fine thing, the future Countess Erlencamp taking a French ship."

"Oh, that's okay." J. C. laughed. "Hitler doesn't mind their playing house at sea in their luxury liners."

"Flowers for the bride, Anne. Pin them on."

Anne held the snowy orchids against her furs. The crowd swept her up the sharp incline of the gangplank. Anne did not look down at the narrow Rubicon that separated the ship from the shore. She did not see the dark, still water that separated her from America.

Lisa had gone to the ship to say good-by to Gottfried Lieber. He was sailing for England to arrange the London production of *Morning Song.* As she walked away from the ship Lisa felt no pang of homesickness for the foreign land. The once lovely Fatherland was now an alien shore.

Lisa watched Anne until she disappeared in the crowd. *She has* gone to the foreign land. And I have come home. Home. In that word my heart embraces the land to which it is no longer strange.

Lisa drove up the highway beside the river. Here the ships have come. The Americans have come on all the ships to freedom. They have come, the dispossessed and the exiled, the frightened and the brave. They have come seeking refuge or adventure, liberty or gold. In the end, beyond freedom's harbor, they and their children have found home.

As the taxi left the highway Lisa turned for a last glimpse of the Hudson. Beyond the steep western shore lies America. The land I have chosen. The land that belongs to all the people. I am alone and I should be afraid. Others before me have come alone. I am not afraid. I, too, in my turn have come home. For me, too, in my time, America is the beginning.